W9-ANF-126
PROSPECT HTS.
3 1530 00072 8591
WITHDRAWN

CRISS
CROSS

Also by Tom Kakonis

Michigan Roll

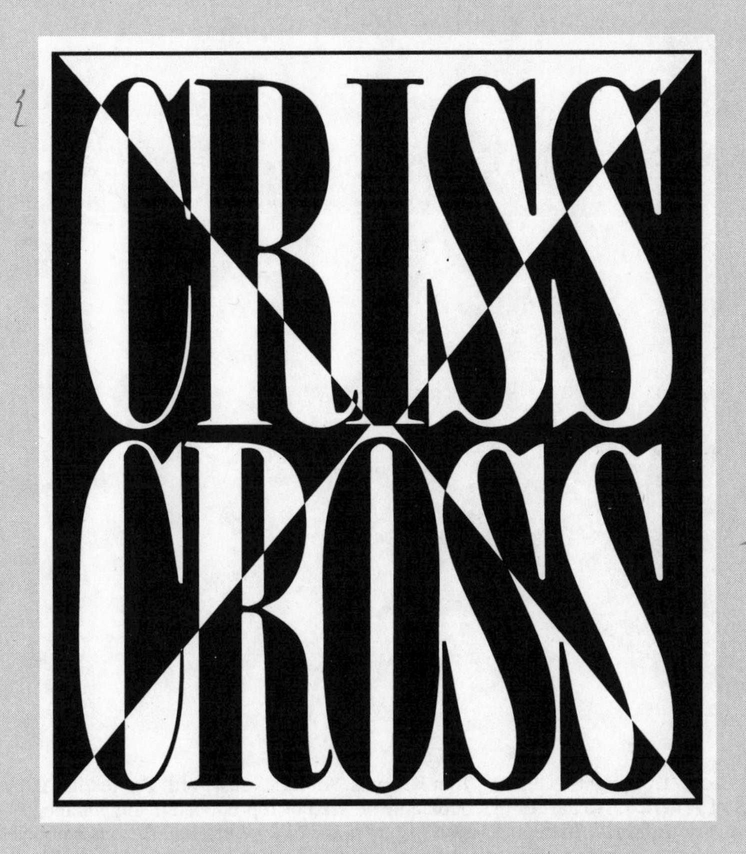

a novel by

TOM KAKONIS

ST. MARTIN'S PRESS • NEW YORK

Editor: Jared Kieling
Production Editor: Andrea Connolly
Design by Robert Bull Design

Library of Congress Cataloging-in-Publication Data

Kakonis, Tom.
Criss cross / Tom Kakonis.
p. cm.
ISBN 0-312-03728-7
I. Title.
PS3561.A4154C75 1990
813'.54—dc20 89-24168
CIP

First Edition

10 9 8 7 6 5 4 3 2 1

NOTE TO THE READER

This novel is a work of fiction. All of the events, characters, names, and places depicted in this novel are entirely fictitious or are used fictitiously. No representation that any statement made in this novel is true or that any incident depicted in this novel actually occurred is intended or should be inferred by the reader.

While the community of Grand Rapids, Michigan, has many fine wholesale and retail outlets, the enterprise known in this book as Fleets, Inc., is not among them and is wholly a product of the author's imagination.

For my father and mother. Also for Don Mackintosh,
a friend when friends were in short supply.

"The man grappling with reality fails to find a serious explanation of anything whatsoever he sees."

—Henri Fabre

PART ONE

ONE

SO IF YOU'RE ALWAYS first up in line at Fleets (like their radio jingles kept bawling at you: "Fleets—wah wah wawa/Fleets—wah wah wawa/It's *you* first up in li-yi-yi-yine") how come he was doing the heels-cooling number behind this peevish grandma with the champagne-colored hair and voice an injured croaking honk? How come? And with the hands on the clock on the far wall ticking steadily, keeping remorseless time to the beat that commenced somewhere down at the base of his skull and rose to settle in an urgent throb behind a pair of scarlet-rimmed eyes. Seven fifty-three. Fifty-four. No way was he ever going to make it now. Physically not possible. Why me, O fucking Lord, why me?

At least part of the answer to that question Mitchell Morse asked himself lay in his positive genius for picking the wrong line, logjam line. Didn't matter where: banks, theaters, ball games, supermarket check-outs, airport check-ins, highway toll booths—name your line. Just fall in with old Mitch and watch it shift into low gear or, just as often (like now), grind to a dead halt. Find a way to market that talent, he could retire a rich man, an island somewhere maybe, or a cabin off in some mercifully silent woods.

Meantime The Great Coupon Debate droned on. That seemed to be the issue here this morning, "coopons," as granny called them. She had two for the same product, one in-store, the other a "man-a-fat-chers." Both, she was insisting, applied against the purchase price. Fleets' rules said no, but she wasn't giving in without a fight.

"Awright. Here's this coopon here clipped straight outta yesterday's *Press*. Where's it say anything about it not bein' good at your store?''

''If you'll look in our flyer, ma'am, you'll see our own specials can't be combined with other discount coupons. That's policy. And it's not *my* store, by the way.''

''Sure, take the easy way out. Not your store. Just doin' what they tell you. Like the Naz-ees, butchered all them helpless people.''

''I wouldn't know about that.''

'' 'I wouldn't know about that,' '' granny mimicked, elevating her pitch. Then, leveling it out flat and accusatory, ''No, easier do nothin' than let some more helpless people get cheated out of what's rightfully comin' to 'em.''

''Maybe you want to talk to Customer Service.''

''It's you I'm talkin' to, young woman.''

Morse had been standing with a pack of cigarettes and a bottle of generic aspirin in one hand, his punished forehead in the palm of the other. But at the introduction of the remarkable historical dimension into the argument, he lifted his eyes to the coupon resting on the counter. It had a value of thirty cents. It was for Tater Tots. ''Look, lady,'' he said, ''supposing you put it on my bill. Would that make you happy? Move you along?''

She turned a rouge-splotched face on him, a face with the tight pinched features of a nettled crow. Vertical creases, fine as hairline cracks in plaster, ascended from a righteous upper lip. For a nicely timed moment she fixed him with a glare and said not a word. And then in the roupy bray that was, evidently, her natural delivery, she said, ''I don't remember anybody askin' your smart-ass opinion here.''

Morse put his free hand over one ear. ''Hey, you want to bring it down a little? I ain't in Housewares back there.'' It got an appreciative snigger from behind the cash register.

''Whyn't you just butt on out, Mr. Wiseass.''

''Yeah, well, I'll do that, you let me butt on by. Believe it or not, lady, there's problems deeper than Tater Tots in this sorry world.''

''One of 'em is people stickin' their big nose in where it don't belong,'' she fired back. By way of clarification, she added, ''Other folks' business.''

It occurred to him to wonder how it was he got himself into

such lunatic squabbles. Another priceless talent. On the candy shelf alongside him was a package of sweets in the shape of flattened rodents, colored in fluorescent yellows and neon reds. He picked it up and set it on the counter by the coupon. "Tell you what. You don't like my first offer, I'll throw in this bag of Gummi-Rats if it'll hustle you along. What do you say?"

"You know what you both can do?" she said, snatching up coupon and grocery bag in one deft furious motion.

"What's that?" he asked. Now the clock said 7:58. He was willing to do straight man if that's what it took.

"You can go piss up a rope, two of you," she declared triumphantly and, fortified by the last word, went harrumping away.

"Welcome to Fleets," said the cashier, putting a touch of ironic lilt into their uniform greeting.

Center stage in the conflict as he had been, Morse had taken no notice of her before. Now he did. And what he noticed first, couldn't avoid, was the hair, astonishing dense whorls of it, circle on circle, dusky brown with brilliant streaks of induced gold coiling over her shoulders and down her back, a tangle of artfully wanton curls. Spectacular hair. Too much. Too much for the narrow face it framed, an elongated foxy face all planed and tapered, the nose set at a steep angle, close to vertical, the skin, an unseasonable tanning-booth bronze, pulled taut over sharply defined bones. It was rescued from hardness by a full mouth, lips varnished a moist pink, and by luminous jade-green eyes shadowed in blue. Altogether, a face that projected a wash of miraculously harmonious color.

"Gives your golden years a bad name," he said, nodding after the departing quarrelsome senior.

"We value all our patrons here. That's policy too."

Voice was pure silk, schooled in retail cheery but with a cool distancing all its own.

"Yeah, I heard. Every day's a sunshine special day at your Fleets."

"You've got the words down. Melody needs some work." She dinged off the cigarettes and aspirin on her register. "Will that be all," she asked him, allowing about a quarter smile that still managed to display an abundance of perfect white teeth, "or did you want the Gummi-Rats too?"

For a moment he didn't reply. He found himself staring at her, God knows why. Here was a cashier. At Fleets, your original grub-and-gimcrack heaven on the cheap. Certainly not a beauty, not exactly anyway. Not that much in the body department either: angular, slight in the shoulders, looked to be all but breastless and with scarcely a trace of a curve in the hips or can. Under the khaki store-issue jacket, she wore a functional blouse of some coarse fabric. Her slacks were a gaudy plaid, shit-kicker boots seriously scuffed. Must do all her wardrobe shopping right here. So why was he standing there gawking like a schoolboy? He couldn't fix it, what there was about her, what it was she had. Call it a flashy radiance, maybe, charged with remote dazzling promise, but tempered by a carelessness that seemed to announce: catch me if you can.

"Sir?"

"Ah, what was the question again?"

"The Gummi-Rats?"

"I don't think so. Unless maybe you'd like them."

"Me? Thanks, no."

She hit the total button, and a rectangular window hooked to the register displayed the amount of his purchase, followed by Have a Super Day! The way he saw it, life had enough unwelcome messages without all these phony chippery ones coming at you out of nowhere. He laid out a five, and some coins came spilling down the change chute. Two more bills were held in her outthrust hand. He looked for the telltale ring. None in evidence, for all that might prove. The fingers, he noticed, were long and elegant, nails lacquered a deep burgundy. Very sensual-looking hand. He checked the time. What the fuck, late anyway. The tag on her jacket read Starla H.

"Miz H.," he said, "I wonder if I could interest you in a cup of something or other. In lieu of the Gummi-Rats, say."

She raised her eyes, busy before with the nimble moves of transaction. There was a faintly amused glint in them, the look of someone been over this terrain before, many a time. "That's very thoughtful, sir. But you see I'm on duty."

"So we call in the second team. Anything can be arranged."

"No, I'm afraid not. Not at Fleets."

Was that a rejection of him, or of his easy solution, or both? No way to tell. Anymore, when the pose he presented to the world suffered a reversal, as it did now, Morse's first line of defense was to shrug it off. Which is what he did, shrug, and offer up a stagy grin. "Another time maybe."

"Maybe," she said doubtfully.

XX

It was going on half-past eight when he pulled his ancient, long-snouted Monte Carlo, big, black, cancered with rust and evil-looking as a tank, into the knot of picketers blocking the gate. The autumn sun poked frail shafts of light through a granite sky. A raw wind raised miniature cyclones of dust and dead leaves in the street. The strikers were doing their zombie shuffle, shoulders hunched, breath steaming the chill air. Most of them had on jeans and flannel shirts, tailored by Big Yank, and hooded sweats or fatigue jackets, though a few hard cases still toughed it out in tee-shirts. All of them, without exception, had the sooty look that comes from a lifetime on the wrong end of a real or figurative shovel. And the ornery faces to go with it, furrowed in permanent scowl masks. They knew him, of course, and parted ranks sullenly, taking their own time. A few birds were flipped his way, but that was routine, the morning ritual. From over by the high metal fence, recently topped with razor wire, somebody called, "Yo, security, don't forget now, plant a wet one on Vanderkullen's fat ass."

Picket-line wit. Ordinarily Morse would have acknowledged it with a chummy wave, smoke them up a little, but with a head out to here and a put-down under his belt already this morning, the best he could do was curl a lip in the general direction of the voice and keep on inching ahead.

It was nervous Billy Schooley who let him through the gate, getting it slammed and bolted hastily, lots of rabbity moves. More than usual, Morse noticed. Also he noticed that Billy was wearing the uniform: dog-stool brown, scratchy wool, the double-A Protective Services insignia stitched into either shoulder, baton swinging from a bony hip. Which was curious, since they'd been working this job plainclothes for a month or better, ever since tempers cooled. Something was up.

And that's what he asked when Billy came bounding around the car and stuck his worried head in the window. "What's up?"

"Jesus, Mitch, where you been?" Billy's voice always had a panting quality to it, not one of his stronger points.

"Fuckin' Lady Di invited me to morning tea, where'd you think. You want to tell me what's going on?"

"Ash come in. He's over to dispatch with Vanderkullen right now. Neither of 'em is exactly leadin' cheers, you not here. Buzz is something's comin' down today."

Billy was maybe mid-twenties, at best, graduated from three years heavy-duty mall patrol. He got on with AAPS last spring, just before Morse, and he was having some adjustment problems, all this big-time security. Didn't help any, the way he looked: beanpole bod, scrawny sunken chest, altar boy features with the chipmunk cheeks and onanist's jittery sliding eyes. Lately he'd developed a tic under one of them. Even in uniform, Billy did not cut an imposing figure.

"What?" Morse asked him.

"What what?"

"This is a vehicle here, Billy, not your fundamental echo chamber. What's—how'd you put it again?—coming down?"

"Beats shit outta me. But they're actin' real weird out there." He specified the "out there" with a thumb wagged at the gate. "Y'know, sort of smiley mean, like they know somethin's gonna happen. I was you I'd scoot on over to the office."

My partner, Morse thought dismally. Speaking of coming down, been a long greased slide for him, past year or so. Nevertheless, he flashed the all-purpose grin and said, in parting, "You're a lot of things, Billy, but one of 'em ain't me."

XX

For this town it was a big operation, big warehouse. A long file of loading docks, trucks backed up to all but a few as he drove on by, forklifts purring about, scabs busily humping beer cases, shifty looking and shameless as ever. Nothing out of order so far. He turned the corner at the last dock, and there, faithful to Billy's alert, was Tony Ash's powder-blue Buick parked under the outsize company sign:

VANDERKULLEN'S RED CARPET DISTRIBUTORS, INC.
WEST MICHIGAN'S LARGEST AND FINEST WHOLESALE BEVERAGE COMPANY

Beneath the boldly lettered words was the design of an unfurled carpet the color of blood, flanked by the emblems of assorted domestic and foreign beers, and beneath that the pronouncement:

THE LEADER IN ALCOHOL AWARENESS PROGRAMS

Lots of class, this dike-jumper.

Morse went inside. There was the customary morning scramble, and the chief dispatcher, a fussy coveralled grunt whose substantial belly betrayed a weakness for the company product, looked up just enough to motion him back to the glassed-in cubicle the boss reserved for himself whenever he descended from the Olympus of the front office to favor his troops with an inspection. Vanderkullen and Ash were waiting, the former behind a sturdy wooden desk appropriate to the hands-on setting, the latter in a lime-green plastic scoop chair along one wall. Both wore three-piece suits. Neither looked elated, even as Billy had warned. Nobody offered him a seat.

It was Vanderkullen who started things up, a real take-charge guy. ''People work for me, they turn in on time. Or they don't turn in at all.''

Sounded like something rehearsed. Probably engraved on the company time clock: our founder's motto. He spoke in one of those growly voices hard drivers sometimes affect, but coming out of that chubby pink face it seemed almost laughable, or would have been if he didn't hold all the head-rolling cards. From the ambiguous set of his eyes it appeared he might be addressing either party in the room, so Morse said nothing.

''For me also,'' Ash seconded grimly. No question who he was addressing.

Morse rolled over conciliatory palms. "Okay, I'm a little late. But Schooley's out there. And the other team, they don't look like they been unpacified yet.''

''Schooley!'' Billy's surname came flying on wings of spittle, and Ash swiped furtively at moistened lapels, breaking his rhythm. ''You're missing the point, Morse. I made *you* honcho here.''

''Looks to me,'' Vanderkullen allowed, stroking his meaty chin, a wise banker now, pondering an overdue loan, ''like we might have ourselves a substantial error in judgment, Tony.''

Ash winced visibly, and not, Morse could guess, from the

implied rebuke alone. His given name was Anthony and, for whatever reason, he despised its familiar form. Maybe he figured people would mistake him for a wop, which is what in fact he partly resembled: swarthy skin, midnight eyes, wide red mouth, wiry black hair that glittered from an excess of natural oils, and an unfortunate penchant for elastic Mediterranean gestures he seemed powerless to control. Just then Morse was having a similar problem, trying to contain a small smile.

Vanderkullen missed or ignored Ash's discomfort, but he was keen enough to catch the flickering smile. "You find all this entertaining, Mr. Morse?"

It was issued as a challenge, CEO style, gravelly tough, and when he didn't immediately reply Ash jumped right in, hands chopping the air. "Well, do you?"

Morse felt the color rising through his neck all the way to his thumping temples. He wished now he had taken the time to pop a couple of those aspirins back at Fleets. But who could have predicted this reception? He hadn't seen either of these wimps in two, maybe three weeks. Now here they were, jerking each other off, competing for stiffest dick of the day, and at his expense. And both of them the kind of people whose side you were ashamed to be on. And not a goddam thing to be done about it. He needed this job. Swallowing hard, he mumbled, "No, sir." Talk about your whale shit depths, he was brushing the bottom of the sea.

Vanderkullen broke out a wicked sneer, so broad it pressed his plump cheeks upward, reducing his eyes to slits. To no one in particular he said, "Detroit hot dog. No wonder they turned that town over to the coloreds." He shook his head sadly, as though mourning the memory of that abandoned city. And then to Ash, directly, he said, "But we got our own town to worry about, correct? The good folks in Grand Rapids going to enjoy your finer brews tonight, my trucks got to make delivery."

Ash started to say something but Vanderkullen cut him off with a no-no finger. "Let me finish, Tony. Take a good look at your honcho here. No uniform on. Needs a shave. Eyes like a couple piss holes in the snow. Way he looks, he'd have trouble keeping order with a pack of cub scouts. My people inform me he's been showing up like this, oh, past month or better. Comes in late, leaves early. Two-hour lunch breaks. I'd have to call that pretty lax security, particularly the fee I'm paying your organization."

Morse stood there like a man eavesdropping on a slanderous conversation about himself. He didn't trust himself to speak.

Vanderkullen went on, spacing his words for effect. "Now, those trucks of mine got to get by that gate today, irregardless what that rabble out there's got in mind. Irregardless. How they do, that's up to you. And your honcho. You're the experts, this line of work. They don't, I'm going to have to do some serious reevaluating, my whole security program. Are we understanding each other, Tony?"

Ash's face wore the distressed look of someone trying desperately and without much success to restrain a gust of flatulent wind. "Perfectly, George. And those trucks *will* roll. You've got my assurance."

"Superb," Vanderkullen said around a nasty smile. "That's just superb." He glanced at his Rolex and bounced to his feet, holding himself ramrod straight the way diminutive men, as he was, will often do. "Well, got to run. Staff meeting, ten minutes. I'm glad we had this little chat, Tony. Get things aired. We'll talk again soon." He let his eyes drift over Morse distastefully and added, "Real soon."

With the brisk stride that implies a merciless schedule, he came around the desk and was out the door and gone. Morse had to step aside to let him pass. Ash was still glowering so there was more yet to come.

"Sounds like the monarch of suds caught his superb dick in the zipper this morning," Morse said, getting in the opening line.

But Ash was not about to be deflected. "You got any idea what this account is worth, Mitchell?"

It was a severe tone he adopted, but by now Morse understood his spongy side: for all the sterling reputation and prosperity of the Anthony Ash Protective Services Agency, its owner-president had himself never been anything more than a rent-a-cop, and he knew it. And in the company of anyone who had ever sported a legitimate shield, he displayed a certain residual awe. If Morse had any edge on him, that was it. And now was as good a time as any to use it.

"Y'know, Anthony," he said (early on he had learned to defer to him on the name, though he always allowed a little insolence to ride along with it), "where I been, a chief backs up his men."

In light of his own bitter experience, the words all but choked him. He said them anyway. Whatever it took to get these crotch-rots to vanish, get his head right again, get by the day.

"Back up!" Ash exploded, face going crimson, arms flagging. "You got the stones to stand there and accuse *me?* Not backing *you?* He was after your ass, you know. You're just goddam lucky you're not swinging a torch, night watchman duty in a nursing home. Who you think you got to thank for *that?*"

Evidently it was the wrong tack. He tried another. "Look, you had any problems since I tranquilized them out there? I'm late, that's one thing. Vanderkullen can't get it airborne over how I look, that's something else. But you know I've kept order here. You know that. And—correct me here if I'm wrong—that's what you hired me for."

It sounded good. Sweet reason. Yet Ash was having none of it.

"The point keeps escaping you, Mitchell, that it's the Vanderkullens who pay the freight. Your salary. Not me. Them. We work for them. You're not rousting your Wayne County spooks anymore. This is *business* we're in."

Morse lit a cigarette and took a mighty drag. First nicotine hit of the day, it about knocked him over. That, and his quicken-the-dead breath, which was not going to qualify him in any auditions for Listermint Man of the Year. They were probably right, probably he did look like your fundamental puddle of upchuck. Day-old variety. All the same, he was getting powerfully sick of this circular conversation. "Everybody keeps talking about points today. Maybe you want to make yours."

"What I wanted was to get to you last night. I was calling your place till after one, all the good it did. Where the fuck were you?"

"I don't remember anybody telling me I was pulling O-T. I was out."

"Out. Okay. Out. If you'd been in, you'd of known to wear your uniform today. Known Vanderkullen's ear passed down the word they brought in some new muscle, going to hit up the first driver to the gate this morning. A test. Throw a little panic in them. Also known about this butt-chewing—Vanderkullen, I'm referring to—which is what I been listening to for the past hour, waiting on you. Trying to defend you. Knowing all that you might have come in looking—looking"—he searched for just the proper squashing word—"professional. Halfway, at least."

While he spoke his hands never stopped moving, like he was signing his speech for an audience of the deaf. His voice, which began on a note of ham-fisted sarcasm, dwindled to a wounded whine. His dusky features looked perilously near to crumpling.

Morse never could tolerate crybabies, and Ash had it in him to be one of the first order. Another small edge. "Yeah, well, since I didn't," he said dryly, "know any of that good stuff you just said, I mean. Since I didn't, maybe you want to terminate this little chat—like our favorite Dutchman calls it—and let me get outside and see about all that world class muscle."

Ash massaged his forehead, an elaborate show of the weight of his entrepreneurial burden. "Yeah, I need you outside," he said wearily, gazing at the floor. "But there's problems running this business, Mitch, nobody can understand."

Oh oh. Chainlock the wallet and count the coins in your pocket anytime Ash goes confidential, trims up your name. "Problems? What kind?"

"Personnel kind. Over at the foundry. Three of my people called in sick, and the line is some union hardhats picked today to get restless. Full drill over there, no tests."

Morse, fresh out of sympathy, said nothing. He had an idea what was coming but he wasn't going to make it easy on him either.

"I got to take Schooley," Ash said finally, really gouging now. Any harder and he'd erase those shag rug brows of his. He didn't look up.

Morse thought about it a minute. Then he said, evenly, that which was indisputably true. "You take Billy, I got nobody looking over my shoulder. He's not much but he covers the glutes."

"I know that. Still got to take him. It's a matter of . . . deployment."

"Deployment."

"Right. Deployment. Y'see, Mitch, you got the experience, comes to this work. You're more, y'know, capable. Than most."

Why Ash was taking the trouble to grease him, he couldn't

tell. "Good words," he said, "but without a backup I'm still parading around in my underwear. Experience or not."

"I know how that is," Ash said, bogus hearty now, "so I got you one." He boosted himself up out of the chair, tugged the vest down over a mounded midsection, and led the way to the door. "Thing of it is," he added, not looking back, "it's a new hire, Mitch. A female."

XX

She was younger even than Billy and she looked about as comfortable in her starched uniform there as a schoolkid about to get herself initiated into the Campfire Girls. Also sort of dazed, like she just got her first taste of joy stick and wasn't sure she liked it or not. Merciful Christus Fuck, Morse asked himself—again, second time around today already—why me?

"I'm really, uh, happy I'm going to be working with you," she said uncertainly. "Mr. Ash told me a lot about you. On the way over."

When he didn't respond she added quickly, "All of it good," putting a hopeful musical ripple in it. Like they were going to be co-hosting the charity bazaar.

"Who?" Morse said.

"I'm sorry?"

"Who was it did all this boosting of me? You just said?"

"Mr. Ash."

"Lesson numero uno. Call him Itchy, he's not in earshot. Ash. Itchy. It's a little joke we make. Get in the car."

Jean Satterfield was her name. Ash had done his brisk Rotarian introductions ("Jean, want you to shake hands with Mitchell Morse. Man with two last names can't be all bad. Haw. He's going to show you the ropes. Take good care and good luck.") and just as briskly sped away, get the fuck disappeared before any protests could be lodged. Left them standing alongside the Monte Carlo watching each other.

She was tall, not all that far off his own height, somewhat big-boned, not fat but kind of square, as nearly as the uniform (which flattered nobody, never mind the gender) revealed. She had straight dark hair, cut short, boyish, sheared off at the neck and cropped close over the ears. A wide innocent face, innocent of makeup, innocent of guile. Lips pale and thin, tight looking, a little prim.

Clear brown eyes that dispatched an appeal: patience, understanding, support. Qualities he had never been exactly famous for. This was not, he decided, his day to be going for the Lotto.

He settled behind the wheel, shook two aspirins from the bottle and chewed them straight, savoring the evil taste. She sat pushed over against her door. He slid the car in gear and drove past the loading docks toward the gate.

"You got any experience," he asked, "this line of employment?"

"Well, an internship the summer before last. At GM, here in town. Ten weeks."

Soft, almost purling voice. Very polite-spoken. "Internship," he said. "You a college girl?"

"I graduated in August. Ferris."

"No kidding. What's that, Ferris?"

"It's a college. North of here."

"Studied to be a cop up there?"

Her lower lip stiffened some but she said, quite levelly, "It was security administration."

Quick enough to catch when she was being ragged anyway. Not an altogether bad sign. Morse had nothing against women. They wanted to get themselves liberated—whatever the fuck *that* meant—fine by him. Go shinny up a phone pole, swing a pipe wrench, pilot a dozer, manage a bank, run for Congress, be a general in the goddam army even—whatever jollied them. No skin off his backside. But not, goddammit, a cop, not even the for-lease variety. No. He'd seen enough of that, Detroit P.D. Seen them hired and promoted over good deserving grunts, all that affirmative action doodoo. Then you get a little hard going, they started calling time out, periodic distress. Pussy was just fine in your face. But not covering your back. Like this one would be doing—trying to do, botching it up for certain—today.

He swung into the employee lot beyond the warehouse, killed the engine and sat there a moment, not moving or speaking. She looked at him puzzled, waiting for direction.

"Okay," he said. "Mostly you just hack around, these jobs. Do your eight with your thumb up your ass. That's the way it goes most of the time. Today though might turn out to be one of them exceptions you probably read about in school. We're going to stroll over to that gate there, you and me. Plant big smiles on our face, even when them gentlemen on the other side get unmannerly. Couple minutes there'll be a truck pull up. I'm going to get the gate, walk on out in front and let him by, into the street. You with me so far?"

"I think I can follow that."

He had been talking into his lap. Now he looked at her narrowly. "That's good. Your following, I mean. So anyway, long as the truck's this side of the gate, company property, everything's cool, what you college people call orderly. Also once it gets in the street, gets accelerated. Then it ain't our problem no more. But in between's that little stretch of driveway there, kind of a no-man's-land, you might say, which is where them cowboys might get grouchy.

"Now, all I need you to do is hang behind me, about three paces off to the left. Truck'll be on my right. Anybody get any cute blindsiding notions, you just shout out. That's all you got to do."

"I know how to use a stick, Mr. Morse."

"Bet you do. Bet you got some of them colored belts they give for jujitsu, too. Tomorrow, day after, you can leap right in swinging. But for this one morning here I'd be obliged if you'd put all that deadly force on hold. We straight on that?"

She gave him a short indignant nod.

"Okay. Let's go administer some of that security you learned in school."

XX

At thirty-four, Morse still had all the moves he'd had some fifteen years back, starting linebacker, University of Michigan. Or almost all. He stood two inches over six feet and went 220, last time he was on a scale, only about five pounds or so up from his best playing weight. All of it pretty nicely distributed yet, too: heavy in the shoulders, spare at the hips, lean and still muscular in the legs. Gut wasn't quite as armor-plated as it once had been, a little suet there, but solid enough underneath. Going into a little scuffle like this one, memory served up some of the loose jauntiness he used to feel just before the first hit of a game, like a flare waiting to go off in his head. He had loved to hit, those days. Sent his share of business the orthopedic surgeon's way. He still loved it.

But he wasn't so fond of the godawful racket—hoots, jeers, catcalls, shrill teeth-clamped whistles, fence banging—that greeted him when they first saw him coming, a uniformed girl at his side. Murder on the head.

"Happiness boy got himself a *body*guard!"

"Sheena, queen of the jungle!"

"Yo, security, furburger for lunch."

"Hey, no dippin' it on the job."

He cranked up a shark grin, put a little malice in it and a little more swagger in his step. He could feel Jean Satterfield closing in behind him, and with a cupped hand at his side he motioned her back. Under his breath he said, "Keep smiling."

He stood there, staring them down. Soon enough came the deep-throated rumble of the first rig chugging toward the gate. He glanced over his shoulder and up into the terrified eyes of the driver. Scab driver, served him right. Morse signaled him to stop, got the lock and flung open the gate. A squad of picketers dropped their signs and fell into a wedge formation in the drive. One of them moved out in front and stood squarely in his path, beckoning him with a waggly finger.

"C'mon, Morse, c'mon out here. See how mean you are off company turf."

It was one of the tee-shirters, pit-bull face set in a combative sneer. Wiry red hair coiled over the neck of his collar, and a couple of ornate tattoos adorned beefy arms. The rest of him was all sausage-roll fat, spilling over a belt with a solid brass buckle that bore the legend BORN TO BASH. Morse knew who he was: your fundamental mouth-breather, megaphone lungs, lard ass, born, if for anything, to captain the bowling team. He knew also this was not the one.

Moving with a consciously lithe, easy stride, Morse proceeded into the drive and got right up in his face. "Hey, basher," he said, "somebody give you a balls implant?"

"Yeah, same fella you're gonna be lookin' up, get yours reattached. Give you his name if you want."

"Why, that's mighty generous, seein' as how your old lady's got his dick in her mouth right about now, speakin' of attaching. Least that's what your buddies there tell me, last one got unspliced from her this morning."

A collective expectant sigh escaped the crew of third-stringers, and they faded back along the curb. All but one, also got out in tee-shirt, black, with tight black pants patterned out of shiny leather, and black snakeskin Dingo boots with stiletto toes. A study in darkness. He was made to appear taller than he probably was by a wide flat chest and sinewy shoulders tapering to a needle waist, no hips at all, slender planks for legs. Firehose veins ran the length of his ropy arms. He had a hard triangular face, glittery vacancy in the eyes. Hair, also black—what else?—was slicked across his skull and tied in an oily ponytail that reached halfway down his back. This now, Morse thought, this is the one. He watched him lay a gentle restraining hand at the elbow of the basher, who was just then advising Morse to go fuck himself.

"Well, I'll likely do that, Mr. Basher, soon as you and your lady friend—I do admire his pigtail, just like a regular Indian squaw—soon as you two step out of the way that truck comin' on. Lots of citizens going to want to get winterized tonight, so we got to get their beer to 'em. You can understand that, tub of guts like that one you're modelin' there."

"What I understand is how you're gonna be shittin' blood, Morse, any minute now. This 'lady' you noticed, he come to have a word with you. And that pussy driver. After you two talk we'll maybe see which one's the lady."

The ponytail moved alongside him. "This is the man?" he asked, voice absent, uninflected, a dreamy quality to it.

Morse turned and faced him, snapped a finger as though in tardy recollection. "That's right, we ain't been properly introduced. No manners, basher here. I'm the guy you come to speak to."

"Pleasure."

"Well, kind of yes and no. Y'see, I'm also the one's going to put your arms in casts, you don't trot right along now. You got any idea the inconvenience that'll cause you? Have to get your sidekick's old lady, wipe out your ass for you. Course she won't mind, right, basher?"

Without looking at him or waiting for a reply, Morse laid a flat hand in the basher's face and shoved hard, sent him reeling.

The other one didn't move. "That's what you're going to do?" he asked mildly. "Break my arms?" His face was expressionless, eyes empty, inward turning.

" 'Fraid so. 'Less you care to join your friends on the curb there."

He shook his head sadly. His shoulders seemed to droop,

arms went slack. And then he sprang up on the toes of one boot and in a graceful pirouette, all the more elegant for its laser speed, brought the other around and caught Morse dead on the jaw, sprawled him across the pavement, the sky a deepening blur above him and a delirious whoop sounding in his ears. Morse got as far as his knees, just far enough to see it coming again, a kind of balletic flying dropkick this time, both boots connecting thuddingly on his chest, flattening him. His breath came in short, strangulated gasps. Blood leaked from his mouth. Through a shimmery glaze he could see Jean Satterfield come charging in swinging her wand, and he shouted, wanted to shout, tried but nothing came out—too much windup!—and the ponytail stepped over him nimbly, barest hint of a smile visible on his face, and opened both his hands in a mock display of fear, and then dispatched the blade of one of them in a short chopping blow across her throat. One more to the side of her head, directly over her ear, and she went crumpling to the ground. He straddled her, wide-legged stance, and made an elaborate apologetic gesture. It excited a rousing cheer.

About a foot from where Morse lay was a rock the size of a fist. He rolled over and grasped it and scrambled to his feet. The cheer abruptly translated to a howl of warning, and the ponytail wheeled around but not quite in time, for in a roundhouse swing, all the force left in him, Morse brought the rock into one side of his face, splintering the bones. An astonished yip came riding a gusher of blood. Morse raised a leaden arm and drove the rock into the back of his neck, watched the knees go buttery, watched him begin to sink, slow motion. The inert figure of Jean Satterfield cushioned his fall.

Morse stood over him, quaking from a curious mix of rage and triumph and pain. And then he stooped down and gripped one limp arm, twisted it at a tortuous angle. Simultaneous with an ugly grinding snap came a piercing screech, repeated once again when he did the same thing with the other arm. "Promise is a promise," Morse muttered, partly to himself but also for the cautionary benefit of the assembly, grown suddenly silent now and shrinking away. Wobbling some, he tracked one of them, a runt, deliberately chosen, and seized at his collar. "Gimme your shank," he demanded.

"I ain't packin' no knife."

"You better find one or you're goin' to be wearin' plaster laundry, same as your champ there."

A pocket knife was produced for him. He flipped it open and took a sideways step and planted a foot in the small of the back of his toppled opponent. He lifted the rope of hair and sawed it loose.

"Thing about your kung fu," he said, raising it aloft, shaking it at them furiously, "it don't take into account the other guy maybe ain't gonna fight fair."

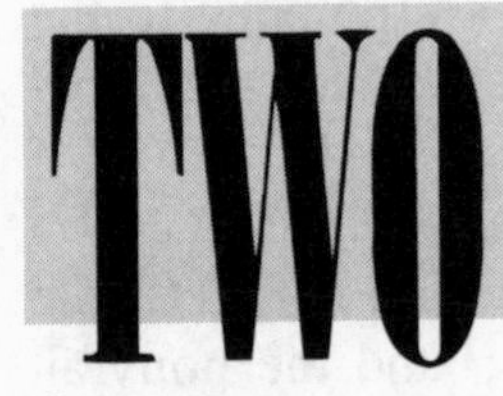

TWO

AT ABOUT THE SAME TIME that morning, a man of extraordinary proportions sat impassively in the front booth of a West Leonard Street eatery that went under the generic name "Grill." He seemed absorbed in some reverie, his gaze shifting between the door and the cup of muddy-looking coffee in front of him, from which he took an occasional noisy slurp. At the rate of about one every eight minutes, he lit an unfiltered cigarette, a Lucky Strike, and smoked it down to a tiny stub. Judging by the contents of the spilling-over ashtray, he had been there approximately an hour and a half. Apart from the coffee, he had ordered nothing in all that time.

Grill was without pretension to elegance. Its feeding area was a narrow rectangle, high-backed wooden booths along one wall, on the other a Formica counter with a file of uncushioned stools rooted to a floor covered with pumpkin-colored linoleum. Water spots stained the ceiling; motes of dust hung suspended in the thick condiment air. In the back a tiny portal opened into the kitchen, and a chef in blowzy whites peered through it like some wary gunner studying the terrain from the observation slit of a fort. Up front, a young waitress with ringlets of yellow hair leaned into the cash register, idly chewing a moist toothpick, shuttling it now and then from one corner of her uncommonly wide mouth to the other. On the wall behind the register was a framed painting supplied by a brewery, depicting a heroic General Custer assailed by a pack of savages, and flanking it were a number of signs that said such things as: IN GOD WE TRUST—ALL OTHERS PAY CASH; KWITCHERBELLYAKIN'; WE GET TOO SOON OLD AND TOO LATE SCHMART; and, THE BUCK DAMN WELL BETTER STOP HERE. In the window was a neon sign, unelectrified at this hour, bearing the stark command EAT. Evidently it was all but universally ignored, for the occupant of the booth was Grill's sole customer.

The waitress hadn't wasted a glance on him before, figured from his Goodwill wardrobe he was just another seat warmer, two percent tipper, if that. After her pick was thoroughly disintegrated, she sighed audibly, hauled herself off the register, picked up a pot and sidled over and filled his cup. He acknowledged neither the courtesy nor her presence, so she stood there a moment, tapping the lineoleum with a sneakered foot. Generally pissed. Letting him know this wasn't your basic shelter for the homeless. "You plannin' to order anything?" she said finally.

Immediately, she regretted it. Never mind his size, which was scary enough, straight out of *Frankenstein*. What about those eyes he fastened on her, very slowly, very deliberately, as though she were some kind of bug he was giving thought to squashing. They were set in dark bony sockets and steeped in a detached malice that seemed to include, without exception, whatever they measured. Over the left one a corded scar arced quizzically into a narrow corridor of forehead. As though in partial symmetry, another scar that appeared to be sewing-machine stitched ran vertically along the right side of his blunt-tipped nose. Above the square prow of jaw the mouth was little more than a thin bitter line, and he made a closed-lip smile with it now and said nothing.

"Reason I ask," she added quickly, backing away, "is because, see, our breakfast special goes off at ten. You get your two eggs, hash browns, choice bacon or sausage, toast or cakes. Dollar eighty-nine. I was thinking you might want . . ." She trailed off, conscious of maybe saying too much. What she was not conscious of was her free hand held in a trembly fist at her chin.

"Yeah, what? Want what?"

"Thought you might be, y'know, hungry."

"You expectin' a crowd in here?"

"No, but . . . No."

"I'm waitin' on somebody. He gets here, we'll eat." His voice was a harsh bass rumble, close to a monotone but for its snarly, wised-up quality.

"Okay. Sure. You just sing out anytime you're ready."

"Sing for my supper, huh. Only it ain't supper time yet."

The smile widened, and though the lips never once parted he produced a laugh in the sound of three short, deep barks. She remembered the ketchup squeeze bottles urgently needed filling, and got out of there fast.

He had that effect on people. He didn't mind. It was comforting to be feared.

Milo Gordon Pitts. That was his name. But for well over half of his thirty-six years he had gone by Meat, a name that testified graphically to his inordinate bulk. He had the neck of a sumo wrestler, the power lifter's thick square torso, nose tackle thighs, pink beefy arms; and all of it came about through no effort of his own, a gift of nature, for he had an aversion to physical labor of any kind, and sports were of no interest to him whatsoever. Unless a patented Meat Pitts stomp-and-maim tuneup qualified as sport; then he had the credentials of an All-American. The wintry glare he had used to send the waitress scurrying, that was another gift, quite uncultivated, cost him nothing in the way of study or rehearsal. Despising anyone not equal to his brutal proportions came naturally to him, which meant in practice he despised just about everyone, either gender.

There was one exception, and four Luckies and thirty minutes later it came through the door in the person of a frail-looking young man who moved with a bouncy, finger-popping strut. He was stylishly outfitted in a frosted denim jacket replete with zippers running at diverse angles, acid-washed jeans with the obligatory rent at one knee, and scuffed hi-top Reeboks, laces flopping carelessly. Large amounts of synthetic gold chain dangled from his neck, and both ears were adorned with pearl studs. He stood at the entrance with thumbs hooked in his belt, squinting through puzzled myopic eyes. Meat regarded him from no more than ten feet away. He gave it a moment and then called, "Hey, fuckdawdle, you lookin' for anybody in particular?"

The young man's face opened in an extravagant grin. "Meat boy!" he exclaimed and came on over and slid into the booth.

Four palms were lifted and joined in a ritual slap.

"Old Ducker," Meat said.

"Meat boy."

They gawked at each other with an awkward fondness. Meat's smile was perilously close to a display of teeth, and so to temper it he said gruffly, "This your idea of eight o'clock? It is, you better think about boostin' yourself a new Timex."

"Hey, what can I tell ya. This little twat last night, she got such a taste for old Uncle Clyde here she liked to flog the poor fella to death." Old Uncle Clyde was identified by a grasp at his crotch. Simultaneously, he made the shrill quacking laugh that, as much as anything, had earned him the name Ducky.

"It's goin' on to two hours I been sittin' here, Duck."

"You got to lighten up, boy. Take things cool. You're a free-worlder now."

"Cool," Meat said, the smile settling into a more comfortable and familiar sneer.

"Fuckin'-a dog, cool. That's how it's done out here among the citizens. How long you been back, anyways?"

"Couple weeks."

"Couple weeks! So how come you don't call till last night?"

"I been nosin' around a little. Also had to get myself orientated, guess." Which was the truth. All those dreamy visions of free-worlding—eight years' worth—and now he was discovering the real thing was stranger even than dreams. Felt like you was walking the streets in your skivs. Or inside somebody else's skin. Felt strange.

"You on parole?"

"C'mon, you know better'n that. I done it all."

As nearly as he could like anyone, Meat liked this young man. Or maybe it was more favored, the way you would a spunky worthless mutt you kept around, got to be a habit, like a good-luck charm. Three of the eight they had celled together, and in quarters that close for that amount of time you either favored somebody or fucked him or killed him. Since he had done neither of the latter two, Meat supposed it must be favored or tolerated—well, maybe it was liked. But sometimes the little popcorn fart could get on his nerves, too. Like now, with the featherhead questions. He shook another Lucky from the dwindling pack and reached for the book of matches on the table between them.

Ducky laid a restraining hand on his wrist. "You want to know how come I'm late?"

"Bet you're gonna tell me."

"Stopped by a Jew-ry store on the way," he said, and from one of the zippered pockets of his jacket he took a small plastic box. "For you. Comin' out present."

"You got me a present?"

Ducky did an elaborate aw shucks gesture, but the radiant grin very nearly split his narrow face. "Woulda got it wrapped except the kikes I nicked it off of, they might not been too accommodatin' that way. Open 'er up."

Meat removed the top of the box and discovered a miniature statuette of a naked woman, silver plated and set in a marble base and poised in an attitude of passionate abandon, arms thrust overhead, breasts at an exaggerated tilt, thighs partly open. He looked at it, mystified. "That's real nice, Ducky, but what am I suppose to do with it? Diddle a hunk of metal?"

"You ain't seein' what she's for. Look down at the stand."

There was a knob embedded in the base and fixed to a thin tubular shaft. "So it comes with a stand-in dick," he said. "Now what?"

"Run it up her legs," Ducky instructed, giggling softly. "Real slow. Watch what happens."

Meat did as directed and when the shaft arrived at the precious juncture its tip burst into a ruby glow.

"What you got there," Ducky explained, shuddering with glee, "is a lighter. Dong hits her cunt and—foom!—here come the heat. Just like real life, huh."

Meat lit the cigarette and shook his head slowly. It was coming back to him, why it was he favored Ducky.

"You like 'er?" Ducky asked him expectantly.

"Oh yeah. That's a real nice present you got me there, Ducko. Real generous. What do you say we eat now?"

XX

Ordering was more complicated than it should have been. Not for Meat, whose frozen glare was enough to persuade the jittery waitress the hours of the breakfast special ought to be extended. But Ducky always had serious problems with choices.

"Count Chocula, that's my favorite. You got any that?"

No Count Chocula.

"Okay, how about some Fruity Pebbles. Or Sugar Frosted Flakes. You got either of them?"

Negative.

"What you got in the way of breakfast food anyhow?"

They had Raisin Bran.

Ducky made a vinegary face. "Forget that. I'm shittin' regular. You know them cream curls, got this shell on the outside, cream in. Take a bite and the cream comes squirtin' out the end." He leered at her. "Got any of them?"

No cream curls either, she had to tell him, reddening just a bit.

"Jesus fuck," he said, genuine annoyance in the squawky voice, "this a cafe or what?"

The waitress pointed an apologetic finger at a pastry case, haloed with sluggish autumn flies, on the counter. The monster man was staring at her coldly, and she hardly dared to speak.

Ducky craned his slender neck, tugged his lower lip thoughtfully and said, "Okay then, gimme one of them jelly-filled donuts, and, uh, gimme one of them with all the crumbly worm turds on top, and, ah, lemme see, better gimme a short stack, blueberry syrup. Glass of your chocolate milk, that'd be good too."

As the waitress hurried away, he leaned across the table and whispered, "You eyeball that mouth on her?"

"Didn't pay it no attention."

"She comes back, check it out. They got a mouth that size it means for sure they got a gash on 'em big as that gorge out west someplace, can't remember the name."

"That's the Grand Canyon you're thinkin' of."

"That's the one. Anyway, makes for a piss poor fuck but a sensational blow job."

"You're sure about that," Meat said dubiously.

"Listen, I'm tellin' ya. It's a true fact. Scientific."

"Meat was thinking about his wife—or ex-wife, or whatever she was now—remembering the shape of her mouth. Astonishingly, now he was free these disjointed images came flashing out of the wilderness of memory with a frequency that was almost alarming. Why now? "Maybe you're right," he allowed.

"Bet your ass. Get her to say Walla Walla Washington around the old wang a couple times, your rocks'll go like a landslide."

For such a keen observer of anatomy, Ducky was remarkably, serenely oblivious to his own appearance. By any standard, it was singular. The mouth was easily as prominent as the one he rhapsodized over now, and was further accented by lips that habitually hung open, and by a recessive chin. The nose had the long spiked taper of a beak, and the eyes, yellowish brown against a backdrop of sunset pink, were quick blinking, birdlike. Straw-colored hair sprouted wildly from a skull so large it was just this side of hydrocephalic, sadly out of harmony with the reedy neck and spindly body it perched on. The entire face, as a consequence, had the squeezed-up look of some kind of waterfowl, which was another reason he came by the name Ducky. He had been christened Conrad: Conrad Marion Pickel. The surname, he insisted, had a final accent, but no one ever listened, so if it hadn't been Ducky it would have been Pickles. Of the two, he liked what he had better.

". . . now you get your really tight pussy on the skinny ones," he was saying, deeply interested in the topic and eager to expand on it. "Take this chickie I was layin' tube to last night. Six-two if she's an inch, can't go over a hundred pounds, and that's drowned. You seen the kind—nose to nose your toes is in it, an' toes to toes your nose is in it. Whatever's in it's gonna get snapped off clean . . ."

Meat watched him steadily. It was like listening to a tireless drunk, so many words to spit out, so much to say. Finally he made a stop signal with a palm of a hand. "You can get your mind off your nuts a minute, I got a couple other ideas to turn over here. Think you can do that?"

Ducky looked surprised, even a little hurt. "Why sure, Meat," he said defensively. "I just figured a man fresh sprung, he'd be itchin' to go sniff some tail. Cheat on his hand a little."

"I'm eight years backed up on tail talk. Lemme ask you somethin' else. Loot-wise, how you doin' these days?"

"Oh, I get by. Little boostin' here, swappin' and peddlin' there."

"I ain't askin' *what* you're doin', I'm askin' *how*."

"How? Gettin' by, like I said."

"How much you carryin' on your hip right now?"

"Now? Oh, I got me a couple deuces, that's about it. You want one, I can loan it to you."

"Deuces," Meat snorted. "Might as well be back in the can, deuces."

"Can ain't so bad, you think about it. Three hots and a cot and the sky ain't dumpin' on you. There's worse places. Speakin' of hots, here comes ours."

Without a word, the waitress laid out their breakfasts and got away, fast as she could. In a series of rapid nibbly bites, Ducky vanished the doughnuts, washed them down with a gulp of chocolate milk, poured a lake of blue syrup over the pancakes and dug in. He ate with a fierce concentration, hunch-shouldered, fork hand moving in metronomic rhythm from plate to mouth, jaws grinding. His extrusive lips smacked wetly, something like a hound lapping water.

"You enjoyin' that?" Meat asked. He had been picking indifferently at his eggs and some black fingers of sausage.

"Yeah," Ducky said, not looking up or breaking rhythm. "Good eats."

"Okay. Lemme try another one on you. How you gonna eat tomorrow?"

Now he looked up. Puzzled. "How? Whaddya mean, how?"

"I mean like in pay for it how."

"Jeez, I dunno. Never thought about it. Something turn up. I know this hooker over to Division, outlaw. Once in a while she lets me roll a john. Maybe I'll scoot over there tonight, roll me a john. You wanna come along? Could be a clean bill in it. We could split."

Meat shook out a cigarette, last one in the pack. He crumpled the empty, dropped it in the eggs and shoved the plate aside.

"Use your cunt lighter," Ducky pleaded. "It's a present."

Meat ignored him, struck a match. "Ducky, how old are you anyway?"

"Be twenty-eight, December," he said around a mouthful of sodden cakes he had gone back to shoveling. "You don't have to get me nothin' though, my birthday."

"Twenty-eight. And you don't know where your next pretzel's comin' from. What you got in mind to correct that?"

"Well, 'bout what I said. I sure as fuck ain't plannin' to sack no groceries."

"Your birthday's twenty-four December, ain't it. Christmas Eve."

"Hey, how'd you know?"

"Remembered it, from when we was cellies."

"You still don't need to get me no present, Meat."

"I already got you one, boy. Comin' in the mail."

A sunburst smile broke across Ducky's face, revealing remnants of the breakfast lodged between tiny stained teeth. "No shit! Present. C'mon, I can't wait no two months. Tell me."

"It's a score, Ducko. Big one."

"Score?" Ducky said, smile waning fast. "That's my present?"

"I ain't talkin' your South Division john rollin'. This is major leagues."

"How big?" Ducky asked. He couldn't keep the skepticism out of his voice, or the fear. He was glad Meat was out, glad to team up with him again. But his whole life was in order now, pretty much. Last thing he needed was grief.

Right away Meat caught the hesitation. It troubled him. For reasons he couldn't comprehend, made no sense at all, he wanted Ducky's approval. More than approval—galloping enthusiasm, like in the joint days when they had a scam going, or a touchup hatched. For Meat, Ducky was like a tuning fork, vibrating to notes forever out of reach to him, the melodies of danger, risk, treachery, fatal error, peril in the extreme; but of luck too, promise and fortune. An irrational music heard exclusively in some inner chambers of that vacant, outsized head. Believing all this, convinced of it, Meat said earnestly, "Three hundred balloons is what I figure, inside. Could be more."

Ducky was wonderstruck at the sum, but no less doubtful. "Jesus, score that big, that'd take a stakehorse. You and me couldn't put enough together between us to pick up a couple cooled pieces. And who'd do the quarterbackin'? Face it, Meat, we ain't neither of us too heavy, that department. We was, we wouldn't earned no first class tickets to Jacktown."

"You got that one correct, little man. But we do got the muscle. And we do got the plan. All we need's a tree to shake and a quarterback, we're home free."

Ducky opened up two exasperated hands. "That's what I just said. I just said that. Where you gonna find couple dudes like that, G.R.?"

"What if I was to tell you I had the both of 'em. Wrapped up in one package." With a conspiratorial wink, he produced a torn scrap of newspaper and held it up in display. "Do a scope on this, see if it don't cheer you up. Come right out of yesterday's paper, sports page."

Ducky glanced at it once, and then his eyes began to flutter and he leaned across the table for a closer look. "Holy fuck. Ain't that the Doc?"

"Bigger'n shit," Meat said with no little pride. He liked what he was certain he saw in Ducky now. The whole feel of things was coming around again.

A thin whistle of air came through the rosy parted lips. "He in?"

"Not yet. But he will be when I lay it out to him. Y'see, Duck, I been thinkin' this one through a long time. Year and a half, be exact, ever since you was walked. This is the one gonna stuff our wallets and stain our fingers permanent green."

"When you gonna tell me what all this rich action is? So far all I'm hearin' is hard noise."

"Real soon, partner. Let's go pay a friendly call on the Doc first."

THREE

ON A NAUGAHYDE COUCH in a corner of the abbreviated reception room of United Hairlines (also known, in subtitle, as the D. C. Kasperson Clinic of Naturopathic Trichology), a young man sat with pen and clipboard in hand, diligently completing a form labeled Personal Data Sheet. In the blanks he printed his name, Doyle Harmon Gilley; his age, twenty-two; profession, which, after some thought, he described as sanitary engineer (he did in fact hold down a key spot on the sanitation crew at a frozen food plant); and general health, to which he could reply, truthfully, excellent, for he worked out regularly and his body was lean and handsomely muscled.

Those were the easy questions. The rest grew progressively more intimate and, in come cases, downright strange. He was asked about his diet, which he rarely paid any mind to as long as he got up from the table comfortably full, and so in response he listed what he could recall of yesterday's fare. His habits: did he smoke? consume alcoholic beverages? indulge in sexual excess? inhale pure air deeply? evacuate his bowels thoroughly daily? think placid calming thoughts? His answers, respectively: no, sometimes, sometimes (he supposed his bed sessions with Twyla now and again qualified as excess), yes, yes (what else to say—you breathe, you shit), most of the time (he was a happy-go-lucky guy, or had been before the hair started going). And that's what he wrote opposite Present Condition of Hair?—going fast.

The next question (When did you first discover The Problem?) stirred painful, humiliating memories. Vivid as a nightmare, he remembered the precise moment and place it was first brought cruelly to his attention. A Saturday afternoon, a tavern up in Comstock Park where he lived, enjoying himself as always, slopping up a little beer and wasting all comers at last-pocket eight ball. Thrashing the piss right out of them, actually, and picking up some nice pocket change at a fiver a game. It was like his elbow was greased that afternoon, and every ball he hit had Doyle Gilley written all over it, just had to fall. Then along came that cocksuck Porky, wore the only crewcut, outside of punkers and World War Two vets, in west Michigan, grew right out of his eyebrows like some kind of ape, or werewolf. Couldn't handle a stick worth a fuck either, which was probably what sparked the shitsack to bawl out, loud enough for everybody in the house to turn and gawk, "Well, I'm maybe losin' my ass here, but least I ain't losin' my hair."

About six months ago, Doyle wrote in the answer blank, and pushed on to the next question.

What, if any, preparations, ointments, treatments have you tried?

Out of a multitude of profitless therapies he had experimented with over those six months, only the most recent name came to him, and he scrawled it now, bitterly: Nil-O-Nal.

He had made the mortifying purchase at the cosmetics counter of a discount drug store. A smirking salesgirl looked him over, her eyes straying to his ebbing hairline as she gathered up the substantial payment. Bitch ought to be losing *her* hair, he thought. Or be bald. A bald female cosmetics clerk, explaining soberly the merits of various restoratives. Imagine that.

He had hurried home to the efficiency apartment he shared with Twyla, locked himself in the bathroom and studied the instructions. He learned Nil-O-Nal was lanolin spelled backward. He learned lanolin was the life-giving emollient of youthful hair. He learned water dried up the natural oils of the scalp. Had he ever seen a bald sheep? Preposterous. The reason? Lanolin—lanolin in abundance in the skin of the fortunate sheep—much the same sort of lanolin in Nil-O-Nal. He was urged to emulate the sheep by working a palmful of the gooey stuff into the roots of his hair morning and night, and admonished to shampoo no more frequently than once a month.

For eight weeks he followed the regimen, till one night, in the rising heat of passion, he was brought thuddingly to earth. Twyla laid a caressing hand on the back of his head and abruptly yanked it away. "Yuck!" she exclaimed. "When's the last time you washed your hair?"

It had been the prescribed month.

"It's greasy. Gritty." She touched at it again, gingerly. "Thinner too. People lose their hair when they don't wash it. Don't matter then if you *do* look a little like Tom Cruise, or how many muscles you got. Nobody can love a baldy."

The following morning he got out a dusty bottle of Prell and dug at his head savagely, and the next and the next after that, on through a week-long orgy of cleanliness. With a flush of the toilet he disposed of the remaining Nil-O-Nal, but while his hair was no longer the consistency of mucilage, it was perceptibly finer and lanker than ever. He wondered desperately where to turn next.

An advertisement he came across in the newspaper, sports page, resolved the dilemma for him. Its headline posed the blunt question WHY BE BALD?, and its text implied that new hope existed for balding heads. It went on to define the science of trichology—the diagnosis, treatment, and correction of hair and scalp disorders. Finally, it introduced and credentialed the founder and director of United Hairlines, Dr. D. C. Kasperson, Trichologist. His photo revealed a man of ripening years, wearing what appeared to be a surgical smock. He was seated behind a substantial desk, hunched forward slightly and aiming a pencil at the camera. His face was fleshy and full but the eyes keen, intense, under hedgerow brows. A thin mustache served as counterweight to a fishy and somewhat slack underlip. His own hairline was ruler-edge straight, the hair itself graying a bit but wondrously thick.

The initial exploratory examination was free, no-obligation, and when Doyle read that line he knew at once he must have it. He clipped the advertisement carefully and tucked it away in his wallet. Now it provided an answer to the last question on the form: Where and when did you learn of my Method? Saw ad in yesterday's *Grand Rapids Press*, he wrote, Monday, October 26. He got up and handed the clipboard and completed Data Sheet to a matronly woman in a stiff white uniform who watched him from behind the reception desk.

"Pen too," she said, unsmiling.

"Oh yeah," Doyle said. "Sorry."

"You wait here," she directed, and took the Data Sheet and disappeared behind a door to an inner office.

Apart from himself, the room was otherwise empty, so Doyle got the clipping out of his wallet and studied it once again, hope and anxiety welling up in him, equal parts.

Coincidentally, at about that same moment, in a booth in Grill on the other side of town, Milo Pitts was showing Conrad Pickel a clipping identical to the one Doyle held in his hands.

XX

"Mr. Gilley? D. C. Kasperson. So pleased to meet you."

A large man, erect and tall and round as an untapered pillar came striding across the room, hand outthrust, smiling genially. Doyle got to his feet, and they clutched palms and squeezed.

"Mrs. Julius," Kasperson said to the scowly woman, "kindly hold my calls."

He ushered Doyle into his office and indicated a chair opposite the desk. Same desk, Doyle noticed, as in the ad. Same waist-length smock, too. And the face was essentially the same, though a little heavier at the jowls and with more droopy substance to the chin. But there was nothing ersatz about the hair; grayer maybe, but if anything more dense and full than in the photo.

"Bear with me a moment, Mr. Gilley, while I examine your Data Sheet." The voice was surprisingly high pitched for so imposing a man, the words meticulously enunciated.

Doyle glanced around the room as he waited. Like the reception area, it was compact and sparely furnished. Behind the desk narrow metal shelves with platoons of squared-away texts reached to the ceiling. The titles were esoteric, treatises on the maladies of man's topmost self mainly, but with some medical books too, anatomies and pathologies of this and that, and some darkly forbidding-looking volumes on, as nearly as Doyle could tell, The Wisdom of the East. Also, sandwiched in among them were a few incongruous and quite unforbidding practical vocabulary builders. On another wall a blank screen like a television monitor hung mysteriously. A window opened onto a view of a warehouse.

At last Kasperson looked up from the form, squinted at him and drew the corners of his mouth into a smile. "Hair troubles, eh," he said gently.

Stammering some, Doyle affirmed that there were.

"And you've come to me."

"Yeah, see, I saw your ad in the *Press* and I thought maybe you could take a look at my hair and give me some idea if . . . uh . . ." Doyle broke off helplessly, his hopes and fears too vast for words.

Kasperson leaned back and cradled his chin in a hand. He crossed one chunky knee with the other and gazed off reflectively. He let a silence hang in the air awhile before he began.

"Mr. Gilley, I'm genuinely glad you have come. That very fact—that you *are* here—reveals a good many things to me: an eager inquiring mind, a capacity for faith and belief, a stubbornness too. You smile, but that's it exactly, a stubborn unwillingness to admit that baldness cannot be conquered. How often do I hear, 'But Dr. Kasperson, we know baldness is hereditary, there's nothing can be done. What possible good can come from your treatments?' Oh, how often! In this very room."

Doyle felt somehow guilty of this clearly erroneous opinion. He looked about unhappily and slumped a little lower in his chair.

"There is a great deal that can be done," Kasperson said, answering the ghosts of all the doubters who had ever passed through the room. "I'd be delighted to tell you something of my unique approach. I ask nothing of you but your attention and these few moments of your time. Agreed?"

Wholeheartedly.

"Splendid. You see, Mr. Gilley, I like to think your coming here today may be the initial step in setting you on the road to healthy hair. A new and more rewarding life, even. Let me explain."

He stepped over beside the mysterious screen and flipped a pair of switches. The overhead light went out and the screen began to glow a pale aqua, illuminating a tangled mosaic resembling an aerial photograph. He picked up a pointer and swept it over the screen. "What you see before you is a highly magnified cross section of the hair shaft and follicle, the papilla, sebaceous glands, and so on."

Doyle stared at it dumbly. He could make out a clamshell on one side; on the other he thought he saw something like a glob of intestines. A long black shaft, thickened at one end, dominated the center of the screen. Looked to him like a limp dick. Kasperson's pointer traveled its length and came to rest at the base.

"Our friend, the hair," he said simply. "Note please the bulb-shaped papilla here. In this bounteous womb every new hair is conceived. Destroy the papilla and you destroy once and for all any possibility of growth for that hair. Destroy enough papillae and you have baldness, my friend."

For a moment a look of infinite sadness darkened his face. Only a moment. "But so long as there's a spark of life in our papilla, just so long can new growth be persuaded. Folks come here with their hair for all visible purposes gone. Lost forever, or so they believe. Often mistakenly. A patch of fuzz, barely discernible to the naked eye, may yet live. Show me a man with a trace of fuzz," he announced triumphantly, "and I'll show you a man with a potentially luxuriant head of hair."

He turned on the lights and stood tapping a palm with the pointer. "Now take your case. Standing here, at this remove, I can say confidently I can help. You're wondering, 'But when will he examine my scalp?' My friend, I've been examining it from the moment we shook hands. I've noted, for example, that the bulk of your hair is still intact and growing nicely. True enough, you've receded. I shan't minimize that. But even a cursory glance revealed to me a trace of that all-important fuzz."

Doyle's hands went involuntarily to the voids at his temples. By God, there *was* a fine down. "You mean you could grow hair back in here again?" he asked. "Where it's gone?" Halting the relentless loss, that was the absolute best he had dared allow himself to hope for.

"Sluggish," Kasperson corrected him. "Dormant. Not gone."

Doyle asked about costs and, swallowing on the word, guarantees. He was electrified with hope, but he was nobody's fool either.

Kasperson drew himself up stiffly. "No man can make guarantees on the human body. Can a surgeon removing a malignancy guarantee the life of his patient? No indeed. Such guarantees belong to a Power higher than our own."

He took a mimeographed sheet from among the papers on his desk and handed it to Doyle. "As for costs, you'll find them here, in detail, your own case clearly marked. Issues of money I prefer to leave to the bookkeepers. My concern is with the hair."

Regretting the question, Doyle pocketed the sheet without so much as a look.

Kasperson extended a parting hand, signaling the conclusion of the interview. "Think over carefully what I've said this morning. I sincerely hope we'll meet again." Before Doyle reached the door, he added, "One more thing. Consider it this way: why *should* you be bald? Think that over."

XX

At the same moment Doyle was leaving the offices of United Hairlines, Meat and Ducky were gazing out the window of a GRATA bus pointed in the direction of downtown. Their immediate view was a blurry succession of warehouses broken occasionally by an abandoned furniture factory or two, grimed with age and neglect. In the distance the skyline was dominated by the Amway Grand Plaza, centerpiece of the community, a wall of glass shimmering against the sky. It was flanked by a handful of office buildings and a high-rise parking lot. The bus turned at the Pearl Street bridge and passed over the Grand River, which rolled sluggishly south, eventually to empty into Lake Michigan some thirty miles to the west of the city. At the intersection of Pearl and Monroe the bus pulled to a stop and they exited through the rear door. Meat checked the address on the clipping while Ducky rubbernecked the Amway Tower.

"How'd you like to be campin' out, ho-tel like that one," Ducky said dreamily.

Meat was unimpressed. "Huh, we hit on that score, you'll be callin' a dump like that a sleep cheap."

Noontime crowds swirled around them: clusters of secretaries, youthful and well turned-out; chattering knots of J.C. students lugging over-the-shoulder book bags; career women fashionably and severely outfitted for success; earnest-looking professional men in tailored suits and topcoats; a few shoppers, refugees from the outlying malls. Traffic clogged the narrow streets. Exhaust thickened the crisp autumn air. Horns sounded.

Once he had his bearings, Meat said, "Okay, let's get movin'. We got a little hike to take here."

They set out walking. After a couple of blocks the crowds

began to thin; a few more and the streets were all but deserted. In front of a nondescript building, six stories of grainy red brick, Meat paused and inspected the number above the revolving door. A bit doubtfully he said, "This got to be the place."

The lobby directory listed a variety of enterprises: financing, insurance, detectives, electrolysis, personal injury attorneys, bail bonding, ghost writers, artificial limbs, Swedish massage, practical nurses, abdominal supports and trusses. United Hairlines was on the top floor. They rode up in a creaky, slow-motion elevator reeking of ammonia. When it came to a shuddery halt at their floor, Ducky looked down the bare dingy hall and remarked, "Looks of this place, Doc ain't exactly livin' in shit."

Meat said nothing.

They checked out the signs on the opaque amber windows, and at the last door in the corridor they found the Kasperson Clinic.

"Come to have a word with the Doc," said Meat, natural spokesman for the pair.

The woman at the desk gave him a look of alarm mingled with distaste. As long as the alarm was there, he didn't mind. She motioned them to the couch, rose, tugged at the hem of her uniform and went through the inside door.

An oppressive silence settled over the room. Inside of ninety seconds Ducky grew fidgety. He unzippered a jacket pocket and removed a package of chocolate-covered peanuts; he shook out a palmful.

"Goober?" he offered.

Meat shook his head and said irritably, "Sit still, fucknuts." There was a rack of magazines beside him so he picked something at random and shoved it in his partner's lap. "Here, look at this awhile."

It was a loose-leaf album entitled *Case Histories: 1985–1987*. Ducky began thumbing through it, and soon he was snickering quietly. He poked Meat with an elbow and said, "Lookit here, you think old Doc's lost his touch."

On one page were bird's-eye photos of heads with retreating hairlines and obscene patchy bald spots; opposite them were those same heads miraculously quilted with rich blankets of hair. Each case came fully documented, though each head belonged to a citizen resident in some distant community. Meat stared at them, nodding wisely. "What'd I say. Man's a fuckin' genius."

A moment later the object of their admiration came through the office door, the frowning woman at his shoulder. At first his benign, ossified greeting smile collapsed, then it recovered, fell again, resurrected itself, like some crazily accelerated warning beacon sweeping the sky.

"Milo," he said, "Conrad. Nice to see you boys again. Come right on in. Mrs. Julius, hold my calls, if you please."

FOUR

IN THE EMERGENCY ROOM of St. Mary's Hospital, another doctor, medical variety, was allowing himself a wry smile as he worked on the ragged gash under Morse's jaw. "You better take it easy the rest of the day," he advised. "Stay out of arguments."

"Yeah, I'll do that," Morse said. "No politics or religion round tables for me the next twenty-four hours."

The doctor, looked like he might be old enough to get served in a bar, was cultivating the weary-wise bedside manner of the man who's seen it all. You know you're starting to calcify, Morse thought, when even the quacks look like infants. Also when you feel as wiped out as he did. Rest of the day off, that sounded half tolerable right about then.

Shortly before noon they released him. He asked about the girl and a nurse told him she was being held overnight "for observation." He got the room number and took the elevator up. He'd had enough exercise for one day.

Morse had no great love of hospitals. Most of his life he'd

been lucky enough to escape them, though once, as an adolescent, he did close to three weeks in one when his appendix nearly ruptured on him. And passing down this corridor, what he remembered dimly from that time—the clashing perfumes of sour bedsheets and antiseptics and ailing flesh—came back to him now. Better to go out lying in the grass with your toes pointing up than to linger in a white world like this one. He walked faster.

Jean Satterfield was drifting in and out of sleep, mostly in. The other bed was empty so he hopped up on it and waited. After a while her eyes opened and seemed to focus, and she gave him a meager smile.

"How many fingers do you see?" Morse said, holding up a middle one.

"You're an evil man, Mr. Morse."

Her voice was a scratchy murmur, would have been a rasp if it weren't so faint. Her face had the pale-blue color of skim milk, except for the purplish bruise splayed all across one side of it. The white sheet was tucked up under her chin, and her short hair was drawn back severely off her forehead. She looked like a cadaver waiting to be iced. Not good.

"Secret of my charm," he said. "Penetrates right to the hearts of you ladies. But you got to promise not to tell."

"It's safe with me."

"Yeah, I figured I could count on you."

It came spilling out before he thought about it. Her lower lip did a slow twitch and her eyes began to cloud over. "I'm sorry about . . . this morning. Sorry. I thought I could help."

"What are you talkin'. You did good. I mean it. Hadn't been for you that ninja would of put me on permanent disability." Morse shifted his glance from her to the wall to the floor. Words of consolation, sympathy, never came easily to him, tasted like so much mush in his mouth, so he added, "You do got to work on your swing, though."

"Or on finding a different line of work."

"C'mon, you're forgettin' the thrill of bringin' felons to justice through scientific crime detection." Tired old line, but it was good enough for another wispy smile and it seemed to hold off the waterworks.

"Will you tell me what happened back there?"

"Not much to tell. You seen the part where he about cold-cocks me. Then you come blitzin' and he dings you, which gives me the time to get regrouped, neutralize him."

"But what about the rest of them? They didn't . . . ?"

"Oh no. Little scuffle like that's a learning experience. Teaches what you might call humility, your Christian forbearance. They were real obliging about orderly dispersal."

"How did we get here?"

"You don't remember?"

She shook her head no.

"My car. First I had to call Ash, listen to him blubber about lawsuits a little. Almost choked him but he did say take the day off. So maybe you got a happy ending here after all."

"Could be a couple of days in my case. They want to keep me overnight anyway, to check for a concussion. What about you?"

"Me? I'm indestructible, didn't they tell you? Terror of the streets."

"That looks like more than a Band-Aid on your chin."

"This?" Morse said, touching at the puffy dressing. "Just a scratch under it, but there's this horny nurse was lookin' for an excuse to get next to me."

"You *are* an evil man."

"Yeah? Lady with a concussion, what would she know." Jean Satterfield had a good smile, Morse decided, the kind that appeared and faded on its own. Best kind. "Look," he said, "I better head out. Got me a ten-K race to run yet today. Tell 'em to treat you right here. Tell 'em I said."

Before he reached the door she said, "Mr. Morse? Thanks for stopping by."

Without looking back he wiggled a hand in a small gesture of disclaimer. But then he hesitated, turned and said, "You might as well call me Mitch. Everybody else does. No respect anymore, your seniority or experience."

"Or your kindness?"

"That either."

XX

Whatever there had been of morning sunlight was long gone, blotted by waffled banks of clouds hanging in an arch of gray sky. He stood outside the hospital entrance, filled his lungs with the chilly, wind-whipped air. Couldn't fault the air here, nothing like Detroit. That much you had to give this town. The rest of its charm escaped him.

He crossed the lot, got in his Monte Carlo and sat behind the wheel a moment, considering what to do with the remainder of the day. He could do the prudent thing, of course, go home—you wanted to call home a three-room apartment looked like it had been tossed, unwashed sheets on an unmade bed, week's worth of dishes piled in the sink, month's worth of dust settled over the garage sale furniture and with his own *Dust Me!* scrawled in it. Or he could attend to any one of the numberless details of the business of living: groceries, laundry, car, checkbook, bills, correspondence—who was he kidding, correspondence, who was there to write? Or he could head for the Plainfield Avenue tavern that, in the past few months, had come to assume the character of home.

No contest.

He swung the car out onto Jefferson, pointed it north, then west on Fulton and then north again on Division which, as he remembered, gave onto Plainfield. In the time he had been in Grand Rapids he'd learned what was needed to get from the apartment to the site of whatever job they were working to the tavern, and not a bit more, believing always in the miracle that was going to pluck him out of here. But for reasons he didn't fully understand—the dismal weather maybe, maybe the near disaster back there at the Beer Factory, something—it was hard to believe in miracles today.

Division, the Grand Rapids version of Sin Street, skirted the ragged edge of downtown and angled into Plainfield. So that one anyway he had right. Driving up Plainfield he passed through unfamiliar residential neighborhoods, rows of close-set, shabby frame houses broken here and there by business blocks, mini-Main Streets. Farther north, the neighborhoods took on a comfortable middle-class look: ranch houses, brick, some of them; wide lawns spotted with trees and well-tended shrubs; lots of church steeples piercing the sky; the occasional wooded slope of a ravine. Abruptly, at the I-96 overpass, all of it gave way to a three-mile stretch of commerce. On the right was a strip mall identified in neon as the PLAINFIELD PLAZA. Many a night he'd come by here and observed the FIELD half of the sign flickered out, and once even the PLAZA dark, leaving only the supremely apt designation PLAIN. A quarter of a mile on the left was the tavern.

Three minutes later he was seated on the same stool he had held down most of the night before, a beer in front of him, lite, more a concession to a body pulsing with aches than to good sense.

"Hey, Mitch," came a voice from down the bar, voice like a slap on the ear. "How come you wearin' that Tampax on your face? Girlfriend bleedin'?" It got a booming laugh from the three or four other juicers in the room.

"That's real comical," he said. "You maybe ought to think about trying out for the teevee." The comedian's name was Cecil, which was as much as Morse knew about him, or wanted to know.

"Little early for you to be punched out, ain't it?" Cecil persisted, and then he added, "That ain't a joke I'm makin'." He chortled anyway.

"Yeah, well, I got promoted to management ranks." Morse stared into his glass as he spoke. He didn't want to encourage this conversation, or any other.

"Good on you. That mean you got the twenty you're down?"

It came back to him now how he'd missed the spread on last night's game. Missed it by two points. Two. Morse turned on his wicked practiced glare and fixed Cecil with it. "You ever been stiffed by me? Cee-cil?"

"No, no. I just figured—"

"Wrong. You figured wrong. Back away. You'll get your money."

Though God knows where, a thought he put quickly out of mind. Time enough for that kind of worry later. Tonight maybe, or this weekend for sure. For now it put a rag in the mouth of scowling Cecil. So he still had the magic, when he needed it.

Or did he?

Sooner or later he was going to have to get it out and look at it. Might as well now. Okay. But for a lucky fluke, name of Jean Satterfield, that poor man's Bruce Lee would have taken him out this morning, chilled him. How many aces could a man hold? First the reflexes go, then the legs. Then the balls. Then what? Vanderkullen was nothing more than a hick-town peddler of beer, but on one thing he was shrewd enough to circle around the truth: who'd want a washout cop, couldn't keep the peace at a Boy Scout jamboree? You knew it had to happen some day, an inner voice scolded him. Yeah yeah yeah—I know. But now it's *happening*.

Next month he'd be looking at thirty-five in the rearview mirror. Thirty-five years, a third of them pension years gone Drano over one stupid, fucking, ignorant, arrogant, grandstanding move. Not a little like the one he'd made today. If he'd learned anything at all, he'd learned that all experience was lost on him; his whole life was testimony to that hard fact. And now it was half over and what did he have on his supper plate? This is what he had: a candyass job in a vanilla milkshake town, a bank account with something under a thousand in it, last time he looked, forty thin ones or fewer in his wallet till paycheck Friday, and then the rent was due. And a creditor who wanted half the forty. Named Cecil.

Where was fair, this world?

Wherever it was, it was not in the men's john (identified as "Roosters' Room") necessity took him to finally, six dismal beers later. As often as he'd been there and toughened as he believed he was, it never failed to stun him, for in any contest for sheer vileness the Roosters' Room had to be a front-runner. The single stall's door was removed, either to discourage deviant behavior or more likely out of simple neglect; and the pitted stool bubbled in perpetual flush, swirling a blend of soggy paper and disintegrating turds. A loop of smirched cloth dangled from the towel dispenser, brushing the damp floor. Exposed pipes under the scarred sink gurgled ominously. Two urinal scoops clung to a plaster wall. Morse straddled one, spraying into extinction the sodden cigar butt beneath him. At eye level was penciled: *Don't drop toothpicks in pisser—the crabs in here can pole vault fifteen feet*.

As he stood dipping his fingers in icy tap water, he read another appeal scratched on the wall alongside the mirror: *Please don't piss in our sink. We don't shit in your bathtub. Thank you, The Management*.

And over by the towel dispenser, a play on the familiar nursery rhyme:

Jack and Jill went up a hill
Each with a dollar and a quarter.
Jill came down with two and a half
And you think they went for water.

For a bleary, beer-fogged moment, he wondered at the anonymous voices behind all this jeering business. Wondered if they were merely the shadowy underside of the same voices directing you to have a super day, mocking you with the sniggery and, when you thought about it, dreadful message: the laugh's on you, friend, the last laugh is surely on you. You want to think they went for water? Okay. Sure. Go have yourself a super day, and fuck you very much.

Unaccountably, he felt a sudden lecherous buzzing in his head. Super day . . . super day . . . Fleets. That was it, Fleets. The cashier this morning, dazzling swag of hair, cool distant knowing voice. Starla.

Maybe there was something after all to these mysterious messages that seemed to be tracking him.

Fleets was no more than a mile or so down the road. There was still most of the afternoon and a full evening ahead, even if it did have to be a Tuesday. He had forty bucks in his pocket, take away what he owed on the beer. The mirror gave him back a reflection distorted by grime, but what he saw was not entirely discouraging. Still had the thick dark hair, all of it, and with only a fleck of sleet here and there. Athlete's blade-honed face. Clear blue eyes his ex-wife had once described as "nimble" (whatever that meant; he assumed it was good). And the bandage across the chiseled jaw bestowed a kind of piratical dash. Few miles on him maybe, but he was road tested, still very much in the race. He settled up at the bar and wheeled his Monte Carlo out into the Plainfield traffic. Headed for Fleets.

XX

"Starla? She's morning shift. Went off at three. You just missed her."

He was looking across the Customer Service counter at a woman with the bulldog features of a female thug. A thin, bleach-resistant mustache trailed across her upper lip like a line of soot. She was wearing her khaki Fleets jacket and one of those brisk, better-you-than-me smiles some people will use to deliver the bad news.

"Three," Morse said. It wasn't quite a quarter past the hour. He could still get lucky. He tried his grin on her. "She wouldn't be in the back, maybe? Changing, or fixing her face, or whatever it is you foxy ladies do?"

"Not Starla," the woman said, laying a finger on the mustache. "No way. Quittin' time, she's outta here."

On the wall behind her was a sign that offered the bold challenge:

QUALIFIED? JOIN THE FLEETS FAMILY.
POSITIONS AVAILABLE NOW. INQUIRE HERE.

"Not a happy family member, huh," Morse said.

"Huh?"

"Uh, nothing, just thinking out loud."

"You a friend of Starla's?" she asked, putting a sly insinuation on the *friend*.

"Manner of speaking," he said, extemporizing, running on the gas of feeble inspiration. "I'm her cousin. From Detroit. Just in town for the day, so I thought I should look her up." He gave it as casual a melody as he could, though he knew the rhythm was off. Too many warmup beers.

"Cousin," the woman repeated skeptically. "Well, you might catch up to her at home." Her eyes narrowed into two tiny beads of spite and she added, "Better hurry, though. Cute little thing like your cousin, she's real popular."

"Yeah, well, that's the problem. See, I don't know where she lives."

"You always got your phone book. She's in it."

Morse did a helpless shrug. "Don't know the name she's going by these days. You know how it is, marriages, divorces. We been out of touch awhile." It was an even-money guess, and he was low on chips.

"You do got a problem, don't you."

"I figured you could maybe help me out."

She shook her head firmly, all the neighborliness gone out of her smile, just the spite left. "No can do. Against policy. Rules is we can't give out no employees' phones or addresses."

"I didn't hear you say last names. And first I already got."

"Can't do that. Against policy. That's why you got just your last initial here on the name tag." She pointed to hers, a B. For Bulldog, he would have bet. Or Bitch. What he said was, "I was thinking you might make an exception this one time. For a family member."

"Unh-unh, can't help you. Even if she was relation," she added, in the tone that says there's nobody gets anything past this shrewd dealer, been around the block a time or two herself.

Morse could recognize a stonewall. He'd been there before, often enough. But experience didn't make it go down any easier either. He started to move away, paused and turned and faced her. "Oh, I seen you noticed this bandage I got on." Which was true, she'd been eyeing it, desperate to ask, all the while they spoke. "You want to know what it's for?"

"None of my business."

"Well, kind of yes and no. What I got is the plague. Contagious variety. Bubonic. Now you probably got it too, which means if you do you got a little under seventy-two hours to live. Hey, have a super day."

Fucking Fleets, he thought as he took the car squealing out of their lot. Thanks for zip and fuck you very much.

FIVE

CURIOUSLY, STARLA HUDEK was thinking something very much on the same order, that same moment, as she lay naked in a tanning bed, frying her flesh a color the strange cross between iodine and rust. Fleets. If it were up to her the whole Fleets family could go fuck themselves to death. She was knocked out, beat, and not in a mood to feel generous toward her employer or fellow workers or the public she served. Who would be? Eight hours on your feet in that jungle of junk, mammoth as an underground cavern and for all the fluorescent lighting somehow just as dank. Chanting the "Welcome to Fleets" refrain ("Your purchase FREE if we forget to say hi!"), dancing to the tune of every bluehead coupon squirreler who came down your aisle, punching out the minutes and days and years of your life on the keys of a Jewish piano—that's what the store manager, Eddie, called a register. It was funny the first time, less so after five years. Ready Eddie, who'd be coming to collect his periodic blow job soon, and she'd have to oblige if she wanted to keep her place on the morning shift, and she did.

And as her thoughts turned to that sort of thing, her hands, with a will of their own, began to move caressingly over her slender body baking in the luminous heat. Her fingers brushed the insides of her thighs, lingered awhile on the velvety, smooth-shaven mound (early on she'd discovered all men were baby fuckers at heart), stroked languorously across her tight belly and traced slow circles of delight around the nipples of her pointy little breasts. So there wasn't much there, so what? What there was was sweeter than honey and cream, and a troop of men would take an oath on that. The feel of her firm body confirmed what she'd always known: she was born for something better than Fleets. But knowing it was one thing; getting it, that was altogether different, altogether baffling.

The Lotto maybe, maybe she'd get lucky, hit the Lotto (so these dreamy ruminations took her). It was up to five million this week, a sum dizzying to other players but not to her. She had parsed it meticulously in her head, many times over; it was how you got through the day. About seven minutes remained on the timer, so she entertained herself with it again now.

Five mil split twenty times comes to two hundred fifty thou a year for the next twenty years. Okay, the government dipped sticky fingers in for a third of it, eighty grand, say. Leaves one seventy. Put one twenty of that aside for just general high living day-to-day—you could live right on ten large bills a month—and that left her fifty a year for a wanton, self-indulgent, spending spree: clothes, cars, perfumes, jewels, restaurants where they served you wines with names you couldn't say, trips to places where the sun shines more than two weeks a year. And men. Men whose breath didn't stink of onions and Tic Tacs, and whose bodies weren't as lumpy and pale as yesterday's rice pudding. Men of her own choosing, like the ones in *Flex* maybe, looked all carved out of quarry stone. She'd have sucked her last managerial cock then, and anything she did from there on out, along those lines anyway, would be for the sheer private tingle of it. Her own pleasures for a change.

Twenty long years of them. And then the well would go dry. It wouldn't matter, she'd be forty-nine, an age as inconceivable to her as a hundred and so not worth wasting any thoughts on. Live that long and you get what you deserve.

She played one ticket a drawing, all she could afford, and her numbers were invariably the same. They were selected to coincide with the years of the most hateful events in her life. Nine: when Uncle Ray first started snuggling into bed with her; fifteen: abortion year; seventeen: marriage; eighteen: first serious cuffing by the old man (strictly, that one should have been seventeen too, but you couldn't repeat a number); twenty-four: first got on with Fleets; and then finally the wild card, which was always different, always the date of the day she bought the ticket. It was a way of ambushing fate, her system, and she had a stubborn faith in it. Once she'd matched four numbers and strutted away with a hundred and six bills. The five mil had to be just around the corner and up the street.

She was about to dissect her ten thousand a month allowance when the timer dinged and the electric lamps above and beneath her suddenly went out. She climbed out of the bed, stretched her limbs languidly, dressed and waved an airy goodbye to a middle-aged woman at the front desk whose skin had the shade and texture of a withered tangerine. Her six-year-old Chevette sputtered on the start (Lord only knew what she was going to do for wheels when it turned really cold) but she pumped it a little and drove on home.

Home for Starla was a rented tin trailer set in a park crammed so full of dead elephants you opened a window and you were just as likely as not to catch a neighborly goose. Which is why she kept her windows permanently sealed, the quality of people there, slithered out from under a rock, most of them. She had been there ever since she came down from that flyspeck home town of hers, forty miles north, town full of huckleberries and horseshoes, called a good time chugging beer and watching barnyard animals hump each other. Down to make a new life for herself, for all that had come to. Big town for her, Grand Rapids; sure, but the same creepy crawlers everywhere you looked, only more of them. The one good thing she'd done, though, was shuck her married name, even if it wasn't exactly legal. She'd never followed up on the divorce, but then who had the juice to pay off a shyster at seventy an hour, tries to cop a free feel on the side? Anyway, Hudek beat Pitts by a back-road mile. Starla Pitts? Made her sound like she had acne or something. So who cared, finally? Long as you were clear of that swamp, who cared what you went by?

XX

"I just spent four hours," Dexter was saying, "trying to coax words out of my head. Four hours, and scarcely a usable line. And you want to go out. Can't you see I'm exhausted?"

Starla had that one figured out the moment he came slouching through the door, face a map of prickly gloom, but it didn't make her any less annoyed. Tuesday night was Friday night to her: forty-eight hours of blissful freedom from Fleets, dead ahead. And here sat this lump grouching about exhaustion. Translated, that meant he was too cheap or too lazy or too ornery, or some mix of all three, to move out of the chair he was sprawled in. Take a derrick now. She lit a cigarette—give him back some of that annoyance—and said coolly, "You may want to remember it was you said we were having dinner out tonight." From him she had learned to call it dinner instead of supper.

"I know I did," he said, batting irritably at a trail of smoke drifting toward him. "But when you're totally engaged in an all-consuming project, as I am, there's no predicting one day to the next. Honestly, Starla, there are days when my life seems barely tolerable."

That was how he talked. She'd picked up a few of his words and phrases, used them on the girls at work sometimes, to show off some class. But mostly she ignored it. "Maybe you should think about getting on with Fleets," she said. "They're hiring, you know." When his scowl only deepened she added, "It was a joke, Dexter. Just making a little joke."

"Some rapier wit you have there."

Now he was staring glumly into the water glass of whiskey she had poured him. Pouting. "Okay," she said, smothering the sigh on a gust of exhaled smoke, "we'll order out."

"I'm not hungry. But if you are, why not phone Little Caesars. You'll get two, and one of them you can freeze."

Trust Dexter Graff, still had his piggy bank under the mattress, to think of that one.

After she made the call she fixed herself a drink, a tall one, and sat on the frayed couch opposite him. His eyes were still lowered. He looked on the fine edge of tears. She was doing a Wallenda with this one, and she knew it. Whiny, rude, foul-tempered, arrogant, he nonetheless represented her most immediate and best—only, actually—hope of tossing Fleets an over-the-shoulder farewell bird. "Maybe later on," she said carefully, "you'll want to play some party games. When you're more relaxed."

He favored her with a languid smile, his look of sad, infinite wisdom. "Oh, I don't know, Starla. Age, that job I'm shackled to, the demands of my real work—they all of them take their toll. I doubt I could do you much good tonight."

Talk about your robbing the grave, at forty-seven he had the age part right. The job was teaching English twelve hours a week down at the J.C., where he was known as Professor Dexter Graff. The real work he was always sputtering about was some goddam novel he was writing, or said he was writing, that was supposed to, in his words, "expose the rotten core of academe." And make that not doing much good *any* night, she thought, saying, "Why don't you let me be the judge of that."

"Ah, Starla. You know me better than I know myself."

Next translation: he was feeling horny but too lazy to do any of the work. By now she knew what that meant for her. She filled his glass and made herself another, a real tightener this time.

What was ahead this evening, she needed it. He was five feet nine inches (in lifts), 240 pounds of loose flesh. His face was rubbery and weak, the features blurred by soft living. Also his teeth were false, and in the eerie light of dawn it was still unnerving to wake and find those clackers grinning at you from the nightstand. But he packed the heaviest wallet she'd seen in a good long while, if you could ever get those alligator arms of his to reach for it. She had ways of doing that, but she was keen enough to know when she had a plump fish on the line. Reel it in very, very gently. It took him six weeks of shuffling through her check-out lane, all cow-eyed and lip licking, before he screwed up the nerve to ask her out, and then she all but had to invite herself. Six more to get him talking seriously about her coming along to Florida on his

Christmas break. Lately he was making some shifty noise about her quitting work and moving in with him after they got back. He lived in a big old house he'd inherited, along with a pile of hoarded money, from an aunt. So she had to play things cautiously, and right. He could be her ticket out of Fleets, a cushy way-station till something better turned up.

Nevertheless, it irked her. If they'd gone out tonight she could have given quick head in the car on the drive, gotten it over with and enjoyed the dinner at least, if nothing else. Now she was going to have to pay the heavy dues.

After another drink the pizzas arrived, and the spiritless professor found it in himself to tuck away one, solo, and no small share of the second. Stringy ladders of cheese dangled from his mouth, which was going nonstop now about The Novel and the terror it struck in the hearts of his colleagues, who had every reason to fear his penetrating insights, and blah and blah and blah. Starla tuned him out, nibbled at a thin slice and threw back a couple more drinks, anesthetizing herself. Finally he put his plate aside and thumped his stomach contentedly. He nodded toward the bedroom and said, "Uh, those games you spoke of earlier. I think I'm up to a little after all. Help me unwind."

A bit unsteadily, she made it to her feet. "You wait here. I'll get things ready."

In the bedroom she lit a pair of candles and some incense, and switched off the overhead light. She put a bath towel on the throw rug by the bed. Then she took a fresh tube of Wildfire Lubricant and a skintight plastic glove from the bottom drawer of the dresser and laid them alongside the towel. And then she stripped off all her clothes, took a few shallow breaths and called him in.

He disrobed in a corner, as far away from the meager candlelight as the tiny room allowed. Without a word he got down on his hands and knees on the rug. She fit the towel carefully under him and came around where he could watch while she squeezed a fistful of the creamy Wildfire lotion all over her breasts and belly and thighs. Then she slipped behind him and emptied the tube on his back and began to stroke gently. He buried his face in the rug, furry ass riding the air. She worked her way south (or maybe it was north, given the angle of his spine), tracing wide circles around his hips and those enormous hams of buttocks, flicking lightly over the parted gate and then under it, teasing the scrotum and the little needledick shaft, already pulsing at her feathery touch.

Once he was thoroughly oiled she mounted him, doggie fashion, and rubbed her hips slowly over his ass and brushed his back with her belly and breasts. A little of that got him purring, and when the groaning began she knew, from odious experience, the rest wouldn't take long.

Time for the main event. She pulled on the glove, lubricated the fingers and then thrust the middle one into the wide open portal. He let out a pained, pleasured yelp, and she slid another finger in, and then another, plunging them in a slow circular motion.

Soon he was bucking and heaving, a mercifully clear signal it was about over. "Now," he said thickly, and she did a quick reach-around with her left hand and, still impaling him with the right, clutched that toy water pistol and gave it a quick tug or two till it squirted all over the towel.

He collapsed on the rug, gasping. She leaned back and gazed at her professor with monumental disgust. It was staggering, incredible beyond belief, what you could bring yourself to do to escape a place like Fleets.

SIX

"FLEETS" WAS HOW MEAT had begun when, earlier in the day, he addressed his attentive audience of two, outlining his plan. He paused significantly, let the full dramatic impact settle in. "Christmas Eve," he resumed, "we take out the Fleets up on Plainfield. Think about it. Here's your Christmas Eve, security's loose, everybody sportin' a big holiday grin, yodelin' 'Joy to the World,' waitin' on Santa. And who comes down their chimney? Us is who. Got to be three hundred long in them tills easy, night like that. We're maybe talkin' more. Think about it."

That's what they appeared to be doing, both of them, thinking about it. Ducky was seated in the consulting chair, features knotted in the effort of concentration, Kasperson behind his desk, chewing thoughtfully on the erasered tip of a pencil. Meat stood facing them with his back to the window. He had appropriated Kasperson's pointer and was slapping a palm with it, rather like a corporate executive unveiling an aggressive marketing strategy of his own invention, awaiting the proper genuflections of his staff. "Well?" he said.

Ducky was the first to respond. "I dunno, Meat, place like Fleets, that's a pretty heavy score, three of us. Somethin' go wrong, you're lookin' at a twenty-year jolt."

"Or a hundred and up balloons in your hip pocket, which is a nice combined Christmas-birthday present for you, Duck." Meat looked at him steadily, then glanced over at Kasperson. "Don't nothin' have to go wrong, you got the right man drawin' blueprints."

Kasperson put the pencil down and made a prayer steeple with his hands. "By that you mean me."

"I was thinkin' along them lines."

The fingers of the steeple began drumming softly. "It's an interesting idea, Milo. But chancy too, as Conrad here suggests. Fleets is not what you'd call a mom and pop operation."

"It's a big store," Meat confirmed.

"With many entrances, no doubt."

"Total of nine. Five loadin' and four customer, three of 'em up front, one in the back. But if it's timed right I figure only the front three would need sealin'."

"Three," Kasperson said after him. He opened the steeple in a gesture of self-evidence. "And I count two of you."

"If you're sayin' we'd need another force man, I already thought of that. We wouldn't have no trouble turnin' up a dude knows slack work. Fuck, anybody got his head right be, y'know, like honored, get an invite to this one."

Ducky's eyes had been shifting between them, in rhythm to

the exchange. Now they fixed on Meat, stricken. "Jesus, Meat, that'd mean another share."

"He makes a good point," Kasperson said. "There's always the risk-to-reward ratio to consider."

Meat's broody face displayed its first faint sign of self-satisfaction. "I got a feeling this other fella, whoever he is, gonna be one of them dudes just natural born unlucky. If you take my meaning."

For a moment Ducky looked vacant. Then a shrewd spark came into his eyes. "Oh, I get it. You're sayin' an ice job. But how would we—"

Meat cut him off quickly. "Them are the kind of details for you and me to work out. Doc, he don't want to clutter up his head. Not if he's quarterbackin'."

Kasperson had picked up a wallet-sized calendar from his desk and was studying it silently. Meat watched him, gave it a while before he said, "If it's time you're thinkin' about, we're lookin' at eight weeks."

"And two days, to be exact," Kasperson murmured quietly, as though communing with himself. "Not all that much for an undertaking of this magnitude."

"Doc, you got to talk American. What's that mean?"

"It means, Milo, that your time frame is tight for the kind of research this score would require. We'd need diagrams, floor plans, schedules, alarm system details, security procedures—that kind of information. None of it easy to come by."

Meat's earlier hint of complacency blossomed in a sly grin. "Supposin' I was to tell you we got a mouse."

Kasperson's eyebrows arched. "You have someone inside?"

"We will," Meat declared confidently.

"Someone reliable?"

"Oh yeah. We'll be able to count on this party."

"Who's it, Meat?" Ducky shrilled at him. "Huh, who?"

"Lady name of Starla. She's my wife."

Now Ducky looked suddenly perplexed again. "I thought she split the sheets on you. Long time back."

"Maybe she did. I never heard for sure. Don't matter none anyways. We was both raised Catholic, eyes of the Church we're still spliced. Good enough for the Church, good enough for me."

"This wife of yours," Kasperson said, "or whatever—she works there?"

"She's there all right, punchin' a cash register. I already scouted it out. Been with 'em a few years too, my home town sources say. She oughta have their drills down good. Also," he added with a trace of bitterness, "she got ways of findin' things out. Real experienced, comes to that."

"And she'd cooperate?"

"Wife got to obey her old man, Doc. That's in your Bible."

"So it is, Milo, in one fashion or another. Tell me, have you spoken with her yet? On this matter?"

"Not yet. First thing tomorrow. Look, you don't have to worry none, that end. Anything you need in the way of thinkin' materials, you got it. And that's a Meat Pitts guaranfuckintee. Lifetime warranty."

Kasperson chuckled mildly. "If experience has taught the three of us anything at all, it's to be wary of lifetime guarantees."

"Doc, I'm tellin' you, this is a walkover plan. All's it needs is somebody get the square edges rounded off. Guy like you."

"You seem to have given it a lot of thought, Milo."

"Year and a half's worth. Plus the last couple weeks sniffin' around."

"How many check-out lanes in the store?"

"Thirty-six up front. Six in the back."

"Uniformed security?"

"Plainclothes."

"What are the business hours?"

"Six to midnight. Holiday, they figure to close early. Probably around seven."

"Forty-two cash registers, thirteen hours, volume, oh, fifteen an hour, give or take some down time, average ticket fifty dollars, say, conservative . . ." Kasperson tapped a forefinger against his lip, as though to advance the calculations. The tapping ceased and he said, "Your three hundred thousand figure could even be a little light."

"What'd I say? Told you I done my homework, Doc."

Kasperson fell silent, chin in hand, eyes gazing into some middle distance, contemplative as a philosopher weaving some intricate system of metaphysics. Ducky and Meat waited respectfully. Neither said a word.

At last Kasperson lifted his eyes and regarded each of them, Ducky first, then Meat. "Milo, I've got to admire you. This is quite an opportunity you've uncovered. And I'm flattered you'd want to include me since, as you well know, I can't count armed robbery among my accomplishments."

"I can hear a 'but' comin' on," Meat said coldly.

"That's right. The way I see it, there's one flaw in your plan. Maybe not in the plan itself but in bringing it off."

"Yeah, what's that?"

"Start-up cash. If my figures are right, we'd need a pretty heavy sum. You've got vehicles to consider, hardware, miscellaneous expenses, general walking-around money to get us by the next two months. And what about afterwards? A hit like this, you'd have to get out of the country, and fast. That means paper—passports and a whole new set of ID's for the three of us. It wouldn't be easy to lay hands on documents like that. Not in this turnip town. And they wouldn't come cheap."

"Well, sure, you couldn't score this big without some kind of stake."

"And you figured I'd have it."

"Right. I seen your picture in the paper, I says to myself, 'Doc's got himself a nice little scam, growin' hair. Ain't goin' to get fat off it but the money's steady, all the bald heads got to be out there.' "

Kasperson expelled a long, doleful sigh. "I'm afraid that's not the case. United Hairlines is, well, marginal, and that's putting the best face on it."

"But we ain't talkin' the large dollar here, Doc."

"The way things stand right now, *any* amount you name would look large to me."

"I said that right off," Ducky put in. "Soon as I seen this rat's nest you're operatin' out of, Doc, I said that to Meat."

Meat silenced him with an angry wave, and there was a note of rising desperation in his voice as he demanded, "You sayin' you're busted, Doc?"

"You might say my cash flow position is not all it could be."

"How about that dustmop head you got workin' your front desk? You pinch anything outta her?"

"Forget that. There's no way she could help us out."

"Already tapped that one dry, huh," Ducky said with an evil grin.

Kasperson ignored him. To Meat he said, "She's a widow, her funds have already been overextended. To say the least."

Meat wheeled around and stared darkly out the window. All those months of plotting, drafting the plan, thinking it through, revising it, running it by in his head, re-revising, slow speed, for fine tuning—and stalled over some pocket change. Cab fare. If you got it. Which he didn't. He turned once more, facing Kasperson. "How much you think it would take, get us heeled and in the startin' gate?"

Kasperson thought about it for a long moment. "About five thou," he said finally.

"What if we could come up with it? You be in?"

"Where we gonna get five big bills?" Ducky squawked.

"Shut the fuck up, Duck. Doc, what do you say?"

Kasperson made a pensive inspection of the ceiling. Then he squared his hands on the desk, engaged Meat's cold stare and said, "Milo, let me explain some hard economic realities your stay with the state may have sheltered you from. It's an inflationary age we live in. Money won't take you as far as it did a decade ago. Three hundred thousand dollars is a nice score, but split three ways it's not as much as you seem to think. Not anymore."

"Bottom line, Doc. And in American."

"The bottom line is that the rewards don't balance out the risks."

"So it's no you're sayin'?"

"No, that's not what I'm saying. Not exactly, anyway. Let me ask you something. How many Fleets stores are there in this town?"

Meat looked puzzled. "Shit, I dunno. Bunch of 'em, I guess. Half a dozen maybe. Why you wanta know? I already told you it's the Plainfield one's where I got the inside track."

"While we've been talking, a variation on your plan occurred to me. One that could make us all rich men. Seven figures, maybe, instead of your six."

Meat's brows tightened suspiciously. "What might that be, that variation?"

"No point in going into it now," Kasperson said, waving a hand with an air of dismissal. "Without the stake money it's all a handful of air anyway."

"So you ain't gonna say what it is then."

"Come up with the money, then we can talk."

"Lemme see I got this correct. You got another idea—"

"Just a logical extension of your original plan."

"—an' if we turn up the stake, you're in? Quarterback?"

"Partners," he said evenly.

"Okay. You got a deal."

Kasperson saw them to the door. "I hope I'll be seeing you boys again. Soon."

"Bet on it," Meat said grimly.

Ducky hesitated a moment and then turned to Kasperson. "Doc, I got to ask you question, been chewin' on me ever since we sat down in here. You really grow hair?"

Clearing his throat in the lofty fashion of an orator about to launch an address, Kasperson replied, "My methods have generated some outstanding results. There's much to recommend them."

A wide innocent leer, preface to a punchline, unrolled across Ducky's face. "Reason I ask, see, is because I knew this fella in the joint could do it too." He made a masturbatory gesture, added, "Only thing is, he'd grow it right in the palm of your hand."

Kasperson pulled himself up archly. "How refreshing to hear your wit again, Conrad, after these many years."

"Figured you'd get a hoot outta that one."

Meat yanked him by the elbow. "C'mon, Mr. Dingleberry Comedian, before you get a rap upside the head. Doc, we'll be doin' some more of that chattin' soon."

"I look forward to it impatiently," Kasperson said.

In the elevator Ducky, still giggling over his excellent joke, said to his partner, "Old Doc, he don't never change. Shit just keeps dribblin' off his tongue, slicker'n spit."

"Yeah, well, you're gonna work with the man, you better quit raggin' on him."

"Little jab here and there don't hurt nothin'. Life's too short to take it all heavy."

Meat, occupied with his own thoughts, made no reply.

"Where we headed now?" Ducky asked when they were on the street.

"Get us a beer. We got some hard thinkin' to do."

"Beer sounds good."

"Also, comes dark, we got a little errand to run."

"What's that one, Meat?"

"Ain't got nothin' to do with our money problems here, but it's a piece of business I need to get cleared up."

" Business? What kind?"

"Punishing kind. Tell you about it later."

SEVEN

ELEVEN P.M., Tuesday, October 27.

Mitchell Morse was sprawled on his living room couch, trying without much success to focus his attention (and his vision as well, what with the new glasses he had to wear for reading) on a book entitled *The Uses of the Past*. Part of his concentration problem could be traced to the lingering effect of the midday beer; part to the dinner that churned relentlessly in his gut (a takeout special billed as: "Two pcs chix—Bisq—Slaw—FF or Mash Pot—$1.99") and whose remnants lay in a sack on the floor; and still another part to the aborted search for one Starla H., stalled by the iron rules of fucking Fleets. Then there was also the nagging worry that maybe he had gone a little too far with the ninja type this morning, which lent a private gravity to the title of the book in his hands and made it all the more difficult to reflect on the lessons of a history wider than his own.

He had picked the book at random from the small collection on the bricks-and-boards shelf kept out of sight in the closet of his bedroom. He owned no television, didn't want one; possessed no stereo or tape deck; subscribed to no newspapers or periodicals. But he liked history, God knows why. All through high school and his two years of college (well, one and a half strictly, since middle of the second they pulled the full-ride scholarship out from under him) it was the only study he found even remotely interesting, and the only one he tried to do something more with than merely squeak by. On those rare occasions, in those years, he gave any thought at all to a life off the football field, a future more distant than the day after tomorrow, he sometimes imagined himself a teacher of history, lecturing with the wisdom and authority of a professor on Sumer, Babylon, Assyria, Egypt. Ancient ruined cities and vanished civilizations, lost and gone. The sweep of the winds of time, and the wreckage left in its wake.

It was a murky ambition at best, as impossible to account for as it would have been to realize. No explaining it to himself, never mind to anyone else. And given the company he kept and the persona he had adopted, out of necessity, at an early age—loose, physical, profane, stripped of sentiment—one best kept strictly to himself. Which he did. But now and again (more frequently lately, it seemed) he caught himself drifting into a reverie in which the years miraculously rolled back and the very site on which he stood (or lay, like now) was the way it had been a hundred years ago, a thousand, ten thousand; and his mind reeled and his senses went numb at the mystery and immensity of time.

And it was in one of those near dreamlike trances his eyes grew heavy and he slid finally into a fitful sleep.

XX

Jean Satterfield was having no such luck with sleep. After Morse left she had dozed most of the afternoon and when she woke, her mother and father were hovering over the bed, wearing expressions that said simultaneously *you poor dear thing* and *we told you so*. Her father was a Steelcase executive, her mother a librarian. Jean was their only child, and at twenty-four she was still living with them in a luxury condo on the east side of town. They were good dutiful parents, had supported and encouraged her through the bewildering variety of careers she had embarked upon and abandoned over the past six years: gym teacher, botanist, nurse, social worker, lawyer—a trail of discarded ambitions and dreams (to say nothing of a small fortune in tuition). But much as they loved her—and she them—they were quietly appalled at her ultimate choice, and before they left that evening they expressed the fervent hope this dreadful experience had brought her to her senses.

She had to smile now, lying there wide awake in the dark, contrasting their earnestness with the cynicism of a Mitchell Morse. She thought about him, swaggering into that hostile picket line. She thought about waking this afternoon to find him slouched across the empty bed, big shouldered and self-consciously tough, grinning at her crookedly and making weak jokes. She wondered about him, how he came by that transparent pose, a grown man like that. Ash had told her something about Morse being a Detroit cop, ex-cop, dropped the broad hint it was some kind of trouble had severed him from the force. Itchy Ash, Morse called him, and she snickered out loud, remembering it now.

Why, she asked herself, this preoccupation with Mitchell Morse? The answer, when she examined it, was obvious. The fact he had even bothered to look in on her today, his fumbling words of assurance, his, well, gallantry—what else could you call it?—were just enough to steady her, teetering as she was on the high wire of self-doubt. She made up her mind that when they released her she was going back on the job she had committed to. No more running and hiding. And when she saw him again she was going to tell him why. Even if it did provoke only an indifferent grunt. She had him figured now.

Out in the corridor a nurse hurried on by, starched uniform snapping a flourish to the brisk stride. The sterilized hospital air settled over the room. Her head still ached some and her throat was still raw as emery paper. But it didn't matter. With this decision made she felt better at once, eager for tomorrow. Eventually she slept.

XX

Starla Hudek, at this hour, was floating in that borderless twilight between wakefulness and sleep, dimly conscious of the professor snoring in the next room. After she got him up off the floor ("For Christ's sake, Dexter, you can't lie there shaking all night") and onto the bed, it had required fifteen minutes of scalding hot shower and three more solitary stiff hits before she was loosened enough to pass out, more or less, transported by fatigue and drink into the timeless regions of memory and disjointed dream.

Now she was in that sanctified country of the past, eight years old, her hand grasped securely in the age-coarsened hand of her grandma, the only person she had ever loved. They were wandering through a dazzling mall somewhere, here it was, Grand Rapids, just the two of them, on her first great adventure to the city. A wonderland, mammoth as a cave, with splashy fountains and trees that seemed to sprout magically from the marble floors, brilliant neon, the sweet fragrance of caramel corn, and everywhere the jostling crowds of people. Now she was modeling a dress, for church or something, school maybe, twirling proudly for the joyous approval of the delighted old woman. She could feel its satiny texture against her skin, smell its fresh-off-the-rack newness. And now they were in some kind of tea room, sipping Cokes and nibbling at chicken sandwiches cut into triangles and crowned with toothpicks. And between sips and bites she was trying haltingly to explain why it was she never wanted to leave, why she wanted to stay here always, live in the shimmery bedlam of the mall and never go back to that gray stucco house of theirs where her mother, cigarette dangling, shuffled around all day in bathrobe and curlers, and where Uncle Ray (as she'd been instructed to call him) took her on his lap for the Saturday morning cartoons and then slowly drew her hand over the bulge in his pants, cackling, "Lookit that Road Runner there, Starla, ain't he somethin'."

In the trailer next door a furious quarrel was erupting, and Starla tossed restlessly on the couch, the fragments of the dream scattering on a pair of images: the glint in Uncle Ray's eyes, and the helpless bewildered melancholy descending over her grandma's grieving face.

XX

For Doyle Gilley sleep was elusive too, but not because of any disquieting images out of a troubled past. Rather, he was bedeviled by visions of a hairless future unless he could find a way to raise the money for the Kasperson treatments. Frightful thoughts crowded in on him. How much longer before his transparent efforts at concealment became obvious to the world? Would they call him Baldy . . . Curly . . . Skinhead . . . Chromedome?

Six months ago, baldness had never occurred to him. Now it dominated all his waking thoughts. Why him? He had a face so piercingly handsome it awed him sometimes, studying it in the mirror. There were people who told him he resembled the movie star Tom Cruise. He could get just about any woman he wanted, but he wasn't interested in any of the featherbrained cunts who touched on his life right now. Right now Twyla was enough for that; his plans went further than that.

About a year back someone in the gym told him he ought to think about becoming a male model, and he learned there was such an agency right here in Grand Rapids. Imagine where *that* might lead. Sometimes, sweating over the endless racks of grubby freezer trays, he followed that vision, to New York City maybe, or maybe out to Hollywood. Why not him? There were homelier faces staring out at you from the pages of those slick city magazines, or from any screen you wanted to watch, large or small. Homelier by far. Money, cars, clothes, women—some of those remote gorgeous twats you see pictures of, looked like they could fuck you till you faint—and all of it in reach for a dude had all the equipment he did.

All but the hair. Lose that and all the dreams and ambitions vanished.

But maybe, just maybe, things didn't have to come to such a desolate pass. If the treatments worked, all his hopes could be rekindled. He would never know unless he tried. And never forgive himself if he didn't. But how could he come up with two thousand dollars? That was the sum total, the staggering bottom-line figure on the sheet Dr. Kasperson had handed him this morning, and given the condition of his accounts it might as well have added up to two hundred thousand. Twenty bills a shot for thrice-weekly treatments of eight months, plus another hundred for something called the "Home Maintenance Kit," and you were looking at two grand and some change. A hurdle so monumental his mind shrank from it.

Doyle recognized he was arrived at a crossing in his life. The treatments he had to have; that was no longer in doubt. Therefore, he had to find the money. Somewhere, somehow. And he was wrestling with this thorny problem still, as he fell into a fretful sleep.

XX

The thoughts of D. C. (Dwight Claude) Kasperson were also focused on money this evening, and with a desperation equal to Doyle's. He was propped in a La-Z-Boy in the living room of the modest home that belonged to his United Hairlines associate and patron, Mrs. Delberta Julius, sipping at a cup of herbal tea discreetly laced with brandy a moment or so after she had padded off to bed, and taking mental stock of his fortunes. Not promising, he had to conclude, not at all good.

He was sixty-three years old and, apart from his tenuous link with Delberta and her rapidly shrinking resources, penniless. The Clinic, launched so hopefully less than a year ago, was floundering dangerously, was indeed about to sink with the dead weight of a ruptured *Titanic*, and with him on the bridge, tuning up for a chorus of "Nearer My God to Thee." A stack of unpaid bills—rent, phone, utilities, supplies, advertising—lay in a drawer in his office desk. He was two weeks behind on the wages for their single employee. Delberta was beginning to make noises about the wisdom of her investment, which amounted to every last nickel of her meager savings and which he had assured her would provide a handsome return. And that was a stern and unforgiving widow, honking herself to sleep in the bedroom down the hall, not incapable of calling in the law once her patience ran out. Not in the least incapable.

He had persuaded her to part with the money through essentially the same logic that imbecile Milo used this morning: the world was full of yearning bald heads earnestly searching for succor. He believed it himself, and with a confidence born out of experience. After all, thirty years ago a similar enterprise in Milwaukee (known there as American Hairlines) did quite nicely for him. He was Dr. Chesney Gottswald in that incarnation, and the science of trichology was young enough and arcane enough to attract a sizable clientele. He might have prospered indefinitely had he not tacitly encouraged his female operators to extend the vibro-massage and electro-stimulation techniques to the lower extremities of their patients, one of whom turned out to be a vice cop. So much for American Hairlines.

But three decades later the principle—new hope for denuded heads—remained valid, should have been just as remunerative. Who could have foreseen an age of hair transplants, inexpensive toupees, and cheap home remedies littering the shelves of every cut-rate cosmetics counter? He had tried to accommodate to this new age by adding the naturopathic dimension to his art. It had a nice ring to it, should have appealed to a health-intoxicated generation. It hadn't succeeded. Nothing, in fact, had worked, and for the first time in a good many years he felt himself swaying perilously on the brink of ruin.

In the old days a crisis of this sort would never have daunted him. He'd have examined the situation with a cool dispassionate eye and then made a dash for the nearest exit, bolted, been out of there and gone in the blinking of an eye and embarked upon some bold new venture before the bus passed the city limits sign. No more. No place to run anymore. Time, wits, stamina, imagination—they were qualities in woefully short supply these days.

With a fond nostalgia, his thoughts glided back to the cemetery lot scam, one of his most inspired conceptions. Made his way all across Ohio and Indiana and up into Michigan with that one before they finally tracked him down. But what an ingenious scheme while it lasted. Came to him one day with all the blinding force of a supernatural vision: peddling nonexistent burial plots to credulous hayseeds. "Pre-need arrangements" was how he pitched it, and done with taste and dignity and a certain doleful countenance that bespoke our universal and inescapable mortality, it seldom failed to touch an empathetic nerve and open a wallet. A dozen closes was a mediocre day—some only two-holers of course, but not infrequently, out in the pastureland, a four- or even six-holer bonanza strike; and at five hundred a hole his pockets were bursting with plunder. Low overhead too: some printing costs, a somber wardrobe, and transportation of the speedy variety. The heavier costs came later though, for a man could forfeit a great deal in five years behind the walls of Jackson. Like his fertile vision, say, his buoyant spirit of adventure, his courage, his heart.

So he had to do something and do it soon. Make a move one way or another, before a fatal paralysis set in. Without question it was hazardous, teaming with a pair of psychopaths like Milo and Conrad. It was up to them to produce the stake; he wasn't about to take a fall over some cotton candy heist. But if they could, then maybe he was still enough of a strategist to turn their five and dime tactic into the score of a lifetime, the mother lode. He had confirmed there were seven Fleets stores in this overgrown cow town and its immediate environs. Seven times four (and probably more than that; Milo's arithmetic was as suspect as his powers of ratiocination) multiplied out to something staggeringly near to three million tax-free dollars. Enough to fix him comfortably for the remainder of his days, and in a style he was by temperament and native wit rightfully born to.

But first they had to lay hands on the operating capital. If they didn't . . . ah, no good to think that way. That way lies madness and despair. He had planted the proper seed this morning, and what seed ripened more fruitfully than greed? He would be hearing from them again, and soon, the proverbial nick of time. A few thousand they could manage; three million, now that was another matter altogether and one best deferred for a later reckoning.

His cup was empty so he lumbered out of the chair and into the kitchen and filled it again, just the brandy this time. A voice muddy with sleep came wafting down the hall: "D.C.? When are you coming to bed? D.C.?"

"Soon, my dear. I'll be joining you soon."

XX

"You get the wheels?"

"Yo."

"Where you parked?"

"In the alley, like you said."

"How about the other gear I told you?"

"All there."

"Took you long enough."

"Man's goin' to do things professional, takes time. Now I done all the spearchucker work, can I sit down and get outside a drink?"

"Okay. Sit down."

Ducky pulled up a chair. The table was in the darkest corner of a large, dark, cheerless and, on this Tuesday night, sparsely trafficked lounge. Meat's position against the wall offered him a clear view of the horseshoe-shaped bar, where a handful of stealthy-looking men sat nursing drinks and watching each other. He had a full bottle of Bud in front of him, three empties, a glass from which he disdained to drink, and an ashtray full of Luckies butts. A tall, painfully thin young man materialized at the table. He wore a dainty frilled apron, and he hovered with the mournful vigilance of a funeral director while Ducky agonized over a choice. "I can recommend our Fuzzy Navels," he said at last and with all the lank enthusiasm of a man suggesting cough syrups.

"Okay, gimme one of them."

"Real sweetie, huh," Meat observed, after the waiter was gone.

"I s'pose you're gettin' around to tell me what it is we're doin' here in swish heaven."

Meat nodded his head affirmatively but said nothing. His gaze was fixed on the bar across the room.

"So? I'm waitin' to hear."

"What time you got?"

"Little past eleven. Why?"

"You think you could open up a door for us tonight, you had to?"

"Hey, Meat, ain't no place folks want to keep me out of I can't get into. That still don't tell what we're doin' here."

"You remember that little errand I mentioned to you? Back at Doc's?"

"Oh, yeah. What was that again?"

"I never said what it was, shitbrain. I'm tellin' you now."

Just then the waiter reappeared bearing a frothy orange concoction. "Your Fuzzy Navel, sir." Ducky laid some bills on the table and responded not at all. The waiter made change and floated away.

Ducky took a tentative sip, smacked his lips judiciously, swallowed some more and made a thumbs-up gesture with his unencumbered hand. "You oughta try one of these, Meat. Like drinkin' dessert."

Meat grunted contemptuously. "Goes with a sissy boy dump like this."

"One thing you got to give your air flyers though, they know how to mix a drink. Can't tell what all's in 'er but she's real sweet. Want a taste?"

Meat moved his head slowly, a gesture part refusal, more exasperation. "You remember askin' me a question 'bout a minute back? You interested in hearin' the answer or not?"

"Yeah, sure. You was sayin' how come we're here."

"You remember Sugar Boy Mottla? The joint?"

"Whoo—ee, do I! Old Sugar Boy. Had a bunghole on him closest thing to a snatch you could find in all Jacktown."

"That's the one."

"I'm tellin' you, if he'd had a set of fun bags on him you'd have half your male population this state standin' in line to do time. Got many a inmate through a long night, Sugar Boy did.''

''Also he got me set up for this zipper I'm wearin' alongside my nose. You notice that?''

''Can't say I did, Meat. Thought you always had that one.''

''You got a nice eye for detail there, Ducky.''

Ducky shrugged his regrets. ''Wonder what ever happened to old Sugar,'' he said.

''If you was to look behind you right now, which I'm recommendin' you don't, you'd find out. He's up at the bar, hustlin' a citizen. Keep your eyes on me, Duck.''

A dawning recognition flickered across those eyes, and a smile full of childish mischief widened the narrow face. ''Okay. I get it now. We're gonna lay on some hurts.''

''Your heaviest kind of hurts,'' Meat confirmed.

''How'd you know where to find him?''

''That part was easy, all them pen pal sweethearts he's got back inside. Studyin' his moves, past week or so, that's cost me some time.''

''So what you got in mind for him?''

''Oh, I got something real special planned for Sugar Boy.''

''That's what the car and all the gear's for, huh. Here I figured you was workin' out an idea for the stake.''

''Nah, not in a hot vehicle, not in this town anyway. I been thinkin' on that though, while you was gone. Got me some thoughts along them lines, just can't get 'em straight in my head yet. This business with Sugar Boy, it's just side action, I know that. But I ain't gonna feel right till I got my accounts cleared. You see why that is?''

Ducky gave him an understanding look. ''Know exactly how you feel, Meat. Anyway, little touchup keeps a man in condition. When we goin' to administer this one?''

''I'd say about any minute now. That citizen get any more excited he's gonna leave his wad in his jeans. Finish off that milkshake you got there and then let's you and me step outside.''

In under a quarter of an hour two men came through the back door of the bar. One of them, the taller of the two and the older, wore a camel coat over a vested suit. The other was outfitted in a skintight leather jumpsuit and killer-heel boots. They held hands and hunched together against the wind. Ducky and Meat stood in a patch of deepening shadow by the building, waiting.

"Now what we got here?" Meat said, moving into their path.

"Look to me like a couple sweet boys," Ducky said.

A shaft of moonlight fell across the face of the older man. He drew himself up in a posture of indignation, but his eyes darted furtively. "I beg your pardon," he said. The younger one squinted anxiously, and then he gasped, "Milo!"

"Hi there, Sugar Boy. How's life treatin' ya?"

"Milo," he said again and took a stuttering step backward. Ducky closed in behind him.

"You got a good memory for faces," Meat said conversationally, "which ain't surprisin' seein' as how you had something to do with the way this one looks. But you got a problem with names. For you, Sugar Boy, it's Capital Punishment."

Ducky uttered a staccato squealy laugh. "Hey, that's real good, Meat. Call you capital punishment."

"I demand to know what's going on here," the older man said, firm as he dared.

Meat turned a cockroach-snuffing smile on him. "Minute ago you was beggin', now you're demandin'. Which one is it?"

"I think you should let us alone. We've done nothing to you."

"That's what you think, huh. Know what I think? I think your wife and kiddies be mighty ashamed of you, fixin' to suck the dick of this boy here. Also police officers wouldn't like it. Goes against the laws of our land, y'know. Bible too."

"What is it you want, anyway?"

"Want? Tell you what I want. Just step out of that fine laundry you're wearin' and you can scoot off right down the alley. Don't have to get yourself mixed up in this business we got with your friend here at all."

The man's jaw went slack. He stood motionless, gaping at Meat.

"You got some shit in your ears, I can help clean it out for you."

Now he looked at Sugar Boy desperately. "Roland?"

"Better do like he says, man." Sugar Boy's best advice.

"But this . . . this is Grand Rapids," he said.

"Ain't it though," Meat said. "And inside a New York minute

you better be standin' there bare ass or you're gonna wish it was anyplace else in the whole fuckin' world. Russia even."

With as much dignity as he could muster, the man got out of his clothes, folding them carefully and laying them in a neat pile at his feet. At the underwear, a pair of tiny bikini briefs, he stopped and clasped his arms around his chest, shivering in the night air. He had a puffy shapeless body, overgrown with bushy tufts of hair.

"Now ain't them cute," Meat said. "I'd of figured you for boxers. Okay. Let's lose 'em."

"But I—you can't—"

"Your minute's runnin' down fast, faggot."

He pulled off the shorts. Tears smeared his face and a hand instinctively covered his crotch.

"You ain't got all that much to hide," Meat said. "What do you think, Duck, that little knob down there?"

"Look like he got to do more catchin' than pitchin', toothpick like that."

"How about you, Sugar Boy. What do you say?"

"Why you jammin' me, Milo? We're on the street now. Let it be."

Meat shook his head sadly and then, with the force of a cattle-stunning mallet, brought a fist into the midsection of Sugar Boy, who staggered and slumped to his knees. "Ain't nobody jammin' you, Sugar. Just askin' your opinion is all." He turned to the naked weeping man. "You. On your horse."

The man went hopping down the graveled alley and vanished in the dark.

"Least he hadn't ought to catch cold," Ducky said, "all that hair on him. Look like an ape."

"Go bring up the car. Put on them gloves first, like I told you before. And bring me mine."

"How 'bout them clothes there. Can I have 'em?"

"No. Just the wallet. Might be some walkin'-around money in it."

"C'mon, Meat, that's a pricy coat there."

"Do like I tell you, Duck. We ain't gonna get hung out to dry on a ten-cent beef. Move."

After Ducky was gone Meat squatted down and put an arm around Sugar Boy's shoulders, which bunched reflexively under his touch. "You gonna be okay?" he asked solicitously. "Ain't gonna blow no chunks, are you?"

What he got in reply was a congested hack.

"You still got that nice white skin on you," Meat said, drawing a hand gently over a cheek. "Smooth as a baby's ass."

"Let me walk, Milo. Please. I'll get you money."

Sugar Boy's face had the peculiar cast of a rodent: close-set eyes, needle nose, receding chin and full red lips that looked to be perpetually moist. Meat's fingers brushed the lips now, and then trailed down the throat. "Yeah, real soft skin," he said.

A glimmery light came into Sugar Boy's eyes. "Or you can fuck me, Milo. I'll make it real good for you. Like nothing you ever had before."

Meat tugged at the zipper on the jumpsuit, got it as far as the sternum, slid his hands inside and ran it caressingly over the frail chest. "Y'know them satin sheets, kind they sell in the titty books. Feels just like they look."

"Take it down below," Sugar Boy urged in a husky theatrical voice. "Go on. You'll love it."

Meat removed the hand and grasped him by the long slicked hair that fell over his neck. Sugar Boy shifted awkwardly on his knees. "Start off with a little head?" he said purringly.

"Maybe we try some dirt instead." Meat drove him face first into the ground and held him there awhile, body convulsing like a fish snagged roughly out of water, scream muffled by the gravel. "Ain't enough dicks in the world, you could suck your way out of this one, Sugar. No, you and me is goin' to have to find another way to settle up."

A car pulled alongside them and Ducky leaped out the door and tossed Meat a pair of gloves, a roll of adhesive tape and a length of rope. Working under Meat's direction, they taped Sugar Boy's mouth, stripped off his clothes, bound his hands in front of him and shoved him onto the floor in the back of the car. Meat took the passenger's seat while Ducky slid behind the wheel. "Where to now?" he asked.

"Go around out front and follow that street north. I'll tell you where. And drive slow. We don't need no heat."

After about a mile Meat said, "See that place up there on the right, next block? Suntan parlor?"

"I see it."

"Swing in around behind."

"How come there?"

"Think about it, Duck. What was Sugar Boy proud of most? Always braggin' on?"

"His fuckin'."

"Outside of that."

The question was too much for Ducky.

"Remember that skin on him?" Meat prompted. "White skin? Think about it."

Now it came to him. "Oh yeah! Sugar's gonna get one of them Caribbean suntans."

"More like a African one. Time we're done, he's gonna look like a pureblood bluegummer. Crispy critter."

A moment later the three of them stood in the darkness at the rear entrance to the building. With one hand Meat clutched the quivery Sugar Boy at the neck, with the other he held a coil of rope. Ducky, stooped in an intense, bomb-defusing stance, tinkered with the lock. He mumbled to himself as he worked.

"Hurry it up," Meat said. "We don't want Sugar Boy to catch no chill."

"You know what a fella ought to invent," Ducky said, bending in closer. "Little patch of hair you fit around a keyhole. Y'know, one of them gag gifts, like a pet rock. Bet you'd make a bundle on it."

"Will you knock off with your goddam inventions and get the goddam door open. Timin' is real delicate here."

"It's comin', it's comin'. Jesus, Meat, don't have to be so crabby. We're suppose to be having' some fun here."

"The fuckin' door, Duck."

In a matter of seconds Ducky said "Bingo!" and they stepped into a narrow blackened corridor. Meat kept a firm grip on Sugar Boy, and once his eyes were adjusted to the dark he said, "Okay, take the first room back here."

"You been here before, Meat?"

"Not *this* one, but one just like it. They got 'em all over town." With a hint of complacency he added, "It's like I told you, Duck. I spent a little time workin' this out."

He hustled Sugar Boy through a door into a small space dominated by a coffin-shaped tanning bed, its top section lifted like a wide-open mouth. Along one wall was a timer. He set it at the limit, an hour, and took an eight-penny nail from his pocket and wedged it under the knob, blocking its movement around the dial. Then he punched the On button and the long tubular lights in the bed flared, casting an eerie bluish glow through the room.

Ducky glanced about uneasily. "What if somebody sees?"

"Ain't no windows, nobody gonna see. C'mon, let's get him bedded down for the night."

Up to now Sugar Boy had been unresisting, but as they forced him onto his back inside the bed he began thrashing violently. His face was streaked with grime and blood, and his bound hands slapped the air in silent panic.

"You hold him down," Meat directed. "I'll get him trussed."

He slipped the rope under the bed and looped it around the shuddering body at the ankles, knees, groin, belly and chest. The last loop he wound tightly around the throat. He gave it a sharp yank and secured the knot. From his hip pocket he took out the roll of tape and, ever so gently, peeled back the lids of Sugar Boy's eyes and laid a thin strip across each lid.

"What do you think of this touch?" he said to Ducky.

With an admiration approaching awe, Ducky said, "Jesus, it's like genius."

"Gonna get a sunburned dick, might as well get it in the eyeballs too. It's what they call an even tan, places like this."

Meat lowered the top of the bed and they stood there a moment, two craftsmen examining their finished work with a detached critical air. Sugar Boy's head jerked furiously. Already his chalky face was purpling under the pressure of the taut rope. Urgent gurgly sounds came from behind the tape, and his eyes bulged with terror.

"You keep floppin' around like that," Meat said in a tone of paternal advice, "and you're gonna choke yourself clean to death." He turned to Ducky, winked broadly. "Course layin' stone still, that might get tough too, eight hours under them rays."

"Tough," Ducky echoed, beaming with barely contained anticipation. "Hope to shit in your mess gear, tough. Can we watch, Meat? Be just like a weenie roast."

"Huh, be more like marshmallow, that skin on him."

"So, we get to stay awhile?"

"'Fraid not, Duck. We're sailin' close to the wind right now, just bein' here. Anyway, this here's gonna take care of itself real quick, is how I figure."

He stooped down for a final farewell, gazed into eyes suspended in a paralytic shock. Tenderly he stroked the clammy forehead. "Don't you worry none, sandman be here soon. So long, Sugar."

As they pulled away in the car, a curious melancholy overtook Meat, like a post-coital is-that-all-there-is. He sat slumped against the passenger door, staring glumly out the window.

Ducky paused in the breathily whistled rendering of an unrecognizable tune and, oblivious to Meat's altered mood, said, "I tell you how much was in that wallet?"

"How much?"

"You ready for this? Close to four hundred!" he exclaimed, banging a jubilant fist on the wheel. "Payback like this one tonight, and a bonus on top. You oughta be real proud, Meat."

"It's a nice little take," he allowed, but with none of his partner's enthusiasm. He couldn't trace it, this peculiar dejection. Like Ducky said, he ought to feel proud now, real good. Instead he felt a shadowy nagging anxiety. He rode in silence awhile, Ducky chattering away gleefully beside him. And then, unaccountably, his thoughts returned to the Fleets adventure, and out of nowhere he was galvanized by a sudden inspiration. "Four hundred, huh. You know anyplace we could pick up a piece? Wouldn't have to be no cannon, pea shooter'd do."

"Know a fella knows a fella. But you couldn't count on it bein' cold."

"Don't matter none for what I'm thinkin' here."

"What's that, Meat?"

"Y'know how you was sayin' a touchup keeps a man in condition. You might be onto something there, Duck boy. I think it just come to me how we're goin' to raise that stake."

PART TWO

EIGHT

EARLY IN THE MORNING of the following day, Mitchell Morse learned his services were no longer required by AAPS, and for the second time in under a year his life was flung into disarray. By any measure, it was not your cheeriest wakeup call: a banging at the door as insistent as the dawn greeting of a Guatemalan death squad. He sat up on the couch heavily, knuckle-drilling his bleary eyes. His clothes had a stale, slept-in odor, and the rest of him wasn't so fragrant either. He got to his feet and shambled across the room, muttering "All right, all *right!*"

There stood the chief himself, old Itchy Ash, come to deliver the mail, wearing an expression half splenetic, half contrite, and all guilty apprehension. Innocent of amenities, like a man picking up his end of a conversation left off midsentence no more than a moment ago, he began, spleen first: "Why'd you have to break his arms, for Christ's sake? That's not our policy. Intimidate's our policy, get 'em to back off, spare the muscle. You know that, I told you that. Now the union's talkin' lawsuit, and that kind of grief I don't need. Vanderkullen's so hacked off he's spittin' bullets, won't let *any* of my people on the property now, never mind you. I'm going to lose that account for sure." His hands were making roving circles in the air, and his head jerked in a kind of spastic punctuation to the tumbling speech.

"I guess we're talkin' about that little scuffle yesterday, right?"

"More'n yesterday, we're discussin' here. Today, tomorrow,

and the day after that. You're a loose cannon, Morse. I can't use you anymore."

"Gimme that again, Anthony, lemme see if I got it right. You can't use me? For doing my job? What you pay me for? For that I don't make your cut? That's what you're here to tell me?" He was doing his best to balance this dizzying news against what remained of his image of himself; nevertheless, he could pick up traces of a wounded tremolo in the questions that came spilling out.

Ash lifted one of the revolving hands in a gesture of nonresponsibility. "Nobody said go that far. Your problem is you never did understand security work. Not the way we do it out here."

"Maybe not. But I understand the reason I'm out here, first place. You wanted an enforcer. Your words. Remember that?"

"Enforcer's one thing, one-man goon squad's another. Those days are over."

"Then why the fuck did you take me on, bring me out to this nowhere town? You knew my jacket."

"I thought you could . . ." He searched for just the right word, settled on "accommodate. People I talked to in Detroit gave you high marks for smart. When you weren't playing cowboy. Which is what I tried to make plain to you: West Michigan's not your frontier territory, and every little rumble's not your OK Corral. But you never could figure that out, Mitchell. Yesterday proved it."

"Look, Anthony, you cut me loose now, I'm suckin' dirtwater. I need a job." Morse had been staring him down, but now he had to avert his eyes. He despised the weakness creeping into his voice.

"You're too high risk for me. Maybe you were on the force too long."

Not long enough, it seemed, to learn the world was just as shifty off the streets as on. But long enough to know not to cringe. No more begging, Morse instructed himself.

"I drew your check for you," Ash said, extending it stiffly. "Tacked on a month's severance pay."

Morse gazed at it. It was as though all his manhood, everything he was, turned on that thin slip of paper. He could accept it, of course; he'd earned it yesterday, and more. And God knows he needed it. Or he could show some class, some balls, and rip it in two and let it drift to the floor between them, an eloquent wordless expression of disdain. The hesitation was not lost on Ash. He nodded charitably, folded the check and tucked it in the pocket of Morse's shirt. Morse mumbled a thanks, wondering if this sea he was sinking into had any bottom at all.

Now came contrition. In a voice softening some, Ash said, "I always liked you, Mitch. Take no pleasure, doing this." The circling hands came to a slow halt, and he rolled over the empty palms of regret. "It's just business, is all."

Sure. Calling it business makes everything right. "Yeah, well, anyway we had a couple grins out there," Morse said, showing him one now, jaunty as he could muster.

Ash tried to hold on to the mournful look, but his face succeeded only in betraying a blessed, home-free relief. He shifted uneasily, looking for an exit line. "You need a reference, whatever, you know where to come."

"Oh, I know you got the good words, Tony. Tell 'em, 'Hire this gunslinger or he'll bust your bones.' Right?"

Ash was too uncomfortable to take issue with the familiar use of his name. He produced a distressed smile and backed away, stammering something about luck.

XX

Luck. If I were to try to count all the ruinous choices that define my luck (thought Morse philosophically), I would surely fail, for the roll call is as numberless as the stars in the heavens or the souls frying in hell. And if ever a man invented his own destiny, I am that man.

These and other dismal speculations went through his head as he sat anchoring his appointed stool in the tavern, sipping brandy and water and smoking steadily, objectively fascinated by his whirling progress toward self-destruction. The place was all but deserted, this early hour, not even a Cecil there to dun him, which should have established that his luck was not entirely departed but from which he took little solace. Along about his fourth shot, the bartender arched the brows on a seamed, world-weary face and delivered himself of the conventional wisdom too much morning drinking was hazardous to the health. No worse than your morning teevee, Morse responded, nodding in the direction of the racketing screen that had held the bartender's transfixed gaze for the better part of the past couple of hours, and that just then featured two toilet lids chattering to each other. The bartender shrugged and backed off. Morse returned to the privacy of his own thoughts.

Those thoughts were eased some by a fatalistic calm descending over him, the mellowing gravity of drink. Meanings are hard to come by in life, he decided stoically, but after the lapse of enough years, patterns are bound to emerge. Out of three and a half decades of blunder, posturing, vanity, miscalculation, misplaced trust, delusions and deceits, he could isolate three (now four, if he included this latest debacle) pivotal points from which the patterns dilated like widening ripples, the pebble in the brook principle, a theorem to explain away the shambles of his life. Three (make that four) errands of violence, linked by the common theme of a tinderbox temper ignited by an irresistible impulse to sculpt his own legend: Mitchell Morse, so bad that bullets bounced off him. Since there was nothing better to think about and now all the time in the world for it, and since the best the screen could offer was a jiggle show masquerading as an inspirational call to fitness ("Lookit the warheads on that one in the back," the bartender remarked to the only other solitary lush in the room) he trotted them out for a morbid inspection.

The curtain raiser was a terse little skit that almost certainly cost him a professional career, and beyond any doubt a college degree. From age sixteen on, everybody kept telling him he was a shoo-in for the pros: high school All State, a dozen colleges lined up at the door, freshman starter—how could he miss? The sports pages were full of the name the writers had christened him with, The Hammer, for the way he drove into opponents half again his size, flattening them. Even the spooks recruited from the inner cities, pumped by steroids and seething with aggressive ambitions of their own—even they were dazzled by his moves. Out there I run where I want to run, was the simple truthful answer he once gave to a worshiping admirer who wanted the secret of his prowess. Across the gulf of the years he could hear the echo of a hundred thousand voices shrieking "*Ham*mer! *Ham*mer! *Ham*mer!" every time he clotheslined some bulldozer fullback or speared some lionized quarterback, whacking the wind out of him, along with his expiring Heisman dreams.

God, those were some days. Some days, those were.

But in the middle of his sophomore season some nowhere team upended them, blew them right out of Michigan Stadium.

Anymore he couldn't even bring back who they were, but he had no trouble whatsoever remembering the game, easily the worst he ever played. And the last, as it turned out.

The assistant defensive coordinator, brought in new that year, was a slack-bellied southerner with a pitted face, looked like it had taken a blast of birdshot, and the mean pinprick eyes of the natural born bully. But he did a nice Assholes and Elbows speech, nice studied menace riding the drawl, and that's how he welcomed them to the Monday practice: "If you was to consult your calendar this mornin', genemum, you see today is National Butt Kick Day, in honuh of all the sissies and faggots ever got out of their panty hose and put on a football suit, and proclaim' by your president, which is me. So that's what ah'm goin' do heah today, kick butt, all day long and on afta' the sun go down, howevuh long it take. Till you either get it right or you turn in your pads, go try out for the ping-pong squad. Contrary to what you maybe hud, there ain't goin' be no more pussies on mah playin' field, bring shame on your team and your school. Like you done last Saturday."

Good speech. A cross somewhere between late John Wayne and early Jimmy Swaggert. There was more, but Morse stopped listening about midway. He'd heard it all before, figured it more effective as drama than as threat. He was wrong. The cracker was all over him all afternoon, steaming, ragging ("Call that a hit, Mo's? Look like a love tap to me, fairy tryin' to cop a easy feel"), literally booting ass a few times, and finally, after a botched tackle, cuffing him on the back of the helmet so hard it dropped him to his knees. A real bell ringer.

"Goin' haf' to find a new name for you, Mr. Hammuh. Maybe Feathuh do, you think?"

Morse looked up into that jeering cratered face. Their glances crossed like blades. And it was there, that moment right there (he recognized now, far too late), he might have made a different choice, prudent one, smothered the whirlwind storming in his head and displayed some cool, some of those smarts he was supposed to be celebrated for. Instead he came up swinging. Through the blur of memory he could hear that astonished hillbilly voice croaking around a mouthful of blood, "Mah jaw! You brok-mah fuckin' jaw!" Actually it was the cheekbone, but it was enough. Good enough for a one-way ticket to cipherland, rocket express. Enough to change the direction of his life forever. Which, if you reduced things far enough, accounted for his being here, this town, this tavern, this very stool.

Also this empty glass in front of him.

"Yo, barkeep, 'nother jolt."

"Yeah yeah, hold your water. I'm learning how to enhance my erotic potential here."

On the screen was a panel of broads animatedly dissecting their intimate lives, talking altogether more confidently than they should have been about commitment, partners, identity, communication, mutual respect and gratification. More and more about less and less. He watched for a moment and then turned away in disgust.

"You oughta listen up, Mitch," was the wry advice that came with the drink, free for nothing. "Them ladies teach you how to get your knob polished good."

A scowl dispatched the wise counselor back to the far end of the bar.

Knob polishing was one thing, but all he ever needed to know about commitment he'd learned from a wife, long ago. Hard lesson.

He didn't like to think about this one much, number two on the roster of ruin. Wasn't exactly a jet blast to a plummeting ego. Nevertheless, he had to wonder where she was now, what she was up to. And who with, this time around. Shannon Shane, sweet Irish girl, seasoned romantic, her whole life a single-minded quest after Mr. Right, a journey marked by innumerable side trips, teasing flirtations, desperate infatuations, calculated appraisals of the available goods in the room. Any room. A perverse image wormed its way behind his eyes: Shannon Shane, got up in harem girl outfit, all tantalizing silks and veils, and transported halfway around the world to perform some swirly sinuous dance for the pleasure of a camel jockey. Well, she'd always longed to travel, so maybe at least some of her dreams had come true. Of course if this one had (and that he didn't care to know), her camel jockey was sporting a few permanent zippers on his swarthy face, courtesy of Mitchell Morse, Minister of Justice and Divine Reckoning. So maybe some things turned out all right, too.

He could extract a certain pride from the climax scene, the whupping, but with the perspective of years he had to admit the action leading to it qualified only as low burlesque, farce even. He worked nights, she had insisted she had to go back to school, "find herself," get a degree in something or other, it was never quite clear. Cheerleading, maybe. Or deception. With a cop's sure instinct, he sensed right away the swindle was on. Too many casually accounted-for trips to the Wayne State Library, too many after-class study sessions, too much nervous primping, and way too much dreamy yearning in those wide-set, crafty eyes.

First he tried wiring her car, and what he got for his trouble was a lot of traffic noise and her occasional warbling along to the strains of some romantic ballad coming off the radio. Then he wired selected rooms in the house and was treated once to an endless dialogue with an Avon lady and, more times than a few, the sounds of her guiltless snores. Next he tried the phone, came up with nothing even remotely incriminating. Married to a cop, she had learned a thing or two about cunning.

He enlisted the aid of forensic science. Every day for a full two weeks he filched her soiled panties out of the laundry basket and took them to the evidence lab for semen testing. Results were uniformly negative. Very puzzling. Even more perplexing was the problem posed by the tests, which turned the panties a neon purple. He had to replace them all and fabricate some preposterous story of doing the laundry one morning and ruining a load with too much bleach. Except for the way she watched him narrowly as the flimsy tale unfolded, her thin lips set in a superior knowing smile, very near a sneer—except for that he would have suspected himself the fool. His instincts told him differently, and seven years on the force and four of marriage had taught him to trust them.

The next day he pulled over on his way to the station, called in sick from a phone booth, and doubled back and tracked her. The trail began innocently enough down the Ford Freeway toward the university, took an abrupt turn at the Lodge, veered off through some winding back streets and ended at a small park on the far northwest side of the city. They were taking no chances, or so they thought.

Morse was dumbstruck when he saw what she was running with. Stretched out languid and jelly-limbed on a blanket in the grass, delicate runty frame all duded up in linen suit, the late afternoon sunlight glinting off sable hair—it was an A-rab, for Christ's sake. Looked like a Baghdad pimp there, fastening her with black eager eyes.

"Shannon, sweetie, you ain't gonna get the discriminating taste of the year award," he said, coming over the crest of the knoll directly behind them. "Not this year anyhow." Must have looked like the wrath of Allah, he thought, remembering it now, or the comic bolt of lightning descending from a sun-flooded, cloudless sky.

"Mitch!" she gasped. Both of them scrambled to their feet. The raghead's inky eyes went steep with fear, and his skin blanched a couple of shades, like a suntan fading instantaneously under the miracle of time-lapse photography. "We want no trouble," he said, "Shannon and I. We ask only for reason here."

Reason, for Morse, took the form of a fist-clubbing, a methodical imparting of pain and a skilled unsealing of flesh guaranteed to leave lifelong scars. He had plenty of practice along those lines. When he was finished, barely puffing and never once touched, he stepped back and examined his work. The A-rab cowered on the grass in a whimpering bloodied heap. "I'm recommendin' you stay with the ladies of the house," Morse said. "You don't do so good with the men."

The particular lady in question was stooped down, cradling the limp head in her arms. Surprisingly, there were no tears, though she trembled violently, her whole body shaking. Hostility pooled in those spiked green eyes that sized him up for a long moment before she said, "You're a sorry excuse for a man, Mitch. Worse than an animal. They ought to have cages for people like you. But maybe you did me a favor today. Now I'm never ever going to have to look at that sorry loser face of yours again in my life, ever."

Which just about said it all. And apart from a divorce court appearance, she made good on that vow.

Six years ago, that was, right around this time of year. Six years, and the memory still smarted whenever he allowed himself to think about it. Like he was doing right now, against all good judgment, focusing most vividly on the cast of her wicked green eyes, swamped with righteous loathing. They reminded him of something he couldn't quite place, something in the here and now, immediate, some nagging bit of business unfinished. At last it came to him: the slippery Starla H., she of the cascading hair and promising eyes, also remote pools of green. And for the second time in as many days, he called for his tab and paid up (noting with foggy alarm the dwindling store of bills in the wallet) and set out for Fleets.

XX

No Starla. He was beginning to wonder if she was merely a figment of his overheated imagination, and he might have believed it too, but Customer Service lady confirmed there was indeed a Starla H. in the employ of Fleets. Sadly, today was her day off. And no, there was nothing she could give him in the way of personal information on Ms. H. Against policy.

The woman he was speaking with was not yesterday's stone-waller, but she was equally stubborn and no less uncommonly ugly. Maybe they were chosen to work this counter on that basis, operating on the theory that a formidable repellent face did little to encourage customer complaints. Yet the hearty invitation to join the Fleets Family remained tacked to the wall, and it occurred to him suddenly he no longer had a job. Place like this had to have security, even if it was your minimum-wage dishwashing job. Nobody was busting down his door with Fortune 500 offers, last he checked. He asked for an application.

Up to this point in the conversation she had been icily polite. Now she regarded him with undisguised distaste. "*You* want an application? For *Fleets*?"

When he left the apartment this morning he hadn't bothered to shave or shower or change out of the slept-in clothes, and his jaw was still adorned with the bandage that by now had to be pretty smirched. Probably his smokes-and-booze breath, offended even himself on the inhale, wasn't scoring large either. "That's right," he said, opening his arms in an expansive, take-me-I'm-yours gesture. "I'm here to enlist."

She shook her head and pushed an application form across at him. He scribbled answers in the blanks, pushed it back completed and said brightly, "When do I start?"

"Procedure is you get a call for an interview. If anybody's interested, that is."

"Don't call us, huh."

"That's how it works."

"Well, I'm sure lookin' forward to workin' with you, ma'am."

"Won't that be nice," she said, and stalked away.

XX

Now he was in a booth in an unfamiliar Plainfield Avenue bar, anther empty glass in front of him, uncertain how he got there and how long he had been sitting there and what time of day it was and what he was going to do next. Some heavy riddles here. First things first. His watch told him it was half past five, a magic acceleration of time. Then the cocktail waitress he beckoned over told him, "All afternoon, I guess. You were here when I came on at three."

"What day is today?"

She cocked her head dubiously. "Day? Today is Wednesday."

"No. Date, I'm askin'."

"Twenty-eighth. If you need the month I think it's time to cut you off."

"Month I got. But you can fill up this glass, long as you mention it."

"You sure?"

"Trust me."

Trust old Mitch Morse. Sure, trust him to pluck disaster from the jaws of victory. October 28. Which made it a year, almost to the day. So he had another drink coming, in celebration of the near anniversary of the most calamitous of all his reckless choices.

By rights, it should have been a routine collar: a walker, escaped from Jackson's low-security South Complex in a laundry truck. Stefón Posey by name, smackhead with a nonviolent jacket and an IQ dipping perilously close to the single digits. A nickel-bag street peddler, needed a favor, rolled over on him and directed Morse and his partner to the east side hotbed where Stefón was holed up. Collecting a dusted-out and cringing Stefón Posey from the closet floor where they found him should have been easy. By rights.

It was that kind of thinking made you careless. Also dead. Stefón produced a sawed-off from under his pajama top and backed them both away and flicked the trigger and stovepiped the partner where he stood. Whack!—one moment he's gaping in stunned disbelief, uttering some pleading sounds, next his head is separated from the rest of him. Not even time for a shriek. Other than the heart-stopping grip of terror and the sudden recognition it was going to hurt and hurt hard, Morse could recollect nothing out of that frozen instant, only his spine nailed to the wall and his arms a pair of I-beams thrust in the air and the stub of a shotgun jabbing at his belly. And then that fierce black face began to crumple in an anguish of panic, and the eyes started rolling crazily, and the barrel was miraculously inverted and thrust inside the mouth, and a finger jerked frantically at the trigger. And nothing happened.

"Looks like you used up your round, asshole," Morse said, crossing the room to where Stefón had retreated and curled in a grovelly ball, blubbering something about not wanting to hurt nobody.

Now if he'd just yanked him up, slapped him around a little, for the sake of the lesson, cuffed him and hauled him in—if he'd done that, used his head for a change, things would have stayed the way they always were, maybe not so good but not all that bad either. Might even have lifted a commendation out of it, for valor, bringing in a desperado like this one. Instead, he'd said mildly, "What you done here was a bad thing, boy. Actin' like you was Godzilla, layin' waste to everything in your path. Only one way I can see to make it right."

Then he got out the sapper gloves he'd carried for the past several years, slipped them on and stroked the naughty Stefón into the likeness of a melted pudding. But what he neglected, all the screaming and scrambling, was to look over his shoulder at the audience gathered in the door, not a white face among them.

They put him on suspension till the outrage of the black community cooled. "Everybody's outraged these days, Mitch," the captain assured him. "Let 'em do their minstrel show for the media, you just keep your head down. Things'll work out." Not to worry, everybody told him. So he didn't. And then at the hearing they dropped him like a bad habit, drummed him out on a charge of excessive force. The captain's parting words of commiseration: "You're goddam lucky you got friends here, Morse. You didn't, you'd be doin' a dime in SPSM yourself, assault with intent to do great bodily harm. Think about that. Ex-cop like you, them darkies over there'd stretch your asshole out wider'n the Windsor Tunnel. So count your blessings, you got off this easy."

Okay, counting, one two three . . . Blessings instead of sheep dip. While they kept him in limbo he was seeing a police shrink, on order. Turned out to be tolerably interesting, those conversations. The shrink was a believer in cyclical patterns, seasonal rhythms, he liked to call them. "Don't you see, Sergeant Morse," the wise physician concluded, peering over the rims of glasses thick as thumbs, "these violent episodes of yours all cluster around the same season? It's as though you have an internal clock, a timer set to explode in the autumn of the year. Maybe it can be traced to your playing days, maybe that's too simplistic. Hard to say. I suspect it would take some intensive therapy to uncover it all. But you need to recognize it, because the consequences of these eruptions are getting steadily more serious. You almost killed a man, a prisoner in your custody."

Yeah, well, maybe you had to be there, too, was Morse's thought. To him it sounded like so much voodoo. The part about consequences, though, shrink was dead on the money with that. Look where he was now. If I'm so goddam lucky, like the captain claimed, then how come I got one foot in the soup kitchen, and how come this empty-handed waitress is hovering over me, gawking like a visitor to the zoo?

"Bart says sorry, you've had enough."

"Who's Bart?"

"Bart's the manager."

There were three men behind the bar. One of them, tall, wide-shouldered, conspicuously fit, stood with bulging arms folded across a deep chest, watching darkly. Bad news Bart. Itching to come over and talk some smack, first sign of trouble. Require something under thirty seconds, take out a mirror athlete like that, in the bag or not. "Lemme guess," Morse said. "Bart's the grim one."

"That's the one."

"Bet he's real mean, Bart."

"He can get mean. If he has to."

"You think I should go quietly? Or put up a fight."

"I'd go quietly."

Morse, at some considerable cost, flashed her a thousand-watt grin and said, "I think you're right."

XX

He sat with his head drooping almost to his lap, like a man offering up a prayer against hopeless odds, impossible forces beyond the power of control. His wandering reflections led him to a commonplace and self-evident truth that heretofore had escaped him. The past is unrecoverable, some say, finished and done. Wrong. The past endures, real as these bleak rooms labeled home are real. The past abides somewhere behind the eyes, like a hardy spore in a forgotten vase in an abandoned greenhouse of the mind, waiting patiently to sprout again in an exotic poisoned blossom. Tamper with it at your peril.

He felt an eerie sense of transience, such as he had never known before. A loneliness he had never believed himself capable of. He felt fear. He thought he heard a soft rapping at the door, but he couldn't be sure. All the synapses in his brain were sedated, and the sound he heard, or might have heard, could have been nothing more than an echo of the relentless drumbeat of time. And then he was gazing into the fond, sad eyes of Jean Satterfield, and the face he remembered as hopelessly plain was transfigured into a lovely vision of deliverance, and he was babbling at her about Sumer, Persia, China, Greece, the heroic vanished legions of the past, while she helped him to his feet, steadied him, guided him to a filthy bed, eased him back and laid a cool hand on his forehead, stroking gently. And under that soothing touch it came back to him who he was, or who it was he had all his life pretended to be, and he patted the soiled sheets and said, "You goin' to lie down with Mr. Wonderful? Plenty room here."

"Nice girls don't do it on the first date."

"This is a date?"

"First of many, Mitch. I think you need someone to take care of you."

NINE

LIKE MITCHELL MORSE, Starla Hudek was plucked rudely out of sleep on the morning of that same day. Like him, she woke to an urgent hammering at the door, and she got up from the couch, pulled on a flannel robe and shuffled across the room, mumbling some vexed sounds of displeasure, also like him. The sight that greeted her, however, was far more alarming than the sight of Anthony Ash had been for Morse. A bolt of fear charged through her and a stricken look crossed her face. She moved back from the screen and said, "Milo!"

"How's she goin', Star?"

"Milo!"

"Hey, you already said that."

"What are you doing here?"

"Well, you know how the joke goes: everybody got to be some place."

"What do you want?"

"Want? Don't want nothin', Starla. Just thought I'd stop by for a little chinwag. Catch up on the old times. Been eight years."

He was bigger even than she remembered him, bigger in life even than the looming presence that had now and again, over those eight years, invaded her dreams. His size was underlined by the scrawniness of the runt who stood alongside him. Both of them smiled tightly, as though they had some secret hilarity to suppress.

"Kind of raw out here," Meat said, filling in the prolonged pause. "I was hopin' you might invite me and my friend to step inside."

Without thinking, she did a quick glance over her shoulder. "I, uh, can't right now. It's not a good time."

Meat followed her eyes. His smile enlarged shrewdly. "Why sure you can, Starla. You got company in there, that's okay. We'll be real polite. Right, Duck?"

"Mannerly," Ducky affirmed.

They weren't going away, that much was clear. And she knew, none better, there was nothing she could do about it. Not with Milo Pitts. Dexter was a heavy sleeper, and after last night's workout he ought to be good till noon; that was how it ordinarily worked. Three hours yet, so said the clock on the wall. If she couldn't get them out of there in that amount of time, then everything she'd worked toward these past months was in serious jeopardy. Maybe she could. Anyway, there wasn't the luxury of choice. She undid the lock on the screen door and led them into the tiny nook of a kitchen, pointed them to chairs at the table. She remained standing, her back pressed to the refrigerator.

From where he sat, Meat could look down the length of the trailer, past the cluttered living room to the closed bedroom door. "Nice place you got here," he said.

"Thanks."

He snapped a finger. "Oh yeah, almost forgot them manners we promised. This here's Conrad Pickel," he said, pronouncing the surname like the vinegar-dipped cucumber. "Call him Ducky. Duck, say hello to my missus."

Starla winced at the marital reference. Ducky threw her a brow-flicking salute, and she acknowledged it with a barely perceptible nod.

"You going to tell me what you want, Milo?"

"Well, some coffee'd be good, starters."

"Coffee. Instant's all I've got."

"Instant be just fine. Duck?"

"You got any pop?" Ducky asked. "Like Dr. Pepper, maybe?"

Meat put a hand to his forehead, an elaborate show of exasperation. "You don't drink pop nine in the morning, fucknuts," he lectured him. For Starla he winked broadly and made the crazy gesture around an ear. Ducky grinned vacantly.

Starla had the uneasy sense of witnessing a rehearsed performance. Everything they did or said seemed to have a trace of irony running through it. She turned to the sink, filled a pan with water, set it on the stove, rinsed out a couple of filthy cups and put a heaping spoonful of coffee in each. When the water was bubbling she poured it into the cups and set them on the table, laid out a sugar bowl and a carton of milk and retreated to the refrigerator. A little domestic ceremony, undertaken and completed in silence. She watched Milo watching her steadily. His eyes were remote, expressionless, a contrast to the fixed empty smile.

"You're lookin' real good, Starla," he said at last. "Like you was freeze dried at seventeen."

Unconsciously she drew the robe tighter around her throat. "Thanks."

The praise continued. "Got a real nice suntan on you." Ducky giggled at that, and Meat said to him, "We know a little about suntans, don't we, Duck."

"We're the experts," he said, spluttering to contain his mirth.

Evidently it was an inside joke, one she had no interest in exploring.

Meat blew at the steam rising from his cup. "Know what this reminds me of, Starla? Reminds me of the old days, sittin' around the kitchen table like this, sloppin' up coffee."

"Milo," she said, about as firm and no-nonsense as she dared, "there's things I've got to do today. Whatever it is you want, why don't you just get to it."

"Yeah," he went on, ignoring the appeal, "we had some times, them days. Remember Teddy and Emily's Liquor Bar? That was the name of the place," he explained to Ducky, "Liquor Bar. Up in our home town. After we was married we 'bout lived there, right, Star?"

"*You* about lived there," she corrected him.

"Remember that time Teddy was gonna boot me out? Got a burr up his ass over somethin', can't place what. He says, 'Meat, you had your last drink in the Liquor Bar.' Like the place was your fuckin' Ritz. I says, 'Teddy, you better think real hard, what you're sayin' here.' Next thing I know he's climbin' all over me with a pool cue, like to brained me. That's how I got this tattoo over my eye."

"What'd you do about it, Meat?" asked Ducky, breathless audience to the tale.

Starla stiffened her face against a yawn. She'd heard the story before.

"Well, after I picks myself up off the floor and swipes the blood out of my eyes, I stroll over to the little turd. See, he can't believe I'm still on my feet and he's all sorry now, sayin'"—and here he did a high-pitched sissy imitation of his antagonist from out of the distant past—" 'I didn't mean it, Meat. You can stay, you want. Don't beat on me.' You can maybe guess I ain't in a mood to hear none of it. I do a quick snuggie on him and march him back to the john. Back there I dunks him face down in the pisser, make him do some garglin'. I tell you, he come that close to drownin'."

He indicated how close was *that* close with a barely visible space between a thumb and an index finger. Ducky slapped his hands overhead, and both of them exploded in hog-calling laughter. Starla had been staring at the floor. She glanced up anxiously at the bedroom door, just in time to see Dexter coming through it, hitching up his trousers with one hand and grinding at puffy, red-rimmed eyes with the other. He was barefoot and shirtless. A buttery roll of fat oozed over his belt.

"What's all the racket out here?" he demanded in a sleepy irritable whine. "I'm trying to—" The plaint broke off abruptly when he spotted the two male figures in the kitchen. "Oh, sorry," he said in a voice that conveyed more suspicion than apology. "Didn't realize you had . . . guests."

Starla moved quickly into the space between him and the table. "They're not guests exactly," she said. "Just some, uh, people I know. Stopped by."

Meat exchanged facial signals with Ducky, and then he leaned out laterally from his chair and peered around her. "More like family's what we are. Whyn't you come on out, get acquainted."

"Lady brew you up a real tasty cup coffee," Ducky added, reinforcing the invitation.

"It's early," Starla said. "I think you should go back to sleep." She put as much solicitude into it as she was capable of, added, "They have to leave soon anyway."

Dexter looked uncertain at all this advice. The company of anyone over the age of nineteen was always vaguely threatening to him, particularly men, and most assuredly cretins like these two appeared to be, as much as he could see of them with Starla so obviously blocking his view. But he was wide awake now and curious over who they were and what they were doing here. And in the pettish tone of someone airing a grievance, that's what he said: "Well, I'm wide awake now. I may as well get dressed and join you." He disappeared back into the bedroom.

" 'May as well get dressed and join you,' " Meat mimicked, reviving his squeaky impression of Teddy of Liquor Bar fame.

Ducky was quietly convulsed.

Starla whirled around and hissed, *sotto voce*, "God damn you, Milo, lay off him. I got something going here and you goddam well better not fuck it up."

"Look to me like an oinker's what you got goin'," he said good-humoredly. And then, with a touch of sadness, "I'm kinda disappointed in you, Star. I'd of figured you for better'n that."

"You son of a bitch. You're going to spoil it, aren't you. Same way you spoil everything."

"Also disappointed," he continued mildly, "to find you betrayin' your marriage vows. Last I knew we was man and wife, and I ain't heard no different since."

Starla stood trembling with powerless fury. Her slender hands clenched and unclenched rhythmically at her sides. She was run out of curses.

Meat presented her with placating palms. "Hey, Starbaby, take it cool, wind down. You pop a blood vessel that way. You don't got to worry, I'm gonna forgive you bein' unfaithful. That's what your Bible say to do, forgive and forget. Am I right, Duck?"

"It's in there somewhere," Ducky certified, mock earnest. What was coming up, he knew he was going to enjoy himself, absolutely.

"So maybe you better step over to the stove there," Meat directed her, "heat up some coffee for your shitbag friend."

Defeated, Starla did as she was told. Everything was certainly lost now anyway. Eight years gone by or not, didn't matter, nothing changed. She knew Milo.

In a moment Dexter came through the bedroom door for the second time that morning, fully clothed in suede jacket with patches at the elbows and shirt with button-down collar, conservative tie. His soft pink face was fixed in a studied, cloud-sniffing expression, but there was a wariness in his eyes too. Meat bounded to his feet, yanked out a chair and ushered him into it with a waiterly flourish. Starla put a cup in front of him and faded back to the counter.

"Like to do the introducin' all around," Meat said. "My name's Pitts. Milo Pitts. Folks call me Meat, on account of my size. Course the ladies, they got another reason for hangin' that tag on me. Ain't that right, Starla?"

She put her head in her hands and sighed.

Meat made a short braying noise, like a trumpet unmuting. "And you'd be?"

"Dr. Dexter Graff."

Meat stuck out a hand and Dexter touched it limply, did a quick release.

"Doctor. Now ain't that one of your coincidences. Y'see, this fella here, Mr. Conrad Pickel—we call him Ducky, guess you can tell why, just lookin' at him—anyway, he's been havin' a serious pain in his shoulder. Ain't you, Duck."

Ducky grabbed a bony shoulder cap and moaned, "It's makin' me crazy, Doc. Can you help?"

"I'm not that kind of doctor."

"Also he got a real bad case of the clap," Meat went on, as though the disclaimer had never been uttered.

Now Ducky clutched reflexively at his penis, made a plaintive face and said, "Uncle Clyde down here, he's gettin' all scabby. You gotta do somethin', Doc."

"My degree is a Ph.D.," Dexter said, trying on a thin distant smile, to demonstrate he was in on the bantering, if not terribly amused by it.

"No shit!" Meat exclaimed. "P.H. and D."

"That spells fud," Ducky volunteered, really catching the spirit of it now.

"That make you a schoolteacher," Meat asked, "that fud?"

"Among other things, yes. A professor."

"Professor same as a teacher?"

Dexter tried chuckling tolerantly. "Depends on who you ask. Most people would say so."

"You don't look like no teacher to me. Teachers I had in school was all scarecrows, blow 'em away with a beer fart. You, you're a pretty husky fella. Wouldn't you say, Duck?"

Ducky's head bobbed in concurrence. "Look like he packed

in his share of the groceries, all right. 'Cept they all went south on 'im."

Enough, thought Dexter. Banter was one thing, arrant mockery quite another. In the classroom, he was the one who did the bullying. He tightened his jaws contentiously and said, "Very amusing, this Mutt and Jeff comedy routine. But I think we've heard just about enough. Suppose you tell us who you are and what you're doing here." He shot a quick glance at Starla, searching for support of his deliberately chosen plurals. She appeared to be studying the patterns in the tile at her feet.

Meat and Ducky nodded gravely at each other, like consulting surgeons simultaneously arrived at the same melancholy diagnosis. Meat fingered the scar that ran like an arrow up the side of his nose. A sleepy menace flickered behind his frozen smile.

"Why sure, Doc, you got a right to know. This is America. See, fact is this lady here, Starla, she's my missus."

"Whaaat? *You?* And Starla? I don't believe it."

"Guess some folks'd call me her worser half. But that don't make us no less married."

Dexter turned to her. "Starla? This can't be—you never said—" His voice fluttered between outrage and injury, and his hands sliced the air helplessly.

She lifted her eyes, but there was an incurious distance in them, a measuring. "If I were you," she said listlessly, "I'd get out of here. Now."

It occurred to Dexter suddenly he was in alien country, friendless, alone, and innocent of the tongue. A sudden lunatic image flashed through his head: a man trapped inside a carousel, encircled by stallions with vaguely human faces set in pitiless smirks. He started to rise but Meat reached over and laid a heavy hand on his bald pate, effortlessly forced him back into the chair.

"See a man come out of your wife's bedroom, bareass practically, that don't look good, Doc. Look like you been committin' the sin of adultery. And sooner or later, man's got to pay for his sins."

"Pay the fuckin' piper, Doc," Ducky declared, a cheery underscore.

"Now, I remember my schoolin' correct, what they use to do, your olden times, was hack off a man's nuts, catch him bangin' another fella's old lady. You're a schoolteacher. That what they do?"

Dexter's mouth was set in an incongrous, clenched-teeth grin, like a novice ventriloquist trying without success to produce a voice. The veins on his temples pulsed visibly. His face had gone chalky.

Meat gave the silence a moment to unroll. "Guess that means you don't know what they did, them days. Well, I s'pose we could do the same thing. Good enough back then, good enough now. What do you think, Duck?"

"I think he'd make a real fine soprano for the school chorus."

"I dunno. These is modern days, so maybe that wouldn't be right either. My thinkin' is we should just shake hands and forget about it. You agree, Duck?"

Ducky was shivering with glee. "Meat," he said, "you got a heart big as all outdoors."

"That sound fair to you, schoolteacher?"

Dexter moved his head up and down vigorously. The ghastly grin was still in place.

"So let's shake on it then."

Dexter put up a fluttery hand and Meat wrapped his own around it, held it securely and squeezed. Dexter leaned forward, wincing in pain. A mischievous glint came into Meat's eyes. He put the heel of his other hand on Dexter's thumb. "Y'know, Doc," he said conversationally, "if I was to spike this thumb here, you'd have a real pro'lem gradin' all your pupil's homework, right?"

Dexter's mouth fell open but no words came out.

"I'm askin' you a question here, Doc."

"Yes. A problem. Yes."

"Show 'im how it's done, Meat," Ducky squealed. "C'mon, show 'im."

Meat took a moment to consider. "Nah, I don't think so. Not this time. Course, I catch you sniffin' around here again, that's how it's gonna have to be. We straight on that, Doc?"

Dexter mumbled something unintelligible.

"Think I heard a yes in there. Sure hope so. Duck, whyn't you show the doc out to his car. See him off. Then you wait out there awhile. Me and Starla got matters to discuss."

XX

She stood with her back to him, gazing blankly out the window at a sky full of low-slung clouds.

"How come I got the feeling you ain't too happy," Meat asked her, "me sendin' your boyfriend packin'? I thought I was helpin' out here."

She answered with an absent shrug.

"You want to throw things, trash the place, that's okay."

Another shrug.

"Maybe you like to come clawin' at me, way you use to when you was pissed. Remember?"

"What's the good of that now?"

"Get the poison outta your system. Then we can talk reasonable."

"Talk about what? It's been ten years since you and I had anything to say to each other."

"Eight."

"Ten. Maybe more. There's nothing between us, Milo, probably never was."

"You forgettin' all them sweet jelly rolls we use to have?"

"Yeah, that's right, I'm forgetting them. Forgot them a long time ago. Why, is that what you're here for? He-man wants his rape?"

"It ain't rape when you're married, Starla. It's what they call the marital privilege."

She turned and faced him and said coldly, "Let me tell you something, Milo. Anything you get off me—a fuck, money, place to hang out, a cup of instant coffee—it'll be rape. You and I aren't married. Maybe the divorce papers never got filed, but we're *not* married."

Meat sat with his fingers laced behind his head. His wide-margined face was fixed in the same glacial smile it had worn since the moment he first appeared at the door. "I hear there's people do it even if they ain't married," he said easily.

Starla slumped onto the couch, lowered her eyes dismally. "You might as well tell me what it is you want. You're going to take it anyway."

"You got it all wrong, Star. I don't want nothin' off you. Nothin'. But I do got a proposition to make to you."

"Huh, proposition. Seems to me I was about sixteen, your first proposition. Look where it's got me ended up. Nailed to a cash register in discount city."

"This one's a business proposition. Spring you loose from that register for good."

"Milo, that *was* my permanent pass out of Fleets you just sent running. Now you've got a proposition that's going to spring me free? Sure."

"You ain't heard this one yet."

He explained it to her. As much as he wanted her to know. He kept his eyes on her as he spoke. She seemed to be absorbing the particulars of the plan, her role in it, thoughtfully. When he was finished he flipped over his hands and said, "Well, what do you think?"

Only after prolonged and cautious reflection did she reply. "Robbing Fleets, that's pretty heavy. You know I've never done anything like that. What if something went wrong?"

"Ain't nothin' goin' to go wrong, Starla. It's like I told you, man we got drawin' blueprints, he's a genius."

"But if it did?"

"It won't."

"I don't know. I'm not like you. I couldn't do time."

Meat tapped a finger against his lip, as though it helped him think, formulate his arguments. "Take a look around, this dump you're livin'. Make my Jacktown crib look like a room at the Hilton. Look at you, suckin' up to a stiff-fucker like that one we just had a word with. Look at that ratty bathrobe you got on. Frederick's of Krakow. You're doin' time, Starla. You just lost count of the years."

She stood up and paced the narrow living room of her tin trailer, four steps one way, four back. She paused again at the window, stared outside. "I don't know."

"I'm offerin' a proposition get you outta here. Get you fartin' into silk, like you got comin'."

The sky had opened in a soft drizzle. The wail of an infant rose from the trailer next door. A biker roared by, gunning the throttle of his chopped hog. The wind picked up an empty garbage can and sent it rattling down the street. The sights and sounds of her life.

"And you're guaranteeing there'd be no strings, you and me?"

"You don't got to worry about strings. Them eight years done something to me. That way." His voice had deepened into a bitter growl. He shook a Lucky from his pack, lit it and blew a fierce gust of smoke at the floor.

Starla came over and took a chair beside him. She studied him, not with sympathy or even much curiosity, but with the fleeting interest of a spectator witnessing a fire or a natural disaster from a safe remove. "They were pretty bad for you, those years?"

He was unable to meet her eyes. He slapped the air in a silent curse. "Ahh, I got by. What can they do, guy like me." He drew deeply on the cigarette. "Anyway, there's better ones ahead, what I'm layin' out to you here."

"I don't know, Milo. My head's too scrambled to think."

"Tell you what we do. You spend some time with it, give it some thought. Couple days we talk again. That sound good?"

"That's good."

"Meantime, you can help me out. Little information I need."

Starla drew back warily. "What information? I don't know any of those things you said. About the store."

"Ain't that kind I'm after yet. You remember how, up home, they use to have that Halloween Day parade. School put it on. All the little squirrels in their costumes marchin' down Main. Practically shut up the whole town for it. Remember?"

"I remember. Why?"

"They still got that?"

"How would I know? I never go back there. That ugly little town." Her nose crinkled in distaste at the memory.

"But you got family up there. You could find out for me."

"I could."

"Want you to do that. Right now. Get on the horn."

Starla made a call. She was obliged to chat for a while, and Meat listened closely, trying to glean from one end of the conversation what it was he hoped to hear. His fingers drummed the table impatiently. "Well?" he said as she recradled the phone.

"They've still got it. Friday this year, since Halloween comes Saturday."

Meat's face brightened in a smile that was now very near to genuine. "Bingo," he said. And then, more pensively, "Friday. Day after tomorrow."

Starla wore an expression of baffled perplexity. "What's a Halloween kiddie parade got to do with anything? What are you up to, Milo?"

"Don't ask." He got to his feet and moved toward the door, paused. "Oh yeah, one other thing. Gonna need the keys to your car. I got to borrow it, couple days."

XX

Driving away in the cramped Chevette, Meat remarked to his partner, "Y'know, Ducks, there's some days a man just can't snag a break, other ones everything you do come up aces. This one's aces."

Ducky, misunderstanding, rolled his eyes lewdly and said, "Hey, I hear you. That old lady yours, she's a real fine-lookin' squeeze. Maybe little skinny, but you know how they say, closer the bone the sweeter the meat. Which you bein' named Meat has got a special meaning."

"I ain't talkin' about that kind of luck, dickhead."

Ducky looked at him, mystified. "What other kind, then?"

Meat took a hand off the wheel, made a pistol of it, aimed it at him and cocked the trigger thumb. "Bang bang kind. You and me is gonna turn over that stake we're lookin' for. First, though, we got some stalkin' to do."

TEN

THE ONLY RUDE SOUNDS to waken Doyle Gilley that Wednesday morning were the ones buzzing in the deeper recesses of his own head. The nagging issue of the absent two thousand dollars essential to the rescue of his hair had not vanished in the night. Gone, however, was his room- and bedmate, Twyla, off to her early-shift hashing job at the Beefaroo. Mercifully. He could do without her chin dribble conversation, the weighty matters facing him today.

After a while he got out of bed and strode purposefully into the living room, picked up the phone, dialed the plant and declared himself too ill to report for work. Which in a way was true, if you thought about it. His affliction was as real to him as any of the thousand maladies flesh is heir to. All he was about to do was seek the funding for treatment, possibly even—if there was anything like fairness or justice in this world, and if Kasperson was the magic healer he claimed to be—a cure.

Later, showered, shaved, extra vigorously shampooed and presentably turned out in sport jacket and tie, he stood before the bathroom mirror and set to work on his hair. These days this procedure required very nearly a quarter hour of meticulous parting and reparting, looping, layering, patting and arranging before he was satisfied that the widening expanse of forehead was at least partially concealed by some wispy strands. Well, not really satisfied, but it was the absolute best he could do, camouflage-wise.

Now he paused and studied himself. He thrust out his hard dimpled jaw, narrowed his eyes, tightened the corners of his mouth and addressed the reflection: "Okay, I'm here to talk business, discuss a loan. I've got an account with you people"—let's never mind the amount in it, another voice murmured in his ear—"hold down a good steady job, got no wife and kids to support, no debts"—not exactly true, the taunting voice reminded him: what about those car payments, hundred and a half a month, thirty-six months?—"of any importance, and a fantastic future ahead"—maybe, the voice sniggered, unless it's all a scam, a grisly joke—"so what do you say, you advance me the two large I got to have?"—Loan you money? came the jeering reply. You? Flush it down the crapper first.

And he was still crippled by doubt as, an hour after that, he parked his car in the bank lot and sat there immobile, paralyzed. A loan for scalp treatments? They'd hoot him right out of the bank. What the fuck was he thinking of? Where was his head? The voice in his ear had been right all along. He turned the key in the ignition and sped away.

For the rest of the morning he drove aimlessly. Numbed. Later, he sat in a Burton Street tavern, nursing beer and the battered remnants of his dreams. Defeated by a sum so insignificant, in the grander scheme of things, it was almost laughable. If you had it. Across the street was a Fleets, and he stared moodily at the throngs of shoppers hurrying toward it. In any single given hour they squandered enough for a lifetime of treatments, and he required only maybe six months' worth. There were a quarter of a million people in this town, something like that. Snap a finger and they'd pissed away more than he would ever need.

Nothing was fair.

A soft rain pattered against the tavern window. Just beyond it some trees, barren of leaves, swayed in the wind. Nature's equivalent of baldness. He wondered if it might be better simply to accept her verdict, pack it in. And then he glanced in the mirror behind the bar and saw the stunningly handsome face staring back at him reproachfully. He imagined how disfigured it would look without hair. No, he told it. No giving up without a fight. Somewhere there had to be the money, and somehow he had to lay hands on it. He ransacked his imagination for a solution.

Two beers later it came to him, so glaringly obvious he reddened at his own thick-wittedness. Sealed in a plain envelope and tucked away in a metal file in a corner of the closet were an even dozen Series E bonds, two hundred dollar denomination, Twyla's legacy from her farmer grandparents. Enough and then some. Just waiting to be tapped. If he could only figure how. He *had* to figure how.

He ordered another beer and put his fertile imagination to work.

XX

" . . . so Darlene don't show up and I'm coverin' two stations, really bustin' butt, and this old fart flags me down and starts in his eggs is runny and his toast is burned and his hash browns cold and it's all *my* fault, if you can swallow that, and he's not gonna pay, da-dit, da-dit, da-dit. And I'm like, wow, pardon me for bein' on the same planet, your fuckin' highness, and he goes, 'Send over the manager, you snotty bitch.' Well, by this time I've had it right up to the eyeballs, so I go, 'Find him yourself, shithead,' and just strut away. Trouble is he does, and then Alvin had to come back and give me his customer relations ass-chewin'. I'm tellin' you, Doyle, this was *not* a good day. And then to top it off . . ."

The thing about Twyla, the way Doyle saw it, was she'd be a

good enough woman if you could somehow arrange to have a sock stuffed in her mouth every morning of every day of her life. Maybe not perfect—she couldn't cook or clean house for shit—but good enough. She had a nice swag of flaxen hair, blankly pretty face, saucer eyes, sky blue, generous mouth, and the plump creamy body of a milkmaid, which in fact is what she was—a country girl raised on a dairy farm over by Greenville, come to make her way in the big city. Also, she could be a hard-driving player between the sheets, so for where he was in his own life right now she was okay, she'd do. But first you had to get past that mouth, never stopped running, never, and that spike-in-the-ear voice, carried all the way up to the UP. And that's what he was trying his best to do just then: dial it down, wait it out. Had to be a breath stop coming up soon; if not (and here a weird image trailed through his head, unbidden) her face would certainly turn blue, eyes begin to bulge, hand clutch the throat, and she'd go down in history as the first and only person in the world to gag to death on her own words.

She was sprawled on the couch, head tossed back, plaid skirt of her waitress uniform riding high on outspread thighs, her exhausted heap posture, something less than ladylike. At the same time, she was managing quite adequately to vanish a bag of Taco Chips, wash them down with a diet Mountain Dew, and keep the Sominex chronicle rolling right along. Doyle, in the chair opposite her, had caught a glimpse of himself in the aluminum toaster on the kitchen counter. The reflection distorted his features, endowing him with an enormous, blade-keen jaw. He made a series of furtive smiles at it, working for a romantic crease in his cheek, and he just about had it mastered when he realized there was a silence fallen across the room. He looked over to find her staring at him.

"What're you grinnin' at?" she demanded. "I ain't got to the good part yet."

"Uh, that toaster there. I was just thinking how we need a new one." It occurred to him that possibly he could turn the feeble reply into a wedge, burrow his way through the flurry of words and arrive at The Issue. There had to be an opening somewhere; maybe this was it. "Wish we had the money for a new one," he added cautiously.

"So that's funny? Lots of things we need, but you know what they say: if wishes was horses, beggars'd ride."

Second only to the incessantly yammering mouth, the thing

Doyle disliked most about Twyla, he decided, was the earthy, turnip-truck wisdom that frequently came out of it, unsolicited and free of charge. The longer view, he reminded himself. "Seriously though, Twyla, talking about money and things we need—"

"Which if you remember we wasn't. I was tellin' you about Maxine and what they caught her doin' back in the cooler. Don't you ever listen?"

"Yeah, sure, and I want to hear all about it too," he said, adopting a wheedling tone. "But there's something real important come up, money-wise, and—"

"What? They can you?"

"No, no, nothing like that."

"Give you a raise, then. About time, I'd say."

"Not that either."

"What else is there, money-wise? You're not gonna tell me we won the Daily?"

"Almost as good," Doyle said earnestly, and since it appeared he had her attention, however fleeting, he launched his story, extemporizing as he spoke. "Y'see, over to the plant there's this supervisor, older fella, works out of the front office but spends a lot of his time back with us. I known him awhile. Didn't seem like a bad dude, for a suit." Her slackening mouth and slowly unhinging jaws appeared on the threshold of a yawn, so he hurried along. "Lately he's been acting real friendly, this fella. Too friendly, if you catch my drift. I figure he's got to be a closet queen, trying to hit on me."

The jaws clamped shut and the eyes narrowed suspiciously. "You never told me nothin' about no fairies, Doyle. How come?"

"Well, that's not the kind of thing you brag on." There was of course no such person, but somewhere he'd heard or read male models were constantly fighting off fags so in a way it was not totally untrue, more a kind of preview of what lay ahead in his life. But only if he could vault this present hurdle. "Anyway, he tells me, 'You want to make some fast money, Doy-boy'—that's what he calls me, Doy-boy—'I can show you how.' "

An expression midway between anger and disbelief darkened her face, but Doyle was catching the rhythm of his fantastic tale. He pushed on. "Course, I'm saying to myself, no way!, not what you got in mind, not this—"

"You're sure?"

"Huh?"

"You're sure that's what you're sayin'?"

"Sure I'm sure. Besides, turns out that's not what he's fishing after anyway. See, he's got a hot line into management and he's heard the company's planning to buy out Wholesome Foods. That's an outfit down in Battle Creek, about to go belly-up. He says, 'Take all the money you got and buy Wholesome stock. Inside a year it'll triple. But you got to move now,' he says, 'before word gets on the street. Every day you wait, it'll cost you money.' That's what he said," Doyle concluded solemnly.

He paused to let it settle in. He was surprised at his own inventiveness, its scope and spontaneity. As far as he knew, there was no such enterprise as Wholesome Foods, and he hadn't the dimmest notion how stock deals worked, how they were traded even. But anything he knew was more than she did. About that he had no doubts whatsoever.

"So what'd you have to do then?" she said sourly. "Let him go down on you, this big stock market tip?"

Doyle discovered himself defending the phantom deviant supervisor, who seemed, wondrously, as real to him now as the two of them sitting there in the shabby room. "So what if he's a swish? Some of them people are plenty smart. Rich, too. It goes with being gay. Anyway, you're missing the point. We could make some good money here."

"Yeah, just how we gonna do that? Where you gonna get the bread to buy them stocks? Maybe you're thinkin' your friend there, he'll say"—she elevated her voice in a lisping whine—" 'Oh, that Doy-boy, he's *such* a cupcake, always good for a quick blow, I'll just *give* him all the money he wants.' That what you're thinkin'?"

The Doy-boy touch, he saw now, too late, was a mistake. "C'mon, Twyla," he said, soothing and sincere as he could pitch it, "nobody's straighter'n me. Who'd know that better'n you?" He took a quick shallow breath and plunged ahead before she could speak. Now comes the crunch. "I wasn't thinking anything like what you said. But I was remembering them bonds you got."

Head to foot, her whole body stiffened. "No. Not my bonds."

"Think about it a minute. What do they come to, twenty-five hundred? In a year you could have seven, eight grand. Maybe nine, even."

"No. Grandpa Leo told me not to cash them in till I was twenty-one at least, and that's another year yet."

"But this is something special," Doyle said, "once in a lifetime." He could hear the desperation seeping into his voice. He tried to steady it. "If your Grandpa Leo were alive, he'd say do it."

"No he wouldn't. He said either wait till you're twenty-one or"—she paused, gave him a sly look—"till you got married. You and me, we been livin' like this for, what?, year and a half now. And we sure ain't married."

Doyle's stomach took a sudden anxiety spin. His fingers began to flick nervously against his thumbs. "Well, that's true too. But we probably will be. Before long." The words came out slowly, painfully, split by lengthy spaces, as though each were extracted with pliers.

"That a proposal?" she said coyly.

The question fell on him like a winter frost. He felt like a man stumbling blindly through a deepening swamp, all direction lost. Reflexively, his hand went to his temples. Under the angled part, the blow-dry deception, they were still bare. Beyond this moment, he didn't dare allow himself to think. Whatever it took, he was prepared to do. Or say he would do. He went over and sat beside her, stroked her thigh. "I guess you could maybe say that." To him it sounded as if he were somehow miraculously disconnected from his own voice.

She gave him a wet, joyous kiss. "C'mon back to the play-room," she said. "I'll show you how to raise something better'n money."

Straddling her, bucking away, he caught the scent of fries issuing from her hair. He wondered if a year from now the woman beneath him would have perfumed hair.

Twyla tapped him on the arm, signal she was ready to move on to a different position. In a moment, over her shoulder, she said in a throaty, panting voice, "Doyle? Honey? Maybe we can take some of that money we'll be gettin' and go see Disney World next year."

He pumped harder.

ELEVEN

IT TOOK TILL FRIDAY, but by then Morse was reasonably certain he was not dwelling among the hosts of the dead. Not yet anyway. No thanks to himself. All the credit (if credit it was) belonged to Jean Satterfield, nice girl, didn't do it on the first date. Or the second either, if her Mother Teresa impression of the past couple of nights qualified as dates. Maybe nice girls didn't do it at all anymore, not that he could have tested that proposition, the shape he'd been in. One of these times he'd have to get around to it, though. Out of gratitude, if nothing else.

Because he owed her something, no getting away from it. Look at the place, all flash and order and spit polish shine, looked all but unrecognizable. Take top honors, a white glove inspection. So he owed her for that. Look at him: dried out, rested, properly fed, even sanitized somehow. Could light a cigarette now, or lift a spoon to his lips without doing the palsy dance. Another score for her. It was a serious drunk she'd brought him out of, the last twirl on a long tailspin, actually; and she'd done it coolly, efficiently, and without so much as a word or look or hint of disapproval. He owed her, all right.

So why was it, then, he felt almost uneasy, sitting there on his own couch in his own remarkably immaculate apartment, waiting not very patiently for her to arrive? Not a bad feeling exactly—couldn't call it that—but not quite right either. More on the order of curious, awkward, unfamiliar, like a man wearing someone else's ill-fitting clothes, and intruding on a stranger's space. Why was that?

No time to explore it. She'd promised to be there by noon; noon it was. Another virtue: dependability.

"You're looking pretty close to human again, Mitch. How do you feel?" She was smiling at him, gravely cheery sickroom smile.

"About half. You?"

It was more than an idle query. He knew she had come directly from a follow-up examination with her doctor, mentioned offhandedly the night before. "Oh, fine," she said, touching self-consciously at the fading bruise on the side of her face. "I'm going to survive just fine. He tells me I've got the skull of a concrete block and the constitution of a plow horse. Very flattering man."

"That's what he said, huh?"

"Something like that."

"Itchy give you any grief, the time off?"

"Itchy was very accommodating. Well, he did have to grouch a little."

Morse studied her a moment. Her close-cropped hair looked as if it had been newly styled, and she seemed to fill out her AAPS uniform better than he remembered, even a curve or two here and there. Unless he imagined it. No imagining the makeup though, some pale color on the lips, thin dusting of shadow on the eyelids, a trace of rosy blush on the cheeks. That was definitely an added touch. Whisper of fragrance, that was new too. She flushed a natural pink under his scrutinizing gaze. "Okay, crimefighter," he said finally, "let me buy you lunch."

"I'm the one employed here. I'll buy."

"Listen, you want to bring evil-doers to justice, first thing you got to learn is to follow orders."

He took her by the elbow and guided her to the door.

XX

"I just love that automobile of yours," she said, glancing up shyly from a menu. She held off a smile but there was nothing she could do about the teasing light in her eyes.

"No kidding? You like it, huh?"

"Fits the image perfectly."

It was a gentle enough ragging, might as well go along with it. "She's a slick one, all right," Morse said. "Fix her up a little, I'd probably get a pile of money off some classic car dealer."

"No doubt about it."

"I tell you though, the vehicle I want to own someday is one of those first Toronados, mid-sixties. Now there was an evil-looking machine. You remember them?"

"Not really. That's about when I was born."

"Yeah, I keep forgetting you're still a bubble-gummer. Be lucky I don't get a statutory slapped on me, just being out in polite society with you along. Bad for that image you were talking about."

They were settled in a booth in one of those restaurants that bills itself as "family" and makes a righteous point of serving nothing harder than Pepsi. Smile-button hostess and employees that had to tell you their names ("Hi, I'm Ginger, I'll be your waitress today"). Morse had let her choose the place, but he insisted on doing the driving. He wanted to test the steadiness of his hands. Maybe a C-minus, he decided, but then the Friday noontime traffic was heavy, and he'd been squinting against a sun-drenched sky on this unseasonably warm, almost hot, autumn day. Perverse weather, this side of the state. The last time he was out of the apartment the same sky was leaking a chilly rain.

After they placed their order her expression went serious, the eyes attentive. Perceptive eyes on her, he thought, intelligent. Quite evenly, she said, "Image is everything, right, Mitch? Image is the man."

"I don't know what that means."

"It means I'm curious about you. About the face you put on for the world."

Automatically, he arranged that face in a mannered grin. "What you see is what you get."

"I don't think so. Example. When I was straightening up your apartment—terminally grungy, by the way; you're going to have to let me introduce you to a box of Spic and Span. Anyway, while I was doing that, I saw all those books you keep hidden in your closet. What kind of hard case reads history books?"

"Oh, I don't read them. They're for show. For when I get a brainy lady, sort of like yourself, come to call. Wows 'em every time."

"In the closet?"

"That's the tidiest spot in the whole dump. Least it was till you got seized by a cleaning frenzy." He said it lightly, but he wasn't so sure he liked the direction this was taking.

"Okay. What about that picture on your bureau, then?"

"That?" he said, no longer grinning. "That's the lady I was married to. Thousand years ago."

"She's very lovely. Why do you keep her facing the wall?"

"So I'll remember never to turn my back on a woman again," he said. This was the kind of talk that always made him uncomfortable. Private space you had to protect, measure out cautiously. "Look, the cleaning I appreciate, but it's not a license to toss the place."

Right away he regretted it. A cloud of injured hurt crossed her face. She mumbled a sorry, looked at her lap.

"What do you say we forget it. Once in a while I flip the pages of a book, once I was in a bad marriage. Neither one's any big thing."

"I don't mean to pry, Mitch. It's just, well, I'd like to know about you, your life . . . more."

"You want to know something, all you have to do is ask."

So soft he could barely hear, she said, "You know who you remind me of?"

"Who'd that be?"

First she hesitated, then she lifted distressed eyes and fixed him with a gaze of unconcealed tenderness. "Nobody," she said, searching for something in his face.

It was the nick-of-time appearance of the waitress rescued him from a direct reply. She laid out plates and cups and bowls, instructed them to enjoy their meal, and vanished. There was a moment of tight expectant silence, which Morse filled by attending to the busy motions of sawing at a sizzler. Then, nodding at the diminutive salad in front of her, he said, "If you're going to be a law-enforcement he-person, you've got to eat more than bunny food."

"Really. I didn't know nutrition was among your many accomplishments."

It was a relief to see she was masking her disappointment with a playful air. "Any problems at all," he said, "you bring 'em to the quizmaster."

"Quizmaster's going to have a clogged artery problem, all that red meat."

"No, you got that wrong. It's this roadkill makes you vicious, which is how you got to be, our line of work." He thought about what he had just said, amended it: "Better make that *your* line of work." And since he didn't want to follow that thought too far, he added quickly, "Speaking of which, how's that going? They got you back at the beer factory?"

"No, from what I hear, Ash may have lost that job. I'm at a medical lab out in Kentwood. Monitoring drug shipments."

"Sounds like scut work they got you on. Who you teamed with?"

"Billy Schooley."

Morse repeated Billy's name around a scornful grunt. "Listen, I got a word of advice for you. Anything Billy says to do, you do it just the other way and you'll make out fine."

"I don't know. He seems all right. A little jumpy sometimes."

"What Billy ought to try out for is meter maid. He'd be sensational at that."

She had been picking indifferently at her salad. Now she put down her fork and said, studiedly casual, "What are you going to try out for, Mitch? What's next for you?"

"Haven't got that far yet. I still got some friends in Detroit. Maybe I'll head back there, see what I can turn up." He knew better than that, but it was a thing to say.

"You know, my father has a lot of contacts in Grand Rapids. I could have him ask around. If you want, that is."

"Yeah, well, that's mighty decent of you, but I don't think it's such a good idea."

"Why is that?"

Purely by chance, a way to explain it presented itself just then. "Look over there," he said, directing her with his eyes to the booth across the aisle. A middle-aged couple sat with palms pressed together, eyes lowered, intoning a grace. Talking to platters of steaming food. She glanced at them and then back at him, questioningly.

"This is a town where grown-up people still say their prayers. Wonder Bread town. It's not right for me."

"Because *they're* saying grace, *you're* leaving town? That kind of logic escapes me."

Morse shrugged. "Logic's got nothing to do with it. I operate best where there's plenty of grit."

She shook her head slowly, sadly. "Maybe you'll think about it awhile."

"Yeah. Maybe."

XX

The phone was jangling when they came through the door of his apartment, twenty minutes later. Morse picked it up and spoke into it, monosyllables mostly, a clipped question or two. He scribbled some notes on the back of an envelope. Finally he said, "Okay, Monday. Ten o'clock. I'll be there."

He replaced the receiver, his face tightening with perplexity. She waited.

"That was Fleets," he said. "They want me to come in for an interview."

She flew across the room and wrapped him in a joyous hug. "Mitch, that's terrific!"

"Man said my credentials were impressive." He looked stunned. "That's what he said. I forgot I even applied."

"I think it's just great! Fleets is the biggest employer in town."

"It's only an interview."

"I know you'll do just fine."

"You think that?"

Still grasping him at the shoulders, she took a step back and looked steadily into his used, handsome, puzzled face. "Remember what I said: there's nobody like Mitchell Morse. Anywhere."

He laid a hand gently on her bruised cheek. "You know what I read once, one of those books you came across? Fella writes, 'Geography is destiny.' Feels now like he was talking right at me."

She covered his hand. "He was, Mitch. Right at you. Come on." Her voice was dense with emotion but her eyes were serene. She led him toward the bedroom.

"This only makes three dates," he reminded her.

"Nice no more," was all she said.

TWELVE

AT FOUR-THIRTY that Friday afternoon, Doyle Gilley signed his name to a check in the amount of $2020 and pushed it across the desk of D. C. Kasperson, Doctor of Trichology. Doyle was perched expectantly on the edge of his seat. Everything about him—the cords of tension in his neck and shoulders, the rigid set of his mouth, the fretful anticipation in his eyes, the tightness in his scalp—announced the zeal of the manic moonseeker.

Kasperson kept up a torrent of small talk as he busied himself with the check and a hasty scan of the Gilley Data Sheet: "Warm one today, eh, Mr. Gilley? Last gasp of Indian summer, I fear. Well, by the time you complete your course of treatments nature's true summer will be upon us, and that's the season most favorable for hair growth. You'll discover yours blossoming under the sun. Source of all our life, you know."

And so forth. Finally he set aside the sheet and squared his hands on the table. Locked in the vigor of its squinty smile, his face fairly beamed certitude.

"Mr. Gilley—Doyle, is it?—may I call you Doyle?"

A quick head jerk signaled assent. What the fuck, thought Doyle, long as you grow hair call me anything you want, late for supper even.

"Splendid. Let us begin. Today we commence a series of thrice-weekly treatments that I feel confident in predicting will alter the course of your life. But first let me acquaint you with some of the philosophical underpinnings of my Method. You see,

Doyle, your, um, condition is merely an outer manifestation of a grossly abused system, a system poisoned and corrupt."

Doyle winced at this intelligence.

"Now, there are some practitioners, charlatans, to my thinking, who douse your head with greasy oils, massage it a bit, and then suggest the problem is solved. Can they change the inner workings of that body temple of yours with their potions? The answer is no, Doyle, and if you trust them, the more fool you."

Remembering the Nil-O-Nal, Doyle squirmed uneasily and said nothing.

"Long ago, through my intensive studies in Naturopathy, I learned that to grow luxuriant hair one must work both from without *and* within. I can provide the essential external stimuli here at the Clinic, but only you can clean up that profaned system of yours. Are you willing?"

Doyle was.

"Think of it this way. Your car won't run if you fill the tank with mud or sand. First clean out the clogging mud, then fill 'er right up with good premium gas and she'll be rarin' to go." Charmed by the homely analogy, he chuckled a bit and then resumed in his natural delivery. "Similarly with your internal organs. Think that over, Doyle."

But there was no real need—or opportunity—for Doyle to give it much thought, for the trichologist was launched immediately on an explanation of the means to unclog that tank, his "dual approach to internal flushing." Its first component was diet, and a battery of grim expressions marched across his face as he enumerated the foods forbidden, most of which were the ordinary staples of his cupboard and the bases of Twyla's haphazard menus, but which now were exposed for the poisonous garbage they really were: mucus-forming cow's milk, soggy white bread, empty refined sugars, devitalized luncheon meats, gummy rice, acidulous pickles. All, Doyle learned, must go; shun them like the plague, he was urged.

Kasperson took a moment's pause. His eyes darkened. Deep runnels of doubt appeared in his forehead. He emptied his lungs, filled them, and pressed on.

"My other approach to internal purgation may be less agreeable to contemplate, particularly if you are one of those people still bound by the old taboos."

Doyle wasn't sure what he was talking about, but he shook his head vigorously anyway, to assert he was not.

"I'm relieved to know that, Doyle. For my part I can find nothing but folly in the refusal to consider and discuss certain functions that are a part of our everyday lives."

Again he paused, looked Doyle squarely in the eye. "What I must do here is give you a plain talk on the ashes of the system. This may not be pleasant," he warned, "but it is absolutely necessary to impress on you the crucial importance of internal purity."

Silent and unflinching, Doyle returned the steady gaze.

"Your colon, my friend, is a great sewer through which *should* pass freely the effluvia of the system. In his natural state, man, like his animal brethren, speedily disposed of this waste. But as he grows more sophisticated, more civilized, he ignores and postpones Nature's call, till at last She tires of prodding and scuttles off to attend other of Her countless chores. Little wonder it is, then, that the walls of the colon are encrusted with impacted waste matter. In some persons the colon is laden with hardened feces as solid and dark as coal, so foul it often becomes the breeding ground for worms. The pity of it all is the blood—that same blood feeding our papillae, you remember—absorbs a goodly amount of this poison. Imagine carrying a full sewer around inside you! I'm sure you'll agree we can't feed the hair with—well, best left unsaid—and expect it to thrive."

Doyle knew of no plainer truth, and said as much.

"How then do we rid ourselves of this abnormal filthy accumulation? Perhaps we must look to the animal kingdom for help. Let me tell you a little story, Doyle.

"Many centuries ago the natives of India observed that certain birds of the ibis family, a long-billed species, returned from lengthy journeys to the interior in deplorable condition. This bird reached the river in a state of near exhaustion, scarcely able to fly from weakness. Then the natives witnessed a startling phenomenon. The ibis filled its beak with river water, inserted said beak into the anal cavity, and injected the water and relieved itself. After several repetitions of this act, the vitality of the bird was completely restored and it flew away robust as ever.

"Now, the old chiefs and priests of the tribe were perceptive enough to draw a lesson from the book of Nature. They rigged up a device and tried it on themselves. The results were simply astounding. Their vigor returned, they entered into tribal business again and"—he winked slyly—"took to their beds young wives. More to our purposes, the Indian is famous for his bounteous head of hair. The correlation is obvious."

"You mean I'm gonna have to . . ."

Doyle was too dumbfounded to finish the thought. He didn't have to. In a voice resonant with inspirational appeal, Kasperson concluded for him: ". . . imitate the action of the ibis! Let that be your motto, my friend."

During the protracted monologue, Kasperson's thick eyebrows had been doing curious things: arching steeply, collapsing, folding in half, crinkling. Now, for a flicker of an instant, Doyle suspected he was in the presence of a madman. He didn't care. He was twenty-two, sleekly built, arrestingly handsome, poised on the very cusp of a spectacular future—and balding. Grasping at this last slender reed of hope, he was prepared to do his part, whatever it took, however bizarre.

The clinic's part was revealed next. Kasperson escorted him to a large adjoining room split by a narrow corridor and divided into tiny cubicles, "treatment booths," in his designation. Doyle's enclosed a single adjustable seat much like a dentist's chair, and a narrow counter supporting a three-angle mirror and some unlabeled vials of jelly. Kasperson eased him into the chair, tilted it and excused himself.

After a moment he was back. "Allow me to introduce Miss Yvonne Reneau," he said, "my chief operator and soon-to-be associate."

In the mirror Doyle saw a cadaverous woman in a spotless white uniform sashed tightly over bony hips. She dipped in a winsome curtsy.

"Miss Reneau has diplomas from a number of institutes specializing in the maladies of the hair—among them the Parisian Academy. She came to us shortly after we opened our offices here, and with this rich background of study combined with a thorough grounding in my Method her services have become, I might say in all candor, absolutely indispensable."

Her reflected face flushed radiantly. The taut skin pinched over the cheekbones and around the corners of the mouth, and when the color faded it took on an unhealthy sallow tinge, indoor pallor.

"I leave you now in her capable hands," Kasperson said. He patted Doyle's shoulder reassuringly, and then he was gone.

The treatment was multifaceted, complex. It began with a mechanically assisted scalp massage. Miss Reneau thrust a strange-looking device in front of Doyle's face and said, "Massager. Fits on the back of my hand like this, see. Little motor here on top makes it get down deep, right to the roots."

Doyle was taken aback by her voice. It was a sinus-tortured nasal with a distinctly midwestern twang. Somehow, with the name and all, he had been expecting something low and cool with maybe an exotic accent.

After the scalp loosening came one of the jelly vials. "This stuff's Dr. Kasperson's own secret formula," she confided. "He makes it up right here. Gets right down into the papillae, he says, and works wonders. See, I rub this all over your head and then massage it in."

She proceeded to do just that. Leaning over him, she displayed not the slightest trace of a bust. There was a musty, aging smell about her, like a first hint of incipient female complaints. Her own hair was frizzy, a dull orange and peaked in random mounds, rather like a used-up scouring pad. While she worked, Doyle ventured a timid question: "Do you think any of this will help?"

"No reason why it shouldn't," she answered briskly. "You just do what Dr. Kasperson says and relax and enjoy your treatments. No reason in the world why it shouldn't."

After the jelly application he was left alone to bake his head under a lamp. "Special ultraviolet," she assured him on her way out, "really does the trick. Takes about a half hour."

A blade of late afternoon sunlight fell across the cubicle. There was the snap of a cigarette lighter from the other side of the partition. Apart from that, all was silence. It occurred to Doyle to wonder where the other patients were, why it was so still. But he supposed the place was in some ways like a pornography parlor, each booth with its shamed occupant indulging his private dreams.

Eventually a timer dinged somewhere and Miss Reneau came back in. "About done," she said cheerily, emptying another vial of viscous goo onto his head and kneading it in. "Just your electro left." She wiped her hands on a towel and held up a wooden-handled translucent glass tube about a foot long, a vaguely obscene-looking instrument. When she plugged it in it crackled and spit. "Don't tighten up now," she warned. "It's perfectly safe."

Sweeping it like a magic wand, she made quick passes over his scalp, lingering on the bare temples and a spot in the back. A prickly painless shock coursed through him. After a moment or two she switched it off, chirped, "That's it," and helped him out of the chair and brushed stray hairs from his collar. Standing face to face, he could see anxious lines buried in makeup splaying out from her eyes and creasing her forehead.

"Well, what do you think of the treatment?" she asked.

Doyle wasn't just sure what he thought, so he said, "Fine. Just fine."

"Fine. Dr. Kasperson's in the outer office waiting for you. See ya next week. Bye."

The reception lady regarded him with stony detachment, but Kasperson's face was arranged in a benevolent smile. He offered some final instructions on the uses of the Home Maintenance Kit and then, grasping Doyle firmly at the biceps, led him to the door. "Congratulations on this first significant step, my friend. Feel free to consult me at any time—on any problem pertaining to the hair whatsoever."

XX

What it is, thought Kasperson, alone at last, all the smile muscles in his face blessedly relaxed, is the pilot light of hope glimmering, however faintly, in every living soul. The seductive treasonous swindle of hope. And what you do to find it is search the eyes. Find that lunatic glint, signal of the closely reasoned madness of runaway dreams, and you've found the means to mint pure gold. That he possessed a God-given talent for detecting it, he had no doubt. The evidence, the Gilley check, he held in his hands right now. No question, he could still produce the impeccable extemporized wheeze on call (the ibis, now that was an inspired touch, exhumed from the tomb of a memory of a TV special on our feathered friends, viewed years ago), ooze it with passion and sincerity. He'd done it for so long it was a part of him now, worn like a second skin, the blustery torrent of words inseparable from the man. Become the man. But the hard truth was he found little pleasure in it anymore.

Beneath a bundle of completed Data Sheets—a sorry roll call of forgotten walkers—in a lower drawer of the desk was a pint of Cutty. He got it out and treated himself to a generous shot straight from the bottle. Jesus, he was weary, felt like a water-witcher combing the Sahara. Worried, too. Certainly the two thou would help, but it was pocket change finally, pay some bills and tranquilize the widow for a time. How long could it keep the wolf away? Answer was: not long, my good and perspicacious friend, not long at all. You aren't going to make it on a single bughouse Doyle Gilley; some erratic drop-ins, twenty thin bills a scalp; and a parade of walkers vanished into air. No, marks weren't what they used to be, not anymore. Neither was he.

Where was the moronic Milo? Three days elapsed and not a word. In those three days he had culled the local newspaper, searching the Metro section for telltale accounts of petty robberies—Seven Elevens, most likely, or Mother Hubbards—that bore the singular stamp of Milo Pitts. Nothing. Well, not exactly nothing. Worse than nothing. It was the "tanning bed murder" getting all the splash, victim ultimately identified as one Roland Mottla, transient, no known address, no leads yet, no suspects. Yet. There now, there was the heavy hand of Milo at work. A meaningless exercise in payback on a witless, penniless hustler. And to no productive end. If anything, it threatened to unravel the threads of the only inventive scheme that ever had flickered through that knucklewalker's dim brain.

This was legitimate cause for alarm, for Kasperson knew something of the history of his potential partners. Jacktown legend had it that Milo earned his ticket by robbing convenience stores armed only with his menacing bulk and a bag of dog shit. The terrified clerks were given a choice: empty the till or dine on the contents of the bag. It was Milo's contention that if he were ever collared (as of course he was, and forced at gunpoint by an unamused arresting officer to eat his own unusual weapon, the legend claimed) at least he could not be charged with armed robbery, not for simply carrying around a sack of your everyday dog doo. The prosecutor and judge disagreed. There was, after all, such a thing as strong-arm robbery, and though it was a fine semantic hairsplitting, it was still good enough for an eight-year holiday.

If it was possible to be even less kindly endowed in the top-floor department, his freak-jacket sidekick, Conrad, surely qualified for such distinction. The story was told of Conrad that at age sixteen he and an older brother stumbled on the discovery that their lives were somehow empty and incomplete without crotch rocket cycles, one each. Since they had no money, and banks did, the solution was self-evident. They selected one at random and charged into it, shotguns at the ready, jabbing and scrambling and shouting, just the way they'd seen it done at drive-in movies. Sadly for Conrad, his finger inadvertently jerked the trigger and opened a fist-sized hole in the chest of the equally luckless brother. That one was a legal puzzler, too. Eventually they settled on involuntary manslaughter in the commission of an armed robbery; and because Conrad was a minor, he spent the first two years of his sentence in Ionia. He refined his sociopathy there with a nonfatal stabbing or two, and was soon promoted to Jackson. Where a whimsical jesting fate put him in a cell with Milo Pitts.

And where the same mordant fate ordained their paths should cross with his own.

Kasperson knew what it was he was up against, the lumpish clay he had to work with: two marvels of classic ineptitude rendered all the more lethal by a viciousness so casual it was almost by-the-way, offhanded, nonchalant. He understood the hazards. So what do you do? You make do. All his life (up to now, anyway) he had been a shrewd yea-sayer; the very nature of his tenuous livelihoods demanded the sort of man who always saw the glass half full. The sort of man he had once been. And for this last and greatest score in a life waning at a frighteningly accelerated pace, he could bring himself to be that way again. One more time.

His thoughts began to drift toward a dreamy vision of the sumptuous new life waiting for him on the other side of the money. Three million dollars, give or take some change. With that kind of plunder a man could fulfill his rightful destiny, feast at the groaning boards of luxury and pleasure and ease. No more of life's manifold insults. Not for D. C. Kasperson. No more wise deliberations over naked scalps. No more of Delberta Julius, her fat ankles and her elephant skin thighs and her glowery eyes and her . . .

Voice. It was the sandpaper swipe of her voice penetrating the door and bringing him back from somewhere: "D.C. Call for you. Line two."

He'd not even heard the ring. Wherever it was he had been, it was somewhere far away from here. He picked up the phone and, remembering himself, oiled out his customary greeting: "Dr. Kasperson speaking."

A rumbly voice inquired, "Doc? You know who this is talkin'?"

"Indeed I do," Kasperson said tightly. He had no idea what he was going to hear.

"Think we're ready to talk the big numbers."

With some effort, Kasperson held in a great relieved sigh. Talk, he thought, is as far as you're ever going to take those numbers, but he said heartily, "Good news, Milo. Very encouraging. Now we can start making some plans."

A meeting time and place was arranged. Kasperson congratulated him again and they rung off. He had another jubilant gulp of the Cutty, replaced the bottle in the drawer, and sprayed his mouth with Binaca. Then he leaned back in his chair and gazed blissfully at the ceiling. His face was wreathed in a beatific smile, quite uninduced.

"I don't know what you think you got to smirk about," snorted Delberta, hauling him back from the billowy clouds of his restored vision. He had failed to notice her materializing in the doorway. He managed a quick recovery.

"And why not, my dear. Today marks the turning point in our venture." In evidence, he held up Doyle's check, displayed it with a confident wiggle.

"Huh. One steady client don't mean we're out of the woods yet. Not by a darn sight."

For the Delbertas of this world, the glass would forever be half empty. And in her case, soon, as though in self-fulfilling prophecy, utterly void.

"In observance of this occasion," Kasperson said, beaming at her anyway, "I propose we dine out this evening."

The widow's unlovely features knotted suspiciously. "Who's that on the telephone? Another collection agency?"

"Quite the contrary, I believe we may have another client very soon now. All the more cause for celebration."

"I'm warnin' you, D.C. I got no more cash to sink into this business. You promised we'd be on easy street by now."

Poor Delberta. Since she had met him, caught her first glimpse of the artful life, her speech had lapsed into a quaint slang lifted, it seemed, from the movie screens of her departed youth. Kasperson got up from the chair and came across the room and laid a benign peck on her cheek. "And so we shall. The street of dreams. If only you'll believe in me a bit longer."

"Well," she said grudgingly, "I guess we could go out and put on the dog. This one time."

"Of course we can. An elegant dinner is precisely what this doctor orders."

"Okay. Lemme just slip into the little girls' room, freshen up."

He patted her ample buttocks and, irrelevantly, an image of the credulous Doyle Gilley, enema syringe buried in his ass, flashed behind his eyes. For the briefest shard of a moment he wondered if there was in him yet any remaining incorruptible place. He supposed not.

THIRTEEN

THEY WERE PARKED on the farthest edge of a small rural outpost a few miles north of Grand Rapids. Behind them was the last block of houses in town, and across the street a broad, nut-brown pasture dotted with cows. For this next to last day in October it was almost uncomfortably warm in the Chevette, and Ducky was grateful for the Super Slurpee he'd remembered to bring along. Between popped Goobers, he gulped it noisily. He had all the peppy nervous enthusiasm of a leashed toy terrier, pumped and stroked and ready to get to it. Though he was no less wired, Meat at that moment sat stonily behind the wheel, his face wrinkled against the fingers of burnished sunlight slanting through the windshield. The muscles in his neck and shoulders were taut, bunched. A Lucky jutted from his mouth, unlit and apparently forgotten. He checked his watch.

"Okay," he said, "it's eleven. Let's run it by one more time, be sure you got it straight."

"C'mon, Meat, we been over it enough. How many times I got to say it? I ain't no retard, y'know."

While it was undeniably true they had rehearsed thoroughly over the past forty-eight hours—covered the route, timed it, considered all the possible glitches and done their best to account for them—Meat was not totally confident of Ducky's self-assessment. He knew him too well. "Many times as I tell you," he growled. "Now do it again."

"Awright, awright, whatever pulls your pud." Ducky held up a hand and, like a child itemizing a list of chores, began ticking the parted fingers in enumeration of the steps in Meat's carefully crafted plan. "Number one is you drop me off here and I hoof it in to the car lot and—"

"And you're packin' what again?" Meat interrupted him.

"My piece, course." He patted the .25-caliber pistol tucked under his belt and concealed by his jacket.

"That all you're carryin'?"

Ducky unzippered a pocket of the jacket and removed a ski mask and plastic gloves, held them up in dutiful display.

"How about your gear? You got that?"

"Got all the gear I'm ever gonna need," Ducky said. Which was a true fact. The Phillips, ignition plunger and alligator clip in another pocket were more than plenty for an easy boost like this one today. Didn't even need his Slim Jim, way these tractor boys up here left their doors unlocked. Trusted everybody. He'd show 'em trust.

"Okay. Anything else?"

"Yeah yeah yeah yeah. I'm luggin' that grocery sack in the back, too."

So far the little fuck had it right, though Meat was not much taken by the wiseass tone of voice. At the same time, he was not disposed to push things too hard either. Some dim instinct told him what was needed here was harmony, attention to detail, a needlepoint focus. The way the Doc would do it. He tried reason.

"Listen, Duck, you got any idea what all's ridin' here? We get by this today and we're one beat away from hogfat city."

"I know it, Meat, but Jesusfuckamighty, you're gettin' worse'n some little old granny, can't remember she took a proper leak or splashed her drawers. Lookit you—look like you ordered a steak and swallowed a turd. C'mon, man, turn that frown upside down."

The tight vertical clefts in Meat's brow darkened ominously, and his hard slice of mouth rolled back in a snarl. Enough of reason. "Turn *you* upside down, assface, you don't shape up here, run through this drill. What's two?"

Ducky gave a hopeless sigh. "Okay. Two is, I gets to the lot, wire me some wheels and slide out the back way."

"First you got your gloves on. First thing, soon as you get to the lot. Don't forget that. Also you're scopin' up front real careful, right? Make sure there ain't no salesman sniffin' around?"

"Meat," he said wearily, "I been boostin' vehicles since I was eleven. You gonna teach me how all over again?"

The way Meat saw it, there were two potential flash points in his plan. This was one of them, and it worried him. He did what he could to bury the anxiety, hope for the best. "Just keep goin'," he said.

Ducky tapped his middle finger, grinned hugely. "Next up's three, old Mr. Stink Finger here, got to be lucky. I come toolin' up the back road—yeah, I'm watchin' my speed, I ain't forgot—till I gets to your home town, thirty-some miles. I see the hotel, corner of Main, and a block before I gets to it I hang right—"

"Left, lollyhole, left! You go right you'll dead end at a gravel pit."

"Okay, left, I meant left. For Chrissake, Meat, up here is your turf. I ain't no country boy." Which was also true. Apart from his sojourns in Ionia and Jackson, he had never been out of Grand Rapids in his life, and all this open space, empty fields reaching to the end of the horizon, made him feel exposed somehow, uneasy, the longer they sat talking about it. All he wanted to do was get this goddam quiz over with and get the job done, so he added quickly, "I go left and 'bout a half mile outside of town there's this little branch bank, right-hand side of the road."

"What time is it now?"

Ducky looked confused. "Time? You just said it was eleven."

Meat seemed suddenly aware of the cigarette in his mouth. He flipped it out the window and laid his head in his hands. "This ain't gonna work," he said dismally.

Ducky squirmed in the cramped bucket seat. "Well, whaddya mean, time?"

"I'm talkin' what time it is when you pull into the bank. You remember *any* what I told you? Timin' is everything here."

"Oh, that kind time. Whyn't you say? It's noon."

"Why is it noon?"

" 'Cuz at noon the Halloween squirrel parade goes down Main. Everybody in town be there, correct? Bank be empty, no customers, one teller maybe, holdin' down the fort."

Now Meat looked up and studied him closely. This was the real spiky point. "And what you gonna do, that teller?"

"Do? What I come to do. Make her roll over all the money, vault and all. Which I load in the grocery sack. Which is why it's only part full."

"But you ain't gonna dust her up any, right? Just gonna use that shooter to spook her a little. So we don't get no heavy heat off this. You with me on that?"

"Yeah, I got that. Just spook her and get the fuck out."

"Okay. That gets you to four. Then what?"

"I truck on over to the expressway, 'bout another mile, swing north. Six miles or so there's the rest stop."

"Which is where I'm waitin'."

"Bigger'n shit, right, Meato? I pops out of my vehicle into this snappy little number, we do a quick turnaround, first exit, and head on home. Couple citizens out for a Friday drive, eyeball the hillbillies. And that makes five," he said, folding the little finger onto his palm to signal the review was finally complete. And least hoping the fuck it was.

"Yeah, that's the way it's suppose to go down," Meat said doubtfully, and then for a moment he was silent. Hearing his scheme articulated, start to finish, he was struck by its essential flimsiness, by all that might go wrong. Too much was turning on his dim-bulb partner. All of it, actually. If he could do it himself, he would, but no way could he show his face up home. Masked or not, his size or voice or something would give him away. Didn't matter, eight years gone by; somebody'd recognize him. He knew small towns. And this one knew him. Up home, he was famous.

But there was no time for convenience stores—his only heavy experience—and no percentage in them anyway, not for the size stake they needed. That risk-reward business Doc said, he got that correct. This bank though, Halloween, the parade—it was like a suit of clothes put together by a Hong Kong tailor. Fit just right. If they could make it go. Ought to net the five long easy. One quick slide and they're to third base. Home plate by Christmas. So flimsy or not, there was nothing to do but hit it. He clapped Ducky on the shoulder, shoved him toward the door. "Okay, Big Time, go grab your best hold."

Ducky drained off the last of his Slurpee and reached over the seat for the grocery bag. He put a jaunty thumb in the air, flashed a cocksure smile and was gone. And watching that fragile figure prance down the street on legs so thin and bent they resembled the limbs of a paraplegic, miraculously restored to strength and mobility—watching him that way, Meat was overtaken by another sudden rush of misgiving, so intense he had to turn away. Directly across the road one of the cows had wandered over and nudged up against the fence. It eyed him sullenly and then, without warning, sprayed an aureate shower at its feet. As an omen, Meat wasn't quite certain how he should take that. Better not to think about it, he decided, speeding away.

XX

Sunlight filtered through the stripped branches of towering trees lined like platoons of soldiers on either side of the quiet street. Piles of leaves layered the lawns and sidewalks. A few, burnt orange, crinkly, big as hands, some of them, still floated on a gentle breeze; and when one drifted near enough Ducky plucked it out of the air and felt it crumble into a gritty powder inside his fist. He liked this time of year. A buried childhood memory returned to him: laboriously assembling great mound heaps of fallen leaves, chest high, and then scattering them in one joyous flying leap. The sunshine recollection brought a smile to his lips. He wished he were free to do that again right now. Instead of what it was he had to do.

Halfway into the second block he came on two little girls jumping rope. As he approached them he was able to make out the words of the shrill, singsong rhyme they skipped to:

Here comes a candle
To light you to bed,
And here comes a chopper
To chop off your head.

They were having more fun today then he was. "Mornin', little ladies," he said.

"Hi, mister. What you got in the sack?"

Ducky was amused by the child's open, spunky curiosity. He paused a moment. "In the sack? Why, I got my groceries, course."

Both of them put aside their jump ropes, and the vocal one stepped up beside him and tugged at the bag boldly. "You got any cookies?"

She had the pinched, freckled features of a peevish elf. Up close this way, her carrot-colored hair looked oily and limp, and her nose was running. A tiny arm struggled to reach the top of the bag.

"Well, let's have a look," Ducky said amiably.

He had no idea what was in it; Meat had taken care of all that. He set the bag on the ground, and she was rifling through it before he could stoop to look. She came up grasping a box of animal crackers.

"*Animal* crackers! That all you got?"

"Lookin' that way."

"How come you got no Oreos?"

To Ducky the question seemed not entirely illegitimate, for he was fond of Oreos himself. But since he had no answer he said simply, "Jesus, kid, I dunno."

"I like *Oreos*."

"Yeah, well, you can have the crackers."

Saying so was a needless gesture, for she had already torn the box open and her mouth was covered by a bulging hand. "Hey, Darlene," she called through it, "you want any?"

The more reserved Darlene shook her head and glanced warily at a weathered frame house across the street. The other one, not at all timid, wiped some moist crumbs from her lips and said to Ducky, "You wanta jump rope?"

"Can't now. I got to get movin'." He bent over to recover the bag, and as he did his jacket crept upward ever so slightly.

"What you got in your pants?"

A distant alarm sounded in Ducky's head. "See you later, kid," he said, juggling the bag and yanking at his jacket. He took one step down the walk, but she scurried around him and planted herself squarely in his path. The freckles in her face boiled up scarlet and she held her ground, canny eyes fixed at the level of his belt.

"You got something in there. Now what is it?"

He tried to move around her but she was much too agile for him. Before he could fully comprehend what was happening, she made a clawing lunge at his midsection. He blocked it, barely in time, and with his free hand caught her by a wrist and gave it a twist, nothing rough, just enough to get her to back off. Which she did, but with a mouth widening in a siren wail. Darlene tore off down the sidewalk, and from the house across the street a woman, full grown but otherwise an exact replica of the howling termagant at his feet, came running toward them, shrieking, "Lois! My little Lois! Lois!"

She swooped up the sobbing child, soothed and cradled her, patted her hair. And then she turned the full weight of her outraged fury on the shaken Ducky.

"What in the name of Christ's goin' on here? Who are *you?*"

Ducky put a flat, defensive hand in the air. "Just mindin' my own business, lady. Ain't nothin' goin' on."

"You'll think nothin' when I call the cops. What'd you do to Lois?"

Holy fuck, thought Ducky, heat is what I don't need now. He glanced at his watch, abruptly conscious of time slipping away.

Still clutching the child, she advanced on him, assaulting him with a fierce onion breath. "Don't go lookin' at the clock, mister. You're not goin' nowhere till I get to the bottom of this."

Lois had reduced the screeching to a calculated whimper, punctuated now and again by some well-timed shudders. Her eyes darted back and forth between the two adults shrewdly.

"If you listen up a minute, lady," Ducky said, or tried to say, "I can tell you what—"

"You damn well *better* tell! I just wish Flip was here. You better thank your lucky stars Flip ain't here."

Ducky was indeed thanking those appropriate stars. His imagination served up an image of the absent Flip: big as Meat and just as mean, tattoos on hammy forearms, fists like mallets, belly like a battering ram inside a tee-shirt with the block-lettered warning, Kick Axe. Or something like that. Anybody named Flip was bound to be bad news.

"All's I was doin'," he said desperately, "was givin' your kid a treat outta my grocery sack here. Animal crackers." He pointed at the shredded box lying discarded in a nest of leaves, mute evidence.

The thin, orange-tipped line that served the woman for eyebrows rose suspiciously. "What you doin' givin' cookies to strange kids for? I bet you're one of them perverts." As soon as she said it the full implication of the charge struck her. She turned a horror-blanched face on Lois, shook her violently. "He touch you, baby? He lay a hand on you? Answer me!"

"He's got something in his pants," the child whined.

"In his pants? Oh my God!"

"Something *hard*."

"My God!"

In a voice spluttery now with genuine panic, Ducky said, "You got it all wrong. It's one of them cans in my sack she's talkin' about."

"It's your raunchy pecker she's talkin' about, you rotten filthy bastard. They oughta lock you up and throw away the key."

"I was just givin' her a treat is all," he pleaded.

"*Treat!*" she bawled at him. "That's what you call it—treat? You sex maniacs run around with hard-ons tryin' to stick 'em into my little girl, and you dare say treat?"

In spite of himself, in spite of the bog of shit he knew he was in, Ducky couldn't restrain a flickering smile at a whimsical inner vision of himself endowed with multiple members, all of them erect and strategically placed for simultaneous penetration of every available orifice on the sour little pissant.

The woman was alert to it. "You laugh! You got the balls to *laugh!* Well, you ain't gonna have 'em long. We'll see who does the laughin'. I'm gonna get Flip."

Lois peeked over her mother's retreating shoulder, thrust out a purple tongue, and flashed Ducky a quick bird. He took off running.

XX

There were four blocks remaining, and he covered them in sprinter's time. At the rear entrance to the lot he squatted down behind a hedge, his breath coming in great ragged heaves. His body glowed like a live coal. Nerve ends prickled under his skin. Along the watersheds of his back and stomach and sides, runnels of sweat flowed south and gathered in sticky pools at the elastic band of his briefs, which were their own source of torment, creeping as they were into his crotch. He looked at his watch. Twenty-three minutes to twelve. Already he was well behind Meat's tightly timed schedule, and who the fuck could guess what would be coming down the street behind him once Big Lois got to Flip.

Got to chill yourself out, Duck boy, he told himself silently, though his lips mimed the thought; settle down here, no going back now. He poked his head around the hedge and scanned the lot. Between the four files of cars he could see a salesman badgering an elderly couple by the trailer up front, hands animatedly batting the air. This time a voiced curse escaped him—at fate; the grinning demons who doled out luck in thimblefuls, and all of it bad, at that; the threesome who blocked his path as squarely as Little Lois had, moments before; and finally at his partner. Damn Meat, he thought bitterly, God damn him anyway, all his fault, sayin' you got to lift a *used* car, be maybe all day long before it's missed and the heat got it on their LEIN. What'd that fucker know, car boostin'. Diddly was what. He'd of left it up to him they'd of picked one off a G.R. street easy, and he'd be toolin' north right now, pork city dead ahead. Instead of this hash he was in. Fuckin' deep thinker, Meat, playin' like he was the Doc with his genius plans. It's his fault, ain't mine.

But establishing blame was not quite the same as producing a solution, and treacherous time, relentless and unforgiving, posted a frantic notice in his head. He scooted down the length of the hedge for another look; different angle, maybe something would come to him. Next door to the lot was a multipump station with the cryptic invitation sign: WELCOME TRUCKERS—GAS EAT BUNKS. It was at just that moment a sixteen-wheeler a few feet from the sales office trailer came to life with a deafening belch. Gears grinding, trailing a cloud of gritty black smoke, it thumped out onto the road and rattled away. There were two more just like it gassing up, and it occurred to Ducky he might be able to get an engine going under cover of all that racket. It was all he could think to do. He pulled on his gloves, grabbed the bag and made a stoop-shouldered dash for the nearest car, an ancient four-door Impala.

Once inside, flattened across the seat, he went to work on the steering column. For what seemed an interminable time, he waited. And then, precisely in sync with the eruptive sounds of the next departing truck, he brought the Impala to a stuttery, chugging start. To keep it from expiring he had to depress the accelerator with the flat of his hand. It wasn't the car he would have chosen, had there been the luxury of choice. He raised himself up, peered around the lot and saw nothing, nobody, the trio responsible for all this grief evidently gone. Which is what he intended to do, ease out the dirt drive in the back and get the fuck gone while he still could. And which he would have done, too, had he not discovered what Meat—God ream out his bunghole with a wire brush!—forgot to account for in all his passionate attention to detail: the price of the vehicle, $995, chalked across the windshield like a *kick me* note pinned to his ass.

He bounded out the door and, hunkering down, tried to reach up and wipe away the numerals with his gloved hands. All he succeeded in doing was to smear a pale film over the entire surface of the glass. He felt a sudden dizzying rush, like he was going to puke or drain his bowels or piss his pants. One hole or another, something was about to give. Piss, an illuminating voice murmured in his ear, you got a load of piss. He clambered onto the hood, dropped to his knees and got his fly. Aiming his organ like a fire hose, he showered the windshield, and with his free hand swiped at the rapidly dissolving chalk. Grim times, grim measures.

"Jesus H. Christ! You're pissin' on our windshield, you sonbitch!"

Best as he could, given the posture, Ducky looked over his shoulder in the direction of the stunned voice addressing him now. It was the salesman. He and the old folks appeared out of nowhere and were gazing at him in stupefied wonder. Sweet Jesus Fuck.

"He's pissin' on our windshield!" the salesman repeated, and the old man's jaw dropped and the lady buried her face in her hands.

Ducky leaped from the hood, cracked open the door, scrambled in behind the wheel, slammed the car in gear and roared off, raising a whirlwind of dust behind him. "You're stealin' our car!"

the salesman, whose talents appeared to lie in description rather than action, called after him. Ducky kept driving.

XX

The bank was one of those squat, toaster-shaped structures, all functional brick and exposed girders and plate glass. From where he was parked, behind it, hidden from the road, he could see into the narrow chamber of a lobby. Empty, but for a single teller. About that, at least, Meat had been right. Also the parking lot was empty, and the only other enterprises nearby—a Dairy Sweet shuttered for the season and a place called Waterbed Wonderland with a CLOSED–PLEASE CALL AGAIN sign in the window—were equally deserted. Beyond them a weed-choked field reached to the fringes of town. The faint throbbing cadences of band music echoed over it like an agitated heartbeat.

So he should have felt a little better than he did. Except it was now half past twelve, which meant he was thirty minutes behind time, and with the trickiest part still ahead. And the stink of urine and his own anxious sweat rising through the car, they weren't helping any either. Or the idling motor, sputtering dangerously, as it had ever since he went barreling out of the used car lot. That was next, he supposed, fuckin' bolt bucket die on him. Way things were going here, it was overdue.

What Ducky really wanted to do was turn tail and run, get out of there before a truly ruinous disaster overtook him. But the thought of facing Meat with a grocery sack empty of anything but just that, groceries, set his already jangled nerves perilously near to tweaking. He'd seen Meat mad, as in serious mad. Awesome sight. Which left him without option and therefore no sound reason for further delay. Mumbling to himself, he pulled the ski mask over his head, shouldered the bag and slipped behind a row of scrawny evergreens at the side of the bank and came through the front door.

A woman of mountainous proportions loomed over the cage like an airborne blimp. She had hair the color of raspberry ripple ice cream, cheeks daubed with rouge, a nipped mouth painted azalea pink, and a series of accordion roll chins. Pendulous drooping jugs brushed the counter beneath her, on which lay a romance magazine whose pages gripped her attention. Ducky glided across the lobby and set the bag on the ledge beside a nameplate that identified her as Lavonne Gunderson. He cleared his throat loudly. She glanced up and her face enlarged in a grin.

"All right, Wendell. You can come out behind the mask. Halloween parade's over."

For an instant Ducky was dumbstruck. This wasn't how it was supposed to go. "Wendell?" he said, "I ain't Wendell. This here's a stickup."

First she did some tongue-clucking, and then in a tone of scolding good humor said, "You're not scarin' me any, Wendell. Now take off that silly mask before somebody comes in."

Fierce as he could make it, Ducky said, "Listen, lady, I ain't here to slap wet towels. This is the real thing." To prove it he yanked out the pistol and jabbed it into her face.

The grin collapsed. "You're not Wendell," she exclaimed, "you're a *robber!*" Both of her arms fired into the air, perfect simulation of a "reach for the sky" response to the barked command of a cinematic desperado.

Now he felt a little steadier. "Fuckin'-a, robber," he said toughly. "Real mean, I don't get what I come after. Now hoist that rhino rump yours off the stool and back away, nice and easy. Watch your toes don't hit no alarm buttons, you want to keep your head on."

He took a few steps to the left, reached over the top of the gate, got the latch and came around behind the wall of cages. He moved in next to her. On her feet this way, she was easily a full head taller than he was and about three times as wide. Whale like that ever sit on you, he thought, you got one flat Duckburger patty comin' up, rare. The image prompted him to keep the gun carefully trained on her.

"Okay, Lavonne," he said, "so far you're doin' just fine."

"I'm not Lavonne," she whimpered, her face weakening toward tears.

"Huh?"

"I'm Wilma. Wilma Hovis. That's Lavonne's station. She's at the parade. Her kids are in it. I just help out here sometimes."

Ducky sucked in his breath. "I don't give a ripped rat's ass who you are. Just get on over and open up that vault there."

"I can't."

"Can't? Whaddya mean, can't? I'm tellin' you do it."

"It's *time*-locked!"

"You sayin' you can't get in?"

"Nobody can. Not till three." Her chunky arms, twin pillars of white fat stabbing the air, began to tremble. Tears coursed over the lumpy cheeks, moistened the rouge and splayed outward in damp rosy rills. "You're gonna kill me, aren't you," she wailed. "I know you're gonna kill me."

Ignoring her, he backed over to the vault and tested the door. It was surely locked. And he was just as sure he was not going to find a way in: anybody do all that blubbering got to be telling the truth. The churning nausea he'd experienced earlier in the day seized him once again. A frightful taunting vision of an enraged Meat cavorted through his pounding head. He shuddered violently. Mistaking it for rage, she burst into a sob, moaning something about mercy.

"Goddam it, Lavonne—Wilma—whatever, shut the fuck up," Ducky snarled at her. "I got to think here."

And fast, a voice in one ear reminded him; and in the other, another voice counseled run run run. And in his own voice, risen now to a high, piping squeal, he said, "How about them cash drawers? How much you got in them?"

"I don't know for sure. I only work part time and when—"

"I don't wanta hear no more about you!" Ducky broke in shouting. "About how much?"

"I don't know. A lot, I think, on account of today is payday out to the stove plant. Please don't kill me. Please."

"Ain't nobody gonna kill you, you do what I say. Dump all the cash in that sack here. Move your ass. Now! Quick time!"

She set to work emptying the drawers, moving rather nimbly, for someone her size, from cage to cage. Ducky stepped in behind her, prodding her with the gun. Mostly it was twenties he could see flying into the bag, but there were some bundles of fifties and hundreds, too. Maybe he was going to squirrel out of this one yet.

"You want the change too?" she asked over her shoulder when all the bills were gone.

"Nah, you get to keep the change. Turn around here."

Slowly she turned. Her sobs had dwindled to a whistling snivel, but her eyes, glinty with fear, were fixed on the weapon held only inches from her face.

"One more thing you got to do for me," Ducky said.

She lifted a hand weakly, as though requesting mercy. "What's that? You already got all the money."

"That's lose all them clothes you got on."

The idea had come to him on wings of inspiration. He remembered its success with the faggot the other night; ought to work just as well here. Jerk out the phone cord, toss the clothes in the lot, and scoot away smart as you please. Be a good long while before a naked barrel of suet like this one want to go runnin' down the road bawlin' help! help!

It was inspired, all right, but it's effect was like nothing he had imagined. A look of terror, stark and absolute, contorted her jiggly features. Her eyes rolled up in their sockets, prelude, it appeared, to a gigantic crumpling swoon. She clutched at the counter for support. Her enormous bosom rose and swelled. "Oh my Lord!" she shrieked. "You're gonna *vi*olate me!"

Ducky, seriously shaken, took one step backward. The gun quivered in his hand.

And then her eyes refocused, on him now, on the level of his hips, and her mouth fell open like an abruptly unlatched chute, and welling up out of it came a piercing cry: "Your pants! *Your barn door's open!*"

Ducky looked down and saw his fly, forgotten in all the distresses of the day, still undone, and the tip of the head of Uncle Clyde peeking mischievously through the window of his briefs; and then he looked up and—for no good reason he could think of then or ever—squeezed the trigger, and the gun shook thunderously in his hand; and when he looked at the wall behind where Lavonne or Wilma or whoever she was stood, what he saw was a blurred outline of her face set against a backdrop of hair and blood and bone chips, sketched as though in watercolors and by a childish, inept hand, and streaming gently now, with comic precision, to the floor.

XX

Meat's greeting: "Where the holy cock-knobbin' fuck you been?"

Ducky had no immediate reply. He was slumped in the passenger seat, jelly limbed, waxen faced, head lolling on his spindly chest as though from a severed spinal cord. His eyes had all the empty vacancy of a cadaver.

Smoke dense as ground fog hung in the air of the Chevette.

The ashtray was heaped with the stubbed-out tally of Meat's prolonged and mounting anxiety. Wielding a cigarette like a dagger, he shifted to face his partner. "I'm askin' you question here, fartfuck. What happened? Where you been?"

Ducky, coming back from somewhere, managed to lift his head and gape at him dumbly. A spark of supplication lit his otherwise blank eyes. "Run into couple snags," he said in a vowel-sloshing whine.

"Snags I don't wanta hear about. Loot I do. You get it?"

Ducky pointed to the bag at his feet. "It's in there."

Meat expelled a twining funnel of smoke. "Okay," he said, "let's bugass outta here."

He turned the key in the ignition and maneuvered the Chevette across the asphalt, down the ramp and onto the expressway. In the mirror he caught a glimpse of the Impala nestled between a Winnebago and an Air-Stream. The rest stop was unattended so it ought to be a while before the abandoned vehicle was discovered. Long enough, anyway, for them to get vanished. So except for the delay, the as yet unaccounted for lag time, everything was running according to plan. Home free, practically. Should feel good. So why was he still all charged, jittery? Ducky was why, sitting there like a fuckin' zombie, not dribblin' out the mouth like he always did. That wasn't right, that worried him. "About them snags," he said. "What about 'em? Hairy?"

Ducky mumbled something.

"Hey, spit that turd outta your mouth, willya?"

"Said nothin' I couldn't handle."

"Then how come you're actin' funny?"

"How do you mean, funny?"

"I mean what I'm sayin', dogdick. Funny. I know you. Anything went wrong, you better own up."

"Ain't nothin' went wrong, Meat." He turned and gazed out the window at the flat farmland rolling away in every direction. And then, as though in afterthought, he added, "Not exactly. Oh yeah, one thing though. Lady back there at the bank, she lost her face."

Meat's mouth opened in an oval of disbelief. "Whaddya mean, lost her face? You sayin' you waxed her?"

"I had to do it, Meat. There wasn't no other way. You'd of been there, you'd of seen."

Ducky had squeezed up by the door, cowering miserably, like a twitchy hound braced against a blow. But it was his own forehead Meat slapped with an open palm, rhythmically, savagely. "Fuckin' cocklickin' ballbreakin' shit," he groaned. "What'd I say? Said don't do no prankin'. What do you got to do? A waxin'! Cock *fuck!*"

Ducky was too terrified to speak.

At the first emergency crossing strip, Meat swung into the median, squealed onto the parallel road and pointed them south, fast as the rattly Chevette would peddle. For a number of miles he was silent, glowering in a fierce concentration. Eventually, a little calmer, not much, he said, "You know something, Duck? There was a way to fuck up a wet dream, you'd find it. You know that?"

Ducky said nothing. It was probably true.

XX

The proceeds of the day were spread out in front of them, stacked in neat piles, by denomination, on Starla's kitchen table. She stared at the money warily, her expressions sifting through a cluster of emotions: doubt, wonder, a curious tingly agitation not altogether unpleasant, awe, dread. Ducky, no less wary, kept his eyes on Meat, awaiting his response. When none seemed forthcoming, he said hopefully, "I got us close to six long there, Meat. And some change. That ain't so bad, is it?"

"Also you got us a stiff," Meat said dourly, "and Christ only knows what kind heat comin' down." He picked up a fistful of bills, riffled them like playing cards. The tight, furrowed look he had worn all day softened some. "But for a general jerk-off, you done pretty good. I think we're ready to put in a call to the Doc, talk the big numbers."

PART THREE

FOURTEEN

AT FLEETS, Morse discovered early on, you get by on smiles and nods and a certain show of lively industry. Those, and a willingness to share the company philosophy, which, reduced to its essence, appeared to be an unwavering faith in the fundamental goodness of mankind. That's what the founder, a Dutch immigrant named Willem Flietsma, believed back in 1912 when he opened the doors of his meat market and greengrocery. Grand Rapids was about seventy-five years old then, grown up from a tiny logging settlement along the banks of the Grand River to a prosperous community famed as the Furniture Capital of the region (some said of the entire nation even). By the time Willem arrived, Grand Rapids had established itself as the economic and cultural anchor for western Michigan. It had a zoo and a hospital and a library and a junior college. It had banks and railroads and electric streetcars. Also it had churches, many, many churches. Its citizens, predominantly of Dutch and German and Scandinavian extraction, were devout, hard-working folks who measured the quality of their lives by a rigid standard of wholesome family and spiritual values. For Willem Flietsma, it was the next best place to paradise.

His sons, Gerrit and Harm, brought their father's cheery philosophy to an expansion of the market that began gradually, with typical Hollander caution, but in the years following the Depression and the war soon became runaway, exceeding even their wildest expectations. By then, within the borders of Michigan, Grand Rapids was second only to Detroit in size and significance. But though it was beginning to have its share of urban problems (not the least of which was the alarming influx of Slavs, southern Europeans, Jews, Asians, blacks), in values it was still a world apart from that blighted, decaying, cynical city a hundred and fifty miles to the east. And it was those same solid conservative values and traditions that guided the business today, rechristened Fleets by the third generation and grown into a vast chain of food and general merchandise stores spanning the state.

At least that's the way they told it at the group orientation for new family members, a day-long marathon of welcoming speeches, slide shows, explications of benefits and responsibilities, and interminable lectures on company history and policy and, of course, philosophy. Among other things, Morse learned that Fleets, Inc. was one of the largest privately owned retail firms in the Midwest, employing close to thirty thousand people in over ninety units (as the stores and their supporting facilities were designated). Name your Michigan community of any substance: there you'd find a Fleets, for sure. He learned he was not an employee but a "partner," as was everyone else in the organization, right down to the lowliest grocery bagger. He also learned a whole set of corporate Beliefs: honesty, fairness, relentless enthusiasm, the virtue of pitching in, preservation of the worth and dignity of each partner, race, color, gender or creed notwithstanding, and—the cornerstone—a respect for the customer approaching veneration. And, oh yes, "profitability," as they called it, that was important too. These principles were the moral glue that held the enterprise together, he was told.

Orientation was conducted at corporate headquarters, a sprawling complex of office buildings and warehouses and training centers plunked down in a pasture on the far western edge of town, a little city of its own bordered on three sides by hay fields and on the fourth by the trailing-off end of a working-class residential neighborhood gone to seed. Forty or more people were crammed in a stark airless room to hear the message, and all of them, Morse included, were doing their level best to project the energy and wholesome good cheer they were soon given to understand was the stamp of the successful (read retained) Fleets partner.

The first thing they were instructed to do was clutch hands with the person on either side and exchange first names (everyone at Fleets, president on down, went by first name). Morse found himself grinning like a demented fool at, left and right respectively, a young woman with the sheared-away chin of a night owl and a black with the rueful disappointed eyes of the man who expects to be cheated and usually is. He didn't listen to either name. Within an hour he'd pretty much stopped listening altogether, though he adjusted his features in the bright absorbed look that said he was.

By noon he had a poison headache; by three his backside, planted on a metal folding chair, felt as if it had turned to stone. Along about five (a day's work for a day's pay, another company Belief) it all came to a close with a rousing sendoff by some positive thinker whose round, gladsome face betrayed a hypertensive flush. The only thing missing, as far as Morse could tell, was a corporate anthem, or at the very least a fight song.

Welcome to Fleets.

XX

Twelve years as a cop had led Morse to the unremarkable conclusion that a job was, finally, an expression of a man's deepest motives. Given enough time, he believed, the job defined the man, became him. And believing this, he wasn't so sure, two weeks into his Fleets family membership, he liked what this one was beginning to reveal about himself. It was one thing to work as point man for an outfit like AAPS; that was shabby enough. It was quite another to steer a cart up and down the aisle of an overgrown grocery store, masquerading as a shopper and snooping out petty thieves. Or to spend a day wedged behind a two-way mirror in a fitting room, watching men undress and, more times than a few, slink out the door with three layers of clothes bulging their coats. Had to tell you something about yourself, that line of employment.

Fleets' security division, which went under the title of Loss Preclusion Management, had a slightly firmer grasp of the flawed nature of the human condition, but not much. You never know (he was catechized) for absolutely certain, that is, if the customer isn't just absent-minded or preoccupied or maybe distracted somehow, fully intending to pay for the item up front. Folks are basically honest, especially here in Grand Rapids, and at Fleets we always give them the benefit of the doubt.

So the drill was to gunsight your booster, track him (or more frequently her) through the check-out, and then yank the chain out in the lot, quietly, minimum of fuss. By the end of his first week Morse had scored thirty-two collars, unassisted. A Fleets record.

Nice work, Mitch, rolling punker teens and pensioners and blue-haired ladies who burst into wrenching sobs at their undoing, blubbering inconsolably about disgrace and jail and overdoses, things like that. Among his tally was a nine-year-old girl, spidery arms and legs and a couple of bee stings under her training bra, who offered a blow job in exchange for her freedom (*and* the Junior Miss blouse she'd lifted—that was to be part of the deal too). When he declined she went suddenly from temptress to banshee, scratching, biting, thrashing, very nearly catching him with a knobby knee in the nuts. Another memorable bust was made on a middle-aged man with the soft placid features of a Protestant minister, which in fact he turned out to be, Dutch Reformed denomination. And which probably accounted for his taking off in a terrified sprint at the moment of confrontation, desperately flinging packets of Control Top pantyhose from inside his topcoat. This one Morse had to bring down with a lunging tackle.

It came as no surprise to him that he was good at this kind of work. He ought to be. Long ago he learned to read the slipsliding glance, the look of calculated nonchalance. To watch for hands that could move faster than thought. To know better than to expect anything but the absolute worst: cunning, deceit, belligerence, treachery, spite, the general naughtiness of his fellow man, never mind your Fleets philosophy. It was a talent you developed, call it a survival skill. There had been a time when his life depended on it, when it meant something. Now it was good for recovering underwear.

Yet the simple exercise of that talent was enough to earn him extravagant praise. After two weeks of shuttling among several stores, filling in, he was assigned to the one notorious in the company for its dismal loss preclusion record. And as chance (as much even as geography an arbiter of a man's destiny) would have it, that one was the Plainfield Unit.

XX

Okay, so the H stood for Hudek. Starla Hudek. Easy enough to uncover when you worked in the same store, but still a hell of a long way round, finding out a name. And now that he had it, what was to be done? Nothing (he lectured himself sternly), nothing's to be done about it, leave it alone. You've got a satisfactory arrangement here: you've got a job (all right, a paycheck then); the sauce under control; a good woman, loyal, fanatically devoted, just waiting to spring the L-word any day now (deal with that when it came). Some order in your life for a change, more than you've had in a long, long time, longer than memory would serve. So the thing to do was leave it alone. It was only a whim anyway, a juicer impulse. Don't even think about it.

That's what he told himself, and for three full days at the Plainfield Unit he was pretty much convinced that's the way he was going to keep it. But on the morning of the fourth day he waited till she took her break and then followed her to the coffee shop upstairs. He wasn't sure what he had in mind.

Morse watched her for a while from across the room. She sat alone at a table by the window overlooking the lot. Her gaze seemed directed at a spot well beyond the horizon, her bronzed blade of a face knit in concentration, some intense inner reverie. A pale November sunlight illuminated streaks of gold in her cascading hair. Now and again she ran a hand through it absently. Occasionally she drew on a cigarette, refocused the gaze on the funnel of smoke rising off her lips, as though to extract some coil of wisdom from it. Every move she made, every gesture, had an undercurrent of lazy sensuality all its own. And after a while longer Morse thought, Well, no harm in being friendly, that's part of the Fleets philosophy too; and he picked up his cup and sauntered over.

"Got to be a serious laundry list you're compilin' in your head there," he said.

Some slick opening. Its effect was to send a twitch running through her like the aftershock of a sudden electrical surge. "What do you mean? Who are you?"

Ice-green eyes searched him with a look that slid back and forth between guilt and alarm. The look of someone indulging a habit nasty or illegal or both. Someone found out. He'd seen it before, many times. He put up disclaimer palms and said, "Hey, just another partner, tryin' to be social."

"Partner? What kind of partner? I don't know you."

"Partner like in Fleets partner," he said amiably. "You know, fellow worker and all? The Fleets family?"

"So what is it you want?"

"Well, I was hopin' maybe you'd invite me to sit down."

Now the look dispatched a guarded relief mingled with some

mild annoyance. The expression of a woman accustomed to being hit on, not unhappy about it exactly, mostly just bored by it. She fluttered a hand at a chair. "You can have the table. I've got to get back in a minute."

Picked a fine morning for social, Morse thought. Same genius that guides your choice of lines. But he'd come this far, so he sat anyway, tilted his head and tested an easy grin on her. "You don't remember me?"

She looked at him blankly. "Should I?"

"The Gummi-Rats?"

Still blank. He wasn't all that surprised—it had been a few weeks—but he was a little disappointed too. There was a time when all it required was one encounter for people, women in particular, to remember Mitchell Morse. Days when any place he sat was the head of the table, when he took up all the air in a room. No more, evidently. "Yeah, well, it was a while back."

"Whatever."

Morse never had the patience for circularity, or any real grasp of it. For him, the geometry of courtship was simple: two points, a straight line. Either you got there or you didn't. And most often when he wanted to he did. Up to now, that is. With this one he wasn't so sure about the want anymore, but she was fast becoming something of a test. So he just went ahead and said, "Look, my name's Morse, Mitch Morse. Happens we met once, sort of, but if you don't remember that's okay too. Chance to get reacquainted, maybe. Like in a drink, say, after work?"

She gave him a long appraising stare. There was an edge of mockery in it, the cool distance of the woman secure in the wizardry of her silky sexual waves, just keeping them tuned up. Calisthenics. "Now why would I want to do that?" she said.

"Oh, I don't know. Little slackener seemed like a good idea. I noticed you been lookin' pretty tense here."

The stare narrowed in on him suspiciously. "What's that supposed to mean?"

Mean? He didn't know what the fuck it meant. It was something to say. He tried an artless shrug.

"You say you work here?"

"That's right."

"Where's your jacket? Tag?"

"I'm a loss precluder. We go, y'know, incognito."

''You're security,'' she said, almost a stammer, not quite, and the alarm he'd first detected came swimming back into her eyes. She made a halting move to get out of her chair, seemed to think better of it, sat down again and tapped another cigarette from her pack. Morse produced a flame and she leaned toward it, touching his fingers lightly. Just as expertly she tossed her head on the exhale, rippling the abundant hair. Treated him to a smile. Very elaborate moves, controlled. Also very transparent. He wondered what was going on.

''So how's the crime fighting business?'' she asked.

''Business is good. Crime, it's a growth industry.''

''How long have you been with Fleets?''

''Not long. I'm a junior partner.''

''You on external losses? Or the internal kind.''

''Ex. Which means you got nothing to be nervous about. 'Less you've got a nicked Snickers bar stashed away in your purse there.''

''What?'' Something very close to fear flickered across her face, and then the faltering smile was quickly restored and she said, ''Oh, you're making a joke.''

''That's it,'' he said, ''a joke. Security wit.'' But he was thinking, This is one wirestrung lady, and not a very subtle one, at that. As a card cheat, she's not likely to do so famously.

''You know, somebody ought to tell you security types that kind of humor's lost on those of us working the register trenches.'' Now there was a trace of a grievance in that adjustable smile. Or maybe it was a remnant of the fear. Hard to tell. She shot a jittery glance at the clock on the wall, stubbed out the cigarette. ''Speaking of which, my time's up.''

''Too bad. I was just starting to enjoy our little conversation here.''

''Well, you know what they say about time and fun. Anyway, they get grumpy down there when you're late.''

''Uh, about that drink . . .''

She slung the purse strap over her shoulder and got to her feet. ''Not tonight,'' she said, putting a practiced tease back into the smile. ''I've got plans. Bye.''

She walked with a deliberate step, not too fast, alert and studiedly casual at the same time, a little measured sway in it, like an amateur actress conscious of scrutinizing eyes all over her. As his, of course, were. He ransacked the files of memory and experience for some replica of the way it was she moved, spoke, stared, worked her smile and her eyes. Even an echo would do. He sat there awhile, thinking about it, turning it over, puzzling it. Because something was going on. All the signals were in place, and he'd been a real cop too long to miss them.

But then there was also that qualifying *tonight* tacked on to the rejection. Not *tonight*. He hadn't missed that either.

XX

An hour later he was prowling Cosmetics, drawing a bead on a pathetic wraith of a woman with the tiny withered features of a delicate doll remarkably grown old. She was honing in on a display of perfume bottles at one end of an aisle; he watched her from the other. Her skin had gone gray as dusk and her mouth was doing strange things: puckering, wriggling, screwing into grotesque stagy smiles at nothing at all, the tongue flicking with an adder's speed. She wore a frayed, ankle-length coat; deep pockets, for sure. A first-timer, also for sure, first foray into the heady world of boosting. His impulse was to let her keep whatever she could lift, but it had been a slow morning and he had a reputation to preserve, so he began maneuvering his cart slowly her way.

Before he got far an urgent hand gripped him at the elbow. He turned and looked into the panicky face of a Customer Service lady.

"You Morse?"

"I'm the one."

"Eddie says get up front right away, chop-chop. We got trouble up there."

"What kind of trouble?"

"Dunno exactly. Serious though. Some colored guy."

He abandoned his cart and fell in beside her, and they hurried to the front of the store.

There was a knot of people gathered in a loose semicircle around the service counter, shoppers mostly, a few employees, nudging each other, whispering, pointing, giggling nervously some of them, delighted as children at a carnival freak show: oh my!—there's going to be *trouble!* Morse shouldered through them and discovered the unit manager, stout little Eddie, flanked by two loss precluders, the three of them backing off from an embodiment of that most nightmarish vision their steady citizen imaginations could ever conjure: a truly badass nigger, King Kong dimensions, snarling at them out of a lumpy face black as bottom soil.

The eyes were deep into a fierce pathology. A thick brush of jelled hair rose off a sinister shelf of brow, adding about half a foot to the slamdunker height. Wrecking-ball fists clenched and unclenched rhythmically.

"Ah, what seems to be the problem here?" Morse said, starting in lightly.

"You're Morse?"

He and Eddie had met only once, a perfunctory handclasp his first day at the store. He signified he was.

"They said maybe you could explain our refund policy to this . . . gentleman."

With a trembly thumb wag he indicated "they" were the two terrified defenders of Fleets, shrinking away fast on either side of him. No help there. And Eddie, slick film of sweat glistening on his upper lip and with an exaggeratedly backward-leaning stance—he didn't look all that lionhearted either. No help anywhere.

So how in the fuck do you neutralize somebody this size and this bad and for certain highballed on speed? Morse had a suspicion reason wasn't going to do it. He glanced about for anything that might serve as a weapon. Nothing in sight. He stepped into the widening space between Eddie and Kong, said mildly, "You got some merchandise to return, sir?"

"You the big bopper here?"

The acid-dipped voice unrolled on a spool of venomous contempt. Facing him, Morse came about eye level with a goiterous bulge of Adam's apple.

"Yeah, you might say."

"Okay, bopper man. See them threads there?" He pointed to a pile of new clothes heaped on the counter. "Don't fit right and I wants my money back. Two hundred forty-four dollars fourteen cents."

"I bet you got the sales receipts for 'em too, right?"

"Paper's there with it."

Oldest scam in the retail trades. Not very inventive, this one. Probably never had to be, all that intimidating bulk. "How much's it come to again?" Morse said, buying an instant of time. He had no clear idea how he was going to manage this.

"What I just say. Two four four fourteen."

"You got it all worked out, huh. Right down to the fourteen cents."

"Tha's right. Now you gets me what's mine or you goin' feel some hurts here."

"You know what I think, homeboy?"

"I ain't you homeboy, little bopper man. Or you blood. Or you sambo. Orvis my name. Orvis the menace. You hear that?"

"You know what I think, Orvis?"

"Wha's that you think?"

"I think maybe you're jivin' me. Think you come by them receipts however you could, and then you come in here collectin' this merchandise and passin' it off as returns. And that ain't legal, Orvis. That's breakin' the law."

"Tha's how you think? Law got broke?"

"Lookin' that way. 'Less a course you want to cancel out right now, walk out that door just another good Fleets patron."

Orvis looked at the door, looked at Morse, and then he moved in on him, loose and easy. The flaccid lips opened in a slow, wicked smile, but the eyes flashed serious sparks, rapid-fire. Here it comes. Hold your ground or you lose it all. One step back and you join the ranks of Eddie and the petrified duo.

"I'm goin' ax' you somethin', bopper, want you to be real straight up with me. Real hones'. Seein' you say I broke the law, you think the nex' thing I oughts to break is you legs?" He paused significantly and then, very suddenly and with surprising speed for a man that large, brought a clubbing forearm across Morse's jaw with the force of a swung bat, sent him staggering into the service counter, still on his feet, but only barely. "Or you face?" Orvis asked, deeply concerned over the choice. "Which one you think I oughts to do?"

Morse swiped the back of a hand across his chin and it came away sticky and moist. Fucking gash opened up again. Going to be a zipper there, for sure. An extended pleasured moan rose from the crowd—blood! real blood!

"Whichever one you think you can, boy," he said, and he reached behind him and grasped a bomber jacket from the pile of clothes; and powered by the gale of fury storming through his head, nothing else, he shoved off from the counter and charged into him, getting the jacket up into his face, blinding him. He tried to get a knee into his balls, but Orvis had all the instincts of a street fighter, blocked it with the trunk of a thigh, shook off the jacket as easily as a dog shakes water from its fur, and wrapped Morse around the chest, mashing the breath out of him. And Morse, operating off similar instincts, seized him by the ears, dug his fingers into the hollows behind them, and yanked. At the same time he lifted a foot and drove it straight down onto an instep. Simultaneously he could feel ear cartilage ripping under his fingertips and a bone snapping under his heel; and what he saw, abruptly released from the strangling embrace, was Orvis doing a comic one-legged dance, both hands covering the dangling ears as though to fit them back in place or to stop off the sounds of his own yipping, ongoing shrieks. Morse sucked in a quick gulp of air, bobbed to his left, and with the move that had ruined forever many a promising runner's career, hurled himself at the knee of the dancing leg in a spearing, sideswiping tackle that brought them both onto the dust-streaked floor. The staccato shrieks swelled and blended into one long deafening bellow of pain. Morse scrambled across him and laid a hand over the distended mouth. Orvis's eyes seemed to spin in their sockets. A puffball of floor dust sat like a holiday ornament in his glittery hair.

"Got a word advice for you, boy," Morse said, gasping it. "Next time go for the legs."

He looked up defiantly, and out of the dizzying blur of faces watching in suddenly stricken silence he could make out one of them, smiling faintly and assessing him from behind shrewd green eyes.

FIFTEEN

FOR MEAT, that morning was considerably less eventful than for Mitchell Morse. A good share of it was spent in solitary brooding on the stone porch of a remote farmhouse some twelve miles east and eight south of Grand Rapids. His steady expressionless gaze took in a vista grim as a fairgrounds the day after the circus had packed up and left town. In the near distance mounds of trash rose like hillocks off a rutted lawn choked with quack grass. At the foot of a gentle slope stood some crumbling outbuildings, a barn with peeling paint, and a desolate-looking silo tilted at a precarious angle. Spotted here and there among the buildings were the rusted hulks of autos, a discarded stove or two, and the burned-out shell of a house trailer. From there the view stretched off across fields mired in mud. A dirt road coiled through them and into the horizon like a length of rope dropped haphazardly from the leaden sky. There are times when, squinting into any horizon, a man is struck with the uneasy sense things are going on just beyond it, things outside his reach, control. For Meat this was one of those times.

Three weeks now, or very close to it, they had holed up here, on Kasperson's directive, keeping down. *Here* was the homestead of the Dokken boys, two brothers, bachelors, twins. Meat had known them, off and on, most of his life, from back into some long departed days he didn't much care to tamper with. The Dokkens were sometime farmers, though the looks of their place suggested the romance with Mother Earth had gone sour. They were also licensed pilots, and on the other side of the stucco house sat a small building that served as hangar for a pair of Cessna Skyhawks.

It was set perpendicular to a long narrow strip of tarmac, and, in stark contrast to every other structure on the Dokken farm, was freshly painted and neatly kept. Crop dusting was how they said they paid their way. Meat knew better. The dust they hauled on their frequent, unannounced and often as not dead-of-night flights was dream dust, for certain, the kind of dust that turns up pure gold, though you'd never guess it, the way they lived. That was okay; what they did and how they chose to live was their business, none of his. When the time came the Dokkens would serve their purpose, they'd do.

Trouble was that time was rapidly closing in, was in fact five weeks from this very night, exactly. And it had been ten days since he last heard from Kasperson. More than that from Starla, for that end of it. Meat kept track of such things. It was Kasperson's idea that the bank snuffing put them and "the project," as he had come to call it, at great hazard. Also the little side action with Sugar Boy, that wasn't boosting their odds any either, he said, and his first condition for signing on was that Meat and Ducky get down and stay there while he worked out the kinks in the plan. Couple of spectacular waxings like that were bound to draw heat. Out here anyway. Over in Detroit they wouldn't lift an eyebrow, be lucky to make the late news. This wasn't Detroit. So Meat couldn't fault that line of reasoning; it was probably correct.

Didn't mean he had to like it any. But after he heard the new revised version of the project, as spelled out by Kasperson, he was even less inclined to argue. Surpassed his most fantastic imaginings, by far. Instead of one Fleets, they were going to find a way to take out all seven. Instead of a four hundred long split, they were overnight looking at maybe three mil, thereabouts. That kind of plunder was incentive to keep Kasperson happy, keep him in. It was Kasperson had all the contacts for the hardware and especially for that paper they were going to need to get into the wind afterward. But he didn't have to like it, and this morning he liked it not at all. The monotony and the unwelcome memories sparked by this dismal place combined to set the worms of doubt burrowing through his head. Prison taught him to be watchful, and like all crafty men he assumed treachery as a norm of human behavior. He had called a meeting for tonight, insisted on it over Kasperson's objections, and tonight, by God, he'd find out how things stood. This was his action, his stake, his score, and he wasn't going to let it slip away. There were a lot of people you could fuck over, this world; Meat Pitts was not among them. Any fucking over got done, he was the one did it.

Thinking this way and for the moment unable to do a goddam thing about it, Meat became suddenly aware of the accelerated rhythm of his own breathing. He tried consciously to slow it down, turn his thoughts some other way. A shift in the raw breeze brought the pungent perfume of manure wafting up from the barn. It reminded him curiously of his childhood, of the lonely little acreage where he'd grown up, as did the sight of one of the Dokkens, he couldn't tell which, Clayton or Duane, take your pick, squeezed under an ancient shark-finned Caddie jacked up on concrete blocks in a shed with smashed-out windows and a swung-open door sagging off its hinges. Down on his back on the dirt floor, hammering and clanking at the engine. Pig-in-shit happy. Gonna make this sucker dance the boogaloo. Niggerwire it, I got to, make 'er squeal and fart and hum, run on watermelon juice. Run 'er out to Hollywood an' one of them rich coon actors on the teevee pay real handsome money for 'er. You see.

That's how they talked, the Dokkens. Meat had mixed feelings about them. They weren't easy to look at: a pair of tall stalks permanently outfitted in seed caps, grease-streaked coveralls, four-buckle work rubbers—probably wore them to bed—and with sun-withered necks, mouths full of broken blackening teeth, red piglet eyes and bullet-shaped heads. But then they never had been, from his first glimpse of them, age nine. And the years hadn't altered their features much, merely amplified them, like a snapshot blown up poster size, the images aging proportionately, enlarged and weathered and coarsened by time. No, not a lot to look at, your Dokken boys.

On the other hand, they came about as close to family as he'd ever known. His old man flew the coop before he could even remember, and Mom kept the place long as she could, renting out the land and going to work in town, cooking at the school cafeteria. He had no brothers or sisters, and the nearest neighbors were three miles away. On weekends the Dokkens came to call, barrel-assing a pickup down the drive in a swirl of dust or snow, depending on the season, Dokken senior, a widower, at the wheel and Clayton and Duane bouncing around in the back. Now you boys stay outta trouble, the elder Dokken instructed them with a sly wink, don't go doin' nothin' I wouldn't do, which gives you 'bout all the space in the county, haw haw. Then he went inside and banged the shit out of Mom for the rest of the day and on into the night. Godawful pounding. Went at it so hard you could hear the groaning right through the frame walls of the house. The twins were three or four years older and their idea of staying out of trouble was to take turns beating on him, and when they tired of that to wander down by the crick and stage a whacking-off contest, see who could squirt the highest. Old man Dokken wasn't a whole lot better. Sometimes they slept over and the next morning he'd sledge all three of them, just for the exercise. Best cure in the world when you're nursin' a head, he liked to say.

All that changed once Meat attained his full height and a sizable share of his bulk at age fifteen. But by then, for reasons never clear to him, he'd come to half tolerate the Dokkens, almost even to look forward to their visits. So except for a few cautionary touchups, to set things straight, show who was doing the tune-calling, he pretty much left them alone, clubbing-wise.

They took along sixers down to the crick, and came home reeling. And the stroke contests gave way to darker explorations, new to Meat. The way he saw it now, across the gulf of the years, Clayton and Duane, they were twins, like two halves of a single mechanism. Being twins, it probably made perfect sense to them, what they did. But it was different for him, he wasn't no twin. This was a part of his history Meat didn't like to dredge around in. Yet there he was, doing it, and he couldn't escape the nagging suspicion that whatever it was went wrong with him that way had its origins in those shadowy, shame-struck adventures down on the grassy banks of the crick. You'd think a man been in Jackson would know better, make allowances, but it was hard for Meat to shake such feelings, even now.

It must have been around that time daddy Dokken checked out for good, real Dokken style, real original. He's out plowing one day and his Farmall runs up against a field rock, stalls. Mr. Secretary of Agriculture steps down to take a look, leaves the tractor going, and somehow it slips a gear and plows the dumb fuck right into his own soil. One thing about your Dokkens, they weren't too heavy thinkers, none of them. Must of grew a bitter crop that year, that particular furrow.

Mom went right after. She never had been too steady upstairs, and when she got the news about old Dokken carving himself up into planting seed she went all wackadoo. Got herself shipped off to the twitch-factory in Traverse City where they brain-fried her right into a zombie. Did it once too often though, and she choked to death on her own vomit doing a turn under the wires. Poor Mom. He'd always been partial to her too, near as he could remember. So after she was gone and the place got auctioned off for debt and he was on his own, scrambling, he just naturally gravitated down to the Dokken farm, for somewhere to stop by once in a while. Twins sold off the best part of their spread to buy a plane. Gonna be fuckin' *aviators*, they said, winking the way their old man used to, make good money without no ass bustin'. Sometimes they took him up flying, only time in his life he'd been in a plane. Other times the three of them just hung around the grungy house, got zonked together. And some of those other things too, from the crick days; their habits never did change. Then he met Starla and got spliced, which seemed like a good idea at the time, and drifted away. He still dropped by now and then, just not as often, at least the way he remembered it. And then came the Jacktown holiday, and he sort of lost touch.

Which more or less brought him right up to now, and just as well. These brambled memories only stoked his peculiar unfocused malaise and set him bristling like a snappish cat, growling to himself, about what he couldn't be sure: the way life dumped on you maybe, the way things turned out. He didn't want to assay the past anymore, any of it. And happily for him there was no need to, for just then Ducky came padding through the door behind him and lowered himself stiffly onto the porch step. He hunched his spindly shoulders against the chill in the air, rubbed at eyes puffy with sleep, unhinged his jaws in a fly-catcher yawn. He looked around distastefully, ejected a mighty orb of spittle. Getting to be a world-class spitter, Ducky was, all this country living. For a moment he was silent, and then he said, "Y'know what I could use 'bout now?"

Meat knew him well enough to make an educated guess, but any kind of break in these bitter, backtracking thoughts of his looked welcome, so he went along with it. "What'd that be?"

"Nice little nooner."

Meat glanced at his watch. "It's closer to one."

"One-er then."

"How come it is I thought that's what you was goin' to say?"

"I'm tellin' ya, Meat," Ducky told him in an insistent whine, "we got to do much more time out here in hog hollow and ol' Clyde's gonna need Oral Roberts, raise him up from the dead."

"Whyn't you go find a cow to hump. They're easy."

"Yeah, I already heard, cows don't tell. Least that's what your friends say. Sound like they talkin' outta experience. Nice class of people."

"Don't knock 'em. They puttin' you up, no questions asked."

"Ain't knockin', Meat, just askin'. How long we got to do this Casper number anyhow?"

"Long as I say. Or till the Doc thinks it's right."

"Easy for him. Right for us could be till Christmas Eve."

"You shoulda thought of that before you iced the money store lady."

"Ahh, f'Chrissake, I tol' you, that was a accident. Coulda happened to anybody."

"Happened to you. Like all them accidents got a way of doin'. Which is why we're here, first place."

Ducky rolled his eyes heavenward at a sky full of ragged gray clouds rushing in on each other like interlocking pieces of a jigsaw puzzle. He wasn't keen on following this avenue of conversation too far, mood his partner'd been in last few days, sour as owlshit. That way was the deep shit for him, since he'd never really gone into all the embarrassing details of the bank shoot, kind of left them hazy. So even though he wasn't exactly thrilled himself lately, three weeks out here in Dogpatch, he figured he'd better turn the talk another direction, see could he cheer Meat up some, lift the gloom a little. How, he wasn't quite sure. He sat for a while, saying nothing, searching his memory for an amusing story to tell. Finally he lit on one.

"Y'know, speakin' of snatch, like we started out doin' here, I ever tell you 'bout this dude I knew in Ionia, real psycho case?"

Meat sighed. "Nah, I ain't heard that one yet."

"Well, he was from down south someplace, South Dakota, I think it was, an—"

"Dakota's out west, pisshead. Didn't you learn no geography in school?"

"West, south, it don't matter to the point of the story."

"Matters to me. Somebody tell me a story, I want 'em to get their facts straight."

"Why they call it *South* Dakota then, it ain't south?"

" 'Cuz it's south of North Dakota. West of here."

"Okay, he comes from West Dakota. You happy now?"

"Least I know where I am."

"Where you are, this story, is a town name of Kadoka, little nowhere bug speck, sorta like that one you come from."

"Wasn't so bad, where I grew up. Air was good up there."

"Nobody said bad. Said there ain't a lot to it."

"Yeah, well, Grand Rapids ain't so hot either."

Ducky threw his hands in the air. "You wanta hear this story or not?"

"I got a choice?"

A ripple of hurt passed over Ducky's face. "Sure you do," he said injuredly, "you got a choice. You don't wanta hear, we can just sit an' watch the paint peel, that barn out there. Or maybe stroll on down, see how Mr. Goodwrench's doin' on his pimp wagon. Listen to some that real intelligent talk his."

"Tell your fuckin' story."

Immediately Ducky brightened. "Okay. One day we're sittin' around, fuckin' the dog to fuck the time, way you do in the can, so I asks him what he took his fall on. He says—y'see, he's got this weird voice on him, don't go up and down any like yours and mine, like normal, just all one flat sound, sorta like your farm animals out here make when—"

"What'd he say, Duck?"

Ducky pitched his voice low and eerie, putting wide junctures between the words, to capture the quality he sought to describe: " 'I-broke-the-Law-of-Kadoka.' "

Meat grunted skeptically. "Never heard of no law like that. This ain't gonna turn out a joke, is it?"

"No it ain't a joke," Ducky said, resuming his natural piping singsong, but with an edge of vexation riding it. This was his story and he wanted to tell it at his own pace. Fucking interruptions weren't helping any. "I'm thinkin' same as you, never heard no law like that. So I asks him what it is. He tells me. Seems out in Kadoka they got this law says you ever find yourself a snappin' pussy, you got to marry it."

"You sure this ain't a joke. I ain't in a mood for humor."

"I'm tellin' you what he said, Meat."

"Well, that ain't no law. That's like a—whaddya call it?—custom."

"Not the way he tells it. Course you got to remember now, he's from South Dakota. Also he ain't rowin' both oars in the water. So anyway, all his whole life he's watchin' out for an honest-to-God snapper. Never come across one till he's out here in Michigan, on the bum, I guess, and sure as fuck he finally runs into one. Ought to be a happy ending here, right? Wedding bells? Wrong. There's a glitch. See, this pussy comes attached to a body 'bout the size of your average whale an' a face like, oh, say, one of your Dokken boys. That ugly. But she's also sportin' a true snapper. And there's this law. What's a fella to do?"

"This is gettin' to be a long story, Ducky."

"Here's how it ends. First though, you got to picture in your mind how this dude looks. He's got these real glassy eyes, psycho eyes, kind look at you and right through you, same time, don't seem to actually *see* nothin' at all. Also wears a little permanent drool on his chin. I asks him how he got this heavy problem solved. Know what he said?"

"That's what I'm waitin' to hear."

"Said"—and here Ducky glided back into his imitation—" 'I-had-to-settle-for-just-the-pussy.' "

"What's that suppose to mean?"

Ducky grinned hugely. "Means he took a axe to her. Hacked off all the ugly parts, which was just about everything else, an' saved himself the snapper hole. Must of figured he was goin' to marry just that part. Obey the law. Course your other laws don't look kindly on that, so he winds up in the joint, lifer, still believin' all's he ever broke was the Law of Kadoka."

Ducky clapped his palms together and rolled them over, signaling the end of the story. Like any good raconteur, he was deeply interested in the reaction of his audience. "Well, what do you think about that, Meat my man? Crazy world, huh?"

"Think you're makin' it up."

"Meat, that's a true story I just tol' you."

All through the telling of the tale Meat had been staring off into the blighted landscape. Now he turned his lowering gaze on Ducky. "Okay, let's say it's true. Say I give you that. You're askin' what I think?"

Ducky nodded affirmatively, though given the scowl his partner wore, he wasn't so sure anymore he really wanted to hear. Some guys there was nothing you could do, change their natural foul disposition.

"Think you spend way too much time followin' your dick around. In your mind, anyway. Think you'd fuck a rock pile, you thought there was a lady snake in it. Think you gonna end up like your Kadoka one-oar, you don't arrange to do somethin' about it. Quick. That's what I think."

The wounded look came back into Ducky's eyes. "Jesus, Meat, all I'm tryin' to do here is jack you up a little. Get your chin off the floor."

"You don't got to worry none, where my chin's layin'. We got a superbowl comin' up five weeks, an' you're talkin' snappin' pussy."

"What the fuck you want me to do? I got us the stake, didn't I? Didn't I get that stake? What else we gonna do, bein' out here, pumpkin center?" With an agitated sweep of a hand he indicated where they were.

Meat had no clear answers to any of these questions. Little fart got one thing right though: they were *out here* and whatever was going on was going on *in there*, in town. Which was the nub of the problem. Which brought his festering doubts full circle. A bit softer, he said, "Dunno what I want you to do, Duck. Try keepin' your mind on business."

"I can do that, Meat, but there don't seem like a whole lot to actually *do*."

"Maybe after tonight might be."

"What's on tonight?" Ducky asked, suddenly alert.

Meat hadn't told him anything about the meeting. Not yet. He'd thought about bringing him along, weighed it carefully and decided against it. He had his own scenario in mind and he didn't need the distraction of looking out for Ducky. Tonight what he needed to do was rivet his attention, watch the both of them, Starla as much as Kasperson, watch for the shimmy in the eye, listen for the giveaway flutter in the voice. Ducky was a useful sounding board—more than useful, necessary, a rabbit's foot—but tonight he'd only be in the way. Going to have to break it to him sooner or later. Might as well be now. "Duck," he said thoughtfully, circling in on it, "what do you think of the Doc's idea on the score?"

"Sounded good, way he told it."

"You think we can swing it, all seven stores?"

"Don't see why not, he come up with the right game plan. What's tonight, Meat?"

Meat skirted the question with one of his own. "Okay, lemme try somethin' else on you. What do you think of the Doc?"

"Brain-wise, they don't come no better."

"That ain't how I mean."

"How then?"

"I mean more, y'know, reliable-wise."

"Seem to be pretty stand up. How come you askin'?"

"I ain't sure. When you're talkin' three mil, that kind of loot, I ain't so sure you ought to show your back to nobody. An' I don't include nobody out of that. Nobody."

Ducky looked at him perplexedly. He'd heard this ominous rumble in Meat's voice before. "What're you sayin' here, Meat? You sayin' the Doc's thinkin' end run?"

"Maybe more like quarterback sneak, his case. Also my better half, who knows what's goin' on there?"

"How we gonna find out?"

"That's what I don't know. Yet. Called a little parley with them two associates ours for tonight. Goin' to scope 'em both real close. See what my instinct tell me."

"Hey, we goin' into town!" Ducky exclaimed joyously. Visions of a fine piece he knew of on South Division, hooker with some real sweet moves, romped through his head. But then, remembering Meat's injunction to focus on business, he added soberly, "You an' me, we got the great instinct, Meat. Anything shakin' down, we'll sniff it out."

"Didn't say *we*, doodledick. You hear me say *we*?"

Ducky's mouth fell open. He couldn't believe he was hearing what he was hearing. "You sayin' I got to stay here? I ain't goin'?" For Ducky, with the time horizon of a toddler, the idea of being left behind was perhaps the greatest calamity he could imagine.

"Not this one," Meat said firmly.

"Why not?" he groaned. "I thought we was partners, Meat. Team." Now his eyes took on a pained accusatory expression, and his shoulders sagged desolately.

Meat looked away. He was about to explain the why not, justify it, when he saw the Dokken boy slide out from under the Caddie and come plodding up the yard toward them. Under his breath he said, "Save it awhile. We don't want them knowin' any more'n they got to."

"Well lookee what we got here," said the Dokken, his mouth opening in a loose nasty grin, exposing pockets of sooty teeth. "Mr. Daffy Duck up off his sick bed, an' here it is only one o'clock in the p.m. How's she hangin', Daff?"

"Straight up, Rufus," Ducky sneered at him. "Don't s'pose you remember that angle though. 'Less a course you got a pig's asshole in front of you." For three weeks the turnip twins had been ragging on him fiercely, and he was getting mighty fucking sick of it. Sick of them. This place. Most of all sick with the news he wasn't going along tonight. He wasn't in a humor to take no shit.

"Hear that, Meat? He call me Rufus. Don't sound like our little Daff too chipper today."

"Lay off him, Clayton," Meat said, but without much force. Playing at peacekeeper was a role that fit him about as well as a Salvation Army suit of clothes, but he had to do it. For a while longer anyway. They were going to need the Dokken boys.

"I'm Duane."

"You can still ease up, huh."

The Dokkens had always been skinny, but over the years they had grown obscene little potbellies that bulged through their coveralls and jiggled like sacks of meal when they laughed, as this one, Duane evidently, was doing now. "Why sure, Meat," he cackled. "I ain't gonna fool with 'im, even if he do have them nice pink lips and that tender handful a ass. He's all yours. Meat's meat."

"Whyn't you go find yourself a nun," Ducky said, "take her out to the asparagus patch for some squat tag. Maybe that'd get your rocks off for you."

" 'Sparagus patch, that's a good one. Grow 'sparagus out here. This boy sure don't know nothin' 'bout farmin'. Bet his idea agriculture is cornholin'. Haw haw haw."

Ducky worked up a globule of spit and fired it with such accuracy it splattered an inch or so from Duane's rubber-clad feet. "Yeah, that could be, Rufus, but at least I can tell a pussy from a knothole. Which puts me one up on you plowboys."

"That'll do," Meat growled, "both of you. Duane, keep your fuckin' mouth shut, things you don't know nothin' about. An' Duck, I don't like to hear you talkin' that way about religion."

Duane, who for all the years gone by still vividly recalled the weight of Meat's fists, muttered, "No offense, Meat."

Ducky merely sulked.

Duane made no move to leave, so to change the subject Meat pointed at the shed and said, "How you comin', the vehicle?"

"Comin' along just fine. Next stop Hollywood."

"Yeah, and after that the circus," Ducky said, "get a job as a geek. Except he'd fuck the chickens before he bit the heads off."

Duane's tongue, big as a sausage, coiled around his lips wetly. Deliberately and with exaggerated care, he undid a button on his coveralls, tugged a gigantic blue-black member through the window of his stained shorts and sprayed a saffron shower in a wide arc across the lawn. Then he leered at Ducky and said, "Funny thing you mention that, Daff, circus. See, I had this dream 'bout you last night. Dreamed there was a circus in your ass, and ol' one eye here tried to sneak in."

Meat put his head in his hands. His teeth were grinding slowly.

"Better you should try pullin' old one eye down and under, see if you can shove him up your own ass," Ducky said. "Might just reach. Be the best kick you ever had, it did. Better'n your brother even."

Duane clasped his organ in both hands and aimed it at Ducky like a weapon. He gave it a wag. "Lookit ol' one eye, Daff. He's winkin' at you. Drippin' a little too."

Suddenly Meat lurched to his feet. "God fuck it, will you give it a goddam rest! Had a bellyful this fuckin' snipin'. I got enough on my mind without playin' referee to a couple flyweight jackoffs like you two."

Duane slipped one eye back inside the coveralls and stepped around Meat cautiously. The lickerish grin had gone sickly, but his eyes slid over Ducky and they were still glittery. "Okay, Meat, cool down. Just funnin' your boy a little is all." He put up his hands in a no-contest gesture and backed up the steps and through the door.

"Nice class people," Ducky said bitterly once he was gone.

"Yeah, well, you ain't doin' nothin' to make life any easier yourself. Why can't you stay outta their way?"

"Stay outta their way? You see how he looked at me? You seen that look, Meat, Jacktown. You got to take me along tonight.

It ain't safe here.'' There was a shrill note in his voice, genuine pleading.

Meat hesitated, wrestled with his own misgivings. Finally he said, ''Tonight I can't, Duck. You'll be safe, I'll see to it. I'll sit 'em down for a little hard talk before I go.''

''Talk? They don't understand no talk. All's they understand is cowshit and cornholes. Why you cut 'em all that slack anyhow?''

'' 'Cuz we need 'em, Duck. It's like I told you, they're gonna fly us outta here, time comes. That's why the slack. For right now.''

''That still don't say why I'm not goin' tonight.''

Meat sat down beside him. He lit a Lucky, inhaled deeply, collecting his thoughts. Then in the most patient and soothing tones he could muster, he said, ''Look, Duck. What're we talkin' here, you and me? Talkin' three double long, right? Sugarland, right?''

''You're forgettin' that's cut four ways, maybe more,'' Ducky said dismally, not really interested. The night of the score was much too far off for him to grasp in any tangible way. Tonight, that was another story. Tonight was real.

''I ain't forgettin'. Just listen up a minute, what I'm sayin'. Three split down the middle makes one and a half, right? Apiece. Think about that, Duck.''

''Thinkin' there's something wrong, your arithmetic. I still count four of us.''

''Come Christmas Eve you can take away two. And them two ain't gonna be us. Which is why I got to step light, here on out, keep ahead of the curve. You understand what I'm tellin' you?''

Ducky's eyes steepened with wonder. ''You sayin' what I think I'm hearin'?''

And through a slight parting of the lips, intended as a comradely smile, Meat replied, ''What I'm sayin' is what the old farmer use to say: 'All's I want is my own land—and everything next to it.' ''

SIXTEEN

AT SEVEN O'CLOCK THAT NIGHT, Doyle Gilley sat under an ultraviolet lamp in a United Hairlines treatment booth, ruminating darkly on life's confounding, multiplying tangles. It wasn't easy, this business of rescuing your hair. It was worth it, of course; about that he had no doubts—well, not many—three weeks into the regimen. But no one could ever tell him it was easy. The only thing easy was tracing the source of all his grief. Twyla. Twyla was the source.

Take tonight, for instance. Thursday was not his normally scheduled night; he shouldn't even be here, though naturally he was grateful he was, grateful they'd agreed to take him at the last minute. He'd missed yesterday on account of some impromptu party Twyla insisted they absolutely *had* to attend. Some goddam Beefaroo bash, probably in celebration of the millionth side of slaw sold, he never did inquire. But what could you do? Come off a treatment with the hair sticky as glue and plastered over the skull—no way could you conceal the shame, go out into the world and face the smirky looks. Bad enough on treatment nights having to come home late (as cover, he'd invented a company bowling league and even supplied a name for his phantom team—the Sanitary Slammers) and creep through the place tense as a cat burglar and slink softly into bed out of fear of rousing her. Lucky for him she was a serious sleeper.

But that was about as far as it went, any luck with Twyla. It took her less than a week to discover the Home Maintenance Kit hidden in the farthest corner of a shelf under the sink. "What's all these lotions you got stashed away here?'' she had called gloatingly from the bathroom one morning. ''You're gettin' to be like a real beauty queen, all your cosmetics. Next is makeup.''

And that was nothing compared to the problems posed by the, uh, internal flushing. Talk about tangles! The diet you could forget. For a week he tried faking a touch of the flu, asked for a vegetable broth for supper and got served canned chicken noodle soup. Fruit for her meant a box of Fig Newtons or a strawberry shake, and a plate of chilidogs smothered with horseradish and BBQ sauce was her idea of a nutritious meal.

And the other part of it, the ibis imitation, that was just as hopeless, living under the same roof with someone of Twyla's earthy, farm-bred sensitivity to odors. He tried the best he could, but mornings were out—no time, what with the Home Kit applications and all—so he had to wait till she slept before tiptoeing into the bathroom and bolting the door. The first night, a treatment night, it worked fine. The second she stayed up for the late show and he had to let it go. On the third he was startled to see her weaving groggily, half asleep, toward the bathroom just as he was finishing up and leaving. Too late for a warning. The door no sooner shut than he heard her disgusted shriek: ''Phew! God, does it stink in here!'' She came stumbling out, clothespinning her nose, gagging dramatically. ''Jesus, you *are* sick! You oughta see a doctor or something.''

No pity, that woman. Empty of compassion or human feelings.

All this was bad enough, but worse by far, and most ominous, was her new assumption they were as good as married. Already she was breaking his balls about a ring—as though he had that kind of money—and talking dreamily of ''plans,'' wedding mostly, but sometimes beyond that even: home owning, furniture buying, babies, lawns, gardens and on and on, into their twilight years. Made him tremble to hear it. But it was her money financing the treatments, even if she didn't know about her investment, so he had to go along with it. For the time being anyway. Once he got his hair back (and he was pretty certain he detected some sprouting fuzz on the naked temples, just the other morning) he'd find a way to wriggle out. There had to be a way. Somehow he'd find it.

These and other like thoughts had occupied Doyle during tonight's treatment, and he had paid scant attention to Miss

Reneau's chatter while she moved her motorized fingers expertly over his head. In the past weeks he had learned a great deal about her and about her life, for she was a compulsive talker, hectic and headlong in personal revelation. She was married and lived with her husband in an apartment on 44th Street. Her name was not Reneau, as it turned out, but rather Plum, Mrs. Harvey Plum, Rhoda Mae the given half. Kasperson had insisted on the change for, as she put it, "professional reasons."

Mr. Plum had heart trouble and didn't work. "He putters around the place," she explained in one of her windy monologues, "and he reads a lot. Oh, he's a great reader all right. You can always find him racked out on the sofa with one of them men's magazines, not the dirty kind, but more adventure."

He had been a house painter and she had worked in a beauty parlor. Between them they were doing real well and a few years back they had a home out in Cooperville. Then he got his attack and they had to give it up and move into town and cut corners. She worked a number of shops until Kasperson offered her this chance to master his Method, with the understanding that one day soon she would manage a branch clinic, maybe even in East Grand Rapids where all the rich folks lived.

Meanwhile her husband continued to lose himself in the pages of adventure magazines. "He's always gettin' crackbrained ideas from them stories. Last one was treasure hunting. He wanted to go up the Orinoco River, in South America someplace. Said there was a big diamond field up there, just waiting to be uncovered. Now this is a man can't even cook himself an egg. He ever get away from electric lights and flush toilets he'd be a goner. And he wants to go into some jungle! But he was so excited he went down to the library and got a bunch of books on it. He even put up a little poem on the fridge. Was there so long I got it by heart:

The road to gold is long and cold
And few there are who mind it.
Come search for treasure while ye may,
For gold is where you find it.

Kinda pretty, huh?"

Doyle agreed it was pretty, and together they chuckled over the lovable foibles of Harvey Plum.

She liked to talk too about her luck in getting on with Kasperson. "I just answered this ad for an experienced beauty operator, and Dr. Kasperson must of picked me out of all them that applied. He asked me all kinds of questions about my philosophy of hair care, things like that. I got flustered but I must of said what he wanted because he hired me right on the spot. That's when he changed my name. I think he decided on Reneau because I went to school at the Paris Beauty College. You know—Paris? France? Reneau?

"He's sure a remarkable man, Dr. Kasperson, and *so* intelligent. Half the time I don't know what he's talkin' about, but he's sure turned my life around. Lord knows where it's all going to lead. Imagine me running my own clinic and working on the hair of all them rich people. Kind of scares me just to think about it. But then I say to myself, Rhoda Mae, they're just people too, like you and everybody else."

Sometimes it amused Doyle, hearing the simple dreams of the Plums. Other times, when he was alone in the booth, assailed by vague apprehensions and the general muddle of things, it occurred to him to wonder if his own dreams were as far out of reach. Times like now.

Suddenly Kasperson came sweeping agitatedly into the booth. He took a wide-legged, almost belligerent stance directly behind the chair and fixed Doyle's mirrored reflection with a dour gaze. Miss Reneau stood timidly at his side.

"Regularity, Doyle," he said snappishly, "the foundation of all success, regardless of the endeavor. With the treatments it's the cumulative effect that finally produces the desired result."

"Well, something came up last night and I . . ."

Kasperson wasn't listening. He laid back Doyle's glutinous hair and examined the scalp, frowning. "Hmm, coming along a bit, but we still require plenty of work. Remember, you can't thread a needle with a clogged eye; similarly can you not grow hair on a clogged scalp. The treatments will relieve that condition, but only if you keep at them doggedly. Your potential is unlimited, Doyle. We're counting on you here at the Clinic."

With that delivered, he spun on his heels and hurried out. Miss Reneau shook her head ruefully and stepped over to the chair and rolled the lamp aside. Doyle was bewildered. He'd never seen

Kasperson like that, irritable and jumpy in the extreme, and it did little to relax his nagging doubts.

"What the hell was that all about?" he asked her.

"I think he's a little upset, you missing last night."

"But I'm here now. Making it up."

"Dr. Kasperson, he likes things neat and orderly."

She got out the massager again, fit it around her hand and plugged it in. A low steady hum filled the tiny space.

"We've already done that, haven't we?" Doyle said. By now he knew the whole sequence. Electro was properly next.

"Yeah, but seeing you weren't here yesterday a little extra won't hurt. Especially this thin spot up here on the crown."

Doyle shuddered once, then went numb with fear. This was a new one to him. Thin at the crown? What the fuck next? Was there any hope left anywhere?

Later, on his way out the door, the receptionist lady, sulky bitch who seldom bothered even to acknowledge his existence, offered a parting warning: "Can't expect any results if you skip the treatments," she said grimly.

SEVENTEEN

ABOUT AN HOUR LATER three people, by three different routes and in three quite distinct vehicles, converged on a north-side motel whose chief amenity, as the marquee announced, was Free Phones. Meat, piloting a Dokken pickup rust-blasted and rattly enough to be the same one that came hauling up the drive of his boyhood three decades ago, arrived first. He signed in under an agreed-upon name, paid in cash and retired to his assigned room.

It had a bed, dresser, television, nightstand with Gideon Bible, two chairs upholstered in tweed, a picture of a mournful-eyed puppy on one wall, Elvis among the angels on another. On the way he'd stopped for a bottle and a carton of Luckies, and now he poured some whiskey in a glass, lit the first of many cigarettes, and settled onto the bed and waited.

Next to arrive was Starla, fifteen minutes late and not in the best of tempers. Her Chevette had given her trouble, barely starting, coughing and sputtering once it did, skidding dangerously on the wet streets, and then plaguing her with defective wipers that smeared a glaze of snow, all but opaque, across the windshield. On top of that she'd spent an hour or so stroking her boss, Eddie, who dropped by the trailer on his way home to the wife and kiddies. He was still shaken over this morning's brawl, even though his only role in it was spectator, and of course he needed a little thawing. That's what he liked to call it, thawing. Guess who got to be the de-icer. Over the past three weeks she'd wormed as much out of him as she safely could by serving up treats ordinarily reserved and doled out only when there was something really worthwhile at stake. So there'd better be a pot of gold at the end of this tarnished rainbow, was the way she figured now. She accepted the drink Meat offered and fell into a chair, gazing moodily at the floor. She was primed for a battery of questions but, surprisingly, all he had to say was, "We'll wait on the Doc." Okay by her; made her jittery enough just being alone in the same room with him. He sat with his back propped against the headboard of the bed. His face was carefully blank, but she could tell he was watching her.

Kasperson, easily the most nervous of the three, was at that moment behind the wheel of an Aries station wagon, maneuvering it cautiously and doing what he could to gather his scattered thoughts. The car belonged to Delberta, part of the legacy of the planted husband, a good sensible vehicle befitting their lackluster union. She had loaned it to him, grudgingly, on the strength of his tale of a vendor in town with a revolutionary new hair ointment, direct from the Orient, in for a night and gone. Opportunity of a lifetime. Fortunately, she bought it, and at least one of his problems, albeit the lesser one of transportation, was solved.

But in no other respect had it been an easy day for your D. C. Kasperson. First came the morning call demanding his untimely meeting, and in the foul-weather tones of mistrust that a lifetime of scamming had taught him to recognize instantly. Then through the afternoon an unaccountable parade of skinheads appeared at the normally tomblike Clinic, lining up for their free exploratory examinations and scrambling his best efforts to piece together some semblance of a plan. And finally, just as they were about to close for the night, who should present himself at the door but the manic Gilley, pleading for a make-up treatment and squashing his last hopes of an hour's uninterrupted thinking. It was the Doyle Gilleys of this world who sabotaged the best-hatched schemes.

Not that he had one, exactly. The sorry truth of it was he had as yet nothing in the way of a coherent plan. He was hardly to blame, given the fragmented scraps of intelligence fed him over the past three weeks. He was the consummate strategist, but he wasn't a miracle worker. Any reasonable person should be able to see that. But he was dealing with a couple of psychotic thugs and a woman whose transparent capacity for treachery shimmered in the green of her Judas eyes. Forget appeals to reason. For tonight, his immediate problem was finding the means to keep them pacified, keep the project afloat. And now, with the motel's neon blinking up ahead through a drizzle of snow, he determined the best—the only—course open to him was to rely on native wit. Wing it.

XX

". . . and while the information supplied me has been useful"—Kasperson, perorating, made a dandyish little bow at Starla—"I think you'll both agree what we've got to have is more precise detail. Particularly for the project we're considering here."

To test that agreement he looked at each of them in turn, like a public speaker portioning out eye contact equitably among his audience. Meat reclined on the bed with a kind of laid-back surliness, examining him steadily, a cigarette dangling from his lips, blue smoke crawling up his broody face. Starla, in contrast, occupied her chair stiffly. On the occasion of their single previous meeting (same motel, same company as now, minus the moronic clown Conrad, mercifully absent tonight), Kasperson had detected in her this same tight restiveness, an unmistakable signal of something brewing under those heavy vapors of sexuality.

"How much do you think I can get you, anyway?" she flung back at him. On the fingers of one hand she enumerated. "I got you floor plans, schedules, an average day's receipts, a little about security, and as much as I damn well could about the cash pickup and delivery. You think it's easy, coming by all that stuff?''

''It's your number five that's still giving me some trouble,'' Kasperson said clemently. ''You see, I need to know more about the armored car drill. Everything's going to turn on that.''

''I've run it right out to the end of the pier with that manager. He may be stupid but he's not a total fool. Any more questions and he's going to tumble.''

Stalling, Kasperson took a sip of the raw whiskey, arranged his face in a thoughtful, brow-creasing look and said, ''Hmm, this is a a sticky one.'' He shot a quick glance at Meat, checking his reaction to all the verbal dodge and weave.

From the start, Meat had said next to nothing, simply listened and smoked and leveled a stony glare. Now a trace of lightly drowsing menace flickered behind it. ''Y'know, Doc, how they say you goose a ghost, you come up with a handful of sheet? That ain't what I want to take away from here tonight. Supposin' we have a little look back. Seem to me I done my part, done just what you said. I raise the stake money and cut out a healthy slice for you, no strings. Then I put you two in touch, get the details washed and ironed. Leave the brainwork to you, which I remember is how you say it's got to be. Ducky and me get down, also like you say. Three weeks we been out of the action. You take a look at your calendar you see five weeks Santa's due. Now I come in tonight expectin' to hear a solid plan, see some return on my money, but what I'm gettin' is smoke blowin' up my ass. That can rile a man, Doc.''

Kasperson shifted uneasily in his chair. Uncharacteristically, he could think of nothing to say, and for a moment he wondered if he hadn't gotten in over his head. Starla watched both of them narrowly. No way was she going to get into this end of it. She remembered Milo, only too well. The hair doctor had his work cut out, sliding out of this one. She watched his mobile face sift through a variety of expressions, settle finally on wounded dignity.

''Milo,'' he said at last, ''I'm sorry you feel that way. In spite of what you seem to believe, I've been doing my share to move this project along. Already I've made a contact for the hardware we'll need. Also some arrangements for the ID and passports—and I can tell you that part hasn't been easy, turning up a quality paper maker in Grand Rapids, Michigan. So you needn't worry about the money you've advanced me; it's going to be well spent. And apart from a few unresolved issues, I'd say my strategy is beginning to fall into place."

"Yeah? Then whyn't you just spell it out here. I got lots of time. Ain't no cell checks down on the farm."

"All right," Kasperson said, clearing his throat and thinking, If ever there was a time for dazzling footwork, now is that time. "Let's review where we stand. We know that ordinarily the armored car makes two stops, one midday, the other at closing. It's reasonable to expect that on Christmas Eve, with the early closing, the money will be collected in a single stop. Naturally, we'll have to confirm that," he added quickly. "One of those unresolved issues I mentioned."

"So? Where's all this 'review' goin'?"

Kasperson wasn't sure himself where it was going. He pushed on anyway. "Say I'm right: The car arrives just as they're locking up for the night. Now we also know the Plainfield store is next to last on the route. Which is a special piece of luck for us. One more stop, over at the Comstock Park location, and then the receipts of all seven stores are delivered to a night depository downtown."

"Smoke, Doc. My ass is suckin' more smoke."

"Smoke? I don't think so. If we can take the car out at the Plainfield site, we're already halfway home. Better than that. Six-sevenths, to be exact."

"Call that spit bubble a plan? All's I'm hearin' is about what you said, last time we talked."

"With one difference," Kasperson said crisply. He was rolling now, had the feel of it. The rhythm. It was coming to him, the way it always did. "Last time my thoughts were, well, murky. Not anymore. Now the fog begins to lift a little."

"Where I sit it ain't liftin' none at all."

"Don't you see, Milo, if we can secure the car *outside* the building, some heavy problems are going to be solved automatically."

"Like what?"

"For one thing, your idea of sealing off the store, which was messy in the first place. For another, the element of time. With the armored car under our control, and posing as guards, we finish the route and make the final pickup. Comstock Park. By then that store will be closed. The only person there will be the manager, and I assume you could handle him. We transfer the total receipts from the car to our own vehicle positioned nearby, in the rear lot, say. We've bought ourselves half an hour, maybe more, before anyone gets nervous downtown. Time enough to get to the farm, where your friends are waiting to fly us to Canada. At which point the proceeds are split, the ID and passports distributed, and we go our separate ways."

For a moment Meat said nothing. Then, in a tone of challenge, "That's your plan, huh?"

"Well, just in general outline," Kasperson said carefully.

"Okay. Let's back up a little. You ever take a look at a armored car? Like a fuckin' tank. You ain't gonna get near one 'less you take out the delivery boy *in* the store and then come at it blindside, ragged out in his uniform and luggin' the store loot. Like we first figured. Which means sealin' the store, also like we figured. What I'm hearin' now, you'd need somebody could get up close to the car without settin' off no fireworks. How we gonna get around that wrinkle, Doc, your nifty plan? Answer me that one."

"If you'll think about it, Milo, you'll see the answer's very simple. You said before that we'd need another man, remember? What I'm suggesting is this party be someone more than just another force man. Someone with special qualifications. Someone, say, recruited from the ranks of the Plainfield Fleets security. If we had such a person with us, all the other details would work themselves out."

"How the fuck we find anybody like that? Force man, that's something else, that we can get."

With his eyes, Kasperson indicated Starla.

Meat followed the glance, screwed up his face, looked back at Kasperson. "Ahh, that ain't gonna work. Not in the time we got left."

Kasperson turned to Starla. "And what do you say?"

For a time she was silent, thinking how it always came back to the same thing for men, remembering the morning and smiling slightly to herself. Finally she said, "I think I just might be able to help you out."

XX

Because neither of them cared to spend any more time alone with Meat than was absolutely necessary, Kasperson and Starla left the motel amost simultaneously. She made it out the door first. Sweeping the caked snow from the Chevette's windshield, she offered up a silent prayer: Please, let this goddam piece of junk kick over. After some vigorous pumping of the gas pedal, her petition was rewarded.

On the drive home she thought about everything she'd heard tonight, and also about the contribution she'd volunteered. She didn't doubt her ability to carry it off; that part should be easy enough. She knew her talents. And from the looks of this Morse character it might be a welcome change from the Dexters and Eddies she'd been stuck with lately. He might even turn out to be the equal of Milo, if this morning's scuffle was any measure, and in the longer view that was far more important. Because she was going to need some serious help to get out of this with her share of the take. She could see that now, after tonight. This Morse, he could be her ace. If she played her hand right.

Other thoughts were stirring as well, and through some quirky association they led her to last night's Lotto numbers. Her ticket had three of the winning six. One more and she'd of been ninety-nine ahead; two more and it was two thousand something. And with *all* of them, she'd of waltzed away with a pot that, coincidentally, amounted to three million dollars. Nice round figure, three million, nice tidy sum. For one person. And she was only three numbers off. She interpreted that as a good omen. . . .

XX

Kasperson had declined Meat's offer of a parting drink, saying, "Better not. The widow, you know." And then getting the fuck out of there fast. He'd had enough of the frosty, vigilant Milo Pitts stare for one night. Now he steered the Aries carefully through the slick streets, and before the heater took hold, his breath steamed the bitter air. He likened it to the ghosts of his unvoiced thoughts. He was not at all unhappy with his extemporized recitation of the evening or, for that matter, with the fertility of his imagination. For astonishingly, these inventive notions were right on the money, the skeleton, anyway, of a feasible plan. That which had eluded him all day. Day?—better make that three weeks. It must have been lurking there, just below the level of consciousness, all the while. It occurred to him that he never really knew his own best thoughts until he heard them said. And now those thoughts, while equally wide-ranging, ran along lines remarkably similar to Starla's. . . .

XX

From the window of the room, Meat watched both of them drive away. Then he poured another drink and stretched out on the bed. He was in no hurry; dump was his for the night, if that's what he wanted. But what he really wanted was a few minutes of quiet, to reflect on all that had been said tonight. And not said. None of that had gone by him either.

About Kasperson, he'd been right all along (except for the genius part; he was beginning to have some heavy doubts there). It was in the eyes and the voice and all the little wiggly motions he made. It was there. Starla, he couldn't be sure yet, but there was no reason to believe she wasn't looking to squeeze both ends against the middle too. That's the way things worked. The warmth of self-satisfaction chilled under this certain insight, and he began making plans of his own. It was just about time, he decided, to come back into town, keep on top of it, never mind the risks. Also to start thinking about some holiday arrangements, those two shifty partners of theirs. He had a few ideas, nothing real tight yet. Once he got them clear in his head, he'd test them out on Ducky.

The sudden thought of Ducky, alone out there with the Dokkens, made him vaguely uneasy. He finished off the last of the drink, locked up the room, and pointed the pickup in the direction of the farm.

EIGHTEEN

IT COULDN'T HAVE BEEN more than a quarter of an hour after Meat left for town before there came a gentle tapping on the door of an upstairs bedroom.

"Yeah, who's it?" Ducky said warily.

"Me, Clayton."

"So whaddya want?"

"Cookin' up some supper down below. Thought you might want some."

"I ain't hungry," Ducky lied. He'd eaten nothing all day long, and the truth was that under the knot of sour grievance his empty stomach rumbled insistently.

"Sloppy Joes," Clayton said with an upgliding inflection. "Real gutbombers."

"Nah, I don't think so."

"Little nipper then? Mixin' our own home special." Same coaxing lilt in the voice.

Ducky hesitated. Drink, some eats—didn't sound half bad. Use up some slow time too. And he figured he was pretty safe now. Earlier, crouched at the top of the stairs, he'd listened to the warning Meat laid on them before he left. Serious warning, delivered like a Jacktown payback guarantee. Coming out of Meat it would scare the holy shit out of Andre the Giant. So he could probably go down there if he wanted. Only thing was, could he stand the company of the corncob twins.

The door opened slightly. Clayton poked his bullet head inside and, as though in echo of Ducky's thoughts, said, "Hey, ain't nothin' to be scared of. Duane and me, we're just a couple of your good old boys. Like to fart around a little, but we don't mean no harm.''

Ducky made a precipitate decision: Getting down was one thing, but a getting down inside a getting down, that was puzzle house, make you crazy. He wasn't in no lockup. ''Yeah, who's scared,'' he said toughly, and he bounded off the bed and came swaggering across the room.

Clayton's face opened in a sunshine smile. ''Atta boy, Duck. Everybody friends here.'' He laid a companionable arm over Ducky's shoulders and together they descended the stairs.

The Dokken kitchen was thick with heat from a cast iron stove on which a pair of blackened fry pans sizzled and popped over burners lit by blue flame. The room was dominated by a scarred wooden table and of course by Duane, who stood at it stirring a plastic bucket filled with a copper-colored liquid. A film of sweat glazed his forehead, and his beady eyes were streaked with red. ''Daffer Duck!'' he boomed jovially. ''Get your sweet ass in here and suck up a Fuck You!''

Clayton disengaged his arm from Ducky's shoulders and came around beside his brother. Their identical faces were wreathed in identical jeering smiles. One of them dipped a tin cup in the bucket and thrust it into Ducky's hands. ''One Fuck You for you.''

It was explained that a Fuck You was a Dokken creation, a mix of any and every thing drinkable in the house: rum, gin, beer, Faygo pop, whiskey, tomato juice, little buttermilk, some vodka—you name it. ''Also that jug Mad Dog wine you keep stashed in the barn,'' Duane added, delivering a brotherly punch to Clayton's ribs. ''Thought I didn't know about that one, huh.''

Clayton made a guilty, found-out face. To Ducky he said, in mock apology, ''Taste a little sharp to you it's 'cuz Duane here pro'ly pissed in it too.''

Duane, catching the spirit of the banter, pointed at his crotch. ''Why not? Only your genuine hundred proof piss come outta this tapper. Drink up, Daffo. Put some hair on your ass.''

Ducky took a tentative sip. Surprisingly, it wasn't bad at all, a little jagged on the pipes maybe. But he didn't want to give the woodchucks too much so he merely grunted, ''Taste more like panther piss to me.''

Duane threw his head back in a short braying laugh. "Hear that, Clayton? He call our Fuck You panther piss."

"Man knows his liquor."

"Hope to shout, he do." He lifted the bucket off the table and set it on the floor. "Well, panther piss or Fuck You, whichever, let's just squat down here and get outside some more of it. Joes be ready pretty quick."

They all three pulled up chairs, Ducky on one side, the Dokkens on the other. Ducky tossed off the rest of his drink manfully. The Dokkens did likewise and cups were refilled all around. Clayton produced a piece of cigar, stuck the sodden end in his mouth, lit the other. "Too bad Meat ain't here," he said. "Use to be he liked to get himself cranked up. Remember, Duane?"

A wicked leer worked slowly, in inebriate slow motion, onto Duane's flushed face. "Do I ever."

"Yeah, ol' Meat. Them was the days."

"He'll be back," Ducky said. "Before long."

"How'd you two boys come to team up anyways?" Clayton asked.

"The can. We was cellies."

"So then you ain't from up around his way."

"Nah. G.R., born and raised."

"See, I tol' you he was a city boy," Duane hooted. "Don't know a cow pie from a cupcake."

Clayton wagged an admonishing finger at his brother. "Be social now," he said. "Duck here, he's company."

Watching them over the rim of the cup, Ducky had the peculiar sensation of a man stricken suddenly with double vision. Remove the stub of cigar and there was no way to tell one Dokken from the other. He was working on a wiseass retort but before he could get it off Duane said, "That's absolutely right, forget my manners," and he snatched the cup out of Ducky's hands, dunked it in the bucket and shoved it dripping back across the table at him. "Y'know, too bad you wasn't here 'bout a month ago, Daff. Coulda had some of that real fine south of the border marchin' powder we fly in."

Clayton rolled the cigar from one corner of his mouth to the other, savaging it along the way. "Shut up your boozy fuckin' yap, Duane."

Duane made his eyes as wide as they would go, which was about the size of a pair of peewee marbles. "What'd I say?"

"Just keep a clamp on it," Clayton said fiercely. Then he turned to Ducky and his tone went mild, conversational. "S'pose there's a lot a ham slammin' goes on, that jailhouse you and Meat was in."

"You get your ladies in there," Ducky said cautiously. "Don't mean you got to be one."

"We ain't never done time, Duane and me. Been lucky that way. But I always figured it couldn't be too bad. Y'know, sorta like how the coloreds say: tight pussy, loose shoe, and a warm place to shit."

"'Cept in the jailhouse," Duane amended, "you got bungholes 'stead of pussies. Right, Daff?"

Ducky wasn't so sure he liked the direction this talk was taking. To turn it, he said, "How about them eats?"

"Boy got a man-size appetite on 'im. Clayton, whaddya say?"

"Say company ready, you better hop to."

Duane got to his feet unsteadily and wobbled toward the stove. Clayton favored Ducky with a broad wink, said, "Talkin' 'bout ladies, you put Duane in a kitchen and he get to be your regular lady of the house."

Over his shoulder Duane said, "Yeah, wouldn't hurt you none to pitch in."

Clayton gave an extended sigh, ground what was left of the cigar under his heel, and hauled himself out of the chair. "Be midnight, I don't give 'im a hand." He reached across the table and took Ducky's cup and filled it again. "You have another little sip a Fuck You while you're waitin'. Supper be comin' right up."

Ducky took a long swallow. A rich glow emanating from the pit of his stomach surged through him. His limbs softened. His shoulders sagged. Sweat beads popped at his temples and over his lip. Some outstanding drink, your Fuck You. Reminded him of Jacktown spud juice, only more fiery, explosive. He'd lost track of how many he'd had. He watched a blur of Dokkens scurrying back and forth between stove and counter. Lost track of them too, which was which. But he was thinking maybe they weren't so bad, Clayton anyway. Couple of dim bulbs, both of them, but maybe not so bad. Then a steaming plate was in front of him, lumps of ground beef bubbling in a puddle of orange grease. He looked up and there were the Dokkens sitting across the table gazing at him, their plates heaped high.

"Fresh outta buns," one of them apologized.

"You want buns," said the other, "you gonna have to sit in it."

Had to be Duane, that one, though both of them erupted in laughter. He tried to fix it in his mind: right side Duane, left Clayton. Just the reverse of how they'd been before.

"Grub down, boy," the one he figured for Duane directed.

"Hold up! Grace gets said first, this table."

Both of them bowed their heads and one, Ducky couldn't tell which, mumbled, "Good food, good meat, good fuckin' Christ, let's eat."

More croaky laughter.

Ducky took a bite and immediately let out a yelp. He grabbed for the cup, swirled some Fuck You around his scalded mouth and tongue, gulped it down. His flat lips worked like a bellows, puffing out scorched air. When he could find a voice he said, "Holy fuck! What you put in this shit anyway?"

The Dokkens looked at him quizically. Left side, Clayton side, said, "Little hot, is she?"

Right side said, "Secret recipe. Ain't free to tell you what all's in it."

Left nudged right, grinned nastily. "Bet you slipped some Spanish fly in there. Smoke the Daff up."

"Did no such thing. Tell you what, boy, it's too hot I'll just stick it in the ice box for you."

"Freeze 'er right up, make you slopsicles."

"Slopsicles! That's a good one."

They chortled in unison.

Ducky shook his head slowly. He drained off the last of his Fuck You, accepted another. And then he watched them, bent to their plates now, shoveling it in, chewing with a relish of concentration. Studied them. Finally he said slurringly, "I know who you are."

One of them, left, glanced up. "Whaddya mean, Duck?"

"You're Clayton."

"No, I'm Duane. He's Clayton."

Right side, his plate clean, lounged back and probed a molar with the tine of his fork. "Don't believe it," he drawled. "He's pretendin' to be me."

"C'mon you guys."

Dokken left, Clayton, or maybe it was Duane, stuck his thumb in a bristly nostril and extracted a greenish nugget. He held it up for display, recited, "First you pick it, then you lick it, then you flick it." And that's what he did, flick it expertly into Ducky's plate.

Dokken right said reproachfully, "Naw, you done that wrong, Duane. First you pick it, then you lick it, then you got to *stick* it before you can flick it. Ain't that how it goes, Daffer?"

Hysteria time.

Ducky swayed in his chair. It was a hall of mirrors he was in, lost and reeling. He needed Meat, find the way out. Where was Meat? He heard the sloshed words, "Couple fuckin' feeder pigs," and a moment of silence elapsed before it occurred to him he was the one who said them.

The howls of laughter seemed to freeze on the Dokken faces. Their expressions shifted abruptly.

"Hear that, Duane? We tryin' to be nice and he calls us pigs."

"Don't pay to be nice no more. All's you get's a kick in the teeth."

"Man don't take kindly, bein' mocked at his own table."

"That's your worst place right there, table. Think maybe Daff got a lesson to learn."

Their mean canny eyes swerved in a silent transmittal. They lurched to their feet and came around either side of the offended table. Four powerful, uncivil hands seized Ducky at the collar and yanked him out of the chair. Two scowly Dokken faces were thrust into his. Uglier than ever, he thought, up close this way. He pointed a trembling finger at them. "You asshole hay shakers better lay off me. You heard what Meat said."

"Thing of it is, Meat ain't here. You see 'im anyplace, Clayton?"

"Nope, he ain't here."

"He's comin' back," Ducky said, his voice shrill.

"Go get the bows, Duane."

One of the Dokkens vanished. The other shoved Ducky through the back door, across the porch and down the steps. Lights flashed on, bathing the yard in an eerie yellow glow. Ducky stood shivering against the bite of the wind. The ground was laced with a crust of snow. More snow gathered in his hair, moistened his face. "Goddam it, Clayton," he called to the dark figure on the porch, "let me be. Meat'll carve you a new asshole."

"I'm Duane. Clayton's behind you, down by the barn."

Ducky whirled around. Sure enough, another figure moved through a cluster of shadows between a shed and the barn. He turned again and faced the porch. "Listen," he said desperately, "I ain't got no quarrel with you guys. What're you gonna do?"

"This here's a genuine Forked Lightning bow," Duane—or Clayton—said, holding it up in evidence. "An' it's legal bow huntin' season, Daff. So we gonna have a dancin' lesson. Ain't nothin' like dancin', learn you city boys polite. You watch out these broadhead arrows now. They bring down a elephant."

Ducky backed away slowly. "Wait'll Meat gets here."

"Oh, ol' Meat, he'd like this kinda party. He's the one learned us how to use a bow. Back when we was kids. Dead shot, himself."

"Wait'll I tell him," Ducky spluttered. "You wait."

A voice rose up behind him, traveling like electric current on the frigid air. "Ready up there?"

"All set."

Ducky heard a sound rather like a whip snapping four times. He fell flat onto the snow. Instinctively his arms covered his head. When nothing happened he peeked out, confused. He scrambled to his feet in time to see an arrow streak across the lemon slice of moon and pierce the snow ten feet behind him. Three others came swooshing in high looping arcs out of the black sky, bracketing him. His scream was carried off on the hiss of the wind.

"That's the first number, Daff. Here come the next waltz."

The whip snapped again, four more times. Ducky ran in a frantic zigzag but the arrows fell around him all the same, and closer.

"Think that do it?" the voice from the porch called.

"Naw, Daff's just gettin' limbered up. Ain't you just gettin' limbered up, boy?"

No chance to plead. Next dance. He darted off to the left, stumbled awkwardly, grazing the snow. He passed a hand over the icy glaze on his face but felt nothing, not cold or fatigue or discomfort even, nothing outward, only a blind animal terror. An arrow landed in front of him, so close he could reach out and touch it. From the angle that it stabbed the earth, he could tell the trajectory had been lowered. Three more thumped into the ground around him. The bracket tightened.

"Last dance, Daffer. Better stay down for this one."

Coiled in a tight fetal ball, temples pounding, fists at his eyes, Ducky lay waiting. An arrow whisked directly over his head. Then another, from the sound of it, dropped a trifle lower. Another, lower still. There was a long, deliberate pause. He heard laughter. He didn't move.

"Keep a tight asshole now, boy."

An instant later the last arrow dropped languidly from the sky and parted the snow inches from his head, twanging in his ears.

A palsied quaking racked Ducky's thin frame. His legs refused to uncoil, fists remained locked to his eyes. He heard the snow crackling under two sets of approaching boots. They came to a halt beside him. A voice like emery paper sanding the silence announced, "Dance lesson's over, Daffo, and you ain't got a scratch on you. This is your lucky day. Lookit here."

A hand pried the fists from his eyes, and through a stinging wash of tears he saw a matched pair of members, two One Eyes, drooping from the coveralls like slumberous snakes.

XX

The yard lights were out and the house was utterly dark. Meat parked the pickup alongside the porch and came through the back door. No sound anywhere. He climbed the stairs and knocked on Ducky's door. No answer. He pushed the door open and peered inside. Slowly his vision adjusted and what he saw was Ducky flopped across the bed, naked and whimpering, head buried in a pillow. He went over and squatted down beside him.

"What happened here, Duck?" he said.

No reply.

He reached up and switched on a lamp. "Duck?"

Ducky lifted his face out of the pillow, showed it to Meat. A bruise inflated one cheek, puffing the eye shut. The other eye was livid, swollen. The lips were torn and caked with blood. He opened them as though to speak. Nothing came out.

"Dokkens did this," Meat said. He stood up and gazed a moment at his quivering partner. A spark ignited in his chest, rose in a firestorm through his throat, swept through his head. ''Can you move?'' he asked.

Ducky nodded feebly.

''Okay. Get your gear together. We're goin' into town now. Tonight. First there's something I got to settle. You wait for me here.''

The Dokkens were sprawled on two ragged couches in the living room downstairs, snoring softly, contentedly. Had they been awake they would have seen the awful figure of Meat Pitts taking shape out of the shadows. When he was finished with them, one Dokken was slumped on the floor, his face swollen, lacerated. The other cowered in a corner, coughing blood and the fractured remains of his teeth. He looked up at Meat, looming over him, and gasped, ''This mean the deal's off, Christmas Eve?''

''Deal's still on. Which is the only reason why you two are still walkin'.''

NINETEEN

THE FOLLOWING DAY, Friday, November 20, Mitchell Morse turned thirty-five. And that evening, in the subdued light of a Chinese restaurant, he discovered a token of the accumulating years: without his reading glasses the menu was little more than a blur. Another reminder was the lingering ache in his ribs from the Orvis scrimmage the day before. Still another, the fresh bandage covering the fresh stitches in his jaw. As inconspicuously as he could, he played with the menu, searching for a focusing distance. No luck. Finally he set it aside and raised his glass. ''Here's to every damn thing,'' he said.

Across the table, Starla Hudek regarded him with a faint smile. She looked good. The frosted denim skirt she wore displayed an abundance of long elegant leg. Her sweater, top button carelessly undone, was a pastel green, pale, nice contrast to the brighter jade of her eyes. A cataract of hair framed the tapered face, swirled in wanton torrents over her narrow shoulders. The drink she held in her hand was something pink and frothy with a tiny parasol in it. She lifted it and touched his glass lightly. "Does that include Fleets?" she said.

"Fleets too."

It was his fourth martini and he was feeling a little drunk, not much. Also a little guilty, about Jean. But he couldn't deny it was convenient. She was gone for the weekend, down in Ohio somewhere, some family thing, wedding, anniversary, he couldn't remember which. He hadn't mentioned his birthday; otherwise she'd for sure be here right now. That was just the way she was. Something new in his experience with women. Unique. And for all the tantalizing prospects the evening held out, he couldn't seem to push her out of his thoughts. Not altogether. Why is that, he wondered, as the warm sheen of drink settled over him; it's not like I'm married to the girl.

"You know, you're something of a hero around there," Starla said, bringing him back. "After yesterday."

"Aw shucks, ma'am, it weren't nothing."

The smile took on some wattage. She indicated his chin. "Does it hurt?"

"Only when I shave. See, I got this blowtorch for a razor."

More teeth showed, white against the bronzed skin. "How'd you manage it anyway, a caveman like that?"

"It's the Fleets spirit—give it your mightiest heave."

"Seriously."

"Serious?"

She gave a sober sort of nod.

Morse shrugged. "Well, that's my job, it's what I do. I've had a little experience at it."

"Really. Before Fleets where'd you work?"

"Another security outfit."

"Here in town?"

"That's right."

"But you're not *from* here."

"How can you tell?"

"Lucky guess. You don't seem like a Grand Rapids type. Where then?"

"Across the state. Pontiac, Detroit, some of your exotic places like that."

"Did you do security there?"

Morse emptied his glass, pondered his reply. "No," he said finally. "I was a cop."

"A cop! No kidding, a cop?"

"Twelve years."

"What happened? That you stopped being one, I mean."

"I'll tell you about it sometime. Meantime I got a question for you: You got a cushy job to offer me, all these interview questions? You do, and the pay's right, I'm your man." He said it around a grin, to show it was a joke, but he couldn't shake the sense of something going on here, behind all the easy talk.

A shadow of alarm flickered across her face and then was quickly gone. "Girl's got to make conversation," she said. "Strange man, first date."

"That's how you *Cosmo* girls do it, huh."

She smiled again, demurely. It seemed to him there was a slight shrinking of the remote distance in her eyes. Also a hint of reward. Unless he was mistaken. He made a signal and a pygmy-sized waiter appeared instantly. Before Starla could reach for her menu he said, "What do you say we have a couple more of these."

She said sure.

Presto, there they were, two more drinks.

Both of them were silent for a while. Quite a while. Morse felt a kind of stiff and unwelcome formality descending over the table, coming from where, he couldn't tell. To put something into the void he said, "You, uh, working tomorrow?"

"No, I've gone to weekends off."

"Me neither."

"That's nice."

More silence.

At last he said, "Look, we can still talk, y'know."

"I'm trying to think what to say that's not a question."

"Questions, they're okay too."

"All right, here's one bound to come up sooner or later. Are you married?"

"If I was would it matter?"

"Depends," she said shrewdly. "There's lots of ways to be married."

"Answer is no. Once, not anymore. You?"

Now it was her turn for the drink-sipping, thinking-it-over number. After a protracted pause she said, "Yes and no."

"Yes and no," Morse repeated. "That's like being half pregnant. Or part dead."

"Papers still say yes. Facts of the whole thing say no."

"I think they got a word for that. Separated."

"Well, I'd have to call it more than a separation."

"He still in the picture, your old man?"

"Why? Would a jealous husband scare you?" She was smiling, but there was a taunt in it all the same.

"Damn right he would. It's those types can get crazy."

"This one you wouldn't have to worry about. Jealousy anyway."

"That's real good to know. Sleep better for it tonight. What's he do, this mystery hub?"

Starla looked at him very steadily before she replied. A measuring look. "Time, mostly."

Morse leaned back in his chair. "Oh oh," he said.

She said nothing, just kept watching him.

"I got to ask again—is he on the street?"

"He's around."

"How'd he earn his ticket?"

"I'll tell you about it sometime. When you tell me why you're not a cop anymore. We'll trade sad stories."

"That sounds fair."

Time out. Cigarettes were lit and puffed thoughtfully. Drink glasses fondled. And then, with a relevance that escaped him, she said, "You're a jock, aren't you."

"About a thousand years ago. Thousand at least. Why you ask?"

"Oh, I don't know. You've got the look of a jock."

"Sorta clean-cut, huh."

She tilted her head, seemed to study him. The light of promise he'd seen in her eyes, or thought he'd seen, it was there all right. He hadn't mistaken it. But what she said was, "No. More like violent. Maybe a little mean even."

"Yeah, well, I'm a good hater, I suppose."

"It's the haters, I hear, make the best lovers."

He wasn't any good at this, this dancing around. "Listen," he said, "how hungry are you anyway?"

And she answered, quite evenly, "There's lots of different kinds of hunger. Just like marriages."

"Time to leave," he said, rising.

She pointed at his glass. "Don't you want to finish first?"

"Maybe they'll put it in a bag for me. Have to be a running capitalist doggie bag in a place like this."

XX

Every hatch and weld and seam on the tin trailer groaned under the force of the wind. She guided him through the abbreviated living room into the bedroom. There was a reddish glow of a night-light from the open door to the bath; otherwise the place was drastically dark. He stood swaying slightly, feeling some of the agreeable languor of all the drink. Unaccountably, an image of Jean Satterfield came rushing into his head, unannounced; and with it the memory, blurring, of everything in his life that was—or had been—comfortable, familiar, ordered and secure.

"Y'know," he said, almost wistfully, "today's my birthday. I tell you that?"

"Really." She took his hands and drew him down beside her on the bed. "Well then, birthday boy deserves a special treat."

XX

Apart from the disaster years with a faithless wife, Morse had never stuck with a woman long enough to establish anything even remotely resembling a history. A month, six weeks—that was plenty, that would do. With women, he had concluded, it was only the journey that mattered, never the destination. The game, not the score. In that respect it was not much different from the other game that had dominated a good share of his life: rules, boundaries, choices, penalties, reversals—the moves, finally. The moves, and that dizzying sense of the ambushed moment only a player understands. That, and the certain knowledge of a scoreboard clock steadily running down.

With this one, Starla, what he remembered through the fog of drink was the extraordinary intensity of that peculiar moment, the fierce acrobatics; though when he woke the next morning to discover her lying there gazing at him, her face was remarkably serene. Tangles of hair spilled over her shoulders. The heavy perfumes of sex rose from under the sheets. From around the drawn drapes at the window, two ribbons of light fell across the foot of the bed. In a voice scarcely more than a whisper, she said, "Happy birthday."

He said thanks. There was a dull throbbing at his temples. His mouth felt as if it were varnished with shellac. With the heels of his hands he ground at puffy eyes. He was wondering if he was equal to the rigors of this game anymore, wondering if this benchmark birthday signaled the time to turn in the jersey and pads.

"Are you okay?" she asked. Must have been reading his thoughts.

"I think so. Last night, that was quite a workout."

"That's good. You're all right, I mean. Because the party's just beginning, Mitch. Just starting up."

"More presents to unwrap, huh."

"Lots more. Seems to me I heard you say you had the weekend off."

"That's correct."

"And so do I."

"Yeah, I remember you saying that."

"What else do you remember about last night?"

"All of it. Well, most of it anyway."

"You remember telling me how they used to call you The Hammer? When you played football?"

"That part got lost somewhere."

A slow smile played across her face. She extended a hand, stroked the inside of his thigh lightly. "They were right about that."

A warmth stirred in his chest and unrolled in leisurely drift through his limbs, and as she settled over him he was thinking, Maybe I am still The Hammer, maybe I still got all the moves.

XX

Thirty-six hours later, when she was certain Morse was sunk in an exhausted sleep, Starla phoned Kasperson.

"That security man you were talking about? The other night? I think I've found him."

"Excellent. I knew we could count on you. When can we arrange a meeting?"

"Better give it a little while."

"Let's not wait too long. Time grows short."

"Look, I understand that. I'm doing all I can."

"I'm sure you are. How much longer do you figure?"

"A few more days is all. Oh, one other thing. This one, he was a cop, so when you talk to him you'd better come at it carefully. Use some of that smoke you're so good at."

"Cop?" Kasperson said doubtfully. "Are you sure that's wise?"

Starla smiled some, thinking about this Morse and all she'd learned about him in the past two days and how neatly things seemed to be falling in place for her. "You don't have to worry," she said, thinking also, Well, maybe not yet anyway.

PART FOUR

TWENTY

FOUR NIGHTS LATER Morse was sitting in a consulting chair opposite the trichologist's desk. With the introductions over, he glanced around the small room, the shelves full of strangely titled books, the mysterious blank screen on the wall, the seedy warehouse out the window. He glanced at Starla, seated beside him. Her expression was unreadable. Reflexively, he patted at his hair. It felt full as ever. He wondered what they were doing here, why she had brought him.

Kasperson was alert to the gesture. "You give your hair a reassuring touch, Mr. Morse. Clearly, you're in no immediate need of my professional services. No doubt you're wondering why, then, on this Thanksgiving night, Starla has gone to the trouble of bringing you here."

"Yeah, it crossed my mind," Morse said.

A faraway look came into Kasperson's eyes. Stretching his lips in a smile kindly and wise, he said, "Consider the hair. With an almost willful perversity it grows everywhere but where we would have it. Back, shoulders, ears, nostrils, the knuckles of the fingers and toes—name your undesirable spot and there it sprouts. Everywhere but the scalp, its rightful place. One of life's crueler insults."

He paused, stroked the underside of his chin thoughtfully, as though waiting for a response to this intelligence. Neither Morse nor Starla had anything to say, and so he resumed.

"Money, my friends, is like hair. Like the hair, money is elusive. Plentiful enough, but always in the wrong places. As a trichologist, I'm painfully aware of this paradox. More so than most. And even as in my profession I strive to reorder the growth of the hair, to put it where it rightfully belongs, if you will, so also would I maintain that certain monies directly accessible to the three of us in this room are in need of a similar redistribution. To parties more deserving. Namely, ourselves."

He made a steeple with his fingers. Peered over it at Morse, who turned to Starla and said, "You want to tell me what it is he's talking about?"

She looked to Kasperson for help.

"All right," Kasperson said. "Plainly, then. What I'm proposing is an assault on the treasury of your employer. Fleets. Precision-timed, precision-executed."

Morse leaned back and studied the ceiling. "You smoke in here?" he said.

Kasperson frowned, but only slightly. "Let me find something to serve as an ashtray."

He got up and disappeared through one of the doors to the room. Morse lit a cigarette, held out the pack to Starla. She shook her head and fumbled in her purse for one of her own. She avoided his eyes. In a moment Kasperson was back with an empty coffee cup and three water glasses. He handed Morse the cup, took his seat and produced a bottle of Scotch from a desk drawer. Smiling genially, he filled the glasses and offered one to each of them.

Morse set the coffee cup on the floor between him and Starla. He flicked some ashes in it. "Let me see if I got this right," he said. "Scoring off Fleets, that's what you're saying?"

"Exactly."

"And you're inviting me along, this king-size heist?"

"The thought was, you see, the project could benefit enormously from your expertise. Needless to say, you'd be compensated handsomely for your contribution. A full share."

To Starla, Morse said, "He always talk like this?"

"He's a doctor," she said.

Kasperson beamed at the acknowledgment.

Morse swallowed some of the Scotch. "Okay," he said, directing his words at both of them now, "that was your first thought. You ever think to take it a little further, all your precision-timing, think what might happen if I was to get up out of this chair and walk out that door and roll over on you?"

Starla toyed with her glass, gazed into it. Evidently she found no answer there, for she said nothing.

But the relentless Kasperson smile never once faltered. "It occurred to me, certainly," he said. "In point of fact, I was reluctant to agree to this meeting. It was Starla convinced me. She described something of your physical talents, your resourcefulness—"

"How about you spare me the Vaseline rub," Morse broke in on him.

"You mistake me," Kasperson said mildly. "Those traits alone would never persuade me. Force men are not hard to come by these days. Who'd know that better than you, given your former profession. Over in Detroit, I mean."

Morse looked stunned, and there was a chill in his voice when he said to Starla, "You told him about that?"

"She did," Kasperson answered for her. "And your, uh, unfortunate experience over there. Even that would not have been enough to recommend you. Not for a project this serious. But she also told me you were a man of imagination, vision. The sort of man who understands that success in life, regardless of the enterprise, requires a willingness to undertake risks greater than, well, say, the purchase of bank CD's. These are uncommon qualities, Mr. Morse. Starla sees them in you. And it's strictly on the basis of her judgment—her trust in you—that I consented to this meeting."

Morse straightened his back against the chair. He looked at Starla. "In a week you come up with all that, huh? What he said?"

With some difficulty, she met his skeptical gaze. "More than that even," she said.

"Yeah, well, it's been quite a week."

It was her eyes rewarded him: a dazzle of light, promise. "That it has," she said.

Kasperson watched both of them carefully, and then he raised a hand as though in the laying on of a blessing. "The natural affinity between you two gladdens my heart. Disrupting it—that affinity—I wouldn't want that on my conscience. If you choose, Mr. Morse, we can terminate this conversation right now. No offense intended, none, I hope, taken." With a sweep of the hand he made a purgative gesture. "Or, alternatively, we can explore the proposition further. The choice is yours."

"Starla?"

"Maybe you should listen to what he has to say."

Morse thought about it for a long moment. "Can't hurt to listen," he said finally.

And Kasperson sketched in an outline of the plan. Forty-five minutes later, in parting, he said, "Think about it this way, Mr. Morse: why go through life counting up the change in your pockets? That's for the proles of this world. Not people like us. Think that over."

XX

Morse pulled the Monte Carlo out onto the expressway and pointed it north on 131. A cold rain fell from the black, depthless sky, dissolving what remained of the gritty snow. Starla asked where they were going. He said nowhere. They rode in silence. At the Rockford exit he swung around and headed back. A shimmery dome of orange light hung over the city. He drove directly to the trailer court, left the engine idling. Neither of them made a move to get out. Rain spattered the windshield and drummed steadily on the roof.

"Are you going to tell me what you're thinking?" she said.

"Thinking about my playing days," Morse said. "Y'know, those days, a clip, blindside hit, I could always feel when it was coming on. It was like I had this radar in my head, sent off these little warning blips, said: Look out, Mitch, dodge, duck, stutter-step, run. Same on the force, Detroit. Saved my ass many a time, that old private radar did. Both places, on the field, and on the sidewalks."

Starla sighed. "Let me guess, now. There's a message in there, right?"

"No message. No. I was just doing some out-loud wondering why it is that radar won't work anyplace else."

"Maybe you ought to explain what that means."

"It means all your moves were right out in the open, and I never caught a one of them."

"Which moves, exactly?"

"Think about it. Man sits down and talks to the lady, trying to hit on her, but friendly-like, easy. She's not much interested. Not till she hears security. Magic word, security. It helps some, but it's not quite enough to take you where you want to go. So he gets in a little scuffle in the store there, gets himself pounded some but he comes out okay, looks up, lady's sporting a smile. Just for him. My hero.

"Comes the next night he's hearing how valiant he is, manly. Your fundamental legend. This is sweet music. Next thing he knows, he's got the key to the candy store. Help yourself, boy, all you want. Load up your bag. Store, it just never closes. Week later he comes up for air, lady says, Oh yeah, by the way, there's this fella I think you should meet. Real intelligent. Doctor. Save your hair for you if you got that problem. You don't, that's okay too. He's also got a real interesting proposition to make you. Never mind he's a little scooters, and so's his scheme. Cost nothing to listen, right? Turns out Doctor and the lady—oh yeah, don't forget, couple other assassin types who for now remain anonymous—anyway, turns out they all got this big score in mind. Want to cut our man a slice of the action. They're not greedy. Especially the lady. He's her hero, remember? Get on the right side of all that loot and it's you and me, kid. Candy-apple dreams.

"So much for radar. That's the hindsight kind, signal tells you you already been blown away. Kiss what's left of your ass goodbye."

"That's how you see it?" she said quietly.

"That's how it looks, this side of the seat."

"Sounds pretty bad, the way you put it."

"Yeah, well, I'm thinking there's maybe more even. Let me hazard a wild guess here. The other two players in it, one of them wouldn't just happen to be the absent husband?"

Starla nodded her head.

Morse snapped his fingers. "Well I'll be go to fuck! Now there's a coincidence for you. A minute ago you were talking about messages. You ever see those bumper stickers, tee-shirts, got that real cute one says SHIT HAPPENS? They oughta make up one says, COINCIDENCE, THAT HAPPENS TOO."

Starla was pressed against the passenger door. She had been looking straight ahead, through the windshield, watching the rain slap her trailer. Now she shifted, faced him.

"You want me to lie to you, Mitch? I can do that. I've done it."

"None better," he said.

"But I'm not going to now. Sure, that's how it started, just the way you said. Except for the part about my so-called husband. That part, what you're thinking, you've got wrong. Of course he's in it. Started out his idea. But there's nothing anymore, him and me, hasn't been for years. Wait, that's not right either. There's spite, maybe, on his side, fear on mine. You'll see that when you meet him."

"You're way out ahead of yourself, that *when*."

"When," she said tiredly, "if, whichever. Doesn't really matter. Doesn't matter how it started, or what you decide to do. Because there's more than that between us now. You know that, Mitch. And that much anyway is the truth."

"No kidding? This is one of those whirlwind romances, huh, like in the movies? Cold-hearted lady swept off her feet? Transformed by the power of love?"

"Nobody talks about love anymore. Knows what it means even. But he had it right back there, Kasperson. You hear that word he used, *affinity*? If it means what I think it means then he's saying we're alike, Mitch, you and me. We've got the same outlaw brand on us. And you know that's true too, even if everything else is a lie."

Morse rubbed his chin, looked into his lap. "I don't think you got that right at all," he said.

"Well, we'll never know for sure sitting out here. Will we." She pulled her thin jacket over her head and opened the door. "You coming in?"

"Not tonight. Give it a rest tonight."

She shrugged and took off sprinting toward the trailer, weaving expertly around the puddles forming in the tiny patch of yard.

XX

Morse sat in the living room of his apartment, nursing a beer from the twelve-pack he'd picked up on the way home. In the dark the place felt unfamiliar, almost strange. It was still clean from the last Jean Satterfield scrubdown, everything in order, tidy. But it was beginning to take on a musty, unlived-in order. Which was not surprising. Except to stop by for clothes and a razor and toothbrush, he hadn't been here in a week. What a week.

The stale air reminded him of something, he couldn't think what. And then a melancholy recollection appeared to him: the house where he'd grown up, Pontiac, and the sheets of plastic covering the windows of that asphalt-shingled two-story, buckling under the weight of age. He remembered the postage stamp backyard, and he saw himself again, squirrel size, and the old man hiking a football at him, drilling it so hard it about took him off his feet. Mean and lean, boy, tough, came the whiskey wisdom riding the whiskey breath; you want to get outta here, see some of that big world out there, you got to have something in your hand.

Wrong again. Wrong about everything, poor old guy. What could he know? Assembly-line rat all his life, it wore him down finally. That and the sauce. Gone now, his mother gone, brothers and sisters scattered, long since out of touch. And the house gone too, leveled over to make room for a strip mall.

He hadn't thought about any of it, not in years, and the echoes sounding through the long corridors of time prompted a small, rueful smile. It was the football in his hands supposed to get him out of there. And where had he been? Nowhere was where. Except for the handful of road games, he'd never been out of Michigan even. Take that back. Once he'd gone along, Miami, extradite a felon. Miami. Detroit with a lot more sunshine and a little more glitz, but not much. Might as well have stayed in Detroit.

One night last week Starla asked him playfully (circling around it, as he saw now, easing her way toward it) where he would go if he had money. How much money? he said, for life had made a literalist of him. All you wanted, all you'd ever need. He had to think about that a while. There's these ruins (he could have said) in the delta of the Euphrates, place called Eridu. Oldest city in the world, Sumerian. I'd like to see that. And in Spain, Altamira, there's these caves with the paintings on the walls, done fifteen thousand years ago—bison, deer, bulls, wild boar. I'd go there. Some other places too. If it had been Jean playing that dreamy game, that's what he *might* have said. But it was Starla he was with, and so he rattled off the easy acceptable names: Vegas, Atlantic City, Hawaii, Bahamas, places you're supposed to want to go. And of course such names had evoked her delighted sanction: Wouldn't it be something to be able to do that, have the freedom and the money to do all that?

Jesus, he should have paid attention to his instincts, listened to them. They'd told him something was going on, right from that first moment he pulled a chair up at her table in the Fleets coffee shop. But who could have guessed it was *this* heavy, scoring an armored car, seven stores' worth of loot? And why would she ever believe he'd be dim enough to throw in with them? He supposed he had the answer to that last one; she'd told him as much, not an hour back, sitting there outside her trailer.

She was wrong, he decided. They weren't alike, not at all. He was a lot of things, some of them not so sensational maybe, but he wasn't an outlaw. That was the other side, the enemy, the evildoers. He didn't belong with them. All those years on the force, he'd never once been on the pad. Okay, free lunch now and then, tickets to Lions games, bottle of holiday booze. But nothing weighty, nothing that counted. And the opportunities were there, plenty of them.

No, they weren't alike. Why was it then he was sitting here in the dark, entertaining the idea? Why? The sex? He'd stopped leading with his dick a long time ago. A bitter marriage cured him of that. Starla, she could make the rockets go off in your head, exceeded even the wildest pornographic dreams, but there'd been enough sack traffic in his life for him to know and understand it wasn't just that. Beauty? In no conventional sense of the word was she beautiful. Charm? Strike that. No, it was something elusive, and he was unable to account for it, the secret of her enormous appeal. And thinking about it now, he seemed to come back always to that same irrational female radiance of risk, danger, spectacular reward. It was baffling, it was hypnotic, it was bughouse. Whoever said women would have a bounty on them if they didn't have pussies was right, but only partly. There were women, a very few, who had something more. Starla was one of them.

It was the jangle of the phone that brought him out of these wandering reveries. His impulse was to let it go, but on the tenth ring he got up heavily and went across the room and lifted the receiver. He had an idea who to expect. He was mistaken. The voice on the other end was calm, even, concerned, without rancor and with only a trace of hurt.

"I haven't seen you for a while, Mitch," Jean Satterfield said.

"Yeah, I know. And I'm sorry about that."

"I called Monday. After I got back."

"Well, I been sort of tied up lately, at Fleets." His own voice sounded slushy. He pulled the cord over by the refrigerator and opened the door. Half the beers had vanished. Miraculously. And he'd been nursing them, too.

"Did they put you on nights?"

"Something like that. You might say." If you were a liar.

There was a pause before she said, "Are you all right, Mitch?"

"Oh yeah, I'm doing just fine. Listen, how was your trip? That wedding?"

"It was an anniversary."

"Oh."

"My grandparents. Fifty years."

"Uh, that's the golden one, right?"

"Right."

"And you had a good time?"

"It was good enough."

"Good. That's good." Where do you go next? The weather? Traffic conditions? The general state of the goods and ills of this cheerless world?

He was spared that decision, for she said simply, "You want to tell me why we're talking this way, Mitch?"

"I don't know, Jean," he said. "It's . . . I've got some things to deal with right now. Work out in my head."

"What things? What's wrong?"

"Nothing. Nothing wrong here."

"You're not going to tell me, then."

"Nothing to say."

"Would you like me to come over tonight? Now?"

"Nah, this is a holiday. You ought to be there with your family."

"That's not an issue, not the point. I'd rather be with you. But only if you want me to come."

He recognized suddenly he wanted—no, make that more like *needed*—to see her, and the no on his tongue came out yes.

And half an hour later she was there.

If she was disappointed to find him drinking, she never once let on. Instead she watched him, a puzzled, tender look on her face, and listened quietly to his rambling, windy, beer-driven monologue, a voiced longing for the past, days when he was somebody, different from other men, harder, faster, shrewder. Mitch the Hammer, living on the edge. And when it was finished, along with all the remaining cans in the refrigerator, she said again, "What is it, Mitch? What's happening to you? What's wrong?"

"Don't ask," he said, and he got up out of the chair and, weaving a little, came over and took her by the hand and led her on back to the bedroom.

How often will life allow you to connect with a woman like this one, he wondered, lying there alone in the dark after the gentle, tranquil loving. Not often. And now that she was up and dressed and sensibly gone (for tomorrow there was work, both of them), he had to wonder at his own perversity, remembering Starla now and their electric bed sessions, and the wicked promising sheen in her wicked green eyes. Earlier, somewhere between the babble and the lovemaking and now—somewhere in there—a thought had come to him. He could go along with it, this heavy score, or seem to, and then on the night of the hit roll on them, take them down. Emerge the hero. Your legend strikes again. And if he did that, brought it off, who could tell where it might lead? A little reward bundle, maybe; his picture in the papers again; maybe even back on the force, if not Detroit then maybe somewhere else.

Until he remembered Starla. Where would she fit in this fine and fancy shuffle? Nowhere, unless he was prepared to roll on her too. And about that he wasn't sure.

The more he thought about it, the more heads it grew. What it came back to was another of those choices you get to make. A slumbering instinct told him this was a crucial one, a money roll. This one counted. But if someone said to him now, Which way is it going to be, Morse?, he knew he didn't have the answer.

TWENTY-ONE

"LOOK," MEAT SAID, drawing on all his powers of reason and commiseration and good common horse sense, "you had a train pulled on you before, the joint. It ain't like you was cherry that way. Sure, nobody likes a butt-fuckin'—outside your punks, course, I'm talkin'. It happens, it happens. Don't make you no less a strutter, real man."

Ducky picked listlessly at a wedge of mince pie topped with billowy drifts of Dream Whip. His eyes were downcast. His shoulders drooped. His battered face was just beginning to heal. His plate of half-eaten turkey and trimmings, chilling in a pool of gravy, was shoved to the side of the table.

They were sitting in a booth in a bowling alley grill that featured a Thanksgiving Special: Home Cookin', All U Can Eat, $9.95. It was four in the afternoon and they had a few hours yet to kill. From the lanes on the other side of the wall came the muffled thump of exploding pins.

"So," Meat said, opening his palms in a summary signal, "what I'm askin' is, when you gonna quit mopin' around like you was some brokedick? Which, like I just showed you here, you ain't."

Ducky gazed bleakly at the pie, put down his fork. "Joint's one thing," he said. "In there man expects to do some of his time with a flamin' asshole. But this is out here, free world. It ain't suppose to happen like that out here."

"I know," Meat said, soothing as he could, "I know. Least I

shoulda known, them Dokkens. It wouldn't of, if I'd been thinkin'."

Ducky lifted disconsolate eyes. "Thing of it is, Meat, it *did*." His voice shook with emotion.

Words of solace, contrition, regret—they didn't come easy to Meat. Nor was he by nature a positive thinker. But he said anyway, "Okay. It did. Nothin' gonna turn that around now. What we got to do now is, we got to get our shit in order, look ahead." He loosened his mouth in a noble effort at a buoyant smile. "Good times ahead, Duck, when you're packin' a heavy wallet. Like you and me is goin' to be doin', come Santa time."

Ducky cuffed the air with a limp hand. "Ahh, that don't change nothin', what happened."

It worried Meat to see his partner so snake-belly low. More than worried, for with a mind bewitched by superstition, he couldn't escape the conviction that Ducky was a weather vane, swinging to the winds of fortune. And the direction he was pointed right now, had been for a whole week gone by, that was straight in the direction of calamity, ruin. So it was important to bring him around, bring back the old Duck. It was vital. For Meat, everything turned on it, everything. He searched his imagination for a way.

"What'd you think of the grub here?" he said conversationally. "Pretty good feed, huh."

"It eats okay, guess."

"You want some more that pie?"

Ducky shook his head.

"Comes with the meal. All you can shovel in you."

"I ain't hungry, Meat," he said crossly.

Food, clearly, was not the way. Meat thought about it awhile and then, nodding toward the alleys, said, "Listen, you wanta roll a couple lines?"

Another negative.

Meat thought some more. He looked at his watch. Finally he said, "Okay. We got plenty time before I ring the Doc, and I know what we're gonna do with it. C'mon."

Meat pulled the commandeered Dokken pickup out of the bowling alley lot and turned east on 28th Street. A bank of gray-bellied clouds scudded across the sky, threatening sleet or rain. The street, ordinarily thick with traffic, was all but deserted this late holiday afternoon. Here and there some neon winked, and about a mile up the road Meat spotted the sign he was looking for, a marquee announcing boldly, if somewhat redundantly: GIRLS! GIRLS! GIRLS! Beneath it, in lettering considerably more subdued, was the qualifying intelligence: *On Screen—XXX Films—Open 24 Hours*.

"How 'bout this, Duck," Meat said with forced enthusiasm. "Nothin' like a little skin flick, pick you right up."

Ducky's response—none at all—was not encouraging. Nevertheless, Meat parked the truck and got out and led the way to the entrance. A woman with coyote eyes and sharp witchy features framed in straight black hair looked out at them from her booth. "That'll be eight," she said. "Each." She snatched the bills out of Meat's hand and peeled off two tickets. "Happy Thanksgiving," she said.

A buzzer released the turnstile gate, and they went inside. For a moment they stood in the back. In a portal directly over their heads a projector whirred noisily, casting a thin finger of light through the inky darkness. Gradually their vision adjusted. There were maybe half a dozen men, no more, scattered about the narrow theater, so finding seats posed no problem. Up on the screen a naked couple were locked in a classic sixty-nine. The camera scanned them clinically. Abruptly the scene shifted to a dentist's office. A thirtyish woman with the prim look of an elementary schoolteacher reclined in the chair. The dentist, a scrawny little man with a hairline mustache, hovered over her. She poked a finger in her mouth and said, "My tooth aches, Doctor. Think you can fix me up?" He grinned lewdly. "Looks serious," he said. "Have to put you under." He covered her face with a mask of some sort and instantly she was out. He lifted her skirt and buried his face in her crotch. His head bobbed furiously. A closeup revealed a bald spot in the middle of his frizzy hair and the tattoo of a heart on the inside of the woman's thigh.

Some nervous sniggers rippled through the sparse audience. Down in the front row someone lit a cigarette. Meat nudged Ducky. "Now there's a real sponge diver," he observed. Ducky made no reply.

On the screen the woman stirred, opened her eyes. The dentist lifted his head and ran his tongue over his mustache. An aspiring thespian, he registered fear. Happily, there was no cause for alarm. She shook her head dazedly, to signify the anesthesia was worn off, smiled broadly and said, "That's *so* much better!" She slipped out of her clothes and drew him up and into her, and they gyrated wildly in the chair. Then she clapped him on the back and motioned him off. "There's a spot up in here you missed," she said, pointing in her wide open mouth. They traded places, the dentist in his chair, the woman on her knees. The camera panned in close as she fit his wriggly joint between her lips. Then it pulled back to reveal a look of heavenly bliss written on the dentist's face. Music swelled. The words *The End* flashed across her bare buttocks, followed by a series of numbers, and the projector whistled to a stop.

A cathedral hush descended over the theater. The glowing cigarette in the front row made a tiny hole in the momentary blackness.

"Well, whaddya think about that, Duck?" Meat whispered. "That stiffen your gear for you?"

Ducky sighed.

"I could wheel over to Division, hire you a little fluff. Haul the old ashes. Whaddya think?"

He sighed again, deeper.

Very shortly the screen was illuminated. Prevues of Coming (the overvoice made much of the pun, exhausted it) Attractions: a kaleidoscopic sequence of images of men and women in inventive, unlovely copulative postures. Meat grew restless, bored. The gynecological shots sickened him. He glanced at his partner, whose face wore the empty disengaged look of a man in a deep trance. "This ain't gonna work," he muttered to himself, and he gripped Ducky at the wrist and said, "C'mon, let's get outta here." Ducky followed him obediently up the aisle, through the lobby and out into the lot.

They sat for a few moments in the cab of the pickup, motor twanging in a rackety idle, heat on, nowhere to go. A chill drizzle leaked steadily from the sky. Meat was fast running out of ideas, until a dim inspiration began to work in his head. He turned it over, examined it, weighed the potential hazards, which were many, and arrived at a decision. "It just come to me," he said, "what we're gonna do, get you toolin' again."

He slid the truck in gear and pointed it west on 28th Street. At the intersection with Division Avenue, he turned north. They passed by block after block of crumbling buildings, boarded-up storefronts, dingy saloons. The whole area looked as devastated as a war zone. When it became clear to Ducky where they were going, he turned his mournful eyes on Meat and said, "I ain't up to no pussy, Meat."

"Pussy ain't what I got in mind."

On a corner up ahead was a chicken and ribs cafe with a YES, WE'RE OPEN sign posted in a grease-smeared window. Meat drove by slowly, surveying the terrain cautiously. There was a handful of people inside, booth loungers, ferret-eyed hustlers, a hooker or two. Out front the street was empty. He pulled into an alley in the back. "Okay," he said, "you wait here. Be back, a minute. An' lock 'er up tight, huh."

Ducky watched him square his shoulders and stride toward the door. Every head in the place turned when he came through it. He saw him standing at the register, talking to a counterman. Both of them moved their hands and fingers rapidly, as though communicating in sign language. Soon the counterman disappeared into the kitchen. Meat followed him. Ten minutes later Meat came out the back and approached the truck, moving very deliberately, glancing from side to side and over his shoulder. In one hand he carried a bottle of Dr. Pepper, in the other a paper sack. Ducky leaned across the seat and got the door. Meat handed Ducky the Dr. Pepper and extracted a clear plastic envelope from the sack. With no small pride he said, "Look what I got you, boy."

For the first time in a week a flicker of animation crossed Ducky's face. "That what I think it is?"

"Your thinkin' is correct, Mr. Ducko. Pure crystal meth. Month's supply. Cost a serious hunk of change, but I'm figurin' it's worth it, bring you back from the dead."

"Thanks, Meat," Ducky said, voice cracking. "Thanks." His eyes were wet with gratitude, joy. He took the envelope and reached for the sack.

Meat blocked his hand. "Unh-unh, one at a time. I'm mindin' this store. Can't have you tweakin' out on me, push-and-shove hour comes."

XX

They were holed up at a Plainfield motel that offered kitchenette rooms by the week. Meat lay on one of the twin beds, sipping a Beam and water. Ducky paced the floor, delivering a nonstop monologue. His arms swung in wide, violent gestures. He smoked furiously. Three hours had elapsed, and the speed had taken firm hold. Meat watched him tolerantly, listening to not a word. At nine o'clock he said, "Okay, okay, give it a rest, a minute. Business time." He picked up the phone and dialed the Clinic.

"United Hairlines," said the brisk, lip-smacking voice. "Dr. Kasperson speaking."

"Yeah, got a hair emergency here, Doc. You make house calls?"

"Ah yes, this would be Milo."

"Hey, that's pretty good, you knowin' it's me right off. How you tell?"

"It's your wit gives you away."

"Guess you know why I'm callin'."

"I know, Milo."

"So? How'd it go?"

"Hard to say. We may have convinced him, but at this point I can't be absolutely sure."

"That ain't good enough, Doc."

A sigh came down the line. "He's considering, Milo. And that's as much as I can tell you."

"Considerin'," Meat repeated scornfully.

"That's the way it was left."

"How do you read him?"

"I think he could carry it off."

"It's the cop part I'm talkin' about."

"*Former* cop, you remember."

"That don't cut no shit with me, that *former*."

"I think it's a potential asset. At the same time, it never hurts to be cautious. Particularly in a project like this one."

"Listen, Doc, you ain't talkin' to one your skinhead marks. You can shuck the lockjaw, say what you mean."

"What I mean, Milo, is we'll want to watch him carefully. Assuming, of course, he's in."

"See, that's another one them words I don't like hearin', that *assume*. Clock's runnin', Doc. We need this jerkoff—now. Him or somebody like 'im."

"Milo, what more can I tell you?"

"What you said," Meat said ominously, "you already tol' me plenty."

"Patience, Milo," Kasperson said, and now there was a rising note of agitation in his voice. "Patience and caution. As it is, your coming into town is risky enough. No more rash action, agreed?"

"Be in touch, Doc."

Meat replaced the phone and leaned back on the bed, pondering everything he had heard. The more he thought, the more the scowl on his face darkened. Ducky stood at the two-burner stove, watching his partner expectantly and juggling a plastic bottle of barbecue sauce in his hands.

"What'd he say, Meat? Everything set? Security dude in on the score?"

"I dunno."

"What's that mean?"

"Means what I just said. I dunno for sure."

The lid on the sauce bottle was loose, and Ducky discovered he could make it rise and fall with a gentle finger pressure. In motion it looked curiously like the flapping trapdoor mouth on a ventriloquist's dummy.

"Hey, lookit here, Meat," he said delightedly. "What I got here's a little dwarf lady. Miss Beebee Cue. She got a crush on you, big fella. She say"—he pitched his voice high and squeaking, made the lid dance in loose cadence with his words—" 'Hi there, you big handsome man. Wanna suck face?' "

Meat's scowl wavered on the edge of a grin. He tried hiding it behind a hand, but Ducky, with all his senses sharpened, detected it easily. Thus encouraged, he had Miss Cue saying, " 'Whaddya say, Mr. Meat Pie? I give great lid.' " By way of demonstration, he lowered the bottle, aimed it at his crotch and made the lid wiggle frantically.

In spite of himself Meat laughed out loud. "Old Ducker," he said.

Ducky giggled maniacally, his head, neck and shoulders a single jerky unit bouncing up and down. "Little Miss Beebee, she's a real spicy squeeze. You like 'er, Meat? She likes you."

A sudden impulse propelled Meat off the bed. "I like her fine, Duck," he said. "Get your jacket."

"Where we goin'?"

"Goin' scoutin'. See what we can sniff out."

"Beebee come along?"

"Nah, you better leave Beebee here. She ain't your average

cunt, she'll wait for you. Fuck the sauce right outta her, you get back."

XX

They drove by Starla's trailer twice and circled it once on foot, peering through various windows, before Meat was satisfied she was alone. He knocked, got no immediate answer. He pounded harder. The door swung open and Meat pushed his way in, Ducky right behind him. Both of them sank onto kitchen chairs. Starla stood there with her hands on her hips, frowning. Looking a little frightened too, which was just fine, the way it ought to be.

"What do you want, Milo?" she said. "You're not supposed to be here."

"Oh, just stopped by, pay a friendly call. Also find out where things stand, the security hired help."

"It's coming."

"Hear that, Meat?" Ducky said. "Can't be all bad, she got him comin'."

Meat glared at him. "Shut up, Duck." He turned to Starla. "Supposin' you tell me what that means exactly, that *comin'*."

Starla didn't answer.

"I'm waitin', Star. You got him reeled in yet or not?"

She shrugged. "Who knows," she said.

Meat got out of his chair and came over and seized her by the hair. He yanked her head sharply off to one side. "Gonna tell you what I told the Doc. That ain't good enough. Fuck-around time is all done."

Starla, wincing in pain, said, "Goddam you, Milo, what do you want me to say?"

"Wanta hear you say it's nailed down."

"It is. It's nailed down. It will be."

Meat released his grip, stroked her hair. "Y'know," he said, as though it had just occurred to him, "you got lots nice hair, Star. Always had. You ever think how it look, decoratin' these walls?"

"Put a frame around it," Ducky said gleefully.

"Told *you* put a cork in it," Meat said. "Off your ass, we're leavin' now." At the door he paused, turned, and said to Starla, who had shrunk back against the wall, "We'll be seein' you again soon, Starbaby. Real soon. When we do there better be a pussy-whipped security man just beggin' to get in on this action."

XX

Meat lay on his back, motionless, eyes wide open. Sleep eluded him. The curtains were drawn, and in the utter darkness of the room it was impossible to distinguish object from shadow. Occasionally he heard the thunder of a cycle burning down Plainfield. Rain pattered on the roof.

Ducky tossed restlessly on his bed. Eventually, predictably, he said, "You asleep, Meat?"

"Yeah."

"I can't sleep."

"No shit."

"You know what I was thinkin' about?"

"Even-money bet you're gonna tell me."

"Thinkin' about snatch."

"Listen," Meat said exasperatedly, "snatch-wise you had your chance back there. Can't turn up nothin' for sale, this time of night. Even down Division."

"That's sorta what I mean."

"Fuck you talkin' about?"

"Y'know something, Meat?" he said morosely. "Plain truth is in my whole life I ain't never had a piece of ass I ain't paid for. Which is kinda sad, you think about it."

"Well, we get around that money, you'll be shakin' 'em off like a bad case of dandruff. Go through twats quicker'n grain through a goose. Free ones too. That's how money works: once you got it, everybody wanta be your friend. So try thinkin' about that. Cheer you up."

"I got a feelin' it ain't gonna happen that way, guys like us. Ever."

Meat was alert to the sound of wistful melancholy creeping back into the voice, and he didn't like what he heard. The meth jolt was running down. He switched on the nightstand lamp and reached under the bed for the sack. He removed a small bottle from it.

Ducky boosted himself up on one elbow. "What you got there?"

"Hold out your hand."

Ducky extended an open palm and Meat shook two pills into it.

"'Ludes!" Ducky gasped. "You got me 'ludes!"

"Who looks out for ya, partner?"

Ducky popped them in his mouth and took them down with a dry croaking gulp. In the dim light his face was set in a grateful smile. "You're the best friend I got, Meat. *Only* one."

Meat rolled over and flicked off the lamp. "I ain't gonna be so friendly in the morning," he said gruffly, "you don't let me get some sleep."

TWENTY-TWO

THANKSGIVING DINNER for Doyle Gilley was a turkey potpie, Banquet brand; some yellowing cottage cheese about a day off of souring; a can of My-T-Fine jellied cranberry sauce, red and quivery; two raw carrots (a concession to the papillae-nourishing diet he was supposed to be on); a glass of milk; and a handful of Gold Rush double fudge ice cream nuggets for dessert. On the refrigerator door a magnetized smile face beamed at him, mocking his solitary feast. An Alps of unwashed dishes rose from the sink. Crumb beads embedded in a thin film of grease gilded the counter. The sliver of sky framed in the kitchen window was leaden, bleak.

Nevertheless, the way Doyle saw it, there was still much to be thankful for. He tallied his blessings. For one thing, Twyla got tapped to work a holiday shift and so, slapdash as the meal was, at least it was eaten in merciful silence. For another, with the day off and her out of the apartment till three, he had the luxury of sleeping in and, later, indulging himself in the leisurely and unfurtive discharge of the home maintenance regimen, including the internal flushing. Finally, and far and away most heartening, he was pretty certain now that his minute examinations revealed a colorless fuzz, fine as fairy dust, sprouting in the gaps of his temples. And with only a month of treatments behind him. Give it another six or so and he'd be on his way, big-time city. So there was reason for gratitude on this day of ritual thanks offering. And he wasn't ashamed to say (as he did, giving mumbly voice to his thoughts) that's exactly how he felt: grateful that luck and his own dogged persistence had shown him the way to the Kasperson Clinic.

In celebration of his good fortune, he popped a can of beer, went into the living room, flipped on the TV and stretched out on the couch. There was a ball game on and he was just getting comfortable when Twyla came stalking through the door.

"Jesus H. Horseapples," she said in greeting, "you'd think turkey day people'd stay home. Where they belong. That's what you'd think, right?"

Her look and tone implied a clear demand for answer, so Doyle hauled himself up, nodded affirmatively and said, "That's what I did."

"That's where you'd be wrong. Every asshole in G.R. who can drive, run, walk or crawl got to show up and feed their face. I been bun-bustin' since seven this a.m., no letup, and I had it up to here." *Here* was a point high on her forehead indicated by a blade of a hand. "I'm tellin' you, Doyle, they got no common courtesy, city people. You'd think it bein' Thanksgiving they'd be, well, cheery, halfway decent at least, have something nice to say. Boy, you can forget *that*. Grouchiest collection of hogmouths I seen in all the time I been at the 'roo."

She was planted in the middle of the room, wide-legged stance, arms akimbo.

"Why don't you sit down," Doyle said, "take a load off." It seemed lately he'd been listening to more than his share of bitching.

"Nah, I'm too hyper to sit, hang around here. Let's go soak up a couple brews. Maybe help bring me down a little."

The contradiction between this suggestion and the original complaint apparently never occurred to her. Which was okay with Doyle; he hadn't been out of the apartment all day, and you didn't look to Twyla for serious logic. "Sounds good to me," he said agreeably, and he got to his feet and beat it into the bathroom.

"Give me a minute," he called through the locked door. "Be right with you."

"Well, don't go givin' yourself a beauty salon treatment in there. We're talkin' about goin' to the bar, not an audition for *The Dating Game*."

Jesus, Doyle thought, she sees through walls and reads your mind too. X-ray vision. Wonder Woman. He was experimenting with a forelock drawn down over his eyes, a kind of tousled romantic look. Trouble was, it left visible bare patches on either side. If only there were some color to the fuzz.

In about ninety seconds, she brayed, "Bars close at two, y'know."

Doyle looked at his watch. Quarter to four. Whatever the fucking rush was, it was a mystery to him. Nervously, he rearranged the dangling strands. Working up a decent camouflage took time, and under pressure he never held up well. He cursed softly, did what he could and came on out. "Ready," he said.

"No kidding? You're sure now?"

Doyle delivered a sigh. "How about lightening up on me, Twyla."

"Huh, easy for you to say. If I was to add up all the time I spent waitin' for you to get yourself unglued from that mirror I could easy take a good six months off my life. God knows what it'll be after we been married twenty years."

That was a topic he didn't care to pursue. He searched for his windbreaker, found it draped over the arm of a chair. "What do you say we get going."

By common and unspoken consent, Twyla at the wheel, they headed for the Comstock Park tavern bitterly etched in Doyle's memory as the site at which all his extravagant dreams and ambitions were first sent reeling. The agent of that mischief, Porky, was not there today—another small blessing to add to the earlier tally. They settled onto bar stools and Doyle ordered two Buds.

"Here's to me and you and moonbeams too," Twyla said, lifting her glass in a toast. By way of explanation she added, "That's what my Uncle Serenias always use to say when he'd swig a drink."

"That was his name, Serenias?"

"Serenias Root," she said proudly. "Pop's older brother."

"What kind of a name is that? Serenias, I mean."

"Uncommon one. Course he was an uncommon guy, real intelligent. Real funny too. Use to make up these poems right off the top of his head, keep us kids in howlin' stitches. One I remember best went like this:

I went upstairs to get me some gin,
And I fell in the molly up to my chin.
I couldn't swim and I couldn't float,
And a big walla walla washed down my throat.

Cute, huh?"

Doyle looked at her blankly. "What's a molly?"

And she looked back in disbelief. "You don't know what a molly is? Boy, I tell you, growin' up in the city you sure do miss out on a lot. Molly's what they kept in the bedroom, do their business in, back before indoor plumbing days."

"So I can probably guess what a walla walla is."

"That one you guessed right," she snickered.

"Yeah, he's a real comedian all right, your uncle."

"Was," she said, suddenly sorrowful. "He died last year."

"Oh. Sorry."

Evidently the finality of his passing was motive enough for a dramatic emptying of her glass. She signaled the bartender for another round, ordered with an accompanying plate of nachos. Gradually the beer, the food, the familiar ambiance of the place all seemed to work in concert to elevate her spirits.

"Y'know," she said thoughtfully, "speakin' of the good life, country, when I was out home to visit last week I got to talkin' with Pop. About the future, our plans. Things like that."

Doyle scooped some nachos out of the basket and began nibbling at them. He had an idea where this conversation was likely to lead. He searched his imagination for a quick detour. Nothing came to him.

Too late anyway. She was launched.

"See, Pop's got eleven hundred acres, seven hundred of 'em his, the other four rented. Some of the best soil in the county, he says. Grows mostly corn and soybeans, some hay too. He runs over three hundred head of cattle, which makes the place your basic dairy and cash-crop farm, both."

Doyle was a little puzzled by the direction this was taking. "Sounds like a nice big farm your dad's got out there."

"Oh, it's big all right. Pop says a spread that size can support two families, easy."

"S'pose it could," Doyle said warily, "all that land." A distant warning flare went off in his head, also too late.

"He thinks," she said, striking straight to the nub of it, "after we get married we oughta move on back, go halves with him."

A spluttery shower of nacho crumbs flew from Doyle's lips. "Wha-a-a-t? You're sayin' *me?* On the farm? Me?" His most savage nightmares, which lately were plentiful, had never taken so dreadful a turn as this, what he was hearing now. A life on the farm!

"Us," Twyla said brightly. "If we was to make it legal by, oh, say, February, March the latest, we could get in on spring plantin' and next year's crop. You could quit that grungy plant and I could thumb my nose bye-bye to the Beefaroo. Course now Pop would want a little up-front money, show we're serious. Not much. But we got that base covered with what we'll make off Grandpa Leo's bonds. Right?"

Doyle had the dizzy sensation of a man walking a high wire in a windstorm, no net. He tried composing himself. Step cautiously now. "Look," he said, "that's a real generous offer, but you know how much I know about farming. Zip is how much. I wouldn't want to, y'know, disappoint your dad."

"Farmin' don't take nothin' but elbow grease and common sense. One season, Pop'd have you broke in."

The notion of being "broke in" sparked a sudden image of himself yoked to a team of oxen, tugging a cumbersome plow through the dry and unyielding earth. He tried improvising. "Thing of it is though, Twyla, I like my job. Doin' real good at the plant. There's even talk of me getting promoted, next month maybe, or before too long."

"Promoted," she snorted contemptuously. "Promoted where? That front office with all the fruits you was tellin' me about?"

"No, no, not there. Supervisor maybe. Sanitation supervisor. Or some other department. I don't know."

"See, right there, that's the trouble with city life," Twyla said, heating up, jabbing a finger in his face to underline her point.

"All the noise, traffic, weird crabby people livin' right on top of you practically—makes you pig ignorant. Here you are lookin' at the chance of a lifetime, chance to be your own boss, make some real money, and all you're thinkin' about is some maybe promotion in some sweatbox food factory. Do you good, work out in the sunshine and open air for a change." Her eyes drifted slowly toward the uppermost rim of his brow, and she added wickedly, "Might even save some of that hair you're worrying about all the time."

Even for Doyle, this astonishing fork in her logic was impossible to follow. It was bewildering. It was vicious. He was dumbstruck.

"You think I don't know? All them hair lotions you got hid in the john? Whatever them nasty things are you do in there? I got a nose, y'know." She tapped the bridge of it, in evidence. "Also eyes. Got to be blind not to see it, way you try to pull what's left over the bald spots. Face it, Doyle, you're not foolin' anybody."

Doyle was stunned, angered, panicked, dismayed—a swirling brew of furious, injured, bottled-up passions. "What're you talking about, my hair? What the fuck's that got to do with anything?"

"All I'm sayin' is, you keep plasterin' on that goo, you're gonna have a reflector up there no time flat."

"What I do with my hair, I don't see that's any of your business, Twyla. And I sure as shit don't see it's got anything to do with the farm. Which if I remember is what we—you—were talking about."

He was willing to do anything, pay any price, to get her off this track: farm talk, future talk, anything to spare himself any more humiliation. He was not successful.

"That's where you're wrong again," she said triumphantly. "Lemme tell you what Uncle Serenias use to tell Pop about fallin' hair. See, Serenias was maybe ten years older'n Pop, and he still had all his hair, not a bit of it gone and none of it gray either. Well, Pop was losin' his, so he sent away for some of them creams—pro'ly like your stuff—and Serenias seen 'em and tells him, 'Otis'—that's Pop's name, Otis—'you're nuts to pay good money for that crankcase oil you're smearin' on your head. Reason your hair's fallin' out is because of them shoes you're wearin'.' Well, Pop, he thought Serenias gone pure bonkers, so Serenias tells him his problem was—I'm talkin' about Pop now—he didn't go barefoot enough in the grass and dirt and—''

''What!''

''Hold on, lemme finish. See, it was Serenias' idea shoes and socks stopped off the natural electricity from the earth. He said it was this electricity made your hair grow. Kept you healthy too, he said. He was always runnin' around barefoot in the yard, Serenias. Never lost a hair on his head, and never sick a day in his life. Up to the time he died. Course his feet never smelled too good either, farm bein' like it is, but the day they buried him he had a head of hair like a teenager. Thick as moss on the underside of a rock. And he must've been seventy, at least.''

Twyla paused, swallowed some beer and awaited his response to this little parable. ''You talk about ignorant city people,'' Doyle said. ''That's just about the stupidest story I ever heard in my life. Electricity from the ground. Jesus.''

''You should laugh. Serenias use to say, 'Look around at your redskins. You never seen a baldheaded redskin, did you? And they ever wear shoes? No sir.' You better think about that, Doyle.''

''Okay. How about your old man? He try it?''

''Oh no. Them days he was a wiseass, like you. Time he was thirty he was a chrometop too—like you're gonna be, you keep partin' your hair with a grease gun.''

Doyle fixed her with an icy stare. A helpless rage surged through him. He wondered what it would be like to feel her plump white throat in the iron grip of his hands, to watch her eyes bulge, face go purple, tongue thicken, protrude, to hear her last gagging breaths.

And under that strange, remote, arctic glare, Twyla wondered if maybe she had taken things just a bit too far. In all the time they had been together, she'd seen him lose his temper only twice. Twice was plenty. Once, at a gas station, he damn near killed a guy for squeezing in ahead of him at the only open pump. That was bad enough, but at least it was directed at somebody else. The other time, though, she'd been ragging on him over something, couldn't even remember what it was anymore, and he just blew like a rocket. Went through the apartment tipping over chairs and tables, smashing glasses. About trashed the place. Like a crazy man. Scared her that close to shitless. She didn't want any more of that.

"So," she said, much more civilly, "what should I tell him?"

"Who?"

"Pop."

"About what?"

"About what we're talkin' about here. Us goin' partners with him on the farm."

Doyle was overtaken by a monstrous vision of himself in seed cap and bib overalls, scraping cow dung off his boots, his skin leathered by wind and sun, hair—for all the mysterious electric rays beamed from the earth—irretrievably gone, dreams gone. "I don't know," he said and, scowling, turned away.

"Well I got to tell him something, Doyle. He's got to know by Christmas, no later'n that. So we can start makin' plans. All of us."

With a will of their own, Doyle's fingers sought the voids at his temples, caressed them. Still untenanted, but for some barely tactile fuzz. Maybe it was all a grisly joke, his hopes and ambitions and dreams. "Plans," he said desolately, and then because he knew she wouldn't settle for that," he mumbled, "Tell him I'll think it over."

"By Christmas, then?"

"By Christmas."

She put a gentle hand on his arm. "Doyle? Honey? C'mon, I didn't mean to hurt your feelings. That Serenias story, that was just a little joke. Don't matter if you got hair or not. I love you anyway. You got me for always."

TWENTY-THREE

EARLY THE NEXT MORNING Morse was jolted out of sleep by the squawk of the alarm. He rolled over and fumbled for the button, then sank back on the pillow, depleted, working his tongue over the dry residue of last night's beer and cigarettes. His limbs were stiff, his head throbbed. It had not been a night of innocent slumber. A haze of doubt and trouble seemed to have settled permanently behind his crusted eyes. In front of them, streaks of wan yellow light entered the room from the window over the bed.

He lay there for a while, not moving, and when he looked at the clock again it read a remarkable half past eight. Which made him already ninety minutes late. Shame on you, Morse: a Fleets family member is, by definition, punctual, as well as chipper and all those other good things. Of course, you're a legend and legends operate outside of time. The legend got out of bed and phoned the stouthearted Eddie with the story this was the morning the stitches were to come out of his chin, be in when he could, forgot to mention it earlier, sorry. There was some grumbling but nothing serious, nothing that mattered. In his line of work shifts were loose, overlapped all the time. They'd get their hours out of him.

For now he had some unanticipated free ones. But since he'd used the medical dodge, and since that little chore had to get taken care of sooner or later, he decided that's what he'd better do. By ten he was cleaned up and ready to face the world, more or less.

He took some back streets to St. Mary's downtown. Lately they had been getting all his business. Give it enough time and maybe they'd establish a Mitchell Morse Memorial Room. Bed, at least. The doctor who unlaced him was different from the one of a month ago, after the beer factory scuffle. This one could pass for thirty easy, though he also affected a wise and wintry bearing. Different too was the fact there was no Jean Satterfield to look in on when he left. Remembering last night, her soothing presence, her willingness to listen to all that wandering beery talk, he almost wished there were. Since there was not, he drove back to Plainfield and pulled in at an eatery directly across the street from Fleets. Already they had Christmas wreaths on the walls and windows. Joyous carols flooded the air. The waitress pushed their Santa Special: eggs, waffles, sausage, hash browns, the works (sorry, no substitutions). He said okay, and ate next to none of it. He dawdled over coffee, smoked some cigarettes.

And now it was half past eleven. Legend or not, he couldn't afford to do in much more time. Yet time was what he needed most, time to think clearly about everything he'd heard last night. Time to deliberate on alternatives, consequences, aftermaths. Most of all time away from Starla.

A melody resonated in his ears, and his mind strayed from the business at hand and supplied the words.

Hark! the herald angels sing,
Glory to the newborn king.

He tried focusing his thoughts, but his gaze began to wander over the booths, down the aisle, out the window. From where he sat, the view of Fleets was panoramic. The three main customer entrances, each with double doors and an entryway between them, faced the parking lot. (There was another entrance at the opposite end of the store, smaller, irrelevant.) One of the three, squarely in the middle of the building, was sheltered by a large steel canopy. Underneath it was enough space for two vehicles to pass, and it was in the outermost of those spaces the armored car invariably stopped. It made good sense: grocery pickups were handled to the right and well behind the car; to the left, on the other side of a knee-high concrete abutment, was another wide traffic lane; and fore and aft the approaches were clean, ready routes for evasive driving or escape, if ever such were needed.

Peace on earth and mercy mild,
God and sinners reconciled.

The car came with driver and two guards, one up front, the other in the rear, all three men uniformed and armed, though out here in the boonies they were too sure of themselves to bother with vests. Once it was pulled up under the canopy, the guard in front got out, locking the door behind him, and walked cautiously toward the store. A security man inside gave him the sign everything was okay (Morse had done it himself a few times), and the guard returned to the car and made the signal knock on the back door. The inside guard opened up and lifted out a handcart, and then he stepped out and stood watch at the back door. The other one took the cart and pushed it into the store. Both of them sported .38s on their hips, with holster straps conspicuously undone. Their eyes swerved suspiciously. Inside, the cart was loaded with coin and currency bags, taken down the narrow corridor linking the business office with the lobby, and from there around the corner and out to the idling car. One guard heaved the bags and the cart into the back while the other scanned the areas behind and on either side. The driver covered the front. As soon as they were finished, one of them got in the back and bolted the door. The other one came around and waited for the driver to open the passenger door. He climbed in the front seat, and off they went.

Joyful all ye nations rise,
Join the triumph of the skies.

Morse had watched the drill before, several times. He took a professional interest in such procedures. There was a crisp efficiency to this one: practiced, vigilant, seamless. Except he knew there was no such thing as a perfectly seamless drill. Football, his years on the force, and all the history he'd ever read had taught him there was always a slant somewhere. The trick was finding it. If that's what you wanted to do. If.

It was close to noon. He paid the check, and the last rousing strains of the carol, a triumphant finale, trailed him out the door.

XX

Starla was working an express lane over by produce, and he had to pass nearby on his way to the back of the store. Their glances crossed. Her eyes were remote, giving away nothing, barely a recognition, though he felt them following as he faded in among the throngs of shoppers. He spotted plenty of busy amateurs but he left them alone. A collar meant a trip up front, and he wanted to avoid that as long as he could. So Christmas came early for all the boosters today.

At least until three o'clock. A little after three he made a quick sweep of the check-out lanes. She was gone. Now he made up for lost time, putting the arm on five luckless lifters inside of four hours, going at it with a vengeance. It got him a rave or two from Eddie. He was legend all right: Mitchell Morse, the scourge of nimble-fingered legions everywhere.

At nine forty-five, having clocked his eight with some to spare, he left Fleets. At ten he was back in his apartment. And at a quarter past came the tapping on the door. Even as he expected. No surprises anywhere anymore. He ushered Starla into the living room and she stood there, regarding him with a value-neutral expression. "Well," she said. A single word, single syllable, that asked it all.

"You want to take off your coat, sit awhile?"

She removed the coat and settled onto the couch. She wore a filmy blouse, brief skirt—not your usual outfit of choice for a raw November night. Nothing was subtle anymore, either. She arranged the splash of hair around her shoulders. Her bare legs had the glossy shimmer of polished bronze. She crossed them, got a package of cigarettes from her purse, lit one, blew a languid puff of smoke, lifted her eyes to him and arched a quizzical brow. Nice moves, all of them.

"Drink?" he said.

No drink.

Morse took the chair opposite her. "Okay, let me ask you something. You ever spend any time in the can? Even an overnight, I'm talking here."

The gesture said no. The face urged him to make a point.

"Then let me explain a little, how it is. Not like the movies you've probably seen, women caged, ladies in chains, gas like that. Y'see, they're not faithful to the facts, those flicks; they leave out the good parts. Take your Huron Valley Women's Facility, for instance, which is where you'd likely go, heist like the one you and your partners got in mind. Those ladies over there, they missed out on finishing school. They just love to see somebody like you coming through the gate. Be lined right up at your cell door. Welcome to Corrections. Some correcting, they'd do. They'd have you on your back with one bull dyke in your face and another with her head between your legs. For starters. When they got enough of that they'd roll you over and—''

Starla cut him off with a shooing motion of her hands. ''What is it you're trying to tell me?''

''Telling you any time you'd do in there, you could count it time and a half. Telling you what to expect if things go wrong.''

A squint of doubt worked into her eyes. ''Why should anything have to go wrong?''

''Why? Because that's how things have a way of doing, this world. Maybe you noticed.''

''I've noticed,'' she said, and there was an edge of bitterness in her voice. ''Better than most, I've noticed.''

''Then you know what you're looking at, both sides of this cute idea of a score.''

''Right. That's right. Also I've noticed what it's like living out your life on the cheap. Grubbing for nickels and dimes. Growing old that way. Missing it all, all of it. Tell me, Mitch, which side is worse?''

For that he had no answer.

Starla gazed at him steadily. ''Let me see if I understand what you're saying. You don't want in on this?''

Morse studied the carpet. ''That's not what I said.''

''What then, exactly? No more games.''

He clasped his hands and laid them in his lap. His eyes remained lowered. A vertical crease appeared between them, giving him the look of a man wrestling with a formidable problem. ''Okay,'' he said, ''no more games. What I'm thinking is it maybe could be done. With a couple corrections on that plan I heard last night. A little luck, that wouldn't hurt either.''

For a moment she was silent and when finally she spoke it was only to pronounce his name. ''Mitch?''

''Yeah?''

''I think I'm ready for that drink now.''

He went into the kitchen and made drinks, brought them back and handed her one.

"Anything special you'd like to do with the rest of the evening?" she said. Now her voice was measured, cool.

"What do you have in mind?"

"Well, I just happen to have some toys in my purse."

"Always ready for action, huh."

"Girl never knows."

XX

Celebration time. Reward time. The night was one long intoxicating embrace, but somewhere in the middle of it, in a distant province of his head, isolated from all the sensations, was the ripening conviction that his options were dwindling and his life mysteriously changing and whatever choice he made, nothing would ever be the same again, ever.

TWENTY-FOUR

AT APPROXIMATELY THREE P.M. the following Sunday, November 29, Ducky came out of the shower and stood naked and dripping in the bathroom doorway, a fevered grin on his face. Using his left arm as a makeshift bellows, he thumped a rhythmic series of farty sounds out of his armpit, his inventive, corporeal variation on *Name That Tune*.

"Guess that one, Meat?"

At the table across the room, Meat, who had been waiting less than patiently, looked up from his stalled solitaire game, rolled his eyes heavenward and declined to answer.

"Give you a hint," Ducky said. "Goes way back. Elvis use to sing it real good."

"I make a guess will you quit jerkin' around and get dressed?"

"You got 'er, Meat man."

"Blue Suede Shoes."

Ducky's jaw dropped. " 'Blue Suede Shoes'! That's your guess, 'Blue Suede Shoes'? Jesus, Meat, your ear musta gone tin on you. 'Love Me Tender,' that was. 'Blue Suede Shoes' is way too fast to get outta the old pit here."

"Yeah, well, the old pit ain't exactly your New York Symphony Band either. Now c'mon, haul ass. We got important business comin' up."

"What's the rush? Huddle ain't till six, you said."

"Rush is I'm gettin' cabin-ass fever hangin' out this dog pound all day. Climb into your fuckin' threads and let's roll."

"Where to, three hours?"

"I dunno. I'll think of someplace."

"Do one more, Meat? Just one?"

Meat gave his forehead an exasperated thwack. He thought about it, but not for long. When Ducky was on the shit, moods could come and go like the Michigan weather. For now the sun was out; for how long was anybody's guess. "One," he said firmly, no-nonsense rasp in his voice. Sometimes his own tolerance astounded him.

"Okay, gonna make this one easy on you, Meater. It's a Christmas song. Everybody know this one."

Meat watched him standing there in the bare ass, toothpick skinny, flesh bluey-white, like a slice of mottled cheese, arm pumping furiously; and he felt a curious mix of annoyance and affection, fondness and contempt. He didn't know what he felt. "That one about faithful," he said. "Forget the name."

The musical arm went suddenly limp. "C'mon, Meat, you ain't tryin'."

"I'm tryin'. That's my guess."

"You're sayin' it's 'Oh Come All Ye Faithful'?"

"That's the one."

Ducky was seized with a fit of howling laughter. " 'Silent Night,' " he said, choking on the words. "Plain as pigshit on a sofa. An' you call it 'Oh Come All Ye Faithful.' I tell ya, Meat, deafie'd beat you, this game."

Meat shot him a scathing glance. He balled up a fist and held it in the air. "See this? It's gonna be doin' some beatin' of its own, you don't get ready. Five minutes you got. I ain't gonna tell you again."

XX

Half an hour later they were driving up Plainfield, Meat behind the wheel.

"Where we headed for?" Ducky asked.

"I dunno. Maybe we'll go to that mall. Good a place as any for time killin'."

Just ahead, a traffic light was turning yellow, and he was about to hit the accelerator, whiz on through the intersection, when a sudden instinctive alarm overtook him. He glanced in the mirror and, sure enough, there was a sheriff's department black-and-white threading through the traffic behind them, bearing down fast. Meat braked the pickup, hissed, "Heat. Keep lookin' straight in front of you. Don't say nothin'."

The black-and-white pulled alongside. Meat could feel the officer's eyes sliding over him. He kept his own fastened on the light. The veins in his forehead pulsed; his fingers drummed the wheel. For a heart-stopping moment, he waited. And then on the green the cruiser eased out in front of them, picked up speed and disappeared in the line of cars ahead.

"Holy fuck," Meat said, "I thought we was blitzed there, for sure."

"Ain't nothin' to sweat, Meater. All you got to know is how to put on the face."

Meat looked over at him, saw a face split in a loony grin. "Fuck you talkin' about?"

"The face. I learned it from this dude, done boostin' all his life an' never once got collared. See, it was his idea when you went to nick something it was your face gonna give you away. So what you got to do was think happy thoughts. Think about pussy, he said. What's happier'n pussy?"

"So you're sittin' there thinkin' pussy while the heat's eyeballin' you? That near to yankin' your chain?"

"Worked, didn't it."

Meat swung the pickup into the North Kent Mall parking lot. "Okay," he said, "pussy face works for you, use it. Whatever. Just don't forget, we gotta keep down."

The mall was overrun with shoppers, a break for them. Meat waited while Ducky bought a bag of cookies and a root beer float, and then they shouldered their way through the crowd. The intersection of the two main corridors was dominated by a circular fountain with four miniature waterfalls splashing into four pools linked by gently curving benches. Meat steered toward it and secured one of the benches. Waves of people swept around them. Ducky took a swig of his float, wiped the foam from his lips and held out the bag to Meat.

"Cookie?"

"Nah, I ain't hungry."

"There's chocolate chip in there. Some sugar ones too."

"Said I ain't hungry."

Ducky shrugged and popped a cookie in his mouth. He sent it down with another noisy slurp. "Y'know," he said judiciously, "this mall's okay, but you don't get your top a the line twat parade here. Got to go to Woodland for that."

"Well we sure ain't drivin' all the way across town so you can stare at cunts."

"Ain't sayin' we should. Just sayin' where you find your best viewin'."

"I'll keep that in mind, next time the urge comes on me."

"When it does," Ducky said, the sage counselor now, all earnest, "what you got to do is, you got to plant yourself at the bottom of a escalator. Sears got one. Hudson's too, but you get your better peeks over to Sears. Don't know why that is. Anyway, I seen this one comin' down there one time, Sears, no panties on her, and I swear, Meat, she had a gash on her looked like somebody took a axe up there. You never seen nothin' like it. 'Bout blew my wad for me right there, I can tell you."

Trying to follow the corkscrew conversation of a speedballer, Meat decided, was like trying to tie your shoe with boxing gloves on. "Look," he said, "whyn't you breeze on down that arcade, play some video games."

"Hey, that'd be a hoot, Meat. You come along?"

Meat shook his head. "I'll wait here for you." He got a twenty out of his wallet and handed it to him. "Take your time."

His head was still shaking slowly as he watched Ducky scamper away, cookie bag in one hand, float in the other. Once he was out of sight Meat slouched back and lit a cigarette, flicked the ashes in the shallow pool alongside the bench. The water was pale green and the bottom strewn with coins, pennies mostly, a scattering of silver. Fucking wishing pool, Meat thought sourly, and he wished he could drop a coin in there and make the crawling time speed up, make it blur on by—the rest of the day, tonight, the next four weeks. Make things fall in line, one two three, bang bang bang, catch a break for a change.

A child came out of the crowd and stood at the pool. He was barely tall enough to peer over the edge. One tiny plump fist curled around a penny, and with a finger of the other hand he touched at the water gingerly, as though testing it for a swim. Meat found himself staring. The boy wore a fleecy parka with the hood dangling down the back, and a diminutive pair of blue jeans that clung to the tight little swell of his cheeks. His hair was yellow, eyes sky blue. He had the smooth stainless face of an angel. He looked up and down, back and forth, a twittery sparrow. Before long his gaze fell on Meat.

"Know what I wish?" the child said.

"Huh?"

"What I wish."

A slow warmth rose through Meat's chest. His throat knotted. "What's that?" he said hoarsely.

"Wish I'd grow up to be a giant. Like you are. Then I could beat up on Bobby."

Meat felt a nameless longing ache. No, that wasn't right either: it had a name and he knew what that name was, and he despised it. Short eyes. There was nothing lower than a short eyes. Nothing. Yet here he was, a part of him wanting to reach over and touch the child, fondle him, and another part saying shame, shame, get up, get out of there. He didn't move. "Yeah, that's a good wish you got," he mumbled.

"Huh?"

"Just toss your penny in, kid. Maybe it come true."

"Did you?"

"Did I what?"

"Put a penny in and get to be a giant?"

Meat lurched to his feet suddenly. He fumbled through the change in his pocket, extracted a quarter. "Take more'n a penny to get to be like me," he said bitterly. He flipped the coin into the water and spun on his heels and walked away fast. His face felt flushed and hot, like the skin had been boiled. An angry, terrible knowledge seemed to be growing inside him and he wondered if things would ever be right for him again, or if they ever had been, and for the first time in his life he wondered also if there was any power in money to change anything at all.

He searched the arcade and found Ducky bent over a buzzing machine. He tapped him on the elbow and crooked a finger in a follow-me gesture.

Ducky looked perplexed, annoyed at the summons. "Where we goin', Meat? We just got here."

"Someplace else. Go to Woodland maybe, go lookin' up skirts. Anyplace. Away from here."

"Yo, Woodland, gashland. There you are."

XX

Two hours later they stood hunched against the cold outside the entrance to the grainy brick building that housed, among its many enterprises, the offices of United Hairlines. Ducky blew into his cupped hands and danced a shivery jig. Meat looked left and right down the deserted street and cursed softly, his profane breath smoking the air. At ten minutes past the appointed hour an Aries wagon pulled into the private lot behind the building. In another moment Kasperson came striding briskly around the corner, hailing them with an uplifted arm. He unlocked an outer door and they trooped inside, huffing mightily all three.

"Winter is here," Kasperson said sociably.

Meat was not interested in amenities. "This huddle was set for six, Doc."

"Sorry Milo. I was detained." Which was in fact true. Convincing Delberta of the existence of a special client, an affluent, busy executive who could schedule treatments only on Sunday nights, had not been as easy as one could have hoped. An image of that starched, dour-faced woman appeared to him now, and he frowned slightly.

Ducky seemed to read his thoughts. "That bluehead squeeze of yours need a Sunday night service, Doc?"

Kasperson looked as though he were deciding on an expression to allow his face to settle into.

"One a them prayer services, bet," Ducky giggled. "Say a prayer you can get 'er up."

The expression Kasperson finally fixed on was one of infinite pity.

"Where's the other two?" Meat said. "We got a meetin' here or not?"

"They'll be along. Why don't you go on up to the Clinic. I'll wait here."

He held out a set of keys. Meat glared at them, and at him, suspiciously.

"Someone has to let them in the door," Kasperson said with a sigh, as though explaining the obvious to a child.

Meat snatched the keys out of his hand. "Okay. But there better be some quick-step action here. We ain't waitin' all night."

In the elevator Meat turned a scowly face on his partner. "Want you to knock off with the wiseass remarks. Keep your mouth shut and listen. You got that?"

"Just keepin' things light, f'Chrissake."

"Light ain't what we're after here. Heavy is. Heavy business tonight, heaviest kind. You wanta do something, help out, keep your eyes open. Watch 'em, all three of 'em. Watch what's passin' between 'em."

"You think something's goin' on, Meat?"

"Dunno for sure. But we ain't gonna get caught with the drool on our chin. Right?"

Ducky put a thumb in the air. "Bet your ass, partner."

At the top floor they stepped out into a hall illuminated only by two pale yellow bulbs, one at either end. They found their way to the Clinic and went through the reception room and into Kasperson's office. And there they waited.

XX

About fifteen minutes later Kasperson guided Starla into the room. Morse came in behind her. Kasperson edged around them and positioned himself at his desk. He indicated Meat and Morse, respectively: "Milo Pitts, Mitchell Morse." Almost in afterthought he added, "Oh yes, this is Conrad Pickel." He had the surname right and Ducky flashed him a grateful grin.

Meat got out of his chair and took a step toward Morse, and they stood there a moment, faced off, two large physical men, measuring each other. No hands were extended, none shaken.

"So you're the big hitter," Meat said.

Morse looked into a pair of black, bullet-hole eyes. "That's the buzz on the street," he said.

A noise that might have passed for a laugh issued from Meat's throat. "You own a watch?" he said.

Morse held up his wrist and displayed a watch.

"That's good, you own one. Now you better learn how to read it by Christmas Eve, you want in on this score. Six means six."

Starla laid a fisted hand on her hip. "We had car trouble, Milo."

Meat didn't look at her. "It's him I'm talkin' to," he said.

Morse seemed almost to smile, but not quite. "I hear you," he said evenly. "But you better listen to her too, you want a reason we're late. Otherwise forget it."

Meat's face darkened. "What? Gimme that again?"

"Said forget it. We're here now."

Kasperson interceded with an elaborate throat-clearing. "Come now," he said diplomatically. "Let's get down to business." His hands made quick fluttery gestures, urging them to their seats.

Meat's eyes narrowed to a fierce squint, but he backed away, saying nothing. Everyone sat. Ducky slid to the edge of his chair and leaned forward for a closer look. Meat had told him to watch, and he was watching.

"Now then," Kasperson began, sharing a conciliatory smile equally with all parties in the room, Ducky even, "our purpose tonight is to take a close look at the project, work out any kinks or flaws. Needless to say, we have a common goal here, and I like to think—"

Meat swatted the air and said, "How about pluggin' the blowhole, Doc. Get on with it."

Kasperson shook his head and elevated his eyes. "Whatever keeps you happy, Milo," he said acidly. He laid clasped hands on the desk, stared at them a moment and then, in the manner of a coach unveiling an intricate game plan, ran it through step by step, reviewing each of their roles and responsibilities. When he was finished he turned and faced Morse. "Well, Mr. Morse, now that you've heard our strategy, all of it, what do you think?"

"Strategy," Morse said, as though he were weighing the meaning of the word. "Most of what I heard's not bad." He paused, massaged an ear lobe. "There's one part in there, though, sucks wind."

Meat expelled the astonished grunt of a man bludgeoned from behind. "What the fuck do you—" he began, but Kasperson directed a staying hand at him. "Which one is that?" he said.

"Comstock Park store. That's out. At Plainfield we stop, make our run."

Kasperson's eyebrow went up. Ducky bent forward, mouth gaping. Starla seemed to shiver. All of them watched the blackening expression of disbelief working its way slowly into Meat's face. "You ain't gonna work out, Morse, this score. *Mister* Morse."

With his outstretched arms Kasperson made a gesture of parting water. "Now I suggest we all—"

"Shut the fuck up, Doc. I already heard all I need to outta this roller."

Morse rested his chin in his hand and fixed his eyes on Meat. "Hear one thing more," he said. "The crunch comes at the car. That's going to be serious enough. You hit that last store, you double your risk. For what? Four hundred balloons? Maybe? Cut that five ways and you're looking at eighty long each, outside."

"Eighty long is eighty long," Meat said stubbornly.

"That won't balance against the risk. Stick your hand in the fire once, you might come out with a singe. If you're lucky. Do it twice and you're just begging for a Jell-o stump. Strawberry flavor. The secret is knowing when to stop."

"Where you get off, tellin' us our business?"

"I've seen my share, your business. Only from the other end. Jacktown's full up with hard cases went to the well one time too many. And what we're talking here is a one-way ticket. Where I sit, eighty K's not worth that ride."

A muscle somewhere near Meat's mouth tightened, lifting his upper lip in a wicked sneer. "That's your problem, huh? Think them inmates might not be so glad to see a roller like you? They know how to treat cops real special over there."

Ducky, unable any longer to contain himself, blurted out. "He'd wanta lay in a heavy supply of Vaseline, right, Meat?"

Barely glancing at him, Meat growled, "What'd I tell you."

Morse grinned at both of them. "Bet they do, your inmates. Bet the two of you'd know all about that. But it's not in my figuring to find out."

A hostile chasm opened between them. Meat tried to say something but Kasperson tapped the desk impatiently, like a schoolmaster calling for silence. He studied Morse carefully before he said, "That's your condition?"

"That's it."

Kasperson's eyes seemed to turn inward, windows on the precise geometry of his mind. Then they focused again, on Meat now. "He makes a reasonable point, Milo."

"You tellin' me you're buyin' into this?"

"You remember the risk-reward equation we talked about? Consider. Six stores should net us something in the neighborhood of two and a half million, maybe more. A half million each. Eighty thou up against another extended stay at Jackson, that doesn't compute. Think about that."

Meat hesitated, and in that shred of a moment Starla's distant gaze slid over him, this man who had been her husband and, if laws and scraps of paper meant anything, was still. His dark broody face looked older, more deeply fissured, the scars more pronounced, as though the strain of holding on to this rooted idea had drained the juices out of him. If it were possible not to hate and fear him, she might have felt a thimbleful of pity. As it was, all she could feel was a sense of tragic waste at the division of the money spelled out by Kasperson.

"I'll do that," Meat said finally, measuring off each word in a deadly tone. "I'll think about that."

"Good. In projects like this it only makes sense to keep an open mind."

Meat's jaw was tight with anger. His eyes blazed furiously. He didn't speak. The only sound coming from that side of the room was the sound of Ducky's knuckles cracking. Kasperson turned back to Morse and said, "What do you think we'll need in the way of hardware?"

"No Rambo gear, Uzis, nothing like that. Three pieces, small ones, twenty-five semiauts, they'd do. Just for show, making a point. We don't want anybody getting hurt here. What we're talking about, that's heavy enough without looking at any first-degree jolts, things go wrong."

"That kind of piece I can get with no problem."

"Also pillowcases for each of them. Just in case."

"Silencers might be harder to come by, but I should be able to arrange it."

"Got to have them. And all this hardware's got to be stone cold, y'understand. No traces anywhere."

"Give me credit for some intelligence, Mr. Morse."

"You know what a flash bang is?"

"I've heard of them. Some kind of nonlethal grenade, isn't it? Used for stunning?"

"That's correct. Which is why it would be good to have one of them along too. Probably couldn't use it, the noise, but it'd be a nice backup."

"That could be more difficult. Sources in this town are pretty limited, as you might expect. I'll see what I can do."

"Course we'll need a van too, and a new set of plates. Got to come off a lot, not the street. Day of the strike, no earlier than that. Response time's going to be slow that night, but we don't want to get tagged with a UDAA."

"Conrad here ought to be able to help us out with that item."

Ducky showed an expense of teeth. He was about to affirm his expertise with an anecdote or two, but a sidelong glance at Meat was enough to make him think better of it.

"How about that paper?"

"I'm working on that now," Kasperson said.

"Going to need those ID and passports," Morse said. "And they got to be the Canadian kind, if that's the first stop after the score."

"That's for me to worry about, Mr. Morse. Don't concern yourself. They'll be ready." Kasperson had been scribbling notes on the back of a Personal Data sheet. Now he looked up and said, "Anything else?"

"That ought to do it."

Kasperson let his eyes wander back to the other side of the room. "Milo? Any questions?"

"Questions." The word came spitting from Meat's mouth like a bitter seed. "Got no questions, Doc. But I'm wonderin' who's doin' the fuckin' quarterbackin' here, you or him."

"We're all in this together, Milo."

"Yeah, ain't we though."

Kasperson squared the blotter on his desk, examined his calendar. "All right. Let's plan to meet again three weeks from tonight. A final session, to gather up any loose ends. In the meantime, I'll see about getting us the hardware, and the rest of it. Mr. Morse, you'll continue to study the armored car drill, watch for any details we may have overlooked. Starla, you'll pick up all you can get on the holiday scheduling from the manager. And Milo, you—and of course Conrad, we mustn't forget Conrad—will contribute most by keeping down. Agreed?"

A general silence seemed to signify consent.

"Very well, then. I think we're done for tonight."

XX

At Kasperson's insistence they left as they arrived, separately. Meat and Ducky went first. On the elevator going down, Meat stared rigidly ahead, his features set stony as a public monument. Ducky darted a cautious glance at him and ventured the hopeful remark, "I was watchin' close, Meat. Like you said."

The response was a sullen wordless grunt.

Ducky tried again. "He's a mean-lookin' fuck, ain't he. That roller."

"Easy to look mean when you're in the saddle. We'll find out how mean he is, come Christmas."

"He's sure in the saddle all right," Ducky snickered.

Meat turned flat hardened eyes on him. "So what'd you expect?"

"Don't expect nothin', Meat. Just tellin' you what I picked up on, which is they're really hard at the double-backin'. See that all over the face of the lady."

"Ahh, you didn't see nothin' there ain't always been there."

"Know what I seen."

"She's just doin' what she does best," Meat said bitterly. "That's why she's in on this, first place."

"Okay okay. You said to watch. Anyway, don't count for nothin' with you anymore, what she does. Right?"

"Right. That's right. Don't mean dick to me. Gonna come to the same for all of 'em anyhow. Tell you one thing though, Duck, saddle talk. You ever hear what the old bronc riders say?"

"What they say?"

"Say"—he pitched his voice a low, country drawl—" 'There was never a horse what couldn't be rode' "—he paused significantly, then rounded off the rhyme—" 'An' there was never a rider what couldn't be throwed.' "

XX

At that same moment, Kasperson was saying to Morse, "I hope you weren't put off by some of the things you had to listen to tonight." He glanced meaningfully at the empty chairs recently occupied by Meat and Ducky.

"Doesn't bother me any."

"Unfortunately, the average sort of person involved in a project like ours is not what you'd call your seminal thinker."

"Work I do, you get what they like to call desensitized."

"Still," Kasperson said shrewdly, "I suspect there's nothing of the average in you. For all the artful pose."

They were alone in the office. Starla, complaining of the stiff-backed chairs, had gone into the corridor to smoke a cigarette. Morse got up and sauntered over to the window. Across the street the warehouse made a black wall against the night sky. Hurrying clouds polished the face of the moon. "Never met anybody yet who wants to think he's average," he said.

"Average is one thing, loutish quite another."

Morse wondered where this was going. He had an idea. To move it along, he turned and said, "Maybe you ought to get to what it is you're trying to say."

Kasperson's face had gone unctuous in a smile. "Let me put it this way. I think it's safe to say Milo and Conrad won't be best remembered for their intellects. At the same time, it would be foolhardy to discount their low animal cunning. What I'm suggesting, Mr. Morse, is that sometimes the best-laid plans have to be shored up by a certain calculated aggression. I expect you realize this."

"Yeah, that came to me, just sitting here tonight."

"Realizing it, you no doubt recognized the wisdom of—how can I put this?—contingency measures."

"That one crossed my mind too."

"I thought so," Kasperson said. A satisfied glow seemed to settle over him. He looked at his watch. "Well, the time gets away from us. I'm sure Starla is impatient to leave, and I must be off myself shortly. I think we should discuss this matter again sometime, you and I."

"Maybe we'll do that."

XX

Starla watched him over the rim of her glass. On the drive from the Clinic he had said not a word; he said nothing now. And it appeared entirely possible he might sit there in silence for the rest of the night. She gave it a while and then she said, "Well, what do you think?"

He looked up blankly, his face destitute of expression. "About what? The drink? Good. You mix a good drink."

"That's cute."

What he was thinking, of course, was the same thing he had been thinking about, wrestling with, for the past three days. And still no answers came to him. It was like being inside a long tunnel: turn one way, there was light; turn the other, more light, but of a different cast. And he could come out either end he chose. Choosing, that was the sticky part. "You want to know what I'm thinking?" he said.

"Seems to me that's what I asked."

They were sitting in the living room of his apartment, Morse on the couch, Starla in a facing chair. He held a glass in his lap. The fingers of his other hand beat a rhythmic tattoo on the arm of the couch. He lifted the glass and took a long deliberate swallow. Some animation began to come back into his face.

"Make no mistake," he said, bearing down on each word, "they're looking to whack us once this score's gone down. Both of us. You too."

Her eyes widened into intense pools of shock. "How can you be so sure?"

About that much, anyway, he was sure. That much of this kind of game he understood. "It doesn't take a palm reader," he said. "You were there. These boys got healthy appetites. Half a mil's not near enough to satisfy them, not when they got two easy erasures like us."

Starla put her glass on the floor. Her hands made small jittery movements fumbling for a cigarette. Milo's capacity for betrayal was something she understood; she assumed as a matter of course he would try to cut her out of her rightful share of the take. And a fear of prison was something else she could grasp, something concrete, real. But except as an abstraction, distant as a black hole in the farthest galaxy, the idea of her own death had never actually occurred to her. "What are you going to do?" she said, an audible tremor in her voice.

"Don't know. First I've got to locate which side it'll be coming from."

"Who do you think it will be? Which one of them?"

Weighing it, Morse decided against saying anything about the conversation with Kasperson. There was still that choice yet to make and until it was made, the less she knew, the better. "Don't know that either," he said. "Could be all three. It's the combinations I haven't got figured out yet."

"And when you do?"

"Then I work on some zigzag moves. World class moves, they got to be."

"Translate for me. What does that mean? Exactly?"

"Exactly? Means we're going to have to find a way to neutralize them. Which, depending on how it all goes down, could mean snuffing them."

Now she sat there a moment, saying nothing, looking at nothing, and now it was Morse watching her. The smoking seemed to steady her some. Her expression went slowly past the shock and through the fear to arrive at a kind of calculating resolution. Finally she directed her eyes a little to the side of his face, and when she spoke all the quaver had gone out of her voice. "Well, at least it should take care of that arithmetic you were talking about back there."

"You notice I'm saying *we* here. I'd need your help. When the time came."

"You know you can count on that."

"Your hubby," he said, looking at her very steadily now, testing, "you got any problems there?"

"Whatever has to be done, that's what we'll do."

That's what she said, coolly and without a trace of emotion. This was a woman who had no problem with decisions. Morse leaned back on the couch and rubbed the bridge of his nose thoughtfully. Circles inside of circles. He had to wonder which of her circles he was in. And if it was true he was a man on whom all experience had been wasted, then he had to wonder also what the swindling gods had in store for him. Whichever way he went on Christmas Eve.

"Y'know," he said in a tone remote, meditative, "in my

experience the best hits—never mind which side of the street you're working, matters not a bit—best are the ones you get religion on. I got a feeling this one's the kind that's going to make you holy. Either that or dead."

Starla gave him a look of puzzled impatience. She was on the edge of saying something when a soft knock sounded on the door. Morse sprang to his feet and motioned her to stay down. Cautiously, and with the chain still locked, he eased open the door and peered through the narrow slit.

There stood Jean Satterfield.

"Hello," she said simply, an uneasy smile on her face.

Morse unlocked the chain and stepped quickly out into the hall. "Hey, Jean." The heartiness sounded fraudulent even to him.

"It's your basic cleaning lady, come to call," she said, trying for some lilt in it but without much success. "I thought maybe your place might not have been dusted for a while."

"Been a while all right."

"I was, uh, hoping I might be hearing from you, Mitch," she said, more seriously now. "After the other night."

Morse looked down. He discovered he was still clutching his glass. "Yeah, well, it's like I was telling you. Trying to tell. Lately I been sort of . . ." He trailed off, and when he looked up again there was confusion in her eyes. They were fixed on a point over his shoulder. He turned and saw Starla coming toward them, putting a little sway in her walk, once she caught a glimpse of Jean, and shaking loose her abundant hair. He turned back and Jean was rushing down the hall, mumbling, "Oh—I'm sorry—you've got company—I—"

He caught up with her at the outer door. "Look," he said, "it's just that I'm . . . ," but he was trailing off again. Nothing, finally, to say.

"It's all right, Mitch. It's okay. I'm sorry. I guess I thought we were, you and I . . . I guess maybe I assumed too much. Sorry."

Her face tightened with the effort at control, and now her eyes were blurry with tears. She took off running down the steps and across the parking lot. He watched her drive away. He had the sudden panicked sense of a man standing on the deck of a vessel listing dangerously on a turbulent sea, the last lifeboat lowered and gone. He understood dimly that something he had been, or might have been, was sinking fast, and for the first time in his life he was facing the full possibilities of himself.

Back in the apartment Starla came over and curled up beside him. "You didn't tell me you had a girlfriend," she said. There was a ring of mockery in her voice.

"I don't. It was somebody I knew. Once."

TWENTY-FIVE

"YOU ORDER THIS WEATHER?" Miss Reneau was demanding of Doyle over the steady hum of the scalp massager. Her vibrating hand worked deliberately over the top of his head. He glanced at her reflection in the mirror and allowed that he was not the one responsible.

"Can't seem to make up its mind if it wants to rain or snow," she said, and then with a kind of cheerful resignation she added, "Well, you know what they say: You don't like the weather in west Michigan, wait a minute. Ha ha."

Doyle had nothing to contribute to these meteorological observations. His life about to come apart around him and she was talking about the fucking *weather,* for Christ's sake.

"Relax," she urged him, "relax. Your scalp's all tight tonight."

She cut off the massager, replaced it on the counter, took a comb from the pocket of her smock and laid his plastered hair back in a series of terraced parts. She lifted it up and off his forehead, and he gazed on a face unmistakably elongated by baldness. Reflexively, he stiffened at the cruel exposure.

"Take it easy," she said in the kindly tones of a nurse

hardened to the sight of leprosy. "I seen receding hairlines before. That's my job."

"How does it look to you?" Doyle asked. He braced himself against the answer.

"Lookin' good," she said airily. She reached for another vial of the Kasperson secret formula. With deft fingers she stroked it into his hair.

"No, I mean really. Seriously. Can you see anything at all happening up there?" He was desperate for an objective, professional opinion.

"Like I say, it's lookin' pretty fair. I think there might even be a little fuzz comin' in. Takes time though."

Doyle slumped back in the chair. Time. What could time mean to her? It was a diabolic time closing in on him now, sealing off all avenues of escape, and the best she could see was a little fuzz that might—or might not—be there. "Maybe I better talk to Dr. Kasperson," he said bleakly.

"Hey, good luck there! He's been so busy lately, seems like we never see him around here anymore."

"Why is that?" Doyle said. An alert sounded in his head. Kasperson was a lifeline, a last link with the fragile webwork of his dreams. "What's going on? More patients?"

"Huh, sure not that. Tell you what I think." She lowered her voice to a confidential whisper. "*I* think he's gettin' ready to open up another clinic. That one out in East Grand Rapids. Course he's not sayin' anything definite yet, but that's what he's been hintin' at." She came around and stood in front of him. Her face beamed with pleasure. "And you know what *that* means."

Doyle looked at her vacantly.

"Don't you remember? Means I'll be managin' it. My own clinic."

"That'll be nice," he said absently.

"Nice! Just change our life is all, Harvey and me."

"Yeah, that's real nice. Say, you think he'll be in tonight?"

"Who?"

"Kasperson."

"Nope, not tonight. Had some errands to run, he said." She wheeled a lamp out of the corner of the cubicle and adjusted it over his head. "Ultraviolet time. I'm just gonna go scrub the stickum off my hands and then I'll come back and keep you company."

"That's okay," he put in quickly. "I mean if you've got something else to do." What he really needed was some silence, a chance to think, deliberate, or at least a letup in the chatter. There was plenty of that waiting at home. More than plenty.

"Oh, no trouble at all. Be right back."

And she was. She came in carrying a stool, set it by the mirrored counter and perched herself on it, crossing her legs and hooking one blue-veined ankle under the other. In her hand, also vein-mapped, was a lighted cigarette. "Smoke bother you?"

Doyle shook his head no, even though it did. People, it seemed, were always dumping on him, one way or another.

"Dr. Kasperson doesn't approve of smoking, so I don't very often do it when he's around. Sometimes, though, the old nicotine fit just comes on you and you got to light up."

"I wouldn't know about that," Doyle said dourly.

She thrust out her underlip in a mock pout, flicked ashes in an empty vial, and reached behind her to lift the window a crack. A thin stream of chill air swept into the cubicle. In a teasing voice she said, "Y'know, I bet the reason why you're so cranky and nervous tonight is because of Christmas comin' on so fast. Bet you haven't got your shoppin' done."

Doyle could affirm that his shopping was still undone. On the list of urgent distresses, shopping was very near the tag end.

"Me neither. Haven't got a blessed thing bought yet, and Christmas just two weeks from today. Boy, I don't know where the time goes to."

Time, again. Far better than she did he understand its mutinous nature. Two weeks remaining. Two. Only a sign from heaven could save him now. Noosed, snared—an awful sense of desperation raged in him, and there was nothing to release it on, nothing. When he tuned back in, Miss Reneau was still prattling about Christmas.

". . . a devil of a time thinkin' up something to get Harvey this year. Usually it's easy 'cause he's always got some crazy project, gonna make us rich, and I just buy for that, whatever it is, keep him happy awhile. Can't this time."

Her prolonged pause was clear signal for him to ask why. In a flat uninterested tone he obliged her.

"His latest one is the *worm* business," she said.

More riddles. Doyle registered an appropriately baffled expression, even though he didn't give a rat's ass about the zany antics of Harvey Plum.

"Night crawlers. He says there's a fortune to be made in 'em, all the fishin' they do around here." She gave a comic exasperated sigh. "That man! Sometimes you got to wonder. Can you imagine a worm farm? In an apartment?"

His turn to say something. "Maybe you could buy him some books on it."

"Oh, he's got all them. Seems like that's all he does anymore is read worm books. Leave in the morning he's curled up with one; come back at night, still at it. Whatever floats your boat, I guess, but I tell ya, I don't think it's healthy, sittin' around all day with your nose in a book. It's not like he was a shut-in. I says to him the other day, I says, Harvey, you oughta get out more, mix with the people, hear some ideas don't come out of a book for a change. Practical ones. You got to be practical to get along in this world. See, he's got a good head on his shoulders but ever since his attack he's been livin' like a hermit, and you do that too long it makes you weird."

His cue again. But he had nothing to recommend. As counselor, he was out of his depth when it came to her husband's peculiarities. He noticed she was staring at him fixedly.

"Y'know," she said, "you oughta think about doin' the same thing, you don't mind my sayin' so."

"Raising worms?" Doyle said. He was making a sour little joke.

She cuffed at some air. "C'mon, you know what I mean. Doin' something besides that job you got, keeps you inside a plant all day. Nice lookin' young fella like you, you oughta be out where you can meet the people and they can get a good look at you. Be a salesman or a lifeguard, something like that."

Or a model or a teevee actor, Coyle thought. He shrugged modestly. If there had to be talk, this was the kind he could find hard to fault.

Amazingly, what she said next was, "First day you come in here you reminded me of a movie star, favorite of mine. Want to know who?"

Doyle's smile was self-effacing, crooked, eager. Could it

possibly be that a droll fate had elected her, Miss Reneau, to deliver the sign he was waiting for, buried in her babble? Cruise, would she say? Stallone? If anything, he had a better body than Stallone and he could be just as tough, if he had to. Don Johnson maybe, old Miami Don. Under the flowered plastic cape tucked snugly around his neck and dangling at his knees, all the muscles in his body had gone rigid as a horseshoe. His eyes fluttered up expectantly.

"Clint Eastwood, that's who. You look just like him. Boy, can he act."

Clint Eastwood! That fossil! Where the fuck did she get Clint Eastwood?

"You got the same long lean face on you, hard look, especially in the eyes, least when you're not in a chipper mood." Playfully she added, "Like tonight."

Face, eyes—okay, what about the hair? An image of that freeze-dried relic came to him, forehead widening, a pincers movement from either temple isolating a forlorn and shrinking outpost up front. That's where she saw the resemblance. Looking down into the dreadful future, not all that distant anymore, that's where she got Clint Eastwood. Doyle was too numb to speak.

"You gonna pay me now?" she laughed. Then, serious once more, she said, "No kiddin', that's a fact, you and him are dead ringers. Except for the age difference, and course you got more hair'n he does. But anyway you see what I mean when I say you oughta be out mixin' with the people more. People *like* nice-lookin' fellas, like to do business with 'em. You'd do good."

There was a silence. She glanced at her watch. "Well, just a few minutes more lamp and then we'll do your electro and you'll be done for the night."

Doyle glared straight ahead, into the preposterous manifestation of himself glaring back, a grown man swaddled in a flower print cape, greased head protruding like a turtle's emerging from under an oil slick. A specter from the past rose out of the tomb of memory and appeared before his inner eye: a turtle, a real turtle, creeping through the tall grass in the vacant lot behind the house of his childhood. He grasped it with both hands and raced on home, delirious with joy at the discovery. No turtles, his stern-faced mother told him, they're nasty dirty creatures and they carry the fever. All his protests, hot tears, childish rage, moved her not the slightest. You heard me, young man. You want a blistering? Get that thing out of here. Now. This minute. The vacant lot was ringed with houses, all sides. If he released it there it would surely fall into the possession of some smirking neighborhood kid whose generous parents would allow him to keep it. Which was unthinkable. The turtle was his or it was no one's. He slipped behind the garage and placed it carefully on the ground. He watched it. In time the head came poking out cautiously. He stooped down and seized the head with one hand. With the other he gripped the shell and with one mighty yank tore it loose; and then he jerked away, the shell still in his hand, gazing at the denuded bloodied remains of the turtle wriggling in agony in the dust, shuddering at his first glimpse of evil gone unpunished.

Doyle shuddered once again, remembering. He grabbed the arms of the chair and hoisted himself up. The ridiculous cape fell in a heap at his feet.

"Hey," Miss Reneau squawked at him, "you're not done. Got your electro yet."

Electro. As though that crackling magic wand could replace all the electricity draining watt by watt, day by day, from his life. Made about as much sense as Twyla's mush-brained uncle wandering barefoot through a manured field. "I've got to leave now," he said grimly. "Skip the electro tonight."

The echo of her scolding voice trailed him down the hall. The receptionist favored him with a scowl. He scowled back.

Fuck 'em. Fuck 'em all. All, an earnest voice in his head pleaded, except Kasperson. If there was a way out of this deepening swamp, only Kasperson could point him the direction, supply the answers he had to have, and soon. No, not soon. Now. He would have a chat with Kasperson.

He stood in the street, wondering what to do with the rest of the night, where to go. At this hour Twyla would certainly be up, waiting for him. A soft sleet descended from the black sky, moistening his gluey hair.

XX

Kasperson, just then, was studying a small arsenal of handguns laid out in neat files on the kitchen table of a west side efficiency apartment occupied by a man named Harley ("Call me Huck") Nance. The guns, about twenty of them, were arranged by caliber,

.22s at one end of the table, .45s at the other. An orderly man, Huck.

"You're going to have to help me out here, Huck," Kasperson said. "Hardware is not one of my stronger suits. Which are the twenty-five caliber?"

"That's them right there," Huck said, pointing. He was a wiry little fellow, fiftyish, with watery gray eyes, a sliver of a mouth that seemed barely to move when he spoke, and a narrow, deal-making face from which nothing could be read. Kasperson knew him from the Jackson days, knew his reputation as a shrewd and well-connected trader. Inside, if there was ever a thing you needed or wanted or absolutely had to have—anything, that is, within reason—Huck was the man to see. The words "Think maybe I can help you out," escaping from that immobile mouth, gladdened the heart of many an inmate. And some others too, for rumor had it that a certain guard captain with a taste for nose candy had been tucked away securely in Huck's hip pocket all the years he did time. Which was how someone like Huck survived and prospered in a place like that.

"And they're the semiautomatic variety?" Kasperson asked him.

"State of the art, Doc."

"And cold?"

"He was alive, J. Edgar himself couldn't track them pieces. None of 'em."

"I'll be needing three," Kasperson said. "With silencers."

"No problem. Wrap 'em up for you tonight, you want."

"I'd rather you'd hold them for another week or so."

"Layaway plan, huh."

"Something like that. What about the flash bang we discussed, how's that coming?"

"Comin' slow, Doc. Firecracker like that's not easy to turn up. I do, it's gonna cost you some."

"Keep after it, Huck. Money's not a factor here. Time is."

Huck nodded. "Speakin' of time," he said, "don't think I'm gonna be able to do you no good, that paper. Not if you got to have it by Christmas."

Kasperson was neither surprised nor particularly dismayed by this intelligence. He had allowed for it in his own private planning. Locked in a lower drawer of his desk were at least half a dozen authentic-looking documents identifying him by as many different aliases. So for him it wasn't going to pose a serious problem. But managing his confederates—whoever among them was remaining at the push and shove hour—that qualified as serious. Hazardous in the extreme. But then that's why there were people like Huck in this world.

"Huck," he said, "let me ask your professional opinion. On another matter."

"What's that one?"

"Imagine a situation in which a person had to, say, take out someone—maybe more than one—by surprise. What would be the weapon of choice?"

"Close range?"

"Very close, yes."

"It was me, I'd want a twelve-gauge sawed-off. Double-barreled."

"No, that wouldn't do, not in the circumstances I have in mind. This weapon would have to be smaller, easily concealed."

Huck thought about it for a moment. "Well, this person, he could use a derringer, thirty-two. Strap it to his ankle."

"How many rounds in a piece like that?"

"Two."

"Two," Kasperson repeated. "Supposing a backup was needed. What could you recommend?"

"You ever seen a pen gun?"

"Afraid not."

"What they are is a peashooter looks just like a ballpoint. Little under six inches, fits right in your shirt pocket. Packs one twenty-two long shell. For what you're imaginin' here, them're good too."

"But are they . . . effective?"

"Dude get hit by one of them, he'll be suckin' worms. Course it's got to be close up. Like in real close. And right on the button too. Same thing with the derringer. Shoot-and-scoot pieces, both of 'em."

Kasperson looked at him significantly. "Do you think you could get me one each? In lieu of the paper?"

Huck's face was carefully blank. "I might," he said. "But it's gonna be pricy. These are collector's items we're talkin' about."

With an impatient wave of a hand Kasperson signified that

money was again no issue. "I'd need to have them before Christmas, Huck. Otherwise they're of no use to me. Oh, and one other item, a Wisconsin license plate."

"What's today? Your eleventh?"

"That's right."

Huck scratched his head. Seemed to frown slightly. Thought some more. Finally he said, "Okay, Doc. Think maybe I can help you out."

TWENTY-SIX

HERE IS HOW it's supposed to go:

Morse has volunteered to stay late and close up the store. This arouses no suspicion—everyone knows he's a bachelor, no family, nowhere to get to. Besides, he's their standup loss precluder now, and he's walked through the cash pickup drill plenty of times. The other security types are grateful; they're in a sweat to get out of there, get home. There's been an all-day party going on in the business office—a store tradition, according to Starla—and by closing time Eddie's likely as not to be in the bag. If he can, Morse will talk him into leaving before the armored car arrives (Morse is overflowing with selfless spirit that night, lots of beaming good cheer); if he can't, then he'll just have to tranquilize Eddie in advance, get the key to the lockbox and get him bound and out of the action.

A little before seven he begins hustling the last customers toward the door. At 7:15 a van pulls into the eatery lot across the street, Starla at the wheel, Meat and Ducky hunkered down in the back. By 7:30 the store is empty, all the holiday well-wishing done and everyone gone. If it doesn't work quite that neatly, if there are stragglers, they still have a window of time, fifteen minutes at least, maybe a little more. With five stops to make before the Plainfield unit, the armored car can't arrive until 7:45, the earliest. Morse knows this for a fact; he's checked their route, timed it carefully. So the store is cleared when the car pulls in under the canopy.

From there the moves have to be flawless, and in this happy scenario that's just how they are. Starla waits till she sees the guard get out, then she eases the van into the street, pulls left and drives to the rear entrance and comes slowly around behind the building. Stops at the back corner, leaves the engine idling. Morse, meantime, has made the okay sign, and the guard has pushed the handcart up to the outer door. Morse lets him in, locks the door, and walks him through the entryway and back to the business office. The bags are loaded. Everything normal so far, routine. But in the corridor outside the office, Morse draws down on the guard, relieves him of his piece, empties the bullets and reholsters it. Gives him a little pep talk here, so he doesn't get any heroic notions. They proceed through the outer door, Morse following along behind, as though he's leaving for the night himself. At the back of the car Morse freezes both guards and puts them in the position, hands on the door, legs extended. Fingersnap speed, all this goes down. He neutralizes the second guard with an easy tap, walks the other one to the front. Morse stays flattened along the side of the car, out of the driver's line of vision. The guard, still under the gun, knocks and the passenger door swings open.

Now a lot of things happen fast. Morse pivots, shoves the guard out in front of him and shows the driver the serious end of his piece. That gets his attention, keeps his hands off the wheel and the radio. The open door is Starla's signal to bring the van around the corner and up next to the car. Meat and Ducky spring out, get both guards and the money into the back. Morse is up front, gun leveled on the driver. This part, the spiny part, is over in a shaved second. Not a shot's been fired, none needed. And except for the guard with a little bump on his head, nobody's hurt.

Starla takes the van out of the lot and heads north up Plainfield. They follow along in the armored car, Morse directing the driver, Meat and Ducky securing the guards in the back. About a mile short of the Beltline there's an empty house on the left, FOR

SALE sign rooted in the front yard. A dirt road alongside it leads into a thick stand of trees reaching all the way back to the Grand River. There are several small clearings just off the road, secluded spots used by kids for drinking, screwing, grass smoking. In the first one, Kasperson is waiting with the paper. They pull over and park the armored car and van back to back. Morse brings the driver around and they put him to work helping with the money transfer. Once all of it's loaded into the van, he gets to join his trussed and gagged buddies in the car. And then they get the fuck out of there.

They have an easy quarter hour till someone at the Comstock Park store gets nervous, makes some calls. Maybe another fifteen before the heat is on to something and out in force. By then they're down the Beltline and onto 96. They head east a few miles, then south. Everybody's been checked out on the directions to the farm—a Kasperson contingency, in case of any snags. The cornmeal twins have the planes revved up and ready to go. In a couple of hours they touch down at an isolated landing strip outside of Toronto.

In a just and divinely ordered world, that's how it was supposed to go.

Between them, Kasperson and Morse had been reviewing the sequence of action and each player's role in it, one last time. Searching for oversights, weaknesses, imperfection. None could be located.

It was nine p.m., Sunday, December 20. Four days till the score. Earlier that night the hardware had been distributed, everything Morse had ordered, with the exception of the flash bang. Kasperson was apologetic: it was simply unavailable on such short notice. Next he had escorted them to a treatment booth, sat them one at a time against a neutral wall and taken the photos necessary for the documents. Be developed tomorrow, he assured them, and all of the paper ready by Thursday night, no problem. And now they were gathered in the Clinic office, Meat and Ducky on one side of the room, Morse and Starla on the other, Kasperson at his desk, presiding. He made a gesture of summation: "Questions?" he said.

"Yeah, I got one for ya, Doc."

Meat sat with his outsize hands laid in his lap, squat and lowering as a stone Buddha. All evening he had been ominously silent, saying nothing, watching everything. The eyes he fixed on Kasperson were keen as drills.

"Yes, Milo."

"What if it kicks up a blizzard that night? What you two deep thinkers got planned then?"

Kasperson ignored the taunt. "A good point," he said. "But it looks like we're going to be lucky on that one. For Michigan, the winter's been mild so far, and the forecast is for more of the same."

"Yeah, but just supposin' anyway."

Kasperson sighed and put his hands together on the desk. "All right, let's suppose. If there was a heavy storm, unpassable streets and highways, obviously we'd have to cancel. But that's what it would take, something that severe. Otherwise we go as scheduled. If for any reasons of weather we can't fly that night, I assume your farmer friends would be willing to put us up temporarily. Overnight, anyway."

"I oughta be able to persuade 'em to do that," Meat said, holding off a small nasty smirk. He settled back, apparently satisfied with the answer.

Throughout the meeting Ducky had been squirming in his chair. His face was gaunt, cheeks hollow, though the eyes, in contrast, were bright, glassy, threaded with streaks of pink. His nose ran constantly and he kept swiping at it with a forearm. His hands twitched. It had been over ten hours since his last hit, and he was on the perilous edge of a serious tweaking. "One thing I ain't heard tonight," he said, "is nothin' about ski masks and gloves. How 'bout them, huh? Every score I been on you wear 'em. An' if we ain't waxin' the guards, like this roller man here says we ain't, then they for sure gonna get a good scope on us. So how 'bout that, huh?"

"I'll take that one," Morse said. He looked at the little runt coldly. "You want to wear gloves, keep your pinkies warm, that's okay, that's in season. But masks are out, they're not going to cover your tracks. Wouldn't mean shit. Even you ought to be able to figure that out."

"Yeah, maybe not for you, your end of it." Ducky's voice, which began on an abnormally high pitch, then went squealy. "Me and Meat, they don't got to make us, lift no prints."

"How long do you think it's going to take them to make

you?'' Morse said evenly. "They'll go from me"—he rolled a thumb at Starla—"to her"—he indicated Meat—"to him, and from there to you, and finally"—using the thumb as pointer again—"straight to our traffic director here. And they'll do it inside of seventy-two hours, maybe a little longer if we're lucky. And smart. Our edge is the next day's the big holiday, things won't move so fast. *If* we don't take out the guards. Ice them and you'll have every uniform this side of the state volunteering for overtime, no pay, just to run you to ground." He paused, gave it a moment to settle in. "Now, you think you can follow that?"

"You oughta know about uniforms," Ducky sneered, "seein' you done all that time in your blues."

"That's right. Pick up a lot of good habits, that line of work. Like how to watch your back, for instance." Morse lifted the corner of his mouth in an insolent grin. "Also how to spot a dream-dusting freak like you."

"Big fuckin' roller," Ducky muttered. He wished his mind would supply him with better words, wished it weren't so muddy.

Morse could tell from the smolder in those red-rimmed eyes he should stop right there, leave it alone. He went on anyway, slipping easily and naturally into the kind of talk a smackhead like this one could understand. "Y'know, speakin' of employments, you ever think of hirin' out to a shooting gallery, one of them carnivals? You should maybe think about that, this hit don't quite come together. You could pass for one of them clay pigeons easy. Suck up enough that bottom-of-the-line *basuco* you're on and them pellets wouldn't sting a bit. Flyweight tooter like you wouldn't feel a thing."

"Come on now—" Kasperson said, but before he could get any further Ducky vaulted out of his chair and lunged across the narrow space in front of the desk. His head was lowered in a boxer's crouch but his fists, only half clenched, were held high and swinging wildly. Morse rose up lightly and blocked a feeble windmilling punch with one arm. He brought the back of his other hand across Ducky's face, snapping it off to one side, and then he made a blade with the hand and in a short chopping blow drove it into his throat, collapsing him. Meat bounded to his feet, but Kasperson got around the desk in time to plant himself in his path. Starla shrank back against the wall. Ducky, sprawled on the floor, choking, went for the knife he kept strapped to his ankle.

Morse knew the move. " 'Less you're real well connected kingdom come-wise," he said contemptuously, "whatever you're reachin' for down there better be a jelly sandwich, 'cuz whatever it is you're gonna eat it."

Ducky hesitated. His eyes, tearful and angry as a child's, darted side to side. His hand fell away limply.

Like a flash fire, it was over before it began. Morse directed his coldest stare on Meat. "Same lunch waitin' for you."

A seismic tremor rolled across Meat's stunned, purpling face. Kasperson took a cautionary step back from him and lifted his open hands, moved them in deliberate circles as though he were polishing air. "Milo, think a minute," he said. "Do you want to jeopardize everything over a little scuffle? All our plans? All that money?" One of the polishing hands dropped in the general direction of Ducky. "Over *this?*"

Slowly Meat's expression shifted. There was no softening in it, only a kind of wolfish measuring, a summing up.

"Milo? Are you listening to what I'm saying?"

"I'm hearin' you, Doc. I'm hearin'."

He stooped down and gripped his blubbering partner under the arms and hauled him to his feet. His burning eyes never once came unlocked from Morse's. With a slow concentrated ferocity he said, "We'll be goin' now, Duck and me. But maybe we'll be talkin' again. Afterwards. You and me next time."

"Yeah, we'll have to do that," Morse said. "Little chat, I'm always agreeable."

XX

About an hour later, Morse was sitting across the table from Kasperson in a back booth of a neighborhood tavern on the far northwest side of town. He had a lite beer in front of him but he wasn't doing much with it. For this conversation he wanted a clear head, wanted not to miss a thing, not an inflection in the voice, a gesture, look, a single sliding glance. Kasperson sipped at a Scotch and water.

"You were able to find this place without any difficulty?"

"Oh yeah," Morse said. "Your directions, they were good."

Those directions had come off the scrap of paper he discovered pressed into his palm in the parting handclasp delivered by Kasperson as they left the office, shortly after the surly departure of Ducky and Meat. Morse had dropped Starla at his apartment, told her he had an errand to run, be back soon. Then, taking a circuitous route, taking care, he had driven here, parked in an alley across the street.

"And you're certain you weren't followed?"

"You don't have to worry any about that," Morse said.

From where he sat he had a clean view of the entrance. Now he scanned the rest of the room warily. It looked okay. A few lonely Sunday night juicers hunching over the bar. A twosome shuffling across the dance floor to the tinny beat of a mournful country ballad. A haze of blue smoke drifting through the air.

"Yes, I remember your saying you'd learned to watch your back. A useful talent in our profession. Still, you understand my concern. Explaining this little private chat to our confederates could be, well, awkward."

"Chance you take," Morse said with a shrug, show of indifference. He had come here to watch and listen, and he was willing to wait it out. He had time.

"Chance," Kasperson repeated, stringing out the word. "So much of life seems to turn on the whim of chance." He took another unhurried sip of Scotch. Let a silence fall.

Morse had time, but he didn't have forever either. "Anything particular you have in mind, this chance?"

"As a matter of fact, I was thinking of our upcoming project. All the split-second timing, surgical precision, all of that is smoke in the wind, Mr. Morse, as you well know. Real robbery, real crime, seldom works that way."

"Lot of it's luck," Morse said. It was something noncommittal to put into the lengthy pause.

"Luck, with an occasional dash of brute force. The calculated aggression I was talking about a few weeks ago. After tonight maybe you recognize the wisdom in that notion."

"Yeah, I pretty much had that one figured out."

Kasperson eased back in his seat, stroked his chin thoughtfully. "Are you familiar with the name of one Dr. Horace Fletcher, Mr. Morse?"

A shake of the head indicated he was not.

"In the annals of medicine there is no more instructive lesson than the tale of Horace Fletcher, M.D. You see, it was his contention that all of our digestive ailments could be traced to improper mastication. He maintained that the chewing of each morsel of food thoroughly—thirty-two times, to be exact—liquefying it prior to swallowing, this was the certain means of relief for our most troublesome gastric woes. Indeed, the theory is called by his name: Fletcherism." He paused again and, as though in homage to the physician, sloshed some Scotch around his mouth before resuming. "Sadly, legend has it Dr. Fletcher himself ultimately expired of chronic stomach upset."

"Maybe he should have tried some Rolaids."

Kasperson produced a small tolerant smile. "Let me offer you another anecdote, then. There was once an intrepid fellow—his name has since been lost to history—who undertook to go over the Falls at Niagara in a barrel. One of the few to survive that perilous adventure. Years later, so the story has it, he came to an untimely end by slipping on, of all things, a banana peel. In Australia, I think it was."

With the fingers of one hand Morse drew circles in a tiny puddle of liquid on the table top. "Y'know," he said, "it's real educational, talking with you. But I had the idea you invited me here to maybe talk some business too. Could be I was wrong."

"And so we are, Mr. Morse, discussing business. So we are. These little fables were intended merely to illustrate a long-held belief of mine. Some men, I think, go a long way to find their deaths; for others it's just around the corner and up the street."

"That may be. The trick, I suppose, is knowing which kind you are."

"Absolutely right. There's the riddle."

"I'm betting you've got some thoughts on it though."

"As it happens, I do. Consider our associates, cases in point. Now, I won't presume to speak for the lady; you know her far better than I. But my acquaintance with Milo and Conrad goes back a long time, and if I had to guess, I'd say they were destined to fall in that latter category. Both of them. Anyway, it does make for interesting speculation, don't you think?"

"What I'm wondering is where you'd put a couple of worthy gentlemen like ourselves in this speculating. You and me."

"To a great extent that would depend on what we're able to arrive at tonight," Kasperson said. He removed a shoe box from under the neatly folded coat on the seat beside him. He set it on the table carefully and pushed it over to Morse.

"Let me guess," Morse said. "Wouldn't be there's a flash bang in there?"

"Seems I was able to secure one after all."

"And you've got some ideas on how to use it."

"When, more so than how. It's not my place to tell you your business. But it did occur to me that at the point of the money transfer, in the woods, this could be useful. There are two of them, possibly even three. And one of you. I'm sure you understand that sooner or later a reckoning is unavoidable. And doubtless sooner than later."

Morse studied the paunchy face. Its expression was at once kindly and shrewd. "You know how these work?" he said. "They stun. They don't kill. Any killing gets done, it's got to come after. Right after."

Kasperson smiled again, broadly this time. He looked down into his glass as though he were gazing at a vision of the future that brought him boundless joy. And then he lifted his eyes and met Morse's stare. The smile went wistful. "It's one of the crueler axioms of our human condition that everyone's death inevitably simplifies life for someone else."

XX

It was after midnight when Morse got back to the apartment. All the lights were out, and Starla was in bed. Very quietly, he slipped out of his clothes and got under the covers. He lay there motionless, feeling the steady rhythm of her breathing. By an effort of will he loosened his taut muscles, made them go slack. No such luck with his mind: it ran riot with all the possibilities closing in on him.

"That must have been a serious errand," she murmured, and though the sound rising out of the dark was faint, it electrified him.

"You're supposed to be sleeping."

"How do you sleep anymore."

"Peacefully. Soundly. Like a baby. Lots of sweet dreams. Any I missed?"

"How about the sleep of the dead?"

"Maybe not that one yet."

Neither of them moved. She was lying on her stomach, her face turned toward him.

"Are you going to tell me what's happening, Mitch?"

"Nothing happening. I've got it all under control."

"You were with Kasperson."

"That's right."

The blackness of the room seemed to intensify the long interval of silence. Finally she said, "They're really going to try and kill us, aren't they. Like you said."

"Heavy on that *try*."

"Before, I didn't actually believe it. Didn't want to believe it."

"But now you do."

"Now I do."

"What convinced you?"

"It wasn't anything he said tonight—Milo. It wasn't that. It was the way he backed off. All the years I knew him, he's never done that. Ever. And he'll never leave it alone now. I know him."

"Anything else?"

"Yes. Kasperson. Your new friend. You see the glitter in his eyes when he talks about the money? You notice that?"

"We've all of us got that glitter," Morse said ruefully. "All of us."

"Not like his. You know he's got to be making plans."

"Yeah, well, we might just find a way to short-circuit all that foxy planning going on."

"We?"

"Us. You and me."

"You're sure?"

If there was a hesitation it was slight, barely perceptible. "I'm sure," he said.

"How?"

How? It was going to take some fast stutter-stepping, that much he knew. Fastest he'd ever done, snakiest. Mitch be nimble. "We've got four days to think on it," he said. "When the time comes, I'll tell you how."

She boosted herself onto her elbows, blinked at the outline of his features shrouded in night. He seemed to be staring fixedly at the ceiling. She came over beside him and put a tentative hand on his shoulder.

"Tomorrow comes early," he said.

"I know. I don't want that. No toys or games or any of that tonight. I want you just to hold me. Can you do that?"

"Sure I can."

He opened an arm and she slipped inside it, folded herself into him. Tangled clusters of her hair fell across his chest. Her fingers brushed his face, traced the lids of his eyes, his nose, lips, the line of his jaw. There was in that gentle touch a clear and simple need, a tenderness even, and Morse was overtaken by an unsteady feeling he understood nothing at all in this world. Nothing and no one. Himself least of all. He held her close.

"I'm scared, Mitch. Really scared."

"Don't be," he said, and remembering Kasperson's fine theory about progress in the universal journey toward death, he said also, "We're not going to get our numbers pulled. Not yet. It's not our turn."

Long after she slept he lay there, gazing into the somber dark. He thought about what he had told her. His brave words mocked him. And holding her in that chaste embrace, he thought about the prison he had fashioned for himself all his life, not of sex certainly and certainly not of love. Not of money even. None of those. But he recognized he was captive all the same, of that blurry sustaining vision of himself he had once tried, haltingly, to explain to Jean Satterfield: Mitchell Morse, The Hammer. Captive of his own legend, and of the lonely impulse to test the limits of that urgent vision. Reckless impulse, suicidal.

Once or twice he slid into that shadowy margin between consciousness and sleep, and when he did he seemed to hear voices calling to him from across the years. Across the distance widening between him and his invulnerable, departed youth. Voices of clarity and strength and, yes, even a kind of skewed nobility. Until an ungovernable spasm shook him back into wakefulness, into the oppressive silence of the room, and he was swamped by a sorrow alien and acute and vast. Because at just that moment he knew his choice had been made, which way he was going to go.

XX

In another darkened room, Meat was wrestling with emotions just as intense though much more clearly focused. From the bed next to his came the querulous bleating sounds of a narcotized whimper.

"You took some hard lumps, Duck, past weeks," he said. His voice was harsh, final. "But it's their turn comin' up now. Four days. Payback time. All of 'em. I promise you."

TWENTY-SEVEN

PUNCTUALLY AT 5:45 the next day, Doyle stepped out of the elevator and turned into the corridor leading to the offices of United Hairlines. Outside it was pouring down another grim sleety rain, and he paused and did what he could to arrange his sadly disheveled hair. When he looked up, he saw a familiar figure hurrying by, swaying ever so slightly and fumbling with an umbrella.

"Dr. Kasperson?"

Kasperson stopped and stared at him blankly a moment. "Oh yes. Doyle. Fortunate we met. Miss Reneau is not available today and so I'm afraid we must postpone your treatment."

Doyle's face seemed to fall to pieces. Kasperson shot a jittery glance over his shoulder and down the hall. "Have no fear, my friend," he said buoyantly. "Your treatments will resume soon. Very soon." He grasped Doyle firmly at the elbow, wheeled him about and led him away. "Here, come along now and join me in a bit of refreshment. We can take this opportunity to review your progress."

Though he was still upset over the aborted treatment, a share of Doyle's dismay faded. For over a week he had been trying to nail down an appointment with the elusive trichologist. Without success (Can't now, he's busy in the lab; No, he's with a patient; Nope, not in tonight). This could be the chance he was looking for: get some final answers, make some final choices.

Downstairs they huddled under the umbrella and set out up the street. Kasperson pointed them to a saloon in the next block. A throng of rowdy drinkers, working-class types mostly, milled through the place. The back bar was adorned with bowling trophies, and a sign on the wall warned: *If you can't be happy here, you won't be happy in heaven.*

They found a table and got themselves settled. Eventually a cocktail waitress sidled over. She wore a silky pink blouse and hot pants a brighter shade of the same hue. Her stumpy legs were sheathed in iridescent fishnet stockings. "What's yours?" she demanded, unsmiling. Evidently the message on the wall had been lost on her. Doyle looked to Kasperson for direction.

"I think a glass of beer would do nicely."

Doyle ordered the same.

Off she sauntered.

"I like to stop in here occasionally for a friendly glass of beer," Kasperson remarked. "Beer or port wine is nourishing and not mucus-forming like your cow's milk. Far more people suffer from the ingestion of cow milk than those who moderately—mind I say moderately—use beer or wine. You would do well to think that over."

Simultaneously did Doyle give it some passing thought and pay for the beers set out before them. Kasperson lifted his glass. "To abundant hair."

Doyle took a short nervous swallow. "Y'know, that's what I been meaning to talk to you about," he said. His voice was shaky. Desperation's quaver. His eyes shifted about the room. "My hair. How you think it's, uh, coming along."

Kasperson put down the glass and opened his arms in a wide acquiescent gesture. "I'm at your disposal."

"See, I know the treatments are helping," Doyle said earnestly. "I know that. But the thing of it is, I got some plans I got to make, and I got to make 'em right away, this week, and these plans, see, they kind of depend on keeping my hair. Getting it back, actually. Like we first talked about. Back in October. And I know you can't make guarantees and all, but I was hoping maybe you could tell me . . . help me . . ." The words, which had come in a tumbling rush, trailed away now in an agony of doubt.

A look of infinite compassion flooded Kasperson's serene saggy face. "Doyle, my very good friend," he said, spacing his own words with a staunch deliberation, "ordinarily your observation would be absolutely correct, inarguable: Guarantees on this mortal coil of ours belong to"—he allowed his pious eyes to drift slowly toward the ceiling—"that Master Craftsman who guides the destiny of each of us." He paused, stifled a rising burp. The look switched abruptly: compassion into triumph. "However! In your particular case I can say, without equivocation and with every confidence, the full recovery—and retention—of your hair is not only a likelihood, it is a certainty."

"But how can you—"

"Be so sure?" Kasperson finished for him. "Oh, I've been studying your condition closely, ever since we chanced on each other at the elevator. It's a habit born out of a lifetime in the profession."

Doyle's eyes widened, as though limitless new vistas unrolled before him. "You mean then—? You're saying you can—?" The word seemed to catch in his throat, formidable as the panoramic vision it inspired: "Guarantee?"

"You have my word," Kasperson said solemnly. "As a trichologist."

The tumor is benign, the operation an unqualified success, the check in the mail has arrived, nick of time, the enemy routed, the gods are securely in their heaven, smiling. Doyle felt all these things and more. At the thirteenth hour this singular, crazy-spoken man sitting opposite him, placidly sipping beer, had come to rescue him. He stumbled over an expression of gratitude.

"No need to thank me," Kasperson said, all humility. "The restoration of your hair will be reward enough."

Doyle was galvanized at the prospect, eager to get from here to there. "When can I make up tonight's treatment? Tomorrow? I could come in tomorrow."

"Oh, you'll want to give it a while," Kasperson said quickly. "Until Miss Reneau is with us again."

"What's wrong with her? Sick?"

"It's the husband. Unfortunate case. Chronic cardiac condition. Nothing serious this time, I understand, but she felt needed at his side. How could I refuse?"

Heartened at his own magnanimity, he emptied his glass and put two fingers in the air. The waitress brought over more beer. "Allow me to get this," Kasperson said, holding up a bill. Change was made. Once she was gone he started in again.

"Splendid practitioner, Miss Reneau. My right hand at the Clinic. A bit weak as a theoretician perhaps, but for my ultimate purposes this is a minor shortcoming. I expect big things from her one day, and I hope to place her responsibly and well."

"Yeah, she's talked about that some," Doyle said around a long hearty gulp. He had eaten next to nothing all day, and another beer on an empty stomach, the warming glow of a settled future, the steamy intimacy of a dimly lit tavern, the sleet pelting the window, Kasperson's easy confidential manner—all combined to embolden him to ask, "What got you interested in this line of work, anyway? You don't mind my asking."

"Not at all. What is it motivates a man to devote his life to an ideal?" His gaze turned inward for a long moment, in search of an answer to the rhetorical question.

"Naturopathy. The foundation of my calling. Consider its etymology: *pathy* from the Greek, signifying treating disease; *naturo* from the obvious root *nature*. Treating diseases naturally.

"I was raised on the farm, you see, and I came early to appreciate the joys and rewards of natural living—*living,* as over against *suffering*. Later, as a youth on my own during the hard years, I was thrust in contact with modes of living utterly foreign to my simple upbringing. I saw the misery that went with them, those modes. And it pained me to see the extent of that misery. It gnawed at me. A lesser man—or possibly a more callous one—would have found his niche and ignored the plight of his fellow man. Not so I. I simply wasn't made that way. Why, I might have been a doctor of medicine or minister of the gospel had the times and circumstances permitted. As it was, I was destitute, enriched only by my desire to contribute, and by—I flatter myself—a keen if undisciplined intellect."

Doyle smothered a yawn. He was beginning to regret his question. Their glasses were empty again. "Another?" he said.

Kasperson nodded affirmatively. As soon as the beers were delivered, he resumed.

"I cast about me for a way to serve. It was clear I could never enter any of the recognized professions, so I put my wits to work on other means of alleviating the general distress. I asked myself: What are some of the causes of unhappiness? And it came to me one day in an intuitive flash, almost an illumination, you might say, that those seldom-considered problems of the hair were the source of more anxiety than perhaps any other single ill the flesh is heir to. I had discovered a vocation.

"I embarked upon a regimen of deep study. I gave over my days and nights to the maladies of the scalp, their origins and treatment and correction. I haunted libraries, pored over ponderous tomes. Then I emerged from my self-imposed ivory tower to observe the work currently being done. I was appalled at the charlatans growing fat on the fears of the innocent. And I determined then and there to preach the gospel of healthy hair as I knew it to be true. As you yourself have found it to be true. Needless to say, my unique approach met with bitter opposition from the established interests. Believe me when I say it hasn't been easy."

Doyle bobbed his head in a display of sympathy, but his attention had wandered to a pinball machine at the end of the bar and the youth with a sweeping, patent leather ducktail who was playing it. When no free games came, he banged it viciously. The scowling bartender told him to ease up.

"Fuckin' thing's rigged, ain't it."

"Get wise, numbnuts. You ain't gonna beat it. It's for fun."

"Some fun," the young man said, and fumbled in his pocket for another coin.

Kasperson, meanwhile, pressed on.

"No, it's never been easy. Wherever I've gone they've fought me, but always there remains the unimpeachable truth of what I do." His voice elevated in proud crescendo. It carried along a trace of a slur. "Rejuvenated heads of dying hair! New thatches of hair where once there had been none! Young men like yourself, and old as well, women too, made whole again, confident!"

He recessed long enough to wipe a bit of foam from his upper lip. "Let's order a pitcher, shall we? Obviate the need for all these troublesome refills."

Doyle excused himself and walked to the men's room in the back. His step was uneven, his head inflated, the scalp prickly. While waiting a turn at the rusted trough of a urinal, he checked his hairline in the mirror over the sink. It looked pretty good. Holding fast and possibly even making some slight gains at the once barren wings. Tomorrow and the next day he'd double up on the home maintenance routine. Fuck Twyla. Nothing for him to worry about anymore. He felt at peace with the world, though he couldn't avoid noticing the message scrawled by some disgruntled naysayer across the facing wall: Lets join hands and piss on the hole fucking universe.

There was a full glass waiting for him at the table. Half the pitcher was gone, and Kasperson was pouring himself another.

"What is more pleasant," he asked mid-pour, "than confidences shared between friends? How long has it been since I've opened the briefcase of my past? Yet I sense in you, Doyle, the same qualities of the idealist and dreamer that quicken my own ambition. Where would we be without our dreams and the grit to turn them into reality?"

Doyle felt a curious warmth, a beery flush of affection for this blustery windbag of a man who had delivered him from a lifetime sentence to Twyla Acres. So what if he was a little crackers? Who could quarrel with success, and he was wearing its badge up top right now. Or would be soon. "Do you, uh, plan to keep on here in Grand Rapids?" he asked. "I mean, after the treatments are over I'd like to, well, maybe just stop by sometime. Say hello." He found himself clearing a thick throat. "I'll owe you a lot, you know."

Kasperson waved aside the acknowledgment. "Quite the contrary, it is *I* owe you and your trust an immeasurable debt. Here, young lady, renew this if you will."

He extended the empty pitcher to the waitress ambling by, then turned again to Doyle.

"Now, in answer to your question I should say both yes and no. By that I mean yes, I will be here a time, consolidating my position, so to speak. And yes, in spirit I will always be here through the work of my people, such as Miss Reneau. But no, finally, when my task here is complete I will move on to my destiny."

The pitcher was set down with a rude thump, sloshing some beer over the table. Kasperson attended to the pouring. Doyle paid.

"The greatest hair clinic in the history of mankind," Kasperson declaimed, an oracular glaze shimmering in his eyes, "staffed by the greatest array of hair-restoring talent the world has ever known, with branches reaching from coast to coast in all the major cities of our land. Eventually—doubtless after I'm gone—fame of my Method spreading to the tiniest hamlet, putting relief within the grasp of every man. *That* is my destiny. That will be my fulfillment.''

Even to Doyle this seemed a trifle overblown. ''But do you think,'' he asked hesitantly, ''there's enough people really . . . interested?''

''In one way or another, directly or through loved ones, the shadow of baldness clouds the lives of us all. They say we must all be bald finally. This I cannot accept! I will prove them wrong. Here, hand me your glass.''

Doyle handed it over and it came back full. ''I don't know,'' he said. ''Do you think people will care that much?''

''They will care. How many men, at this very moment, in this single community, are dousing their heads with some unproductive slickum? They will care. You cared.''

In all his life Doyle had never encountered such singleness of purpose, and it made him feel impoverished somehow. In the face of it his quibbling seemed mean of spirit. Still, he ventured one last doubt. ''What I mean is, don't you think your average man—y'know, the kind who doesn't have a whole lot to hope for, look forward to—don't you think he's sort of given up? I mean, I've seen guys who don't seem to mind being bald.''

''They will care, when they *know,*'' Kasperson intoned.

The pitcher was empty. Kasperson sat silently, pondering the augury he seemed to take from his drained glass. Shortly he heaved a great sigh, belched softly. ''The hour grows late and the little woman worries.'' He wobbled to his feet and offered a parting hand. ''I can't tell you how gratifying it's been, Doyle, sharing our goals and reflections this way. We must chat again soon. Till then, au revoir.''

Using the umbrella like a walking stick, he moved deliberately toward the door.

XX

He drove the same as he walked: with exaggerated caution. No tripping on a DWI. Not now. Come this far. The expressway was thick with traffic. Cars swooped down on him and hurtled on by, either side, kicking up muddy slush. Pigtails of smoke curled from their exhausts. Their receding lights made tiny paired holes in the night. Sleet lashed the windshield. The wipers strummed a steady hypnotic beat.

His exit came into view and he edged carefully into the right lane and coasted onto the ramp. He steered the station wagon through side streets lined with frame houses. Christmas trees glowed in their windows and, on many of them, colored lights wound over porches and eaves. Here and there a manger scene decorated a lawn. Up ahead was the Julius house. He swung into the driveway. A touch at the genie button and the garage door rose. He eased the wagon under it and brought it down behind him. Reflexively, he sprayed his mouth with Binaca before he went inside.

The house was dark, blessedly silent. No sour widow waiting to grill him tonight. Or ever again, for that matter. He collapsed into a living room chair. Very tense, very weary. A little loosener might be good, short one, glide him off to sleep. But inertia decided him against it. Inertia, and a head pitching from all the beer and all the Scotch before that, tossed down in the solitude of the Clinic office. A hail-and-farewell gesture. Dead soldier now, that comforting bottle of Scotch, casualty of the inevitable melancholy that overtook him whenever a scam was coming to a close.

Still, there was solace in the knowledge that everything was in order, all the pieces securely in place. More or less securely. Reflecting on it cheered him some, and so he directed his thoughts that way. Run it by one more time, see how it plays.

The hit itself was out of his hands. Natural selection would determine who survived the encounter in the woods seventy-two short hours from now; all he had to do was keep down. Right now his money was on Morse, but even if he was wrong he was confident Morse would take out at least one of them, either Ducky or Meat. If he were lucky maybe the three of them would cancel each other out. And if he weren't, well, the provisions he'd made for that final hurdle were quite adequate. Drastic, maybe, but equal to any eventuality.

The widow was safely out of the picture. Yesterday he'd waved her off on a Greyhound to Coldwater, a holiday visit with the daughter and family. A week of cooing over grandkiddies, bouncing them on a fat knee. Coldwater. Apt destination, given her temperament. He was to bring the wagon down Christmas Eve, join the festivities. Grandma's business partner and special friend.

Sure. A sorry day it would be when you found the likes of a D. C. Kasperson in a place called Coldwater. Don't wait up.

The Clinic was shuttered for good. Tonight's errand. Dealing with Miss Reneau, that was something of a ragged end. He owed her back pay, and his share of the stake money was dwindling fast. Just enough remaining, in point of fact, to get him out of town, should things go badly. A prudent man always had an alternative waiting in the wings. And he was nothing if not prudent. So the way to handle the issue of Miss Reneau, he had wisely concluded, was to do nothing at all. Avoidance had its merits too.

Likewise with that persistent worm, Gilley, though admittedly his appearance tonight was mildly discomposing. He had forgotten the eminently forgettable Gilley altogether, and he certainly wouldn't want to tangle with anyone built like that. Lucky he intercepted him at the elevator, turned him around. Rather tidily, at that. Nothing serious. Nothing a little bromide-seltzer couldn't manage. Some inspired smoke-blowing. And of smoke there was an inexhaustible supply.

So all the bases were covered. Slider time. Get on the good side of the money, a six-hour run to Milwaukee, a few days under wraps—plenty of places there—and presto! it's goodbye bone-chilling rain, blue snow, balding heads, and hello tropical sun, white sandy beaches, blissful ease. Sweet release.

So why was he still feeling desolate? Why? He knew why. It was the seductive lure of the shuffle, the sport of it, the game. A world full of eager fish, like the pitiable Gilley back there, waiting to be reeled in. Begging for it. And all it ever required was the dazzling verbal blitz that rose spontaneously to his lips. An unstoppered voice inside him. A torrent of words. There was a genius in what he did, what he had. A gift. Life, for him, was one long mischievous prank, and when the pranking was done, *he* was done. Sweet release? He knew better. Not so long as there were words to give breath to, and witless ears to hear.

PART FIVE

TWENTY-EIGHT

AFTER THE FIRST DRINK she felt a little better, not much, but into the second her spirits began to droop again and she brought the conversation around to the topic uppermost on her mind. Across the table, Billy Schooley listened with a show of sympathetic interest, even though he was getting a little sick of hearing about Mitchell Morse. Still, the way he figured, the best thing to do was just wait it out. Right now they were friends is all, buddies, but you never could tell what might develop. Maybe tonight wasn't the night, but maybe it wasn't so far off either. He could wait.

"How long's it been since you seen him?" Billy asked.

"Three weeks," she said glumly. "More than that, closer to a month."

"He still with Fleets?"

"Last I heard."

"How about you? How you holdin' up?"

"Not so good, Billy."

That's not how he saw it. Miserable or not, Jean Satterfield was looking good lately, slimmer, more makeup on her face, hair growing out and fashionably styled. They were sitting in the 44th Street tavern he had recommended when she suggested a drink after work. He liked to hang out there sometimes, a working man's joint, full up tonight with hardhats getting themselves zonked for Christmas Eve. Coming through the door in their AAPS uniforms, they'd had to listen to some ragging. "Hey, Billy," somebody had called, "there's a real bad dude on the loose tonight. Fatty. Long white beard. Wears a red suit. You an' the lady better skate on back out there, collar 'im.'' It got a big hooting laugh all around. After enough of it he'd cranked up his badass look, the one he learned from watching Morse, and that slowed the comedians down a little.

So he was feeling pretty mellow right about now, Billy was, couple beers in him, holiday arrived, long weekend ahead. Except Jean, she was still sad-eyed, downcast. He wished he could think of something funny to say, pick her up. Since he could not, he tried another route.

''What you got going for Christmas?''

She gave a slack-limbed shrug. ''Nothing much. Nothing. Some people coming by tomorrow. Relatives, friends of my parents.''

''Do your present opening tonight?'' His thought was, if he kept talking long enough maybe he could bring her out of it.

''In the morning,'' she said in voice that seemed to be running down.

''How about the rest of the days off?'' he said cautiously. ''You got anything, uh, planned?''

No immediate reply. Her eyes had gone blank, assumed a kind of mournful, mid-distance stare. Like she was half in the bag already. From a few other after-work stops like this one, Billy knew she was no drinker, but Jesus!—two brandies? Finally she said, ''Billy, did he ever talk much about women?''

''Who's that?'' he said with something of a sigh. Of course he knew perfectly well who. Tonight was definitely not the night.

''Mitch.''

''Well,'' Billy said, going worldly now, macho, ''you put a couple guys together, partnering, there's going to be women talk.''

''That's not what I mean. Exactly. What I'm asking is, was he seeing anyone? Anyone special?''

''Nobody I know of.'' Which was in fact true. In fact, the real truth of it was that Morse had never revealed much of anything about himself, at least not to him. But all along Billy had let on to her that they were really tight, so he added slyly, ''Course a fella like Mitch, he's bound to keep a, y'know, stable.''

A sudden anger flashed in her eyes, displacing the hurt. ''Why do you say that? You don't know that.''

Billy put up defensive hands. ''Okay, okay. I don't *know* it. Not for sure. You asked, I'm telling you my opinion.''

"I don't believe it."

Billy was getting fed up with this line of conversation. "One thing I do know," he said exasperatedly, "is guys like Morse, they just naturally bounce from one broad to the next. You notice I'm saying broads here, which you sure as hell aren't. And if you don't mind my saying, straight out, friend to friend, I think what you ought to do is forget all about him. Face up, he dumped on you."

"Dumped on me?"

"What else are you going to call it?"

She was remembering the last time she saw Mitch, the stranded look on his face as she drove away. Dumped on her? Maybe. But maybe there was something going on then he couldn't tell her, trouble of some kind. It was possible, even with that woman there in his apartment. She'd never actually given him a chance to explain. Maybe now was the time he needed her most. She remembered also something he'd said on another occasion: Anything Billy says to do, you do it just the other way. A dim idea, fueled by the drinks, began to take shape in her head. "I don't know what to call it," she said, much more gently.

"Call it like it is and let it be. That's my best advice. Anyway, pretty girl like you can do a whole lot better."

Jean glanced at her watch. Driving into work this morning she'd heard the radio announcement of Fleets closing early tonight. For what she had in mind, there was some time to do in yet. She reached over and laid an apologetic hand on his arm. "I'm sorry I snapped at you, Billy. And I'm sure that's good advice. What do you say we have one more drink? I'll buy."

Billy looked at the hand resting on his arm, thinking, Could be I was wrong about tonight. Shit, no way to tell with women. "Never turn down a drink or a lady, either one," he said, producing a hearty laugh to go with the clever line, first one he'd been able to get off all evening.

XX

Laughter was rippling through the business office of the Plainfield Fleets, that same moment, some of it the high, tinkling, slightly boozy variety; the Christmas party was well underway and Eddie, with a broad wink at policy, had doctored the holiday punch. Needs a little fortifying, he announced rakishly; Christmas only comes once a year. Desks and tables heaped with mounds of unsold bakery goodies completed the festive spread. Tinsel garlands snaked around the walls, and over in a corner a perfectly symmetrical metallic tree glittered like a silvery beacon. A sprig of mistletoe hung from a doorjamb, inspiring long wet kisses, giggly butt pinching, a copped feel or two. The room was crammed with people: office personnel, been at it the better part of the afternoon; cashiers and baggers and shelf-stockers, in and out on their breaks; wholesalers and suppliers stopped by to join the fun; friends and assorted well-wishers—the extended Fleets family. Lots of flushed, joyous faces. Some of the merrymakers, lingered too long at the punch bowl, were already reeling; all of them were bubbling over with fellowship and boisterous good cheer.

All but one.

Morse stood by himself in the corner by the tree, clutching a plastic cup filled with the treacly punch. Occasionally he sipped at it—but mostly he just smoked and, when it was necessary, opened his face in a stiff smile and said the things you say at frolics like this. Eddie came over, draped an arm across his shoulders and urged him to lighten up, drink up. Once a year, he reminded. His eyes were going shimmery, voice slurry, and a jewel of a sugar crumb sparkled between his front teeth. Morse grinned for him and lifted the cup to his lips. Whatever it took.

He was tight as a coiled spring. Behind all the forced beaming he attended closely to his own thoughts, focused them. Preview of coming attractions.

The squeeze, he concluded, in this final preview, could come at either of two points (three, actually, but Kasperson he figured he could handle afterward, minimum of force). They might try to take him out at the moment of the hit on the armored car. They might, but he didn't think so. Too much confusion, getting the guards secured, getting the money in the back, getting away clean. Also they'd know a quick hop into the front seat would put him safely behind bulletproof glass, and with the driver under his gun, and therefore the car under his control. So it wasn't likely they'd try anything cute by the car. For certain, he'd have to watch himself there, but Kasperson was probably right, probably it would be coming at the money transfer, in the seclusion of the trees off the road. There now, there was your squeeze, right there. Slice-and-dice time. The moves he threw (and he'd rehearsed them in his head a hundred times: slow motion, fast forward, freeze frame, the whole screening) were going to have to be his best ones, best he had in him. The error margin was exactly zip. Miss even one and he could suit up for your heavenly choir.

They could hold the robes. There was nobody'd seen all the Mitchell Morse moves yet. Not yet. He could still dazzle them.

Time crawled by. He was ready to get on with it, get it done. All the gear was in place: sapper gloves in the outer pockets of the jacket stashed in his locker, a loaded .25 semiaut in one inside pocket, silencer in the other. The flash bang lay on the locker floor, along with a roll of heavy tape. No way would it fit in the jacket, too conspicuous to the guard coming through the door. So he'd worked out another little idea, going to require another big league move. Had to do it; the flash bang was his ace. But an ace, he understood, none better, was only as good as its play, and the longer he thought about that the more wired he got.

After a while he edged through the crowd, dodged around the kissing bandits stationed like ambushers at the mistletoe, and went out onto the floor. Last-minute shoppers thronged the aisles. Cash registers jangled. Feverish music—piped-in carols—seemed to trumpet off the ceiling. He walked over to the line of pay phones by an exit and dialed Starla's number.

XX

Starla came sprinting out of the bedroom and lifted the receiver on the second ring. Her greeting was upward inflected, a twittery searching question.

"Me. Mitch."

"Mitch? What's happened? Something's happened."

"Easy, nothing's happened. Just checking in."

"Oh."

After a sufficient pause Morse said, "Well?"

"What?"

"I'm asking how you're doing."

"I don't know," she said. Not quite true. She knew exactly how she was doing. Fogged, numbed, dazed, fumbling like a nightwalker down the passageways of perilous dreams: that was how she was doing. Infected with dread. It was one thing to think about this deadly exercise, plan it, talk it through endlessly, rehearse it, fix it in the mind's eye; it was another to arrive at the crossing, no turning back.

"You're going to do fine," he said.

She repeated she didn't know.

"You got everything in order?" he asked, coming at it from another angle.

"I think so."

"You packed?"

She looked through the open bedroom door. A single vinyl bag, empty, unzippered, its top lifted, sat on the bed. Disordered piles of clothes circled it, most of them hers, a few his. "Almost. I can't get much in just one."

"One's all we need. Traveling light. Feathers in the wind, remember?"

"I remember."

"Couple other things I told you, too. Remember them?"

"I think I do."

"Look, Starla, I got to hear something better than *think*."

"I do. I remember all you said."

"I'm hoping that's the case. Counting on it. Otherwise we can book rooms, your mortuary arms. Pine box suite. Both of us. You follow what I'm saying here?"

"I follow."

"Good girl. Now, you remember what you're going to do once we're in those trees?"

"Yes."

"Whyn't you tell me again."

"I watch for your signal."

"Which will be coming when?"

"When the last money bag's in the van."

"Then what?"

"Then I slam the back doors shut, behind me, fast, and drop to the ground."

"Doing what?"

"Covering my head."

"That's it. Good. Anything else?"

"What else?"

A heavy sigh rode down the line. "The keys, Starla. The keys to the van."

"Keys, right. The keys. I've got them on me. Taken them out."

"When?"

"Before I open the back doors."

"That's a swing point. You know Kasperson's not going to dirty his hands, any of this action. More'n likely he'll be up front, passenger seat. Forget those keys and we'll be standing there with our jaws dropped, looking at his exhaust."

"I won't forget them."

"Thataway," he said, "play the anthem and get the ball in the air. We're ready to scrimmage."

There was an interval of silence. Finally she said, "Mitch, are we going to make it?" It was a needful question, urgently phrased.

"Course we are. Think loose. Loose is what does it every time."

Either he misunderstood or, for reasons of his own, chose to dance around it. She tried again. "What about . . . after?"

"Be in Detroit by midnight, easy. Just like I told you. Get down, wait for the climate to cool. No problem, that end. Detroit's my turf." He spooned out the words carefully, patiently, a tutor drilling a slightly backward child.

Once more she tried. "No, after that, I mean."

"Ride the wind, after that."

Dancing. She let it go. And she recognized, with a certain melancholy resignation, if there was a breach anywhere in this circle of betrayal, tightening fast, it was going to be up to her to discover it. Find her own way out. Like it always had been, all her life. "I'd better get off," she said. "They'll be here soon."

But she hesitated, gripping the phone, and gazed through the kitchen window at the trailer next door, silhouetting moment by moment in the waning light. In a voice no longer stricken but puzzled somehow, uncertain, she said, "I can't, you know, get it into my head it's really about to happen. I mean, it's hard to get it to make sense. Can you understand that?"

"Yeah, well," Morse said, and in his own voice there was something almost wistful behind the dry sardonic edge, "what we're doing here, you don't ask it to make a whole lot of sense."

XX

There was another, similar, review going on just then in a room in a northside motel, Meat the tutor here, Ducky the fidgety incurious pupil.

"Okay," Meat said, concluding his summary, "you think you got all that down?"

"Bet your ass."

"Better give it to me again."

"Why again?"

The question provoked a wordless growl.

Ducky elevated a hand in a sloppy salute, testing the limits of his partner's indulgence, and in a high chirpy voice played back the steps he had committed more or less indifferently to memory. But as he warmed to the recitation, straying from the script here and there, extemporizing, a kinetic surge propelled his arms in twitchy, puppet gestures. The sallow skin drawn tight over the fragile cheekbones took on a flushed pinkish cast, and behind all the spasmodic blinking a fierce glint seemed to invade his eyes.

Meat watched him narrowly. Triple hit, administered less than half an hour ago, was beginning to seize hold. Give it another few minutes and the little fucker's brains would be boiling, every spark and cylinder in that puny wiry frame running on overload. Which was how it had to be, get him up for tonight, get him pumped, viper mean. Get back the old Duck, good-luck charm. It was chancy, rocket ride like that. Dice roll, gamble you took. Plenty of time to bring him down easy, after.

He hadn't been paying much attention to the Ducky monologue (they'd been over it enough; it was just a way of chewing time) and about midway along he stopped listening altogether. His thoughts began to wander. Earlier in the day he had driven, alone, out to the Dokken farm, squared things away. The plane, he learned, was gassed up and ready to go, flight conditions looking okay. Skim in low over the border and they'd be touched down in Canuck country before midnight. Arrangements were made to leave the pickup at a designated spot in town. Last piece of Dokken business was the bow. The distance he'd be firing from, no way could he rely on a handgun. Rifle was out of the question: too much racket. But the bow, now that was an inspired solution. If he could drop a running deer at fifty yards—and he could—then nailing the guard at the rear of the car be nothing. He borrowed a Forked Lightning and a couple broadhead arrows, told them he'd leave the bow in the pickup. Fuck, tell 'em anything. Wouldn't mean shit anyway, after tonight.

They had sealed the bargain with a sweaty handclasp. No

hard feelings about the, uh, other, he'd been assured. The twenty long supposed to change hands, that covered a lot of hurts, both sides. See about that *supposed*. Dokkens, they had a little to answer for yet too, and as long as it was a night for score settling, might as well make it a sweep. Leave your whole house in order.

Coming back into town he'd driven by the dry cleaners and checked out the vehicle one more time. Big Ford Econoline, cargo van, clothes hauler, sliding panel on the side, wide back doors. Just what they needed. They'd scouted it, over a week now. Cleaners closed at five, van parked out back. Piece of angel food cake.

". . . then after we lift that paper off the Doc we learn him a lesson, how you change a five in threes, and then we—"

Meat raised a hand in an emphatic gesture that said stop.

Ducky stopped. He had been pacing excitedly, arms fluttering, mouth flapping tirelessly. Now he turned an anxious face on Meat and stammered, "What? . . . that ain't right? . . . that part? But you said we was—"

"Nah, you got it right. Sit down, give it a rest."

Ducky dropped into a chair. He reached an arm behind him and, like a restless chimp, scratched a shoulder blade. He brought the back of the other arm across his damp nostrils. A foot tapped an agitated beat on the floor.

"You got your piece?" Meat asked him.

He patted the right-hand pocket of his jacket.

"Pillowcase?"

He pointed to the left pocket.

"How about your whittler?"

He lifted the tapping foot, displayed an ankle.

"Look like you're all set."

"Hey, you're scopin' the sandman here, Meato," he said, face creasing in a wicked toothy grin.

Meat looked at his watch, then lumbered to his feet. "Okay, sandman. Whaddya say we get off the fuckin' dime, get 'er done. Go get ourselves a van and a couple million fish. Payback to boot. Whaddya say?"

Ducky sprang out of the chair. "Say, look out world, here come two hard-case homes. Baddest this side Jacktown."

"Jacktown shooters, that's us. Like the old days."

For a moment the flare in those glistening eyes seemed to

dim, and in a dwindling voice Ducky said, "Couple real shooters, we was. Them days."

"Still are, Duck. We still are."

Meat extended open palms, Ducky gave them the ritual slap, and they were on their way.

XX

After the comradely chat with Kasperson, Doyle was convinced he was on his way too—until he arrived at the Clinic shortly after five that evening and discovered the lights out and the door securely bolted. Same as it had been the night before. The tremolo of doubt that had sounded in a distant chamber of his head then, twenty-four hours ago, rose now to a crescendo of fear. Almost a week gone by since his last treatment. Why wasn't it open? Where could they be? Maybe it was nothing, he reasoned. Holiday week, Christmas Eve tonight, they were probably closing early. Had to be some kind of logical explanation. And he kept telling himself it was certainly nothing as he searched frantically through the empty corridors of the building for someone, anyone, who would confirm his conviction.

On the ground floor he found a custodian, grouchy old fart with a withered leg (but also an abnormally thick swag of silvery hair, Doyle couldn't help noting), who answered his query with, "Beats shit outta me. Been shut up all week."

"*All* week?"

"What'd I just say? You deef?" And then, scenting the dismay his words inspired, he added spitefully, "Look to me like they flew the coop. Always figured 'em for crooks."

Doyle's belly knotted and his lips began to twitch. An awful panic seized him. He spun on his heels and got out of there, hurried down the street. He turned in at the tavern, site of his last conversation with the man who had promised him deliverance, took a barstool and ordered a beer. Had to chill out, puzzle it through. Might be there was still an answer he'd overlooked, something obvious, something he'd get a chuckle over, remembering it later, six months from now, say, after the treatments were done and his hair restored and his life back on track.

The place was quiet except for the pinball freak, at it again, same dude from the other night, all that slicked greasy hair. The cocktail waitress stood behind him looking on, and the bartender glowered at a Christmas special on the television.

Maybe it was an emergency, Doyle thought, calling Kasperson out of town. Some family crisis. Could be that. But where then was Miss Reneau, why wasn't she there? Miss Reneau. Of course. He glanced around for a pay phone. None in sight. There was, however, a phone on the back counter and he signaled the liverish bartender and asked to use it. "Business line," he was admonished, "make it quick." Doyle pointed at the directory and it was thumped insolently onto the bar. "Merry fucking Christmas to you too," Doyle muttered, but softly and under his breath.

He scanned the R's. Nothing, no Reneau. And then it came back to him: the ailing husband, Harvey Plum, hatcher of pathetic deluded schemes. He found the Plum listing and dialed that number.

"This is Plum's," a rough male voice announced.

"Is, uh, Mrs. Plum there?"

"She is. Who's callin'?"

"Name is Gilley, Doyle Gilley." He felt obliged to add, "I know her from the Clinic."

"Huh, *that* place. Okay, hold on."

He heard footsteps falling away. There was a short silence, then a rather shrill "Hay-lo."

No mistaking, it was Miss Reneau. Doyle identified himself again.

"Oh, hi. How are ya?"

"Well," Doyle said, straining to subdue the flutter in his voice, "tell you the truth, I'm a little worried. I been to the Clinic and, well, it looks closed."

"You're worried. How do you think *I* feel?"

"What do you mean? What's happened?"

"Dunno. I been in every day this week and it's been locked up tighter'n a drum. I tried callin' and they tell me the phone's disconnected. Dr. Kasperson's not in the book, and nobody answers out to Mrs. Julius'. You heard anything?"

"God, no, that's why I'm calling you. I was just up there. But I saw him Monday night, Dr. Kasperson. He must be here. Maybe he's sick."

"Yeah. Maybe. Sure hope it's not serious. See, he owes me a month's back pay and we're gettin' short. Christmas and all."

"Who's that person you said, that Mrs. Julius?"

"The receptionist. See, her and Dr. Kasperson are sort of—" The rest of it got drowned in a bellowy whoop, for just then the pinball freak hit a run of luck. He danced a delighted jig around the clattering machine, howling, "Fifty free games! I busted the fucker! Fifty free ones!"

"Miss Reneau, I can't hear. Can you talk louder?"

"Say, you might try callin' her house again. Name is Delberta Julius."

"Look," Doyle said desperately, "you're sure there's nothing else? No note left for you, message, letter? Nothing like that?"

"Nope, not a blessed thing. Guess I'll have to look around for another spot if I don't hear something soon. Course that won't be hard, beautician can always get work. But I really was countin' on my own clinic."

In view of the catastrophe that had overtaken them both, she seemed remarkably stoic. Easy enough for her, he supposed; it was just another job she was out, not a future filled with soaring dreams.

From down by the racketing machine the bartender bawled at him, "Get the fuck off there. Somebody might be tryin' to call in. That's a business line."

Doyle thrust a defiant middle finger in the air. A look of grim satisfaction crossed the bartender's scowly face, and he wiped lumpy hands on his apron and started toward Doyle.

"Miss Reneau, I got to go now. You hear anything let me know, will you?"

"You bet. And you do the same. Let's keep in touch. You have a nice Christmas now. Bye."

Doyle replaced the receiver in time to look up into a pair of smoldering eyes.

"What'd you just do?"

"Okay, okay. I'm finished, aren't I."

"Asked what you done."

Doyle backed away, maneuvering for the door. Too late. The bartender got around the counter and grasped him by the collar. "Don't nobody flip me off, my place," he said. An open palm stung one side of Doyle's face, back of the hand the other.

"Smash his ass, Victor," the waitress cheered, and Victor, encouraged, balled a fist, drew back his arm and threw a roundhouse punch. Doyle ducked under it and, operating instinctively, out of some agony of terror, brought his knee squarely into Victor's balls. Victor gasped, clutched at his groin and fell to the floor; Doyle dashed through the door and into the street, the screamed curses of the waitress trailing after him.

He stood there a moment, cheeks burning, and then he took off running, where, he wasn't sure. Away from there. Two blocks down he came on a phone booth, and on a last expiring hope he popped inside, got the Julius number and dialed. Twenty times, by close count, he let it ring.

He ran back to his car and pointed it in the direction of home. An impotent heat kindled inside him, rising through his chest and constricted throat, gathering force, strength, and igniting in a fierce blaze behind his eyes.

XX

Kasperson was squatted down in the garage, busily fixing the Wisconsin plate onto the wagon, humming tunelessly as he worked. From the open door that led into the house, he could hear the phone rattling. Interminably, it seemed. He ignored it. Anyone he wanted to speak with now, this eleventh hour, he'd do the calling.

Eventually it stopped and the house and garage fell silent again. He secured the plate and went back inside. In the bathroom he scrubbed the grime off his hands, brushed his teeth, gargled with Listerine, and relieved himself. In the bedroom he gave his various accouterments a final check. The bag was packed with all the necessities for a brief retreat. The driver's license, vehicle registration and insurance proof all identified him as Terrence Lightfoot, which name, whimsically selected from his collection of aliases, seemed appropriate enough. On the bureau was the derringer and a silver ballpoint pen gun. Stout fellow, old Huck; good as his word. He fixed the loaded derringer to his ankle with a Velcro strap ("No charge for the strap," Huck had told him in a burst of generosity). Next he fit a .22-caliber long shell into the pen gun, the way Huck showed him, and slipped it inside his shirt pocket. The five remaining shells on the bureau went into the pockets of his neatly pressed suit.

Preparations were complete. The rest of it was in the lap of the gods. He stood before the mirror, adjusting his tie. A pensive smile stuck on the reflected face. It was only a quarter past six, well over an hour yet before time to leave. He went into the kitchen and poured himself a drink, very light, mostly water. Carrying the glass, sipping from it, he made a last nostalgic tour of the Julius homestead. Another chapter in his life closing. Already he was beginning to think of the shrewish widow with a certain tolerance. Give it the distance of time and the memory might even turn fond. It was his nature to forgive.

In the living room he paused and gazed out the window. Three days of unseasonable rain had swept most of the thin icing of snow from the streets and lawns. The night was chill, damp, clear—conditions very near to ideal for the enterprise ahead. A lustrous splinter of moon materialized on the blackening sky, and he chose to read it as an omen of success, a benign fortune smiling on her elected son.

TWENTY-NINE

BY 6:30 JEAN SATTERFIELD, her mind made up, was feeling tight with anticipation. Or maybe it was anxiety. Also just a little lightheaded, three drinks being about two more than she was used to. Billy was chattering away, reciting AAPS war stories, himself the hero of most of them. She liked Billy and she owed him for helping her arrive at a decision tonight, however indirectly. But she wasn't paying much attention, though the face she showed him said she was. Too busy with her own thoughts, searching for just the right opening. Pleading, of course, was out. She could be casual, offhanded, flippant even. No, that wouldn't do either; he'd see right through that. Direct, maybe: Mitch, we've got to talk, you know that, if there's something or someone—

"Huh?"

It was Billy, looking at her curiously.

"You was saying something?"

She fluttered a hand in the air. "Ah, no . . . it was nothing." God, she must have been voicing her thoughts, mumbling out loud. No more drinks. She didn't want to come on like someone who needed bottle courage. This last one she'd just nurse along until it was time to go.

As though he were reading her thoughts, Billy pointed at her glass. "You do another?"

"This one's fine yet. Go ahead if you want."

"Think I will," he said, grinning rakishly, devil-may-care. "Christmas Eve." He signaled a waitress and soon another beer was set in front of him. He drank straight from the bottle, manfully. After a while he said, "You okay now on that Morse business?"

"I'm okay, Billy."

"Hope so. Let me tell you something along them lines."

Now he was launched on the subject of man-woman relationships, advising out of his own experience, which he implied was vast. Reduced to its essence, the gist seemed to be there were plenty of fish in the sea, no good to get strung out on one person, lot of times you do better with somebody you got more in common with—things like that. Edging around the proposition.

Jean was doing her best to listen more closely. She didn't want to get caught mumbling again. Anyway, there'd be time to rehearse something on the drive to the Plainfield Fleets. Time. She realized suddenly and with a sudden rush of panic that time, under the magic acceleration of drink, had deceived her. The clock on the wall read five minutes before seven, and Plainfield was on the other end of town.

"I'm sorry, Billy," she broke in on him. "I've got to be going."

"Hey, I thought we was, y'know, talking here." He looked confused, and more than a little crestfallen.

"We'll talk again sometime. Soon."

She got to her feet and pulled on her AAPS jacket. If she moved fast enough she might make it yet. Billy's eyes, puzzled and disappointed, followed her to the door, where she paused, turned, and called back to him, ''And Billy—thanks.''

Women, he thought sourly. Go figure.

XX

At 6:32, about half an hour ahead of schedule, a Ford Econoline van pulled up behind Starla's trailer and Meat and Ducky appeared at the door.

''You're early,'' she said snappishly. ''We're not supposed to leave here till seven.''

''Yeah, well, big night like this, me'n Duck like to allow for plenty of time.''

With a curt nod she motioned them inside, and they waited in the entrance while she carried the bag from the bedroom. She set it on the floor by the couch and turned and faced them. She wasn't much cheered by what she saw: Meat regarding her with a fixed stare, mouth set in a thin icy line, simulation of a smile; and a slack nasty grin laid across the face of the other one. Neither of them spoke, neither moved.

Something was up. She knew him. ''So what do we do now, Milo, the next thirty minutes?'' She tried to keep her voice steady, even, reasonable. All the snappishness was abruptly gone.

''Look like you're all packed,'' Meat said, indicating the bag but keeping his eyes on her. ''Ready to go get rich.''

''You said one bag. Somebody did.''

''Yeah, somebody say that. One each. Where's your boyfriend's?''

''I . . . I don't know.''

''Might be you got his things in there?''

''There's a couple of shirts. I think.''

''Couple shirts. Now that ain't much for a long trip. What do you think, Duck?''

''Won't take 'im far a-tall,'' Ducky agreed. '' 'Less course he's plannin' to wear his underwear inside out.''

Meat let out a short contemptuous bark. ''Big-time roller, outta Dee-troit? He wouldn't do nothin' like that. Would he, Star?''

''Look, if there's a problem with the bag—''

''Ain't no problem,'' Meat said. '' 'Cept you went to all that trouble for nothin'. Shame. See, you ain't gonna be needin' no bags along tonight.''

Starla felt a hollow space opening up inside her. She took a shallow breath, adjusted her face in what she hoped was a neutral expression. "What's going on, Milo?"

"Been a little change of plan."

"What kind of change? What do you want me to do. Just tell me. I'll do it."

"You're a real special piece of work, Star. One of a kind. All we got to do is name it, huh. Well, we get to that part pretty quick. First though we got to be sure—in our minds, I mean—you're dealin' with us straight up."

"I don't know what you're talking about. What do you mean?"

"Mean me and Duck feel a whole lot better, we know you wasn't packin' nothin' you shouldn't be. Shank, say, or maybe even a piece."

"I'm not carrying anything like that," she said. "You know that."

"Yeah, *I* know. It's my partner here. He got a natural suspicious mind. Don't trust hardly nobody. That right, Duck?"

"Wouldn't turn my back on my own gram-maw," Ducky affirmed.

"So we gonna have to administer a little patdown. Ain't nothin' personal, you understand. More like insurance." He made a signal with his eyes.

Ducky took a step toward her, hesitated. "She's your old lady, Meat."

"You do it."

Ducky gave a helpless shrug and came across the room and stooped in front of her. He ran his hands over her tight jeans, up one leg and down the other, inside each thigh. He rose, bringing the hands lightly over her cable knit sweater, front and back, lingering at the breasts. Starla went rigid under his touch, gazing numbly into the watery eyes. A goatish leer lit his sallow features. "She's clean," he said.

Starla's gaze shifted onto Meat. "You satisfied now?" she said bitterly.

Without a word he came over and seized her by the wrist and twisted sharply. A yip of pain escaped her and she sank to her knees, one arm suspended in his tightening grip, wrenched at a wicked angle. She lifted her eyes to the figure looming at some enormous distance above her. ''Please, Milo,'' she said, the words coming out breathy, tumbling. ''I don't know anything. I haven't *done* anything. I swear.''

With his free hand Meat reached inside his jacket and took out a .25-caliber pistol. Its silencer was attached. ''Open your mouth,'' he said.

''What?''

''Said open up. Wide.''

An epileptic shudder knifed through her. She opened her mouth. Meat fit the elongated barrel inside it. He hooked a finger around the trigger. From somewhere off to one side came a high-pitched, ripply giggle.

''That'd be a blow job and a half, Meater,'' Ducky snickered.

Meat didn't seem to hear him. ''Now close it,'' he said.

She brought her lips together. Her jaws quaked.

''Now I want you to listen up, Starla. Don't try sayin' nothin' till I'm all done. Your roller man's got some foxy moves planned for tonight. You know it, and you know I know you know it. So it looks to me like you got a choice to make here. You can go along with me and Duck, do exactly like I tell you. Do that and you be just fine. Come outta this smellin' like a fuckin' rose. Happy ending. Other thing you can do is what you was thinkin' before, which was to try chumpin' us. That gets you the sad ending. Gets you this special blow job Ducky just said. Either way, it's up to you. This is America, you gets your free choice. Now, it's Duck and me, shake your head yes; other way, go no.''

Starla moved her head up and down vigorously. She made some gagging sounds as the barrel was slid out of her mouth. Meat released her wrist and she crumpled to the floor.

''Sorta figured that's how you'd go,'' he sneered. ''Figured I still got my brand on you. How'd you call it, Ducko?''

''I was hopin' see some fireworks.''

''Well, don't you worry none, partner. Plenty fireworks, comin' right up.'' He looked down at Starla. ''On your feet now, quick-time. We got some moves to make, our own.''

On the drive to Fleets, Meat ran them by, those moves, one last time. ''You know what you're gonna do now?''

''Fuckin'-a,'' Ducky responded confidently. He occupied the passenger seat. Starla was behind the wheel, Meat hunched down behind her, his gun trained on the back of her head.

"What you gonna do?" Keep him talking, was Meat's idea, so the little fuck didn't get spooked and do something dumb.

"Jesus, Meat," he whined.

"Say it!"

"Gonna slide in there and get down and—"

"Where, down?"

"Back in Housewares, like we said."

"Then what?"

"Then I wait'll the lights go out, give it some time, be sure the place is clear, and then I snake on up front."

"Where abouts, up front?"

"That check-out aisle right across from the middle door. Where the roller be waitin' for the guard to come in."

"Okay, guard's in. Now what do you do?"

"I let 'em get the loot loaded on the cart, then I do some blitzin'."

"Who, this blitzin'?"

"Who? The roller's who. Gonna make that one sting a little, too."

"Do what you want, just be sure he's down. How 'bout the guard?"

"I do what the roller was suppose to do, before he got himself iced. Walk 'im out to the back of the car, leave the cart, and then move him around to the front door. Soon as it's open he gets a hole in 'em, let the driver see what'll happen if he goes for that radio."

"An' you ain't worried none about the guard in back. Why is that?"

" 'Cuz you already dropped him, right?"

"Correct. Four minutes I'm givin' it, after the first one's inside the store. Four exactly. Then he goes down. So you gotta move fast in there."

"You know me, Meat. Quicker'n catshit."

"Okay. I get the two stiffs an' the money dumped in back, you're up front with the driver, I'm back in the van. Now what?"

"I just have 'im follow along behind you an' her. Out to the woods where the Doc's waitin'. Home free."

Two blocks ahead, the Welcome to Fleets sign came into view through the windshield. Meat nudged Starla with his gun. "Swing in back there," he said, and she brought the van to a stop outside the rear customer entrance. It was five minutes to seven. To Ducky he said, "You gonna remember all that?"

"Hey, Meato, sandman up here. Remember?"

Sand flea more like, Meat thought, remembering instead the Halloween bank score, but he said, "Okay, let's get mean, sandman. Dog-ass mean."

XX

At 6:46 Eddie's sloshy disembodied voice burst in on a snappy rendition of "Here Comes Santa Claus."

" 'Tenshun, shoppers. Store'll be closin' in fifteen minutes. We all of us here at Fleets wanna thank all you beau-ful people for . . . shoppin'. Here at Fleets. An' we wanna wish you and yours a really happy, uh, holidays season. New year too. So Murr' Christmas everybody an' thank you ver' much. Closin' in fifteen minutes. Hope to see you soon again. Thank you ver' much."

"That person sounds *intoxicated,*" a wispy little woman said to her companion, a stoop-shouldered male with canny, roving eyes. "So what," he snapped irritably. "Christmas, ain't it."

They were in Frozen Foods, Morse a few paces behind them, eavesdropping, watching. Out of habit, habit's gravity. The man had just slipped a strawberry cheesecake inside his topcoat. Earlier, in Beer Wine and Liquor, he had boosted a pint of Old Crow, and before that a pack of Merits off a cigarette turntable up front. Smokes, drinks, dessert—going to make a night of it, it appeared. Merry Christmas and thank you very much. Silently, Morse wished them luck.

He stepped around them and went through the storage rooms, locking all the doors in the back. Then he returned and made a final sweep of the aisles. All clear. By 7:07 the last laggard shoppers were threading through the check-out lanes and trudging toward the exits. He walked to the front of the store and stood by the Customer Service counter. He waited. Ten minutes passed. Mid-carol, the music broke off and a silence descended over the main floor. Banks of fluorescent lights flickered out. The few remaining employees scrambled for the door. Everyone was in a hurry to get away. Everyone, it seemed, but Eddie and a pair of young cashiers, frizzy-haired bimbettes he'd been groping at the party. The three of them came stumbling awkwardly out of the business office, arms tightly twined, like a set of Siamese triplets joined at the shoulders and waists, Eddie blissfully sandwiched in the middle. He caught sight of Morse, hailed him and guided the linked trio over.

"Mish, you know these girls? This one here's Edna"—he bobbed his head to the right—"an' this"—bob left—"is Janine."

Morse lifted the corners of his mouth in a stiff smile. Three of them, that could be gluey. He hadn't figured on three of them.

Eddie completed the introductions. "Mish-ell Morse. Best gadam security man we ever had, Plainfield unit. Pro'ly best in the whole Fleets family."

"I seen him around," Janine said skeptically. "Always looks half-pissed off."

"You be piss' too, hadda collar slimeball thieves all day long. Thas' what you security guys call 'em, right. Mish? Slimeballs?"

"Mostly just thieves," Morse said.

"He comin' along?" asked Edna in a voice so shrill it echoed through the deserted store. Her eyes were glassy. Several of the buttons on her blouse were undone.

"Sure is. See, Mish, what we're goin' do is go down the street, lil' Christmas whistle wettin'." He inclined his head toward Morse and in a stagy whisper added, "Maybe the old whacker too. Wettin', I mean."

This provoked howls of laughter from Janine and Edna. When it subsided Morse said, "Somebody's got to wait for the car, Eddie."

Eddie's flushed face registered a sudden recollective concern. "Tha's right. Be another half-hour, least."

"Half-*hour!*" Edna groaned. "What're we gonna do for a half-hour? Punch's all gone."

Eddie disengaged his arms, turned up his palms and gave a weary, burdens-of-management shrug. Janine delivered a testy wheeze.

"Tell you what," Morse said casually, as though it had just come to him. "Why don't you and the ladies go on ahead. I'll take care of the pickup, close the place up and meet you later."

Eddie's forehead creased in lines of doubt. "I dunno," he said. "I oughta be here."

"Nothing to it tonight. Store's cleared and we're all locked up in back. Be glad to do it for you."

"You think you could handle it?" There was still some uneasiness in the voice, but he was wavering.

"No problem," Morse said. "I got the drill down perfect." He rolled over his wrist and checked his watch—7:23. He had to get them out of there, and fast. "Go on," he said jauntily, "go ahead. Just scoot on out now. Enjoy. It's Christmas, right?"

Eddie seemed to brighten. "S'pose it be okay, this one time." He reached in his pocket and handed over a set of keys. "You're a good shit, Mish. Know I can count on you."

Morse made a gesture of reassurance. "Nothing to sweat, Eddie."

"An' you be along right after?"

"Soon as I finish up here."

"You promise now? We're goin' to make it a party tonight."

"Promise."

Five more precious minutes went down in haggling over a meeting place. Finally he got them out the door, secured it, and ran back to his locker. He slipped on his jacket, got the flash bang and tape off the locker floor, and sprinted to the middle exit. There was a dim light above this exit and lights still on in the business office. The rest of the store was black as a cave. He went through the inside door, and with two strips of tape fixed the flash bang at a spot shoulder level along the outer doorjamb. The remainder of the tape he discarded in a trash barrel in a corner of the entryway. Then he took out his gun, fit the silencer around the muzzle, and returned it to an inside pocket of his jacket. Checked his sappers. And then he waited, gazing into the parking lot. Except for his own car, it was empty. Stalks of light poles embedded in concrete and spaced at even intervals cast a yellowish sheen over the asphalt.

At 7:35 another car turned in at the far end of the lot and came slowly down one of the files of light poles. It pulled up next to the Monte Carlo. A figure got out, glanced around, seemed to hesitate a moment, and then started for the door. From this distance Morse couldn't make out who it was, though there was something familiar about the walk. A rush of scenarios passed behind his eyes. None of them made any sense whatsoever. All of them were perilous. And as the figure approached nearer, an alarm that began as a distant buzzing in his head rose to an urgent dissonant squawk. He flung open the door and stepped out under the canopy. A chill independent of the night air seized him, drove straight to the bone. In a voice astonished, rattled, and genuinely shaken, he said her name: "Jean!"

XX

About ten minutes after the lights went out, the lid of a plastic forty-four gallon Rubber Maid trash can lifted cautiously and a pair of rapidly blinking eyes peered over the rim. As soon as his vision adjusted to the dark, Ducky set the lid on the floor noiselessly, untangled his arms and legs, and extricated himself from the can. He stood in the aisle a moment, shaking his numbed limbs. Fuckin' Meat oughta try this end of it, he was thinking; find out how easy it is. Except for him they'd need a goddam tub or a vat, his size.

Once he got the circulation going again, he began moving very deliberately out of Housewares, edging crabwise through Small Appliances, Sporting Goods, Jewelry, Pet and Garden, Ladies' Apparel. Taking his time. Near the front of the store he crouched behind a rack of bulky woolen coats and scoped the situation, the way Meat had told him to do it. Situation looked good. A tiny shaft of light fell across the corridor leading to the business office. Another small light over the middle door, money door. Nobody in the entry beyond it. The roller nowhere in sight. Probably back in the office, watching for the car, counting up the loot in his head. Another few minutes the dumb fuck be countin' the slugs rippin' open his gut, Ducky thought grimly.

He got out his piece and screwed on the silencer. Then he darted across the open space between the rack and a check-out lane. He squatted down inside the cashier's booth and peeked around the corner. The door was no more than twenty feet away, a clean shoot. Don't get any cleaner'n this. And remembering the roller's wiseass crack about a shooting gallery the other night, he snickered softly to himself.

But all the snickering stopped at the next thing he saw: the roller materializing suddenly in the entry, coming in from the *outside,* f'Chrissake, and with some uniformed cunt along with him, mouths running on both of 'em, arms flagging, arguing, it looked like. Jesus fuckin' rat farts, who was she, what was she doin' here, an' what the fuck was goin' on? After a minute the cunt threw up her hands and came through the inside door, roller right behind her, trying to grab at her. Fragments of their heated speech reached him:

". . . got to get out of here—now!"

"Not till we've talked . . . right to an explanation . . . owe me that much. . . ."

She got that part right: explanation be good for everybody 'bout now. This was sure as shit not in no plan he ever heard. Meat never had nothin' to say, something like *this*. Fucker never around when you needed him. Sittin' in the van out behind the store, probably had his old lady goin' down on him while he waited. And here I am, Ducky thought bitterly, wadin' in the deep stuff. Asshole deep.

The clock on the wall said 7:39. Car be here any minute. This one he was going to have to grease out of all by himself.

"Listen to me," Morse was saying, "you've got to listen. You're in danger here."

She swiped at the tears welling in her eyes. Tears, furious argument—this was not the way she intended it to go. Something was very wrong. "Please, Mitch. All I ask is—"

The sight of a spindly little man rising up out of a cashier's booth, gun in hand, leveled on them, silenced her. Morse turned, following those hurt, widening eyes. Ducky stepped carefully into the narrow check-out lane and came toward them.

"Hey, you wanna hold it down, you two," he said. His face opened in a mischievous leer. Might as well enjoy himself, long as he had to get it done anyway. "All that racket wake up the fuckin' dead."

XX

As he came down the hall Doyle heard (or thought he heard—maybe it was in his head—hard to distinguish anymore) a faint whirring sound sifting through the door to the apartment. Inside, he discovered it was not a hallucination but had, rather, a real and identifiable source: Twyla at the kitchen counter carving a tube of hard salami with an electric knife. She was stylishly dressed in red and white plaid miniskirt, vermilion sweater over white blouse, and burgundy dip-side pumps. Her plump cheeks were painted into targets of rouge, lips varnished scarlet, and hair, freshly shampooed, a lustrous chrome yellow, framing the dumpling face. A brilliant splash of primary colors.

Her disposition, however, was peevish. She switched off the knife and turned to him, glowering. "Where the hell you been?" was her holiday greeting.

He went directly to the refrigerator, extracted a can of beer, popped it and took a long swallow. His hands, he noticed, were still shaking.

Hers were planted on her hips. "Well?"

"I got tied up."

"It's Christmas Eve, Doyle. Don't give me no overtime smoke."

"I stopped for a beer."

" 'Stopped for a beer,' " she mimicked in a nasalized singsong. "That's real cute. What kind of stunt is this?"

"What?" It was a genuine question. He had no idea what she was talking about.

"*What?* We was suppose to be out to the farm by six o'clock."

"For what?"

"For *what!* For supper. For present openin'. For *Christmas,* for Chrissake. You know my folks celebrate tonight. Whole family be there. I *told* you."

Her voice ascended in a grating whine. Her bill of grievances multiplied. Your life crumbled, future canceled, another insistent mocking voice nagged at him, and she babbles on about supper, presents, family, Christmas. The barrage of words, inside the head and out, dazed him. All he wanted was for it to stop. He made a signal of surrender. "Look, I'm sorry. I forgot. Let me finish this one beer and then we'll go." Anything to make it stop.

Twyla thrust out a pouty underlip. Her eyes, unsoftened, measured him, as though totting up a balance sheet, assets versus liabilities. Assets, evidently, prevailed, though not by much. "Okay," she said sourly, "but hurry it up. I'm gonna call home, tell 'em we'll be late."

She flounced out of the room. One voice arrested, one down. Now if he could only silence the other maybe he'd be able to think clearly, find a meaning in everything that had happened. He drained off the beer in a series of urgent gulps, disposed of the can and got another, quietly and quickly. Stalling. Numbing himself.

In a moment she was back, bearing a package adorned in gaudy Christmas wrap and laced with ribbons. She thrust it at him. "Present for you," she said. "Special one. Just for here." The look of appraisal had gone out of her eyes but in its place was a peculiar glittery light.

Doyle put down the beer can and accepted his mystery gift.

He stared at it blankly. Twyla, leaning against the counter, reached behind her for a slice of salami. Around an energetic chew she directed him to open 'er up.

Doyle complied. He stripped off the outer layer of paper, split the tape binding the middle seam of the exposed box and laid back the two sides. What he saw was a cheap toupee. Alongside it was an advertising flier of some sort, with two photos prominently displayed on the cover, one of a man with a slick skin highway trailing across his skull, the other of the same man, hair miraculously restored. The legend read, *Terry Topper—The Only Sure Cure For Baldness*.

"This isn't funny, Twyla."

To her it was. She burst into raucous laughter, clapped her hands together gleefully, like someone applauding the hilarious antics of a pratfalling clown. "We was tradin' gag gifts—out at work," she said by way of spluttery explanation. "I seen this—thought of you first thing."

"It isn't *funny*," he repeated.

The inner voice, never quite stilled, seemed to take on a shape, a presence dark and vengeful, a faithful comrade urging him to right all the wrongs life was heaping on him. He let the box fall and lunged across the narrow space between them, pinned her, forcing her shoulders onto the counter.

"Doyle, for God's sake, what're you doin', can't you take a—"

The raspy sound of the knife flooded her ears. Her scream broke on his palm flattened over her mouth. She felt a tearing sensation across the knuckles of one hand, followed instantly by a current of pain streaking along the wirework of her nerves, dispatching a message of agony like nothing she had ever known. And the very last thing she saw was the blur of the matched blades descending across her throat.

It was a curious, almost comical sight, Twyla there on the floor, jerking and shuddering like some oversized battery-operated toy, the power running down fast. Watching it, Doyle was struck by the fragile nature of our link to life, all of us. Consider Twyla: one moment here, ragging, jeering, a head full of plans and dreams, mouth full of hard salami; the next—poof!—vanished. In a fingersnap. Curious.

The thrashing stopped. She settled back peacefully, limp as a rag doll. A hand, its fingers laid open to bone, seemed to grasp at the lacerated throat. The eyes were rolled up in their sockets. A pool of blood, deep red, widened slowly under the head and neck and shoulders. Blood, white bone, complementing the gaily colored outfit.

Doyle experienced the onset of an emotion he could not immediately identify: relief? remorse? fear? dismay? exultance? He couldn't be sure, and he felt too stunned to wrestle with it just now. So he went into the bathroom and examined his hairline instead. No mistaking—it was receded. The fuzz he had seen—or imagined he had seen—was microscopic, imperceptible. He took a hand-held mirror and positioned it behind and above his crown. The reflection in the glass in front of him revealed a tiny pinkish bare spot no bigger than a quarter. He pictured its steady, remorseless dilation in monetary terms, a fifty-cent piece next, silver dollar after that. The gradual minting of the dispossession of his hair.

Simultaneously, magically, the elusive emotion came into focus: a rage, gathering with an ominous intensity. From a shelf along the wall he produced an electric razor, plugged it in, popped up the sideburn trimmer and, beginning at the temples and working down and over the ears, shaved a set of whitewalls into the flat flanks of his skull. Hair drifted over his shoulders like a shower of black confetti. He studied his likeness in the mirror, angling his head left and right. The results were unsatisfying. Too much dark stubble yet. A solution occurred to him. He ransacked the cabinet under the sink and found an ancient straightedge razor, a family relic passed down from grandfather through father to son. He found an aerosol can of shave cream, lathered the stubble and scraped it away. He ran a hand over the naked skin, either side. Perfectly smooth, with a fine glossy sheen.

Now he was satisfied, now he was ready. He rinsed the blade, toweled it dry and slipped it inside a pocket of his jacket. He went back into the living room and leafed through the phone directory till he found the Julius listing. He scrawled the address on a scrap of paper, put it in the pocket next to the razor. It was a place to begin.

And then he left the apartment and drove away, all his attention telescoped, searching for the author of all his grief. D. C. Kasperson, Doctor of Trichology.

THIRTY

"SPREAD OUT AND ASSUME THE POSITION," Ducky growled in a voice low and snarly as he could pitch it. "Ain't that how you rollers say it?" He already had the roller's piece, but he figured he'd better give them a quick patdown, like he'd done back at the trailer. Never could tell what they might be packin', either one of 'em.

Morse and Jean laid their palms against the wall, arms extended, legs parted. Out of the corner of his eye, Morse saw a proficient hand pattering swiftly over her body. Then the hand fell on him, lifted the sappers.

"Well lookit what we got here," Ducky said. "Couple knockout mittens. What was you thinkin' to do with these, boy? Gonna use 'em on Meat an' me, was you?"

When Morse made no reply, Ducky dropped one glove on the floor, kicked it away, slipped the other on his free hand and punched him once, hard, in the kidneys. Morse staggered, but he kept on his feet.

Ducky took four steps back. "Want you to stay right the way you are. Make one move—even one—and you gonna catch the heavy weight. Both you."

Neither of them moved.

Ducky pulled off the glove, emptied the bullets out of Morse's gun and stuffed them in his pants pocket. He recovered the other sapper from the floor, turned slightly and heaved gloves and gun into the dark aisle behind him. A brief clattering shattered the silence, and then it was still again. Now he was all set, knew just how he was going to play it. Meat be proud, he could see this action.

"Okay," he said, "lady can step back this way."

Jean started to turn and he barked, "Keep facin' front. Hands on your head. Walk backwards."

When she was about a foot from him, he sprang forward and slipped an arm around her throat, tightened it. She made some gargling sounds and he let up a little, not much. "Now you can peek, Mr. Roller Man."

Morse turned slowly, and what he saw was exactly what he expected: Jean's head twisted at a punishing angle, her eyes darting furiously, the muzzle of a gun trained on a spot just over her right ear.

"Dunno who this bitch is or what you figure you had goin' here," Ducky said, "but it don't make no difference anyhow. Even you oughta see it ain't gonna wash. Not 'less you want me to open her up, spill some brains out on the floor. Get her uniform all messy too. That how you want it to be?"

Morse put his hands in the air, signaling compliance.

"Sing out!" Ducky shrilled at him.

"No, that's not how."

"That's good, you got your thinkin' right again. Now, me'n her gonna get down in that booth while you step over by that door—inside one, where I can see you. You gonna wait for the car, an' when it comes you gonna go get that outside door, bring your guard buddy right on in. Same thing you was goin' to do before. Only thing different is, once you get inside I wanta see them arms of yours pointin' at the ceiling. Any cute ideas you got, just remember this cunt here, she can lose her face real quick. You got that now?"

Morse nodded affirmatively.

Ducky jabbed the gun against Jean's head. "Wanta hear you say you got it."

Morse said it. And as he watched them sink behind the booth, out of sight except for a pair of pink-veined eyes watching him back over the rim of the counter, he was swamped with a sudden rush of desperation. Where were all his fine moves now?

XX

At 7:48 the armored car pulled up under the canopy of the Plainfield Fleets. Following their routine procedure, the driver and two guards unsnapped their holsters, and the one in the passenger seat came out his door, locked it behind him, walked to the back of the idling car and did a perfunctory visual sweep of the area. Nothing out of the ordinary. He approached near enough to the store entrance to see a familiar figure, one of the security boys, beckoning him on. He was not in good humor tonight, brooding over how unfair it was, getting tagged to work Christmas Eve. Naturally, he was in something of a hurry.

He returned to the car and made the signal knock on the rear door. The lock turned, the door swung open. The inside guard lowered the handcart, emerged, closed the door and positioned himself behind it. He scanned the parking lot but his thoughts were elsewhere, totaling up Christmas bills in his head, wondering how the fuck they'd ever get paid. Both guards were large men in their late forties, thickset and broad of beam, with weathered faces and crosshatched bull necks. The driver, a younger, slighter man, was also preoccupied, calculating how much longer it would take to finish the route and wrap it up for the night. He gazed through the windshield at the lights strung like pearls up and down Plainfield. Except for an occasional passing car, the street was all but deserted.

The first guard pushed the cart up by the entrance and stood tapping a foot impatiently while it was unlocked. "See you got dumped on tonight too," he said in greeting. Worse even than dumped on, Morse thought as he let him in. He pulled the door shut but didn't turn the key. If there was any chance at all of getting this far, he didn't want it locked on him. The guard continued through the entry, and in that diced instant his back was turned, Morse reached along the doorjamb, yanked the flash bang free of the tape and stuffed it inside his jacket. He had no idea how he was going to use it. Or if there'd be a chance to use it. It was all he had.

"Rest of the world havin' a good time," the guard was grouching as they came through the inside door, "and we're humpin' other people's—"

The words froze on his lips. He glanced quickly at Morse, whose hands were already in the air. He lifted his.

Ducky was out from behind the cashier's booth, shoving Jean ahead of him with one hand, jabbing the gun with the other. His eyes were narrowed to glinting pinpricks. The muscles in his face twitched. His gun hand quivered. Covering all three of them, that wasn't gonna be no baby food. Gonna have to get it done fast. "Okay, move away from that cart, backs up on that wall, both you. Move!"

They flattened their backs against the wall.

Ducky was conscious of his voice, risen to a squeal. He tried to bring it down. "Now you," he said, indicating the guard, "reach over with your left hand and ease that popper outta your holster. Two fingers on the butt end. I see three an' I'll drop you where you're standin'."

Very gingerly, as though he were handling a sliver of jagged glass, the guard removed the .38 with his thumb and forefinger. He dangled it in the air.

"Set it down easy and kick it over here."

The .38 came sliding across the floor. Ducky felt for it with his foot, found it, and sent it spinning back through the check-out lane behind him. Now he was feeling better, looser. Minute there, he was right on the edge of tweaking out. No more. This one was nailed shut. Wait'll he told Meat.

"Your turn now, roller man. You got some keys I'm gonna need. Want you do just like your friend there, get 'em outta your pocket, one hand, left one, an' scoot 'em on over."

Morse brought his left hand down and across his waist, fumbled in his right pocket for the keys. The smackhead eyes followed the movement, never once shifted. No slack here. Not even a prayer. He dropped the keys on the floor and shoved them over.

Ducky cuffed Jean in the small of the back. "Pick 'em up," he said harshly. She stooped down in front of him and reached for the keys. Ducky aimed his gun squarely at Morse's crotch. His face was lit in a wicked, lunatic grin. "Look like you just sevened-out, boy. Hard way too."

Jean lifted her eyes to Morse and made a slight motion with her head. "No!" Morse bellowed, but she lunged backward and drove herself into Ducky's knees, buckling them. He fired twice, wildly, before he went down. One bullet caught the guard in the chest, dropped him; the other pierced Morse's right thigh as he pushed off the wall. A searing pain shot through him, and he stumbled and fell. Ten feet short of the two of them grappling on the floor.

Ducky tried wriggling out from under her, but she was all over him, pummeling him with balled fists. He tried swinging the gun into the side of her head, but she blocked his arm and brought an elbow down into his face, dead on his nose, cracking it. He screamed. The gun went sailing. Both of them scrambled for it, but it was Jean who got there first.

Ducky was on all fours, looking down a barrel no more than three feet from his terror-stricken eyes. Blood leaked from his shattered nose. His face registered a stupefied gape. He couldn't believe any of it was happening, and happening to him.

"Whack him!" Morse bawled at her.

Jean hesitated. Ducky bounded to his feet, spun around, and in a frenzy of fear ran for the door, thinking, Jesus, sweet fuckin' Jesus, let me make it to the van, just as far as the van. . . .

"Whack him!"

She hesitated too long. Ducky got by the inside door and sprinted through the entry. Morse hauled himself up and came over and snatched the gun out of her hand. In a bouncy, stiff-legged hop, he took off after him.

XX

The guard standing watch at the back of the armored car was still mentally sorting out his tangled personal finances when a razor-sharp broadhead arrow, fired from the open side panel of a van that had eased slowly around the back corner of the building, came whisking through the air and pierced his uniform jacket and his heart. He made a short chugging sound and his hands clutched instinctively at the arrow in his chest as he fell, face down.

Meat had given it the proscribed four minutes, even a little more. He decided he couldn't wait any longer.

He didn't have to.

No sooner was the guard down than someone burst through the store entrance and came tearing toward the van. Meat dropped the bow and picked up his gun. He squinted into the deepened shadow of the building. It was Ducky, running like a chased cat, legs pumping, arms flying frantically. "Fuck's goin' on?" Meat called to him.

A moment later Morse came through the same door, planted himself on his good leg and squeezed off a shot. Wide right. He fired again, several times. One of the slugs entered the back of

Ducky's neck and erupted through his mouth, propelled by a gush of blood. Ducky toppled over and flopped across the wet asphalt like a writhing fish. Morse wheeled around and there was Jean, right behind him. "Get back," he shouted. "Down!" She stiffened against the door, and he lurched toward the front of the armored car, dragging his bloodied leg.

When Meat saw Ducky fall he howled out his name. He reached over and thumped the back of the driver's seat. "Go get him! Drive!" Starla was too petrified either to comprehend or to act. Her hands seemed frozen to the wheel. Meat stuck the gun in her face. "Drive, goddam you. Duck's down."

Her foot pressed the accelerator and the van pulled up by where Ducky lay. He was no longer shuddering. Meat yanked the keys out of the ignition. "Don't move," he said. "You fuckin' move and you're fuckin' dead." He leaped out the side panel and grasped Ducky under the arms, then dragged him into the van. He laid him out gently on the floor. "You be okay, Duck," he mumbled feverishly. "I'll get you outta here." He gazed into the childish, startled, wide-open eyes. A distant gurgle sounded through the ragged hole of what remained of the lower half of the face. "Get that cockfucker did this, first," Meat said.

Morse was banging on the passenger door of the armored car, flagging it forward. "Out of here! Out!"

The driver's face was stunned, incredulous.

"It's a hit. Roll!"

The face went terrified. He understood. He slid the car in gear and took it squealing through the lot and into the street. A bullet twanged off the canopy girder, and Morse turned and saw Meat leaning out the panel of the van, thirty yards away. Firing at him. Morse lifted his piece, aimed and squeezed the trigger. And got a hollow click. Empty. He heard the van's engine turn over, and he stuck the gun in his belt and hopped toward the entrance to the store. Halfway there his foot struck a pool of water and he slid, arms wagging like semaphores signing a frantic call for balance, and went sprawling. He looked up at the van bearing down on him. His vision narrowed on it, as though he were seeing it through the wrong end of a telescope. And what he saw, through that constricted vision, was Starla at the wheel and Meat draped over the seat, gesturing furiously. And if he could have heard, he'd have heard Meat roaring like a man gone mad: "Splatter him! Splash his fuckin' roller guts!"

Five feet from where he lay, the van swerved sharply to the right, angled across the lot and headed for the back exit. And for the second time tonight his life had been saved, by two very different women.

XX

"Is it over?" one of those women was asking him now. "Mitch?"

"Over?" he said, still staring, wonderstruck, at the taillights of the van, dwindling in the dark. "Not quite over. Give me a hand here, will you?"

Jean helped him up and he started for his car, dragging the leg best as he could. She fell in beside him. "Where are we going?"

"Not we. This one I got to do myself."

"No way. I'm coming with you."

"There's a couple men down there."

"Dead, both of them. I already checked. Anyway, you can't drive. Not with that leg."

The barbed pain in his thigh told him she was probably right. Felt like a railroad spike had been driven into it. His pants were sticky with blood. His mind raced frantically. In the near distance, a wail of sirens rose through the night. He had maybe two minutes, no more. There wasn't the luxury of debate time. "Okay," he said, "we take your car. But you got to do it like I say. Exactly like I say. You got that?"

She looked at him very steadily. "I hoped you'd know you could count on me, Mitch. By now."

"I know," he said. "Maybe I'll get a chance to tell you yet."

They drove north on Plainfield, past the road leading to the rendezvous spot in the trees. For a fleeting moment Morse wondered about Kasperson, where he fit in all this. Didn't matter finally, not for what he had to do. At the Beltline they turned, followed it to 96 and then turned again, pointing east. The Christmas Eve traffic was thin, only a few cars on the highway up ahead. Impossible to tell if any of them was the van. That didn't matter either; only one place where they could be headed now, and that was the farm. And they didn't have that much of a start. He knew the way; Kasperson's directions, at least, were good.

Apart from relaying those directions to Jean, Morse was

silent, calmer now, staring through the windshield at the shimmery slice of moon in an enormous black dome of sky. Calculating the odds, which were not so good. If he had been thinking straight back there, thinking like the cop he once had been, he'd have lifted the piece off the downed guard in the lot. Too late now, far too late. Ducky's gun was still in his belt, useless utterly, except maybe as intimidator, bluff. He reached inside his jacket and felt for the flash bang. Still there. It was a weapon, of sorts, something in the hand. Never show an empty hand, someone had told him once—his father, was it? a coach? some wise old cop? Someone.

At the sight of a landmark billboard Morse said, "Hang a right up there."

She turned onto a narrow county blacktop. "Where is it we're going?" she said.

"Better you don't ask."

"But I *am* asking."

"Don't. You've seen enough already."

"You were in it, weren't you."

It was not a question, and he didn't reply.

After a pause she said, "I thought maybe I'd, well, earned something tonight, Mitch."

"Earned more than you'll know, Jean Satterfield."

She laid a hand on his arm and kept on driving.

He watched the odometer clicking off the miles: four, five, six, six point three, point four—"There," he said, "left there," and she swung the car down a winding, rutted dirt road. "Go to your parking lights," he directed her, "and go slow."

Another mile and he said, "Now kill 'em altogether."

"But we can't see the—"

"Just do it. We're almost there."

She switched them off and they drove another half mile, inching through the dark. Up ahead, the outline of a silo loomed like a fragment of the night. And beyond it the lights of a van, just now pulling off the road, fell across the yard behind the stucco house.

"What we're going to do now," Morse said, pointing, "is cut through there, get in behind them."

Jean looked stunned. "But it's a . . . field. Open field."

"Try it anyway. Surprise is the only edge I got."

She jerked the wheel sharply, and the car lurched and

bounced over the open rugged ground. When they reached the silo, he signaled her to stop. "This is the part where you do it like I tell you. Which is to wait here."

"I don't think so, Mitch. I've come this far."

He shook his head slowly, regretfully. "Guess you have at that." He lifted the gun out of his belt, handed it to her. "Can you just stay behind me, then? Cover my back?"

"I can do that."

"That's an empty you're holding. All it's good for is show, making a point. If you have to, can you do that?"

"That too."

"Okay, let's go sling a couple moves."

XX

Meat had swatted her once, open palm, hard but not hard enough to break her grip on the wheel.

"You missed him! God *damn* you, on purpose you missed him!"

Starla jiggled her head violently. Words of denial caught in her throat. Her bronzed skin had gone bone white.

Meat laid the gun against her stinging cheek. His face stiffened in outrage and disbelief at the utter wreckage of all his plans. "Drive," he said.

"Drive where?"

"Farm. Ain't noplace left to go. An' hit the dome light, so's I can see back here."

Once they were on the highway, he sank back on the floor and took Ducky's head and cradled it in his lap. The shattered mouth was frothy with blood. A soft-focus glaze clouded the astonished eyes. The lungs expelled faint puffs of air. Meat's shoulders shook, and all the way to the farm he kept repeating in one of those rapidly closing ears, "You be okay . . . you see . . . get you outta here . . . hang on, Duck boy." An anguished chant. His vision blurred behind a wall of tears.

The van came to a grinding stop alongside the stone porch. "Get the back door," Meat said. "You gonna help me with him." Starla reached for the door handle and felt the gun barrel, cold on her neck. "Not that way," he said, voice guttural, snarly. "Over the top. Where I can see you. You ain't gonna chump me twice."

She climbed over the seat and edged around him. At the sight of Ducky, she hesitated. "He's dead, Milo."

Meat jabbed the gun at her. "He ain't dead!" he said fiercely. "But you gonna be, you don't get the fuckin' door."

She crawled to the back of the van and swung open the double doors. Someone sprang out from behind them, grasped her by the arm and yanked. She went tumbling into the damp grass.

Morse pulled the pin, pivoted on his good leg, and flung the cylinder down the length of the van. He ducked behind the door. He saw a brilliant phosphorescent flash and, in afterimage, behind tightly squeezed eyes, forky streaks of lightning. The explosion rocked the van, echoed through the yard and on into the dark fields like remnants of some distant blast. He gave it a quick three-count, spun around in time to see a gust of smoke surging out the back, and a heavy figure staggering through it, pawing for the door. Meat. It was Meat, crouched, swaying, but incredibly still on his feet. And if he made it outside, it was all over. No contest.

Morse boosted himself up into the van, and in an awkward chop block drove a shoulder dead on at the wobbly knees. From above him he heard a sudden howl of pain, and then he felt the full weight of Meat crumpling onto him like a bag of wet sand. He scrambled out from under, stumbled over something—couldn't tell what—and fell across him. Somehow Meat wriggled over onto his back, and for an instant Morse was looking directly into eyes glassy but still open, blinking in an effort to restore focus. The head lolled off to one side, the mouth gaped. Their faces were so close he could smell the hot sour breath. A gun was clutched in an outstretched hand. Firing blindly. Bullets ricocheted off the ceiling.

Morse seized the wrist, banged the hand against the wall of the van, and the gun went rattling across the floor behind them. But the other hand, balled in a fist and wildly swung, caught him on the back of the head. It swung again, this time in a narrower arc. He tried to dodge, but it connected squarely with his jaw, sent him reeling.

From across some great distance, Morse heard grunts, growls, the sound of his name chanted around a medley of inventive curses: "Gonna open you up, suckwad . . . empty you . . . drain you out, Morse. . . ." And through the gradually clearing smoke, he saw Ducky sprawled out on the floor, not three feet away, and

Meat groping at the lifeless legs, searching for something. Some dim instinct rising through the fog in his head told Morse what it had to be: the shank that was surely strapped to one ankle or the other. And the same instinct told him he had a sliver of a second remaining, and not a bit more. He hurled himself at Meat, wrapped an arm around the throat, threw all his weight and all he had left in him behind a backward-wrenching lunge, and snapped the neck.

Morse sagged back against the seat. The fumes stung his nostrils. Under the pale dome light he saw the bodies of Ducky and Meat, grotesquely twined. He looked at them. And seeing them that way, he felt as if he knew them both in some intense personal way, beyond time and place and circumstance. A mangled reflection of himself.

A buzzing of voices came to him from somewhere outside the van. He clambered over the bodies, grabbed Meat's gun, and lowered himself stiffly onto the ground. Jean was backing Starla and a pair of carbon-copied males up toward the porch. She made quick stabbing gestures with the powerless gun. A promising actress, Jean. He limped over beside her.

"I think this is all of them," she said excitedly. "We did it, Mitch. We *did* it." Except for the gun, which she held steady, her whole body was trembling.

"You did good," Morse said. "Real good. I want you to trust me now, this last bit of business we got to transact here. You do that?"

She moved her head up and down.

Morse turned to the two males. "You'd be the pilots, right?"

"That's right," one of them muttered. "And who'd you be?"

Morse lifted his gun and weaved it back and forth between them. "I'm your fundamental redneck-snuffer, things don't go my way. You got a phone in there?"

Both of them said yes.

"Jean, I want you to go in and call the cops. Sheriff's department, make it."

She looked at him, then at Starla, then again at him, searching for something in his face. "Will you be here when I get back?"

"I'll be here. Go make the call."

Starla waited till she was inside, then took a step toward him. "Mitch, you've got to—"

"No, I don't *got* to do anything anymore. I'm the one holding the piece, remember?'' He held it up, as though in evidence, and motioned her back. ''You heard it now,'' he said, ''all of you. Twenty minutes, half hour on the outside, heat'll be here. That plane ready?''

''Plane's ready,'' one of the Dokkens said. ''How about our money?''

Morse made a short, harsh laugh, not a trace of mirth in it. ''Money? You oughta be glad they're not kicking dirt on you. C'mon, your time's running down fast. Move.''

At gunpoint he marched them around the house. Only one of the Cessnas was out of the hangar. ''Looks like a full passenger list wasn't part of your figuring,'' he said.

''Just doin' what Meat told us to,'' a Dokken said with a helpless shrug.

''Get in.''

The Dokkens climbed into the plane. One of them turned the switch, and the engine cranked, sputtered. The propeller began to spin, slow motion. Starla didn't move. One of the Dokkens looked over his shoulder and said to Morse, ''She comin'?''

''She's coming.''

Starla turned to him. ''Mitch, listen, listen to me. I'm sorry. I didn't plan any of it.''

''There's a couple of iced guards who'd be real relieved to hear that. Also those two stiffs in the van.''

''They're the ones who did it, Mitch. It was Milo, it wasn't me. They forced me. There was nothing I could do. I'm sorry.''

''Sorry's a sorry word, Starla. No need for it anyway. I don't know how far you were in on this end of it. Never going to know. Doesn't matter. What you did back there at Fleets, that was worth something. Clears the books on us.''

''Come with me, then. For what we had. Still have.'' A chord of desperate pleading resonated in her voice. The plane's fuselage shuddered behind her. The sound of the engine rose to a steady, urgent roar. In the backwash of the propeller, her hair fluttered wildly.

''Not this time,'' Morse said. ''From the start we were a bad match, you and me.''

''What'll I do? Alone, Canada, no money—I need you.''

He reached into his hip pocket, extracted a small roll of bills and pressed it into her hand. ''There's about eight hundred there, maybe a little more. My assets, sum total. Long way off that three million you were counting on, but it'll have to do."

She gazed at the money blankly. Her face was streaked with tears. "But what will *I do?*"

"I'm betting you'll find another Fleets up there," he said. "And another Mitchell Morse. Get in now."

The plane taxied onto the tarmac, stood poised for an instant, and then went racing down the narrow strip. Morse watched the wing lights diminishing in the black sky. A sudden silence fell over the fields. A collision of emotions buffeted him. He felt someone touching at his arm.

"*Now* it's over," Jean said.

"Now it's over."

"Who was she?"

"A mistake," he said. One in a lifetime of mistakes. The worst one? That he didn't know, but he was certain it was the one he would remember after all the others were absolved by the charity of time.

"And me, Mitch? What about me? Am I another mistake?"

"No, I'm thinking with you I got things right. For a change."

"You won't be sorry."

She was telling him, with her eyes and her voice and her touch, his terrible secret was safe. So maybe they both were right. Maybe he wasn't going to have to take the weight on this. Meat and Ducky dead. Starla gone. Everyone accounted for. Everyone but Kasperson, and there was a better than even chance a shrewd player like that would be in the wind just as soon as he got the bad news. If, that is, he was still breathing. They could have taken him out earlier in the day, before this shuffle got underway. For now, there wasn't a damn thing he could do about Kasperson. He'd made it this far, maybe his luck would hold up. "Come on," he said. "I'm run out of moves. Let's go in the house there and find ourselves a drink while we wait. I'm buying. I owe you one."

THIRTY-ONE

THERE WAS NO WAY Morse could know it just then, but where Kasperson was concerned he had no real cause for alarm. About ninety minutes earlier the trichologist, lugging his bag, came stepping briskly into the garage, humming softly. He hit the genie button on the inside wall, and the garage door began to rise. His eyes widened in astonishment and the humming stopped abruptly and an incredulous crimp came into the corner of his mouth at what he saw: a young man rushing at him, face expressionless, hair bizarrely sheared from the sides of his skull, a straightedge razor in one hand. Kasperson dropped the bag and fumbled for the pen gun in his shirt pocket, but he was much too slow. And just before the razor sliced through the density of flesh beneath his chin, his brain registered automatically—*Gilley!*—and in the last instant of his life he thought, however briefly, about the sly malice of chance. His knees went splashy, the ceiling began to spin. He felt a vertiginous sense of teetering, falling. And then he felt nothing at all.

On the sidewalk in front of the house a group of carolers had gathered. They were young people, members of a church fellowship, and their clear voices rose exultantly on the night air. But at the sight of Doyle shambling through the garage door, a razor wet with blood in his hand, their song dwindled away and they fell back toward the street. Doyle crossed the driveway and stood in a patch of soggy grass. He flipped the razor onto the lawn indifferently. He thought he heard someone wailing, but he might have been mistaken. It didn't matter.

And then a sudden exhilarating notion occurred to him. He stooped down, unlaced his shoes and kicked them off. He removed his socks. And remembering Twyla's uncle—whatever his name was, something crazy—he started walking, moving in deliberate purposeful circles.

And that's how they found him, slogging barefoot through the slush and the pockets of dirty snow, a stranded smile on his face, mud oozing between his toes, and a fierce joy quickening his heart.

THIRTY-TWO

"SO HOW DOES IT HAPPEN you're the only one in the store when the armored car arrives?"

"Eddie—he's the manager—asked me to stick around and take care of the cash pickup. There'd been a party and he was half in the bag. Wanted to get away early, I guess. You can talk to him."

"Right now it's you we're talking to, Morse."

There were two of them, both in plainclothes, standing on either side of the hospital bed. One was short, dumpy, placid faced. Chewed a toothpick. The other, the one doing the questioning, was lean and gimlet eyed, with a spray of freckles on his cheeks and a shock of fiery hair rising off his forehead. A young man, hotdogger, working on his certificate in hardass. Morse knew the type. Also the game: Detective Nice and Detective Ice, here to play Ping-Pong. Search out the holes in his story, which he'd already recited for them, a couple of times. It was well past midnight and he was bone weary. But he had to stay alert. Lying on his back, he was at a considerable disadvantage; so even though his leg stung fiercely, he pushed himself up against the back of the bed.

"So you're saying he just leaves you there? Rent-a-cop, in charge of all that money? Must of had a lot of faith in you, Morse."

"Must have."

"How do you suppose one of 'em got inside *after* the place was locked?"

"Beats the shit out of me. I'd secured all the doors. All I can figure is he found a spot to get down before the store was cleared. There's plenty of them in there. It's a big place."

"But it's your job to check the aisles, right? You do that?"

"Yes. On both questions."

"You sure you didn't just happen to miss one of them aisles? Think hard now."

"No, I covered them all. Standard drill."

For a moment the detective said nothing, merely gazed at him with a practiced scowl. His dumpy partner got out a package of cigarettes, shook one loose. "Smoke?" he said.

"They let you, in here?" Morse asked innocently.

"We got like special privileges."

Morse accepted a cigarette and a light. Waited for Detective Nice to take his turn.

"The leg hurtin'?"

"It smarts some."

"Bet. Doc down in emergency said you lost a lot of blood."

Jesus, Morse thought, these boys need new material. Or better rehearsals. "Yeah, they told me that," he said.

"Bet you're beat, too."

"It's been a long day."

The detective worked his face into an attitude of sympathetic concern. "What we'd like to do is get outta here, let you get some rest. But y'know, that was a pretty heavy hit. Fleets store. Four men dead. A hole in you. You can see why it is we got to ask some questions here."

"No problem. I want to help."

Detective Ice snorted at that. His partner said, "Good. That's good. So, whyn't you tell us a little more about the girl."

Morse wondered where they had Jean right now. And how she was holding up. Talk about rehearsals, they could have used a few more themselves. "Sure," he said. "What, exactly?"

"Well, you could start with what she was doin' there, first place."

XX

In a waiting room down the hall, Jean was answering the same question. For about the fourth time. The room was ordinarily reserved for children and its walls were covered with posters of cuddly animals. A playpen stood in a corner. Various toys and games littered the floor.

"It's like I told you," she said. "I came there to have a talk with Mitch. We were intending to have a drink after he got off work."

"But I understood you to say your relationship was, well . . ." The detective put a flat hand in the air, wiggled it in a tentative gesture. He was a fiftyish man, square framed and big boned. Grandfatherly. His voice was remarkably soft, almost a whisper, the expression on his leathered face kindly. He sat on a couch facing her chair.

"That's true," Jean said. "We'd had our problems. That's why we'd arranged to meet, talk things over."

This was not precisely the version agreed upon back at the farmhouse. But there had been so much to cover, so many details, so little time. She assumed that sooner or later the police would get to Billy Schooley, and when they did it would all come out anyway. Better to anticipate it now, was her thought. She could only hope Mitch was thinking along the same lines.

"When was it again, you got there?"

"Sometime after seven. Probably closer to half-past."

"And the armored car hadn't arrived?"

"No."

"That's the reason you were inside the store?"

"Yes. He let me in. To wait."

"Isn't that a little, uh, unusual?"

Jean indicated her uniform. "You can see I'm in security, sir. I don't present what you'd call a serious risk. Anyway, it's cold outside."

Both of them held Styrofoam cups filled with bitter black coffee. The detective took a sip of his, nodded gravely. "What I still don't quite follow, Miss Satterfield, is why you were meeting there. At Fleets, I mean. Why not a bar? There's a lot of them up on Plainfield."

"We were planning to go to his place."

"Why not there, then? You don't have a key?"

Jean looked at him very steadily. "No," she said.

He took another sip, made a face. "Pretty foul coffee," he said.

No disputing that. She didn't reply.

He set the cup on the floor and stretched his arms overhead. He sighed. "I know you're tired, Miss Satterfield. So am I. But being in security, you know how these things work. Let's go through it again, just one more time. The robbery part."

XX

"We were thinking to have a drink," Morse was saying, directing his answers at the dumpy one. "Celebrate Christmas Eve."

"Sort of like a date, huh?"

They were trolling for something here, he wasn't sure what. "Yeah, you could call it that. Why?"

"We're asking the questions here, Morse," the freckle-faced detective snapped. His partner made a little shooing motion at him. To Morse he said, "No special reason. We was just wondering how you two was getting along."

"We've had some ups and downs," Morse said carefully. They'd squeezed something out of her, that much was clear. It came to him suddenly what it was. Their breakup. If she'd opened up about that, then what was she doing at Fleets? Maybe it was a small inconsistency, maybe not. They were ready to leap on anything they could get. "Lately, though," he added, extemporizing, "things have leveled out." He hoped to Christ she was sticking with the rest of the script.

"Know how it goes," said Detective Nice wisely. "Oh yeah, whereabouts was you planning to have that drink?"

"Wherever."

"Bar someplace?"

"I hadn't thought about it," Morse said, buying an instant of time and thinking about it now, second-guessing what she might have told them. "Bar, or maybe my place." He winked. "If I got lucky."

The cop shook his head and backed away. Freckles moved in.

"I'd say you were mighty lucky, Morse. Girl saves your ass. You and her take down the bad guy and—"

"Mostly it was her."

"Lemme finish here. See if I got it straight. He makes it outside and they take off in the van. What I want to know is how come you didn't get to us right then, instead of chasing them down. Your jacket says you were a cop, once upon a time. You'd know better."

"Call it a reflex. I knew one of them was winged, and I was still holding his piece. Both guards were dead, nothing we could do for them. Armored car was safe, going to get you on the radio as soon as he turned the corner and hit the street. We had a car in the lot. And the van wasn't that far out ahead."

"Gonna be a hero, huh. Save the day."

Morse just shrugged. That wasn't a question.

XX

"And that's how it went down," Jean said, concluding her account of what happened inside the store.

There was a short silence. The detective was leaning forward, listening intently, watching her. Finally he said, "That was a pretty brave thing you did."

"Not really. It was an opportunity. I took it. From the looks of him, we weren't going to get another."

"No, I suppose you weren't," he said solemnly. "All right. Let's pick it up from there. After Morse recovered the gun and pursued the subject, what did you do?"

"Checked the guard. When I saw he was dead, I followed Mitch through the doors."

"Why didn't you call us? There's phones in there."

"I thought he'd need help."

"But you had no weapon."

"No. But he'd been hit."

A thin smile creased the detective's face. "Caution to the wind?" he said.

"I suppose you could put it that way," she said stiffly.

"Okay, let me back up a minute. When Morse went through the entry between the two doors, did you see him stop for anything? Did he, you know, pause? Stoop down?"

She knew what this was all about, and she was ready for it.

"As a matter of fact, I did. He told me later, while we were following them, he'd picked up a flash bang in there."

"This flash bang, where do you think it came from?"

"The man must have dropped it when he was trying to get away. He was really panicked, you could see that."

The detective tugged at his lower lip. "I see. What about after you were outside?"

"By the time I got outside, the armored car was out of there. The van was cutting across the lot, heading for the back exit."

"So you didn't see much of what went on out there."

"Nothing, actually." This was the way they'd rehearsed it. From this point on, the less she saw, the less to trip over. "Except for the other guard down. The one with the arrow in him. I checked him, too. He was dead."

"And Morse was running for the car?"

"More like stumbling, with that leg."

"He insisted the two of you follow the van?"

"I was the one who insisted on coming along. He thought we should at least try to keep it in sight." When he looked at her skeptically, she added, "He was a police officer himself, you know. Once."

"We heard."

Another silence. The detective lowered his eyes. For a time he seemed to be studying the patterns in the tiled floor. Jean waited it out.

"You trail them down the highway and then out into the country," he said, resuming. "When did you first realize he was going to try and take them?"

"When the van pulled in at the farm."

He stroked his chin thoughtfully, still gazing at the floor. "See, this is the part keeps giving me trouble. Morse has a round in him. Gun's empty. You've got no weapon. Far as you know, they're still armed. One of them, anyway. You got no idea who else might be out there. Seems like awful heavy odds."

"He had the flash bang."

"Yeah, that he did. Piece of luck, coming across it that way."

Morse had warned her about these nonquestions. She said nothing.

"So you stay in the car while he gets up behind the van. Why was that? You were along to help, I thought."

"He wouldn't let me come any farther. Said it was too dangerous."

"After what you did for him back at Fleets?"

"It's what he said."

"Okay, you hear the explosion, then come running." He paused, lifted his eyes and fastened them on her. "Now this is real important, Miss Satterfield. Want you to think carefully, try and picture it in your mind again. When you got there, did you see *any*body? Outside of Morse, I mean, and the two chilled perps. Anybody at all?"

Jean moved her head slowly, side to side. "Sir, there was nobody there." And she maintained an unwavering eye contact as she said again, "Nobody."

XX

"Okay, you got 'em tracked all the way to the farm. Now comes the heavy fireworks. Tell us about that flash bang. Where'd that come from again?"

It was hot in the room. The color in the detective's face was so high he seemed to be blushing through the freckles. His partner leaned against the wall, still sucking the wet stub of toothpick.

"Had to be the inside man was packing it," Morse said. "Probably figuring to use it on the driver. He must of dropped it when he made his run for the door. I picked it up in the entry."

"Real convenient, huh?"

"Piece turned up empty. The way things shook down out there, it was damned convenient."

"Why do you suppose they pulled in at that farm, anyway?"

"Hard to tell," Morse said evenly, though his heart was clubbing in his chest. This was where it got thorny. "My guess would be, the one who got clipped was in bad shape by that time. He'd taken a pretty serious hit, maybe he's doing a lot of howling. The other one swings off the road first place he comes across looks safe. Like this one was: no lights, nobody around, looked to be deserted. He climbs in the back to see what he can do for his buddy. Or maybe he's figuring to dump him there, which is why he gets the back doors. This is strictly a guess, you understand."

"Oh yeah, we understand. So there was just the two of 'em when you got up there and slung the pipe. Nobody else in the yard?"

"Didn't see anybody."

"House either? Afterwards?"

"Not there either."

"Y'know, Morse, that's the funny part. See, there's a couple bib overall boys live on that farm. Turns out they're pilots, got their own planes. And along comes this van with our two desperadoes in it, making straight for their place. Peculiar, wouldn't you say?"

"It's peculiar *if* that's where they were headed. That's what makes me think—guess—they just rolled in there because it was a likely looking spot to pull over."

"But supposing that wasn't the case. Suppose they knew exactly where they were going. You were a cop, what're you gonna deduce from that?"

Morse wrinkled his brow. Thought about it a moment. "Farm boys had a piece of the score?"

"That's real good. Except you're saying nobody was out there waiting. Now don't that strike you as kind of funny?"

"Maybe they got spooked. If they were even in it. I don't know. You're the detectives."

"Yeah, that part you got right, Morse. What do you say we run it by again. From the top."

XX

Over the next few days they questioned him again, many times. Morse stuck to his story, and it held up. It didn't hurt any that Jean could substantiate all the particulars. Along with all the indisputable forensic evidence, her testimony established beyond any doubt that it was Meat and Ducky who had killed the guards. And since none of the money was lost and the two apparent perpetrators accounted for, eventually, grudgingly, they had to accept it.

Of course it didn't take them long to connect Starla to the aborted robbery, even as Morse had once predicted. All the same, she was never apprehended. It was as though she had dropped off the farthest end of the earth. The Dokkens were reported seen in Canada's Saskatchewan province, at a place called Moose Jaw. Another report had them in Hermosillo, Mexico. Neither report was confirmed. After that the trail grew cold.

As for Doyle, he was remanded to the Forensic Center at

Ypsilanti, Michigan, for psychiatric evaluation. The doctors there found him incompetent to stand trial. After the fifteen months prescribed by Michigan law elapsed and he was still judged incompetent, he was committed to the Kalamazoo State Hospital, where he remains to this day.

The Grand Rapids Press featured the robbery under the headline VIOLENCE ERUPTS ON HOLIDAY EVE. Kasperson's bizarre murder made the Christmas Day news all the more lurid, though no one ever put the two incidents together. For a day or so, Morse's picture was all over the front page of the newspaper. Jean's too. A couple of local heroes. He didn't get any monetary reward from Fleets, but he got a special commendation from management and, later, the offer of a promotion, which he declined. Inside of a month he turned in his resignation, but he didn't leave town. Jean moved in with him, and her father helped Morse get into a private security outfit, a major competitor of AAPS. It was administrative work, a desk job, but the pay was good and the benefits considerable. He and Jean got along well. They moved to a larger apartment and began to talk seriously of marriage. He gave up drinking altogether, joined the Y and took up lap swimming. Most of his other leisure hours were spent reading history, long into the night.

But while he was generally content, there were times—shaving, say, or preparing a report, or just idly strolling from place to place—when a peculiar emptiness seemed to settle over him, as though all the electricity had suddenly gone out of his life. And in fact, after taking the slug, he was never quite the same again. He walked with just a trace of a limp. Sometimes, when it rained or the weather was damp, a dull ache pulsed in his leg; and whenever it did he found his thoughts returning to the events of that night, sorting them out, puzzling them through. But to no satisfactory conclusions. Sometimes those thoughts would focus on an image of Starla Hudek that even yet lurked behind his eyes, vivid, stubborn as a phantom itch in a lost limb. A reminder of what he had been, or almost been. And now and again they led him further still, those same thoughts, to a curious melancholy reflection on the bewildering workings of chance and geography and time, and the lessons to be found in the narrower history of his own life.

ABOUT THE AUTHOR

Tom Kakonis was born in California, squarely at the onset of the Depression, the offspring of a nomadic Greek immigrant and a South Dakota farm girl of Anglo-Saxon descent gone west on the single great adventure of her life. He has traveled widely and worked variously as a railroad section laborer, pool hall and beach idler, army officer, technical writer, and professor at several colleges in the Midwest. His first book, *Michigan Roll,* was named by the *New York Times Book Review* as one of the ten notable crime novels of 1988. Mr. Kakonis makes his home in Grand Rapids, Michigan, where he is completing his next novel.